Traci Harding lives on the Hawkesbury River, with her husband David and their two beautiful children, Sarah and John.

Traci has written three trilogies — The Ancient Future, The Celestial Triad and the Mystique Trilogy — as well as three stand-alone novels, *The Alchemist's Key*, *Ghostwriting*, and *The Book of Dreams*.

For information about Traci Harding and her books, plus all the latest science fiction news, visit:
Voyager Online: www.voyageronline.com.au
the website for lovers of science fiction and fantasy.

Books by Traci Harding

The Ancient Future Trilogy
The Ancient Future: the Dark Age (1)
An Echo in Time: Atlantis (2)
Masters of Reality: the Gathering (3)

The Alchemist's Key

The Celestial Triad
Chronicle of Ages (1)
Tablet of Destinies (2)
The Cosmic Logos (3)

Ghostwriting

The Book of Dreams

The Mystique Trilogy
Gene of Isis (1)
The Dragon Queens (2)
The Black Madonna (3)

Triad of Being
Being of the Field (1)

BEING OF THE FIELD

TRIAD OF BEING
BOOK ONE

TRACI HARDING

HARPER
Voyager

Harper*Voyager*
An imprint of HarperCollins*Publishers*

First published in Australia in 2009
This edition published in 2010
by HarperCollins*Publishers* Australia Pty Limited
ABN 36 009 913 517
harpercollins.com.au

Copyright © Traci Harding 2009

The right of Traci Harding to be identified as the author of this work has been asserted by her in accordance with the *Copyright Amendment (Moral Rights) Act 2000*.

This work is copyright.
Apart from any use as permitted under the *Copyright Act 1968*, no part may be reproduced, copied, scanned, stored in a retrieval system, recorded, or transmitted, in any form or by any means, without the prior written permission of the publisher.

HarperCollins*Publishers*
25 Ryde Road, Pymble, Sydney NSW 2073, Australia
31 View Road, Glenfield, Auckland 0627, New Zealand
A 53, Sector 57, Noida, UP, India
77–85 Fulham Palace Road, London, W6 8JB, United Kingdom
2 Bloor Street East, 20th floor, Toronto, Ontario M4W 1A8, Canada
10 East 53rd Street, New York NY 10022, USA

National Library of Australia Cataloguing-in-Publication data:

Harding, Traci.
   Being of the field / Traci Harding.
   ISBN: 978 0 7322 8123 6 (pbk.)
   Harding, Traci, Triad of Being; bk1.
   Previous ed.: HarperVoyager, 2009
A823.3

Cover design by Kerry Klinner
Cover images: forest © Jorma Jaemsen/ Corbis;
woman by Nina Buesing/ Getty Images
Typeset in Goudy by Kirby Jones
Printed and bound in Australia by Griffin Press
50gsm Bulky News used by HarperCollins*Publishers* is a natural, recyclable product made from wood grown in sustainable plantation forests. The manufacturing processes conform to the environmental regulations in the country of origin, New Zealand.

5 4 3 2 1   10 11 12 13

*For Selwa, Sue and Steph.
My dream team!
Thanks for all your guidance.*

CONTENTS

AMIE Layout ... ix
List of Characters ... xi

Part 1: Oceane — Water Planet
    Chapter 1   AMIE ... 3
    Chapter 2   The Crew ... 12
    Chapter 3   Anomaly ... 26
    Chapter 4   Reasonable Force ... 44
    Chapter 5   Bearer of Bad News ... 68
    Chapter 6   Propagation ... 87
    Chapter 7   Interrogation ... 108
    Chapter 8   Homeward-Bound ... 129
    Chapter 9   The Void ... 162

Part 2: Frujia — Tropical Planet
    Chapter 10   Castaways ... 195
    Chapter 11   The Invitation ... 204
    Chapter 12   Appearances ... 221
    Chapter 13   Unguarded Moments ... 243
    Chapter 14   Precognition ... 257
    Chapter 15   Disclosure ... 273

Part 3: Phemoria — Planet of Women
    Chapter 16   Stowaway ... 293
    Chapter 17   Damage Control ... 306
    Chapter 18   Naked on the Inside ... 321
    Chapter 19   Best-kept Secret ... 336
    Chapter 20   Fem-Libertine ... 358
    Chapter 21   The Two-fold City ... 388
    Chapter 22   Angels in Fast Motion ... 415

Part 4: Sermetica — Desert Planet

Chapter 23	Provocation	441
Chapter 24	Anathema	465
Chapter 25	Tryst	493
Chapter 26	Snatch	510
Chapter 27	Ghost Ship	518
Chapter 28	Heavensgate	531
Chapter 29	Cross	544

Bibliography	557
Planets of the United Star Systems	558
The Powers	560
Acknowledgements	563

Astro Marine Institute Explorer

Module F - Top
- Flight Deck/Bridge
- Bio-Containment Labs
- Launch Bay/Pod Bay
- Lift to Module A
- Spare Parts Hold
- Stairs to Module B
- Suiting Station
- Launch Bay Control Deck

Module B - Middle
- Hospitality/Kitchen
- Cafeteria/Mess
- Function Room
- Housekeeping/Laundry
- Maintenance/Rubbish
- Lift to Module E
- Stairs to Module F

Centre
- Power Cells
- Fresh Water
- Fuel

Module A - Middle
- Crew Accommodation
- Reception/Administration
- Offices/Conference Room
- Medical Rooms/Sick Bay
- Lift to Module F

Module C - Middle
- Greenhouse
- Biology Labs
- Nursery
- Fishery

Module D - Middle
- Pool, Track & Gym
- Amusement Arcade
- Cinema
- Sauna & Spa
- Meditation Rooms &
- Float Tank Centre
- Exterior Docking Door
- Science Labs

Module E - Base
- Marine Module Control Deck
- Sub Bay/ Suiting Station
- Kitchen/Mess
- Crew Accomodation
- Marine Labs
- Crew Lounge
- Lift to Module B

A.M.I.E.

LIST OF CHARACTERS

Ship — AMIE (Astro-Marine Institute Explorer)
Anomaly Expert — Taren Lennox
Captain — Lucian Gervaise
Lucian's Wife — Amie Gervaise
Project Manager — Swithin Gervaise
Lucian's Personal Assistant — Aurora (Rory) DeCadie
Pilot — Zeven Gudrun (Starman)
Co-pilot/Navigator — Leal Polson
Ship's Doctor — Kassa Madri
Systems Engineer — Bonar Colbers
Youngest Tech — Raggus
Botanist/Horticulturalist — Ringbalin Malachi
Physicist — Eleazar Kestler
Marine Botanist — Ayliscia Portus
Head of the United Star Systems — Jabez Anselm
Anselm's Viceroy — Khalid Mansur
Stowaway/Systems Tech — Kalayna Zuri
The Being of the Field — Azazèl-mindos-coomra-dorchi
Phemorian Queen — Qusay-Sabah Clarona
Phemorian Viceroy — Jalila Lamus
Presidential Guard — the Valoureans
The Grigori — Azazèl, Armaros and Sammael

PART 1

OCEANE —
WATER PLANET

CHAPTER 1

AMIE

After achieving eight different degrees at the University of Esponisa on Maladaan, Taren had finally scored a research visa and a six-month stay on the esteemed land, sea and space vessel that had been the brainchild of Professor Lucian Gervaise.

Gervaise — whose explorations of space Taren had long admired — was captain of the mobile institute that he had designed. The professor had named the craft the Astro-Marine Institute Explorer, or AMIE, after his wife, Amie Gervaise, who was a well known marine-biologist herself. The AMIE project worked in cooperation with the University of Esponisa, and their home base office here on Maladaan was located on campus. AMIE's earthbound operations and research centre were run by Lucian's older brother, Swithin Gervaise, who raised the finance to fund the AMIE project.

Taren thought it a damn shame that Lucian Gervaise was a happily married man as, besides being a brilliant scientist, writer and inventor, he was remarkably good looking, charismatic and, from all accounts, a pleasure to work with.

One last briefing and Taren would be getting the lowdown on Gervaise from a personal perspective. She couldn't wait to be off this overpopulated planet and exposed to the vast wildernesses that space and the planets of the neighbouring star systems had to offer.

Taren's job on the mobile observatory — to study and advise on space anomalies — had been specifically created for her because of a recent discovery that those in the know at the Astro-Marine Institute's headquarters on Maladaan were not disclosing to anyone outside the presidential office and the Dean of the University on Esponisa. It was widely rumoured that most of AMIE's major discoveries had not been made public as yet; the mobile institute had only been in space for five years, although the project had been in existence for closer to ten. Apart from the construction of the mobile institute, AMIE also built a planet-bound port and maintenance dock for the institute, its recon vessels and its interstellar pod transport system.

Taren was dying to get on that vessel and be made privy to AMIE's discoveries herself. She'd have top-level security clearance soon — well, top-level clearance so far as astro-marine research went, and that's what she was interested in.

The majority of Taren's peers and teachers over the years had questioned the value of the subjects she chose to investigate. She had studied everything from genetics and cell communication to quantum theory, astrophysics and extrasensory perception in hopes of proving her inter-dimensional field theory.

Taren was convinced there was an ocean of microscopic vibrations connecting everything in the universe. This ocean — or field — influenced, and was in turn influenced by, every single particle within creation. The field could control you, or you could control it, unconsciously or consciously, for better or for worse.

The flora and fauna of the natural world was instinctually connected to the field and utilised it unconsciously to their advantage — especially pack animals and those that moved in schools. A large majority of human beings in Taren's day and age, who lived in high-rise cities, had lost their connection with the natural world and the macrocosm. Most liked to believe that life was a string of fated events, because in this belief they need not take responsibility for their own sickness, misfortune, or misguided acts; it could all be blamed away on others or circumstance, but not the self.

So of course, all the serious scientists and scholars at the university of Esponisa had found the concept that they created their own reality and were responsible for everything that happens to them in life a bit confronting. They had ridiculed her theories that all life was telepathically connected, that disease is caused by emotional and mental imbalance, and that it might be possible to influence the past.

Intriguingly enough, after ten years her peers on the research funding board at the University of Esponisa had stopped laughing and had been questioning her about her research with some interest of late. Then, out of the blue, Taren was invited to apply for a grant and a visa to study on board AMIE. This was Taren's greatest dream come true. She'd never bothered to apply for a visa before now; knowing her work was not regarded seriously, Taren strongly suspected she'd be rejected.

Now the heads of AMIE on Maladaan were offering her a job.

The large office where Taren was receiving her final briefing was minus many of the board members she'd been dealing with regarding her place on the space station. The chairman of the board at AMIE home base, Swithin Gervaise, was present.

In Taren's opinion, he was not as appealing appearance-wise as Lucian. Swithin was a serious businessman and came across as very cool and very confident. He was still a bachelor and, by all accounts, was always very charming when in female company. His light brown hair with blond sun-streaks and his tanned skin made it obvious that Swithin was more interested in the marine side of things at AMIE.

There were also a couple of other professors and doctors from Taren's past who she'd not really expected to see at this meeting ... or this institute.

'Dr Lennox,' Swithin Gervaise began as soon as she was seated. 'Before you commenced your study here at our institute, you did some work for the MSS. Is that correct?'

The MSS was the Maladaan Secret Service and it was the last thing Taren wanted to discuss at this meeting — especially if people were finally beginning to take her research seriously. 'Yes, that is correct ... but I don't see —'

'This work was of a psychic nature, was it not?' Gervaise cut to the chase.

'Look,' Taren began to fret that her trip to the stars was going to be cancelled, 'I haven't used anything in regard to my research that —'

'I believe you,' Gervaise cut her short again, though seeming polite, 'but I would like you to assist the board and the AMIE Project with your rare talent.'

Taren was frowning. 'I don't understand.' Why was a doctor of hypnotherapy present for this conversation? *What has he got to do with AMIE?* She had recognised the elderly and well-known fellow from her time with the MSS, where he had often been employed. Taren figured he must have told the board about her business with the secret service.

'Allow me to explain.' Swithin rose and walked around to sit on the front of his table, which joined others to form an arc in front of her chair. 'We at AMIE believe that there may be a spy on board our research vessel and we'd like you to use your talent to help us pinpoint this person.'

'How —'

'Do we know there's a spy?' Swithin pre-empted her query. 'Information about some of the project's discoveries has been leaked to sources other than those that we officially reported to.'

'Then couldn't the leak come from inside the government rather than from on board the craft, or even come from this office?' Taren reasoned on behalf of her soon-to-be crewmates.

'Do you have a vibe on that?' Swithin asked in a condescending manner. Taren felt put on the spot and did not respond, so he continued. 'We do have those areas under investigation, but we need you to be our eyes in the sky, as it were.'

Taren didn't like the idea of having a hidden agenda when she'd have her hands full trying to accomplish her research goals in the six- month period she'd been allowed. 'Do I report to Captain Gervaise?'

'No,' Swithin quickly replied, and gave a half laugh at his own eagerness to make that clear. 'Lucian doesn't know about the problem. He'd have a fit if he knew any of his precious research might be going astray, or that one of his team out there might not be faithful to him and the rest of the crew. None of his people are aware of the spy, nor are they to become aware that you are seeking one.'

'And if I refuse?' Taren had already realised this was a stupid question.

'You do want to go, don't you, Dr Lennox?' Gervaise proved to be predictable and Taren gave a heartfelt sigh.

'So what do you need a hypnotherapist for?'

'To ensure you cannot be unwittingly persuaded by any said spies into not reporting your true findings to us,' Swithin explained. 'That's been a bit of a problem in the past, I understand?'

'I'm not going to let anyone screw around with my brain any more!' Taren had quit the MSS and studied hard to get away from all the cloak-and-dagger crap she'd had to participate in as an agent.

'According to your own theories, Dr Lennox, all mental and emotional activity is stored outside the brain in a great field of consciousness. Therefore, we won't be screwing around with your mental functions as they are stored and preserved on some microscopic part of the universal superconscious.'

What was the point in arguing? Both she and Swithin knew that she wasn't going to walk away from this golden opportunity to be taken seriously and work on AMIE.

'It's your choice, of course,' Swithin prompted her to commit.

Taren had had this type of hypnotherapy performed on her before and had a good part of her childhood memories go missing, along with all her MSS training and mission knowledge. The little she did remember suggested she had been lonely and miserable, so she didn't consider the missing memories any loss at all. 'I guess I'm your stooge then,' she conceded, none too thrilled by the honour.

'This particular mission will not be as distracting as you think,' Swithin assured her with a smile. 'Your research is much more important to us, believe me.'

According to Taren's calculations they must have had her under for about half an hour. Lord knows what they'd been asking or telling her — she didn't want to know. All that mattered was that she was on her way to the dock to get suited up and shipped out.

She was flying express to AMIE via the institute's own deep-space pod system. Her top-level clearance brief stated that AMIE was in the neighbouring binary-star system and was presently stationed off a planet that was primarily covered by deep ocean, and had so been named Oceane. Taren had had a short test run around her home planet in a single-occupant pod, but the thought of being shot into deep space in one, for a journey of some weeks, was a wee bit scary — it was a good thing she'd be in stasis for the entire journey! As she dressed in her battery suit, Taren did her best not to think about the voyage and focused on how good it would be to arrive.

Suited up, she reported to the launch tube, where her luggage and equipment were being loaded into the storage section of her pod.

'Dr Lennox?' queried the man standing by her transport. Taren guessed him to be the launch supervisor.

'Yes, indeed. How did you guess?' she asked, looking down at her strange rubber suit with hoses sprouting out of the body and heat sensors scattered all over it.

'The octopus suits you.' He chuckled at her discomfort.

'You're too kind.'

'Are you ready for the ride?' He motioned her to the cockpit.

'As I'll ever be,' she replied, trying not to wince.

'Then hop inside! I'll hook you up and strap you in.'

As Taren was plugged in, turned on and harnessed, the butterflies in her stomach proceeded to increase.

'You know how this works?' the middle-aged supervisor asked in a calm voice, obviously used to nervous passengers.

Taren nodded. 'You're going to launch me into space and once the initial boost has dissipated, the heat gathered from my body and converted by my battery suit into energy, is going to fuel my pod the rest of the way.'

The launch supervisor gave her a friendly wink as he finished fastening her in. 'There's a homing beacon on the pod that will find AMIE, and AMIE's own tracking system will pick up on your pod as soon as you're through the inter-system gateway. They know precisely when to expect to see you on their scopes and should you not arrive on time, we'll be notified and a search team sent out.'

'So how often does a pod go astray?' Taren said, doing her best not to sound fearful of the answer.

'If you go missing, you'll be the first.' He watched as the pod door lowered to encase her. 'Enjoy the ride.' He gave a very reassuring smile.

Taren gave him the thumbs-up and then the pod door was locked. The subtle lighting of the pod's control panels was rather nice actually and she had a sensation of being safely wrapped up in a little space cocoon.

'*Dr Lennox . . .*' A soothing female voice came through her headset. '*We're going to put you under now and prepare for launch.*'

'I'm good for stasis,' Taren confirmed, wondering how long it would take to knock her out.

CHAPTER 2

THE CREW

What seemed like seconds later, Taren awoke. Everything was white.

'Welcome to AMIE,' said a woman with a velvetty voice that was immediately calming. 'You have arrived safely and are in fine health. The perception of white light will pass as your eyes adjust to being open. The lighting in this room is very dim, but to eyes that have been closed for weeks, it's blinding.'

'Who are you?' Taren asked, all her other questions having been answered.

'I am AMIE's medical practitioner, Dr Madri. Call me Kassa.'

Taren loved the sound of Kassa's voice; it was warm and friendly. Normally she'd probably feel more distressed at being blind in an unknown place, speaking with a total stranger who could have been an alien creature with six heads for all she knew.

'And you are the infamous Dr Lennox,' she chuckled, though not in an offensive way. 'I've been telling Lucian to get you on the AMIE project for years!'

'You've known about my work for years!' Taren was surprised. 'I didn't think my work had been that well publicised ... my reputation, yes, but my actual theories? I thought they were only read by those who had to assess them for further funding.'

'Ahh ... but they kept giving you funding,' Kassa pointed out. 'They knew you were onto something.'

Taren didn't know what to say as she was flattered speechless. She had judged from the voice that this was a mature woman of middle age ... maybe a couple of hundred years old. Taren was a relative baby at fifty. Still, she'd done a lot of living and learning during her short life. But a woman and fellow scientist of true importance was excited about her work! Taren had to wonder if she was still in stasis, dreaming.

'People in stasis don't dream,' Kassa informed.

'Because they're in a suspended —' Taren gasped so deeply she nearly choked herself. 'You read my mind!'

'I did.'

'You have the Powers,' Taren stated surely.

'Well, one of them,' Kassa replied.

'So do I!' Taren blurted out, instantly realising she was telling her deepest secret to a stranger she couldn't see.

'I know,' Kassa replied. 'That's why I've been watching you.' She sounded a little excited. 'If anyone is going to prove that we heretical psychics have been right all along, it's you.'

A flush of pride made Taren smile broadly. 'I had no idea there was another psychic on board.'

'That's because no one else knows,' Kassa explained. 'Although I think some crew members might suspect.' There was a smile in her voice. 'I wasn't as brave as you, Taren. When I was a student, all theories and investigations regarding the supernatural were strictly taboo. It was bad enough being one of the few females actively involved in the interstellar space program.'

'Well, up until a few weeks ago, I was beginning to think my open aspirations were a bad idea, but lately they seem to be paying off.'

Her sight was registering shadows, and after blinking for extended periods, the recovery room finally began to take shape. Taren looked around until she spotted Kassa, still something of a blur to look at. Kassa appeared, at first, to have short auburn hair streaked with grey, but upon gaining a slightly better focus, Taren realised that the bulk of the doctor's hair was twirled into a roll at the back of her head. She was tall and slender and her face had a very pronounced bone structure.

'Your persistence has most certainly paid off,' Kassa agreed, with a warm smile of greeting. 'Welcome aboard, kiddo.'

When Taren felt recovered enough she was taken to a change room with a shower tube. A small-size crew uniform hung on the wall and looked as if it might be the right fit for her. Taren knew that no one was required to wear the uniform. It was more a memento of a stay on AMIE, a gift from the project management. The three-piece wet suit — pants, a vest and a jacket — were all deep blue at the bottom fading into aqua blue in the middle and then black at the top. A zip ran all the way down the outside of both legs of the pants, making them easier to put on and take off when wet. The singlet top and the jacket bore the project emblem of a dolphin jumping over a planet.

There was a pair of fairly heavy-duty work boots that would certainly come in handy — even a sun hat and spaceglasses.

* * *

Showered, changed and suited, Taren felt a little more human, but the uniform fitted her slender body rather more tightly than she was normally comfortable with. She didn't like to advertise her femaleness when she was working — it was hard enough being ridiculed for her theories, so she actively tried to avoid being hit on as well. She also wore glasses she didn't need just to appear more like a scholar and less like a potential love interest.

The truth was, she just hadn't met that many wonderful men. All the men in the MSS were self-involved bastards, and a majority of her fellow scholars at the Astro-Marine Institute on Maladaan were narrow-minded buttheads. She'd had a few short relationships, but her obsession with her work seemed to leave all her men in the background.

'Ah, bugger men.' She finished braiding her long dark hair back and gave her reflection the once-over in the mirror. She loved the way the two new purple streaks at her temples intertwined with her black braid; it made her look all the more the mad rebel scientist. She missed her dark-rimmed glasses though, as they were with her luggage, which would have been taken to her quarters.

She was suddenly hungry for solid food, having been on fluids for weeks. Taren looked at the electronic map on the wall. 'Map me a path to the closest eatery,' she requested.

As her path from the change room lit up on the map, she listened to a set of verbal directions.

Outside the door, Taren headed right as instructed and nearly collided with a dark-haired girl who was even shorter than she was. 'I'm sorry —'

'Dr Taren Lennox, I presume.' The petite lass straightened her zany iridescent glasses over which passed a rainbow of soft vibrant colours every time she moved her head. 'I'm LG's personal assistant, Aurora DeCadie, but folks around here just call me Rory because I'm so vocal.' She smiled warmly. 'I was just coming to get you. The captain and some of the guys you're on the star shift with are having dinner — or, rather, their breakfast — in the mess. LG thought you might like to meet them and eat, as you're probably hungry after your trip.' Aurora finally took a pause, although she wasn't out of breath in the slightest.

'That would be great.' Taren felt overwhelmed by this small bundle of energy. Rory oozed a vibrancy that was almost exhausting and had little short pigtails sprouting all over her head — so short that there was barely anything to attach the hair elastics onto.

Rory noticed Taren admiring her hairstyle. 'I got the shits, cut it off ... big mistake!' She rolled her eyes — heavily made-up with black eyeliner — and moved off, indicating Taren should follow her. 'I'm trying to encourage it to grow again. Your hair is amazing! I like the purple. You'll fit right in around here.'

At the far end of the Mess Room was a group of men seated around a table arguing, jeering and laughing at the top of their voices.

'Aren't there any females on the night shift?' Taren was a little taken aback about the prospect of working with these guys; she'd expected a lot of cerebral scientists not a bunch of mavericks.

'Nope,' Rory advised. 'Besides the Doc and me, there are only two other females on board. They're both in the Marine Department, and they're staying on the daylight side of the planet this evening. The star shift boys aren't this bad when they're working, but at mealtime the pilots and the technicians meet and that's never good. Most of the scientists on board eat early and avoid this ugly, ugly scene.'

'I'll remember that.' Taren felt really uncomfortable in the uniform now and rather naked without her spectacles.

Rory led her by the food dispensers, which had quite a good variety of pre-packaged and fresh foods. Taren managed to get herself a salad.

'Hello.'

Taren found a stocky, handsome young fellow waiting to make her acquaintance.

'Just couldn't wait, could you, Starman?' Rory jeered.

'You must be Dr Lennox, the anomaly specialist we ordered.' He held out a hand to Taren, ignoring Rory's comment. 'I'm Zeven Gudrun, the pilot of this fine vessel ... we'll be working together for a bit.'

'Oh ...' Taren wondered why she would be working with a pilot. 'I'm pleased to meet you.' She shook his hand briefly, whilst juggling her tray. 'And we'll be working on?'

Zeven smiled and shook his head ever so slightly. 'I'm on strict instructions from the captain not to disclose that information at present, although I will tell you that I think you'll find it's pretty impressive.'

'Starman meant the project is impressive, not working with him,' added a second man who had wandered over to join them. 'Leal Polson, co-pilot and navigator.'

'You guys!' Rory objected to their eagerness to meet the latest female addition to the crew. 'I was bringing her over.'

Taren could feel her face becoming flushed from the attention and she really hoped it didn't show. 'I'm very excited to be on AMIE and I look forward to hearing about whatever it is I'm here to investigate, although I do have many of my own experiments to conduct.'

'It's rumoured that you have the Powers. Is that true?' Zeven queried, and Leal served his younger, shorter crewmate a jab with his elbow.

'Give her a break. I'm sure she's sick to death of being asked that.' Leal gave Taren a friendly smile after coming to her defence.

'You have *no* idea,' she emphasised, deciding to take her tray of food to a table and put it down before anyone else wanted to shake her hand. 'I'll just be focusing on the pure science side of my work while I'm here, if it's all the same to you guys.'

'Fine by me,' the blue-eyed co-pilot assured her as the gathering followed Taren to the table.

Leal may have been approaching middle age, but he had a very pleasant face and demeanour, and was still in fine form — as everyone she'd met so far seemed to be. Taren thought the active, stimulating lifestyle must be what kept them all twinkling so. Leal's blond spiky hair was only slightly tinged with grey and the lines on his face seemed more from a happy life in the outdoors, than age.

'So that would be a "yes", then,' Zeven concluded, unfazed by Taren's reluctance to discuss the matter of her Powers.

Normally, Taren would have been annoyed by his persistence, but Zeven, too, had a disarming manner, full of cheek and fun, and she really didn't want to put her crewmates offside just yet. His wide, light brown eyes expressed warmth, and when he smiled broadly a dimple appeared in his left cheek — Taren just loved men with dimples ... it just made them seem more innocent somehow. Zeven's hair was dark, fairly straight and long enough to keep falling in his eyes. He had traces of a wee beard and a moustache growing around his mouth, which was obviously being cultivated in the hope it would make him appear older.

So, instead of being rude to him Taren fixed him in her gaze. 'Would it bother you?' she asked, staring deep into his large clear eyes.

'Hell, no!' He laughed at her implication, although he did take a step backwards and break eye contact with her. 'I'm just interested in that kind of stuff.'

'I see.' Taren didn't for one second believe his claim. This was an attempt to flirt; she could sense his amorous intent. 'Just because I study the supernatural doesn't make me a psychic, now does it?'

'A sci-chick,' one of the technicians said as he walked past on his way back to work. 'I like it! New nickname, people.' He pointed both his index fingers towards Taren.

Please no! Taren thought to herself, pretending she hadn't heard the comment. Here she was, supposed to be keeping that side of her life under wraps, and she gets nicknamed sci-chick — that would go down *really* well with Swithin Gervaise.

Rory saw Taren cringing, and leaned close to whisper: 'Don't worry. *His* nickname is blockhead.'

Taren smothered her amusement, while Rory did not, and so they managed to keep the tech from pursuing the conversation in their company.

'Who was that?' Taren asked once he'd disappeared from the room with three other men in tow, all agreeing that sci-chick was a good name for their new crewmate.

'That's Bonar Colbers, head systems tech,' Rory informed her. 'You won't have much to do with him.

These two, however,' she glanced at Leal and Zeven, 'you are stuck with.'

'Oh, like you're such a pleasure to work with, Miss I-have-to-get-a-paragraph-out-in-every-sentence,' Zeven ribbed Rory.

Rory appeared ruffled by the jest. 'At least I'm sure of my own mind,' she muttered under her breath. 'I'm gone,' she announced, seeing the displeased look on Zeven's face. 'If you need anything just call. I'm contact thirteen.' Rory slapped a communicator in Taren's hand, waved and headed for the door.

The tension between Zeven and Rory seemed to suggest a failed romance? Or perhaps it was just workplace tension? Taren got a vibe on the former.

'Don't worry about them.' Leal took a seat so that Taren might feel at ease to do the same. 'They've had a longstanding love-hate relationship.'

'She started it,' Zeven pointed out in his own defence. 'Why is she always trying to make me look bad?'

'It's called attention seeking.' Taren sat and opened her dinner package. 'Or energy sucking. I'd say she likes you.' She stuck her fork into the salad and mixed it around as Leal chuckled, amused by the insight of Taren's statement.

Zeven was immediately intrigued by Taren's reply and sat down on the chair beside her. 'But I don't want her to like me.'

Taren grinned, knowing that wasn't true. 'Then why were you trying to suck her energy too?'

'I wasn't!' Zeven defended. 'I was just defending us.' He motioned to Leal to include him in the equation.

'Really?' Taren said flatly and looked to Leal. 'Did you feel threatened or insulted by Rory's jest?'

'No,' Leal confirmed, smiling broadly.

'Did you feel compelled to retort in any way?' Taren further questioned.

'I did not.' Leal and Taren both looked to Zeven.

'Oh, I get it. You've done psychology too, huh?' Zeven scoffed. 'That wasn't in your résumé.'

Taren shook her head. 'Through my own research I've discovered that we directly affect all that happens to us, either consciously or unconsciously. Your past, present and future intentions act on probability and determine what events actually come into being. If someone is bothering you it is only because you are allowing him or her to do it, or even willing them to do it. Your reaction to outside stimuli creates what you deem to be real and decides the course of your next action. Leal knew Rory was just having fun and maintained a positive view. He didn't bother wasting his vital energy on creating a negative charge with which to respond to the situation. You, however, chose to take offence, which created a negative charge in your field that you found undesirable. You chose to cast that draining energy back at the cause of your annoyance. Rory, upon having this negative charge tossed at her field, felt suddenly drained and thus took offence also. Not wanting to entertain that negativity either she threw the emotional hot potato back into your lap. Now you feel shitty. Am I right?'

'Yeah, but only because your theory still makes me look like the bad guy,' Zeven grumbled.

'You said it yourself, Zeven. You don't want her to like you,' Taren pointed out. 'So you go out of your way to make yourself unlikeable in her eyes.'

Leal burst out laughing. 'She *is* psychic!'

They didn't usually have this kind of conversation around here and Zeven didn't know what to make of it — since he hadn't understood half of what she'd said anyway. He liked Taren, though; she was really *deep*, and good-looking — a dangerous combination by his reckoning.

'Your theories are really quite something.'

All eyes turned to Lucian Gervaise, who'd been quietly standing nearby listening to their conversation. 'And does this communication we have with reality extend beyond the human condition through to animals, vegetable, mineral, molecule?'

Taren swallowed her mouthful and put down her fork. 'My research supports that theory, yes.'

Lucian smiled. 'You are the answer to my prayers,' he stated confidently, offering her his hand.

His smile made her heart skip a beat, or perhaps it was just the honour of meeting the man whose work and career she greatly respected.

'And you are the answer to mine,' Taren managed to reply graciously, as she rose to shake his hand.

Lucian shook her hand with both of his. 'Someone with an open mind and new ideas will be a welcome addition around here.'

'Hear, hear,' Leal and Zeven agreed.

Lucian pulled up a seat and sat down, gesturing for Taren to do the same.

'I employ all these fresh, young, scientific minds and they're still spouting last century's theories at me,' the captain complained.

Taren couldn't help but feel elated by his attitude. 'My theories are in fact much older, professor,' she admitted boldly. 'They were just hidden carefully in myth, legend and theology for the inquiring mind to decode.'

Lucian smiled at her lack of faith in current orthodox scientific investigation. 'I suspected you'd be just like this. And please call me Lucian. We're all pretty informal here.'

His deep green eyes were so engaging!

'Kassa warned you about me,' Taren guessed.

Lucian shook his head. 'I've read everything you've ever written —'

Taren gasped. 'Ditto,' she explained, to cover how flattered she was and how shocked.

'I was particularly interested in your study regarding the human ability to communicate and manipulate anything via a quantum field of microscopic vibrations. Eighty-seven per cent success rate with the subjects on that study.' Lucian sounded very impressed. 'Did you test your own ability to manipulate the Field Fluctuation Recognition Device you created to prove your theory?'

Taren was rather thrown by the sudden curve in the conversation. 'Well, I used a mixture of people. Some psychic, some with no history —'

'But you were one of the psychics,' Starman butted in.

'I proved capable of triggering the needle on the FFRD to the positive or the negative at will, if that's what you mean?' Taren found herself on the defensive. Why were they so interested?

'Due to all the practice you'd had wielding your psychic talent for the MSS,' Starman concluded.

Taren wanted to scream. She was never going to live her past down.

'She's a spy,' Starman concluded, when Taren did not defend herself straightaway.

Taren laughed. She couldn't help it. 'Why would the MSS be interested in the AMIE project?'

'You tell us,' Lucian invited.

'You think I spent ten years studying so that I could finally get a visa to work on AMIE, in order to spy on the project for the MSS?' Taren rose from her seat, angered and insulted. 'Well, I hate to tell you this, people, but the MSS just doesn't have that kind of long-term vision, nor do I have any passion for the MSS and their investigations. I was invited to apply for this visa,' she reminded them. 'What the hell am I doing here if you don't think I'm legitimate?'

All three men present seemed to relax after her outburst.

'We do believe your work is legitimate,' Lucian said. 'I just needed to establish that we all know you've shown an aptitude for wielding the Powers in the past.'

'So I am to spend this entire sabbatical being catechised by my peers? Geez, I might as well have stayed at home.' Taren was really fuming now. Instead of being treated seriously, she found herself caught up in another interrogation. 'If you want to conduct a third-degree, I'm leaving.'

'Over my dead body,' Lucian stated warmly. 'The truth is, we need you and your unusual expertise. Don't worry about the grilling — everyone on board has been through it. Do you think I would bring anyone aboard this vessel without knowing their entire life story? There is much at stake ... you will soon realise how much. But first I need to know that you're one hundred per cent faithful to this project. If you know of any outside interest in what we do here, I need to know about it.'

'Do I know of any interest in AMIE outside of your organisation, Professor Gervaise? The answer is no, I do not.' Taren stared Lucian in the eye. 'I am not a threat to this project ... may the field strike me dead if I lie!'

'I believe her.' Leal cast his vote.

'Yeah, she's a bit creepy,' Zeven decided, 'but we're stuck, so I'll give anything a go.'

'Oh, thanks very much.' Taren regained her humour. 'What are you stuck with?'

Lucian pressed one of the buttons on the belt around his waist and the shields on the windows in the mess room began to retract. The evening sunlight from the twin suns on the other side of the planet streamed into the room, while the gigantic cloud shrouding the planet over which their craft floated was the most prominent feature of the panorama.

'Oh, my stars.' Taren moved closer to admire the view. She'd never seen a planet from space before. 'It's beautiful ... overwhelming.'

'Yeah, and mysterious too,' Starman added.

'Mysterious in what way?' Taren's eyes remained fixed on the view for she'd noticed a patch of glowing cloud on the night side of the planet and this illuminated area was filled with explosive splotches of different-coloured light. 'What is that?' It looked like a solar light storm, but it was located around the equator of the planet, not at one of the magnetic poles where this kind of anomaly would normally manifest.

'That's what we're hoping you can tell us,' Lucian threw the ball back in her court.

Taren's eyes lit up. 'Can we get closer?'

Starman smiled and rose to make a move to the flight deck. 'You bet we can.'

CHAPTER 3

ANOMALY

'I didn't mean this close,' Taren grumbled from the passenger seat located behind Starman's cockpit in the small tandem spacecraft.

'Come on, Doc. We all agreed that the only way we're going to discover anything is to get a sample to analyse,' Starman reminded her.

Taren looked at the huge glowing storm spreading out over one small portion of the misty planet below — an island of colourful undulating light amid an ocean of darkness. 'This is so dangerous.'

'If you want to break new ground, conquer new frontiers and all that, you've got to be prepared to take a few risks,' Starman said cheerily.

'Now *you're* sounding like an MSS agent,' Taren jeered, and Zeven laughed. Taren surmised he'd been all for going and investigating the mysterious glowing mass sooner, but was held back by Lucian until the anomaly expert arrived — her. But Taren had no idea what the anomaly was either! 'I just want to go on record as saying that I think this has the potential to be a quarantine hazard. The substance could be highly unstable, even explosive, when contained!'

'*Noted,*' Lucian's voice advised via her headset.

'Speaking of negative charges,' Zeven said, raising

an earlier topic of conversation, 'you're a real downer on a field mission, you know that?'

'You're right.' Taren got over the horror of what she had agreed to, knowing that if she didn't maintain a more positive view then she might as well have stayed on AMIE. 'One thing's for sure ... this is one hell of a first day at work. I mean, I thought I'd at least get to rest after the trip, unpack my equipment —'

'*All you've done is rest for two whole weeks,*' Lucian said from the base, defending the urgent schedule.

'Yeah, Doc, you need to be out and about.' Zeven rolled their craft and had it right side up again before Taren even knew what hit her.

'Pleeeease!' Taren begged him. 'Do you want me to make a mess in your pretty spacecraft?'

'See,' Zeven commented into his mouthpiece. 'I told you a woman would prove unsuited for this kind of investigation.'

'Ah, may I remind you,' Taren retorted, 'that without this woman your investigation would still be on hold.'

'*She's got a point there, Starman,*' Leal agreed from the pilot's seat back on AMIE.

'So, they call you Starman because you're the pilot?' Taren decided this was the time to satisfy her curiosity.

'Nah,' Zeven corrected, 'it's 'cause I shine at night.'

Taren rolled her eyes to the sound of Lucian and Leal's laughter echoing through her headset.

'*He only ever surfaces at night, more like,*' Leal informed. '*We strongly suspect he could be a vampire.*'

Taren was carrying a handheld FFRD in order to note whether there were any changes in the quantum world during their flight and she had been glancing at it often.

'So what is that gadget?' Zeven wondered at its purpose.

'This is a Field Fluctuation Recognition Device, which I invented to detect mass fluctuations in the electromagnetic field,' Taren replied, predicting the pilot's bemused response.

'Come again?'

'It measures random states of molecular order in the normally chaotic behaviour of the molecular world,' Taren attempted to simplify her explanation.

'How can it do that?' Zeven was a little cynical, 'and why would you want to?'

Taren shook her head, feeling he was going to find that answer very tedious. 'Are you sure you want to know?'

'Sure I'm sure,' he encouraged her to enlighten him.

'In the quantum theory, particles are represented by fields that have quantifiable normal modes of oscillation. In quantum electrodynamics we study photons being either emitted or absorbed by these fields. Usually these fields function in a random, but stable, manner, exhibiting even amounts of negative and positive charges which cancel each other out and produce no charge for my FFRD to detect. But, if for any reason there is a sudden imbalance in the field, either in the amount of photons being emitted or absorbed, my FFRD will detect this as either a negative or a positive event.'

What Taren's research indicated was that these fluctuations in the field could be affected and controlled by certain individuals — those referred to as having 'the Powers'. She had also discovered that every individual could affect the behaviour of the quantum field, but those with 'the Powers' consistently had more success because they consciously influenced the needle in her FFRD device to sway into the negative or positive register as desired, because they had a much stronger belief that they had that power over the external world.

Taren had used quite a large cross-section of people to test her FFRD, and her research suggested that everyone had some Power, but that not everyone was aware of the field or their connection to it and so were unable to influence it with any conviction.

Taren noted that Starman's acrobatic roll of their craft had registered on the FFRD as a slight positive charge. She realised this had been generated by the thrill, or the 'high', that was experienced by both herself and Starman during the event. If she had truly been scared during the stunt, nothing would have registered on the FFRD: her negative reaction would have cancelled out Starman's positive reaction and the chaos of field would have remained balanced. However, as both Taren and Starman had had the same reaction, a slight positive charge had been recorded.

Taren really didn't expect to register any fluctuations from the glowing rainbow-coloured gaseous mass they were approaching, but as they drew nearer, the needle on the FFRD meter began to shift to the negative.

'Hey, people.' Taren kept her voice reasonably casual, trying to sound unconcerned. 'I'm registering a negative charge here on the FFRD ... Wow!' she exclaimed, as the needle just kept inching further into the negative.

'*Should we be concerned?*' Lucian wanted to know.

'Well ...' Taren took a couple of seconds to assess what the data could mean. 'Either Starman and I are so averse to being here that we're registering enough negativity to match that of a whole stadium of people whose team just lost the grand final, or our cloud of gas knows we're here and it doesn't like it.'

'Are you trying to tell me this mass of gas has consciousness?' Zeven scoffed.

'No,' Taren replied. 'I'm just telling you that that's what the quantum electrodynamics from this readout suggest. There is a ghost in my machine ... a very, very big ghost. The chances of this kind of fluctuation continuing for this length of time are approaching the million-to-one-against mark. I've never seen this kind of control over the quantum field before. It's unprecedented!'

'Could your machine just be experiencing a failure of some kind?' Lucian proffered.

'An overload more like,' Taren replied in all honesty.

'Could the FFRD be picking up this readout from something other than us or the anomaly?' asked Lucian.

'Sure, if you'd like to entertain the notion of there being another large mass of intelligent, or at least sentient, consciousness hanging out around here somewhere.' Taren felt very uncomfortable suddenly, full of dread, guilt and fear. 'In my professional opinion, this cloud mass does not want us any closer.'

'It's okay,' Zeven assured her. 'I can get a sample from this distance.'

'What are you storing it in?' Taren inquired.

'A cryogen-cooled, collision-free vacuum trap,' Starman said. 'I shoot the trap down into the mass. The trap cools to absolute zero and provides the emptiest space possible in which to store some of the gaseous energy.'

Taren wasn't going to argue with his plan; she just wanted this joyride over — she'd never felt so scared.

When the trap was sent down into the spectacular light mass another huge negative charge registered on the FFRD. 'Hurry up, Zeven,' Taren urged. 'Bring it back and let's go!'

'I'm there,' he assured as he reeled it in. Minutes later, with the trap in the ship's hold, Zeven swung the craft around and headed back to AMIE.

When a bit of distance was put between them and the anomaly, the negative charge ceased to register.

'The FFRD reading has stabilised,' Taren said with a quiet sigh of relief.

'*I guess we got away with it then,*' Lucian concluded with satisfaction.

Taren could tell from the captain's voice that in his perception of events — that is, via the onboard cameras of their craft — the mission had been without incident. 'I truly hope so, Professor,' Taren said warily. As usual, it would be up to her to prove that anything extraordinary had taken place.

The return flight gave Taren the opportunity to see AMIE from the outside and she beheld a very impressive and beautiful vessel.

AMIE was a huge craft comprised of six interconnected modules, smooth and elegant, like spheres stretched to an almost flat shape, each one having observation windows all the way around the outermost rim. The body of each module had a metallic fibreglass-looking finish that turned a pale pearly pink tinged with gold in the ship's exterior lighting. If that exterior lighting was turned off and the window shields were down, Taren imagined the highly reflective surface would camouflage their vessel in space and render it virtually invisible.

Starman explained that the module at the top of the vessel was the command section that housed the flight deck and the docks for their air and land exploration craft. The four modules clustered around each other in the centre housed the bulk of the labs, observatories, offices and living quarters for the staff. There was also one major observatory in the centre of the exposed side of both the upper and lower sections. The base module of the vessel was the marine module, which launched the submersibles that the marine department utilised in their research and this module was a submersible itself, as was the entire craft. The marine module wasn't attached this evening as it had been left on the warm stormy surface of the planet tonight along with the marine department.

'A smooth ride, yes?' Zeven asked in a seductive fashion as he helped Taren down the ladder from the cockpit.

Taren felt patronised but thankful for the aid. Her legs had gone to jelly. 'As that was my first time, I have nothing to compare it to,' she retorted, reluctant to feed his already oversized ego. Although the look of disappointment on the young man's face when she gave him the cold shoulder told Taren that his ego was just a false front. 'But I'm sure you're very good,' she added, in more friendly fashion. 'And as I'm back here in one piece, you're a bloody hero in my book.'

For the little flattery it cost her, the smile on Zeven's face was well worth the effort. When he was happy or exhilarated, his whole being vibrated with an amorous, upbeat energy that was nice to be around.

'Easy now,' Bonar Colbers instructed his team as they unloaded the trap from the small transport into an incubator trolley.

Taren approached Colbers. 'That's going straight to the quarantine lab, I presume?'

'Yep, chicky-babe, those were my instructions.' Bonar winked at her and the younger techs smothered snide laughter.

'Fabulous, honey-munchkin,' Taren replied with a good serve of humour, and this set all the men to laughing out loud. 'I'll meet you there.'

'You handled that well,' Zeven commented as Taren passed by him on her way out of the dock — most of the women they'd had on board were offended by the tech crew's chauvinistic remarks.

'Lots of practice,' she explained and kept going, eager to start analysing their acquisition.

Lucian was awaiting Taren inside the quarantine facility, where all her paraphernalia had been delivered.

'I took the liberty of having your equipment brought straight here,' said Lucian. 'All your personal belongings have been taken to your new living quarters.'

'Which I might actually get to see before I leave AMIE, right?' Taren joked, foreseeing much work in her immediate future.

The cryogenic vacuum trap was being transferred into a bio-molecular quarantine room. This was an observation area isolated from the main lab by a couple of sets of shield windows which had a bio-molecular scanning area in-between. The sample was ejected into a transparent containment tube; it could be observed from the lab visually, and could also be monitored by the computer systems in the lab that would be analysing it.

Lucian smiled at Taren's jest. 'It will take a while for the sample to adjust after the cryo-containment, so I could show you around now if you like?'

Taren looked horrified by the notion. 'You don't want to leave an unanalysed sample hanging around your ship, surely?' She was concerned that it might leak, or that some spy might attempt to nick some of the sample. She began searching through her cases for the equipment that she needed.

'That observation room is constantly monitored by AMIE's systems and will be ejected from our craft at the slightest indication of a leak,' Lucian advised her with a proud twinkle in his eye.

Taren was impressed. 'Who has access to this lab?'

'You can register the entry code on your way out,' Lucian assured, as Bonar and his crew stepped into a biomolecular scanning room, situated between the observation facility and the lab, which scanned the crew for any biohazardous chemicals that may have escaped during the transfer. 'Whoever you give that code to has access.'

Obviously getting a negative for viruses, parasites, radiation, and similar dangers, the tech crew moved into a de-suiting room, dragging their trolley containing the empty trap behind them.

Taren had found her hard drive containing the programs that would give her an initial analysis. 'Just give me a couple of minutes to plug in my system and I'll run a spectrograph while we're away. I want to know what kind of quanta we're dealing with. My system will beep me when it's completed graphing the molecular activity of the sample.' She plugged her hard drive into the lab's system and proceeded to initiate her program.

'I can see why you've come so far so fast, Dr Lennox.'

Taren's typing slowed as she absorbed his flattery. 'In my field, wasting time can cost you proof of a miracle. If you're not onto it, you miss out.'

'All too true. And on the subject of miracles, I want to discuss your FFRD reading during the mission today.' Lucian raised the subject somewhat warily.

'I expected you might want to forget it,' Taren proffered. 'Unless, of course, you wish to discuss it in order to find a way to dismiss the incident?'

'On the contrary!' Lucian's tone appealed for her to have a little more faith in him. 'When you analyse the data on the FFRD, I want a copy of the report. I'll reserve any argument until we have some data worth arguing about.'

Good comeback, thought Taren. Lucian Gervaise was certainly a lot more open-minded than any of her associates to date. 'Of course.' She pressed the 'run' button and rose. 'I'm ready for the tour now.'

Lucian motioned to the door that Bonar and his crew were now exiting through. 'Then let's start with how to program your entry code and go from there.'

Taren was truly impressed with her living quarters — her rooms were large with breathtaking views of space.

'Even royalty would be happy staying here,' she commented, as Lucian demonstrated all the mod cons.

'When confined to a vessel, people need their own space,' Lucian explained. 'This may seem like a large area right now, but in six months it could feel all too small.'

'Best accommodation I've ever had,' Taren complimented the captain. 'Good luck getting rid of me.'

'Having you aboard is a welcome diversification for the project. I doubt we shall be in any hurry to kick you out.' Lucian hinted that a more permanent arrangement might be on the cards.

Taren raised both brows, but the professor knew as well as she did that until she proved her aptitude for this type of fieldwork, there was no point in discussing the issue further. Space-work was not for everyone, and there was always a six-month trial period involved. 'Careful what you wish for, Lucian.' It felt wonderful to be on a first-name basis with the legend of cutting-edge astro-marine research. 'I seem to induce a condition commonly known as "red cheeks" in most of my supervisors.'

'I know you've been given a hard time in the past, Taren.' Lucian's tone was serious. 'We're different here on AMIE. Anything goes, all theories welcome. Proof is also very important, naturally, but we are patient and will support your theories unless someone can prove you wrong.'

Taren nearly had heart failure at his words. This guy wasn't a total sceptic — he was being straight with her, she could tell. His energy felt very clear and refreshing; Lucian exuded such integrity that one felt like an arrogant ingrate not to believe him. 'That's comforting to know, Lucian. Thanks for the vote of confidence.'

He smiled, pleased to have set her at ease. 'Come, I'll show you where the offices are.'

Taren's jaw dropped. 'Don't tell me I get an office too?'

'You'll have to share with one of the other solo researchers here.' Lucian led her into the curving corridor. 'He's a nice, quiet bloke. I'm sure you'll get along.'

Taren entered the code that locked her living quarters and then caught up with Lucian. 'What's he studying?'

'Ringbalin is our botanist and horticulturist-cum-geneticist,' Lucian replied. 'He's the reason the salad is so good here.'

'He grows food in space?' Taren assumed.

'He grows *great food* in space,' Lucian corrected, 'without pesticides due to the pest-free environment.'

'I have to agree my salad was pretty good.' Taren followed Lucian down a corridor that led into the heart of this module.

Lucian continued his guided tour explaining that in this module all the living quarters were around the exterior of the module, to take advantage of the views, and all the offices were in the central chamber of the module.

They entered a round chamber full of reference databases and communication systems, one end of which was Aurora's reception area and beyond that the captain's office — the only office with a view of space. But there were doors all around the walls of this office area — bar where the two entrance corridors were located — and these were the private staff offices. Lucian approached one of these and the door slid aside.

'This will be your office.' Lucian indicated one side of an enclosed office which was almost triangular in shape, as the curved back wall was wider than the entrance.

Taren looked over to her new office mate's side of the room where all manner of plants were displayed in long glass tubes. Some plants were growing under lights, but others were both in water and under light. 'Wow!' she exclaimed, thinking they were too beautiful to be scientific experiments.

Her side of the room was spotless and barren, except for the database system on her desk.

'You won't see much of Ringbalin as he spends most of his time in the greenhouse in Module C,' Lucian informed her. 'You might want to seek him out there if you get the urge to cook for yourself.'

'I thought I saw you wander through.'

Taren looked up to see the most stunningly beautiful woman standing in the doorway.

She was tall, slender and graceful. Noting the way she and Lucian regarded each other, Taren knew that this woman was Amie, Lucian's wife.

'I was just showing our new recruit around.' Lucian motioned to Taren, but Amie was already approaching to shake Taren's hand.

'We are so very pleased to have you aboard, Dr Lennox. Your research has been an inspiration to many of us here.'

Oh, shit! Not only is she beautiful, but she's a lovely person, Taren thought, feeling jealous. Lucian was the perfect man; it just figured that he was already married to the perfect woman. 'The pleasure is all mine, Dr Gervaise.' Taren shook her hand, trying to think of something nice to say in return. 'Please, call me Taren.'

'Amie,' she concurred, then turned to address her husband. 'I've just notified Zeven that my team want to be picked up and the storm has cleared. We'd best grab them while conditions are good. We've got an hour of daylight left.'

'Very good.' Lucian smiled and squeezed her hand as she moved past him. 'I shall meet you at the flight deck presently.'

'Aye, aye, Captain,' she replied in a playful manner.

Taren might have been imagining things, but their dialogue sounded like code for 'Meet you in the bedroom in five minutes'.

'We'll speak soon, Taren.' Amie gave a wave as she departed.

''Bye.' Taren managed to keep a straight face and waited for Lucian to excuse himself.

'Unfortunately, I'll have to cut the tour short,' Lucian began, 'as I have to prepare for the pick-up of Module E.'

'I understand,' Taren replied, trying to hide a smile. She just knew he was fibbing.

'What?' Lucian was intrigued by her amusement.

'Nothing,' Taren insisted. 'I'm fine, really. You do what you must.' Taren struggled to suppress her laughter. Maybe she had space-lag and was overtired?

Lucian cocked an eyebrow, suspecting that somehow Taren knew he wasn't being entirely honest about where he was going. 'You really are psychic, I think.'

'No,' Taren regained her composure. 'I'm not, truly.'

Lucian didn't look convinced and now he too was suppressing a smile. 'Feel free to explore, the locals are very friendly.'

'So I've noticed.' Taren nodded in agreement and baide him farewell.

Lucian, exiting the work cubicle, glanced back at Taren with a look of delighted query on his face.

'I'm not!' Taren insisted and waved him on.

The couple left a lovely ambience in their wake. That's what true love felt like, Taren considered, and even though the man of her dreams was not available, it was kind of comforting to know that there was such a thing as a perfect marriage, especially where science and a relationship were concerned.

One of the glass tubes on Ringbalin's desk was holding Taren's attention. Atop a little mossy mound was a miniature tree. The amazing detail demanded a closer look, and that was how Taren came to be so close to the glass when the light suddenly shut down and it began to rain inside the tube. The shock made Taren squeal and chuckle with delight. 'That's amazing!'

'*Allocasuarina torulosa*,' said a voice. Taren looked around to see a small-framed man with fine fair hair that was pulled back from his face in a ponytail.

'Pardon?' Taren hadn't quite caught what he'd said.

'Forest oak.' He pushed his reading glasses up to rest on the bridge of his nose and pointed to the tree inside the tube.

'Oh,' she said, enlightened. 'You must be —'

'Ringbalin Malachi.' He held out a hand to shake hers. 'Looks like we're roommates, Dr Lennox.'

'Taren,' she corrected as she shook his hand.

For some reason, she'd envisioned a big, broadly-built fellow. In reality, the scientist was around her height and had more of the physique of a boy than a man. Taren figured he was probably a bit younger than she was, but he had that quiet unassuming boy-genius thing happening.

'Sorry.' Taren felt she had to explain the grin on her face. 'I'd thought Ringbalin was your second name.'

'I know, it's a mouthful.' He sat down on his chair, which was built onto a track running the length of the desk. 'Most people here just call me Balin.'

With a nod of approval, Taren tried out her chair. It moulded well to the body giving good support. 'Very nice.' She slid her chair the length of the track behind her desk.

'It's great here,' Balin assured. 'When I first arrived, I thought, *wow* ... this is such a perfect work environment that there must be a catch. But there isn't. I've been with the project for six years and I still haven't found anything that would make me want to leave.'

He did look very comfortable in his grotty overalls and boots.

'Do you like plants?' Balin queried.

'Oh, yes,' Taren said passionately. 'I did a three-year study involving plants.'

'Then this is for you.' He picked up the tube-tank she'd been admiring and placed it on her desk. 'A bit of colour.'

The sweet gesture nearly brought a tear to Taren's eye. 'How lovely, thank you. I wish I had something to give you in return.'

'Tell me about your plant study.'

Taren took a deep breath. 'It was on morphic fields and biophoton emissions,' she began. 'That's cell —'

'Coordination and communication,' Balin cut in, letting her know she could cut to the chase.

'I was looking for a low-intensity electromagnetic field that could be orchestrating the growth pattern of the cellular body at a quantum level ... weak biophoton emissions that were orchestrating the body growth. My theory is that these light emissions are the self-organising properties of biological systems from molecules to bodies to societies.'

'Advancing the idea that a low quantum frequency, a light-field, might be responsible for getting proteins to cooperate with each other and carry out the instructions of DNA.' Balin pushed his glasses back up his nose once more.

'Yes.' Taren smiled. She still couldn't get used to people not looking at her like she had two heads and spoke a foreign language when she explained her work.

'And you found electrical fields in seedlings which resembled the eventual adult plant,' Balin concluded.

'Yes, I did.' Taren was further stunned, until she realised: 'You've read my work?'

'That system,' he pointed to the tank, 'is based on much of your research and some of my own.'

This news was also very touching for Taren; someone was basing their research on her work!

'I have been measuring the different photon emissions of many plants,' Balin continued, 'and I have discovered that you were right. The living system must maintain a delicate equilibrium of light. Any excess is rejected, for too much light can inhibit the ability of cells to do their job. Photon emission varies from one living organism to another, depending upon its position on the evolutionary scale. The more complex the organism, the fewer photons being emitted.'

'Meaning ... the more evolved the organism the more light being absorbed and maintained by the cells of the body. Very interesting stuff, Balin,' Taren said, most impressed.

'Your findings on response to positive stimuli on cell growth ...' Balin kept the mutual admiration theme going. '... and the high biophoton emissions of healthy food have been invaluable to my work. So you see, you've already given me a gift.'

Taren had never been so elated in all her born days. Her hard work was finally making a difference to someone. 'I'm honoured that you could put the research to good use.' Taren's beeper went off. 'Oooh, that's my analysis.' She stood to excuse herself.

'Drop by Module C some time, and I'll show you my little oasis in space.' Balin returned to his side of the room.

'I'll certainly do that,' Taren assured him before heading back up to Module F where her quarantine lab was located.

CHAPTER 4

REASONABLE FORCE

Taren followed the same route to the quarantine lab that she had taken with Lucian earlier; she was sure there was a faster route there from where she had ended up, in the offices, but she would investigate later.

She stepped out of the lift at the rear of the flight deck. This control centre housed the pilot seat for AMIE and the navigation station that was open to the lift and the observation lounge behind it. It was here that Taren ran into Rory, who was waving a file around. 'These are the specs on the atmosphere of Oceane, the planet you took the sample from. Lucian thought you'd probably want to compare them to your analysis.' She handed the folder to Taren.

'Whose sample?' Starman butted in as he passed by. He took the pilot's seat behind the huge semicircular console in the flight deck. 'I was the one who bagged it.' Zeven began flicking switches and punching in commands all the way around his console.

Taren knew the young pilot was just fishing for attention, but she played along. 'Then we shall henceforth refer to the sample as Starman's stuff. How's that?'

'That's more like it!' He worked the hand controls whereupon the entire ship began to descend.

'Whoa.' Taren froze on experiencing the odd feeling of moving without movement. She walked over to the large shield windows to observe the gigantic cloud-covered orb while they headed towards the daylight surface of Oceane. Taren could barely feel the motion of the craft in which she stood, although their speedy path through space was plain to see, and she had to give him his due. 'You are elite, Zeven.'

'There's no point in doing anything if you can't excel at it,' he flirted, placing AMIE on autopilot while he left the pilot's desk to duck over to the scanner to get a lock on their absent module.

'He's a bloody show-off, is what he is.' Rory left, having seen it all before, passing Leal storming into the flight deck.

'You could have waited for me to get here.' Leal took up his place and Zeven returned to the pilot's seat. 'What's your urgency?'

'We're running out of daylight in our pick-up zone,' Zeven justified. 'And since I didn't know how long it would take you to drag yourself away from your girlfriend —'

'I don't have a girlfriend,' Leal insisted. 'I had a stomachache. I needed to see the doctor.'

'Yeah, right ... I've never known anybody to get so many minor ailments as you,' Zeven teased him.

'Well, Kassa is a very good doctor,' Leal replied winningly, then spotted Taren standing by the shield windows. 'Hello, Taren.' Leal, feeling embarrassed, looked at Zeven to get a little of his own back. 'Now I see what the urgency was.'

'I'll just be getting along,' Taren decided. She was none too keen on being in the middle of their payback session and made a beeline for the corridor that led to the launch bay and adjoining labs.

The initial analysis of Starman's stuff proved very interesting when compared to Lucian's reports on the overall atmosphere of the planet.

Oceane was basically volcanic, but covered by deep water kept boiling by volcanic activity on the ocean floor. They had yet to find life on Oceane, nor did they expect to, due to the mixture of carbon dioxide and nitrogen in the atmosphere; without other productive elements it lacked the ability to create amino acids, the building blocks of proteins that are the base ingredients of all terrestrial life.

However, it seemed that within their sample of gas a primordial soup was being stirred, for there were traces of methane, hydrogen and ammonia, which did have the potential to yield amino acids and thus proteins. The spectroscopy report was all over the place, showing periodic bombardments of everything from infrared to x-ray and gamma ray wavelengths going on inside the great rainbow cloud of matter.

'If this is correct,' and Taren couldn't think of any reason why it wouldn't be, 'we might well have the perfect scenario to witness the miracle of spontaneous generation!'

How life on her home planet had evolved was still a mystery, as scientists had yet to discover the elusive force that transformed a molecule into a living organism — or rather, they'd failed to discover how nature could have perfected this complicated process by accident.

It almost seemed as if this substance was performing the function of an incubator. Taren was now extremely curious as to what was taking place *below* the cloud mass.

The buzzer on the lab door alerted Taren to company.

'Come in, it's not locked.' She looked up from her screen to see who her visitor was. 'What are you doing here?'

When Taren awoke she was aching from sleeping hunched over at her desk. 'Ooo-ah,' she moaned, having a good stretch. 'I must have been zonked.' She couldn't recall feeling fatigued or dropping off to sleep. 'Now where the hell was I?'

Taren looked around to get her bearings and noticed that the arrowhead of her handheld FFRD monitor was bouncing at the negative end of the indicator, just as it had been when they'd first approached the anomaly.

'Oh no,' she mumbled, trying to get a grip on what living matter might be causing the huge quantum disturbance in the room. There was nothing and no one in sight. The entire crew could not cause such a huge fluctuation to register, so she alone had no hope.

She looked at the gaseous substance of undulating colour held in the transparent tube in the observation room. 'It couldn't be.' She looked back to check the reading to find the needle drifting back over the zero, or centre point of the FFRD register and into the positive. 'No!' She glanced at the sample and quickly back to the monitor which did a little bounce in the positive.

'It's communicating!' Taren gasped, and jumped back from the desk. 'No, that's impossible. It's just a gas!'

* * *

'Dr Lennox?'

Taren woke with a start, gasping with fright. She looked directly to the handheld FFRD sitting on the desk where she'd plugged it into a data history analysis machine — the needle was sitting dead still at zero point. 'Oh, thank heavens.' She held her chest, relieved beyond belief to discover she'd been dreaming.

'I think you were having a bad dream,' someone said. Taren spun around in her chair to find Lucian standing in the doorway.

'Caught sleeping on the job, hey?' Taren winced. 'That doesn't look too good, does it?'

Lucian didn't look worried. 'You've had a full day,' he said. 'If our sample is not an immediate threat, why don't you get some sleep?'

'I've got some very interesting information regarding —'

Lucian held up a hand. 'We'll meet at breakfast this evening,' he decreed. 'Just because a lot of people on AMIE are up at all hours doesn't mean we have to be. Go to bed,' he ordered, over her impending objection. 'Good morning.' He raised a hand in farewell. 'See you at sunset when I arise.'

Taren didn't want to go to bed. Her strange gas was all too interesting. 'We could be discovering the as-yet-undetermined, elusive substance that has the potential to create an energetic reaction sufficient to transform a mixture of molecules into something with the basic characteristics of a living organism, and he wants me to sleep!' Was there a connection between her field theory and this substance? By her reckoning everything evolved through interaction with the field. Could it be that this substance was just her field made manifest? Or perhaps this substance was an instrument of the field?

'Questions that must wait for the morrow.' She closed her folders, and switched off any system that was not needed. 'I guess I have earned a rest.' She yawned — her brain may have been on overdrive but her body sure needed sleep. 'Now all I have to do is remember where my living quarters are.'

Out through the windows in the flight deck the only thing to be seen was the steam rising from the hot-water surface of Oceane fogging any other view. And night was closing in.

On her way to get some rest, Taren stopped to admire Zeven at work, battling high seas and zero visibility to lock onto E module and fish it out of the water. Lucian had obviously been distracted from his date with a pillow by the action. Amie and Leal were also present.

Zeven struggled with the hand controls, trying to line up the module's hatch with the corresponding hatch on the bottom of AMIE. 'These waves are really pissing me off,' he grumbled, remaining focused on the targeting monitor in front of him. 'Maybe we should submerge for pick-up?'

'You've achieved dry dock in worse, Zeven.' Amie encouraged him to keep trying.

'There're some serious currents that are going to cause you just as much grief underwater,' Lucian added. Airborne, they had better manoeuvrability on their side.

The seals on the hatch were magnetic, set to attract each other, but with the rise and fall of the steamy waves, it was proving rather hard to get the right approach angle.

'Sonofabitch!' Zeven took the craft up with the rise of the wave and prepared for the next decline. 'This time I'm in for sure,' he announced, very determined about his aim.

'That's the spirit,' Leal encouraged.

'I'm going down,' Zeven informed one and all, whereupon Lucian, Amie and Leal looked at the second targeting monitor at Leal's station.

'You're looking good, Starman, hold it steady,' Leal urged, although Zeven could clearly see how he was doing. Leal found that Zeven performed better when egged on. 'And he takes aim and ... he scores!' the co-pilot cheered, as the hatches locked together and sealed.

'We're outta here,' Zeven advised, engaging AMIE's automatic pilot to take the ship up and into the outer atmosphere of the planet.

In Taren's experience there was always something incredibly attractive about watching someone engaged in an activity they excelled at, as this was when many people were most in tune with the field.

'You are a legend, Starman,' Lucian told Zeven, before waving goodnight to everyone.

As Amie accompanied Lucian from the flight deck he kissed her. 'Have fun with your analysis,' he told his wife as they parted ways.

'I might see you in a few days,' Amie replied in all seriousness. She blew her husband a kiss and headed off to meet with her marine crew.

Taren sighed. What she wouldn't give for a man who was willing to be a lover but then leave her alone to do her work for days on end.

'I didn't realise I had an audience.' Zeven left the flight deck to speak with Taren.

'Oh, yes.' Taren felt uncomfortable being caught watching him work twice in one day. 'I was just on my way back to my living quarters ... I'm afraid I haven't found a short cut yet.'

'Well, I'm just about done here.' Zeven looked over to Leal, who smiled and waved to imply he'd finish up if Zeven wanted to go. 'I'll escort you if you like. We're neighbours, after all.'

'Sure,' Taren replied, feeling she had no reason to protest. 'I'm still a bit lost when it comes to the layout of this ship.'

'Would you like to get something to eat first?' Zeven led off.

'Um ...' She was a bit hungry, but Taren didn't want him getting the wrong idea. She wasn't on AMIE looking for romance. She was here to look for answers to the riddles of the cosmos. Still, they were working together.

'I'm not asking you for a date,' he clarified, when Taren couldn't decide. 'Just if you're hungry.'

'I am,' she smiled, pleased he had cleared that up.

'Do you prefer to eat alone?' He entered the lift down to Module A.

'Only when I'm working,' Taren replied, foreseeing where the conversation was headed.

Zeven liked her honesty. 'Then would you mind very much if I joined you for something to eat?'

The pilot may have been young, about twenty years younger than Taren, but he had 'how to be charming' down to a fine art.

'Some company would be great,' she concurred.

The food was good, the view was excellent and the company wasn't too bad either. Zeven was proving to be a rather pleasant bloke: he told great stories, was fairly open-minded and had a good sense of humour. An hour after they'd finished eating Taren found herself still sitting there chatting with him.

'I want to know more about the Powers.' Zeven raised the topic again. 'Which ones do you have? And how many are there? Has anyone ever had all of them?'

'Everyone has the Powers to a differing degree.' Taren grinned, shy of the topic. 'And after seeing the way you fly these craft, I know why you're so interested.'

Zeven grinned also. 'How do you mean?'

'You displayed one of the Powers during the pick up of the marine module today.'

'Which one?'

'Psychokinesis,' Taren advised before defining the term to rid Zeven of his frown. 'To deliberately change the position, form or elements of objects of a specific energy field, with disciplined concentration of the conscious or subconscious mind. To direct one's will to act on elementary atoms of the third dimension in an intentional manner.'

Zeven scoffed, amused. 'No offence, Taren, but what happened was just technical training, skill and a lot of luck.'

Taren shook her head to disagree. 'I don't believe that there is any such thing as luck, just the force of probability versus the will of intention. If my theories prove correct — and they will — genius and talent are just a greater ability to access the infinite field of creation. Our intellect, creativity and imagination exist due to our degree of interaction with the field and our ability to exert our will, consciously or unconsciously, over circumstances. The way I saw events unfold is, once you got determined about the hook-up, your will came into play and exerted your influence on the quantum field of probability in favour of obtaining your desired outcome. The fact that everyone around you also desired the same outcome would have contributed to the success. But as the pilot, it is your will that would have affected the outcome the most. The unified field is a reasonable force that usually favours the will of the most influential motivating energy.'

Zeven smiled; he liked what she was implying but ... 'That's going to be hard to prove.'

'I have research data to support my theory.' Taren was very confident about her premise, and whether or not anyone else believed it didn't matter. Taren was the greatest authority in the field of quantum fluctuations and unusual phenomena, and she challenged any fellow scientist to prove her wrong. Her peers were too afraid to test her theories, or try and duplicate her experiments, as they were afraid they'd discover she was right. Then they'd be forced to rethink and rewrite the time-worn theories that had been the cornerstones of scientific investigation for a long time.

'And you've nicely avoided my questions, yet again,' Zeven noted in conclusion.

'There is nothing I can tell you that you cannot discover for yourself,' Taren defended. 'Your talent is more extensive than you realise, mark my words.'

'Won't you at least tell me which of the Powers you have?' Zeven flashed his dimple in a simultaneous smile and a frown of appeal.

'Are you afraid I might be sitting here reading your thoughts?' Taren teased, disclosing nothing.

'No, you're not telepathic ... as you most probably would've slapped my face and left by now,' he said rather daringly. 'However, you sure do read something about people.'

'You're very perceptive yourself,' Taren granted, amused by his directness, although he was probably telling the truth about what he was thinking. The energy he radiated was very seductive, full of fun and allure. Should she put him out of his misery and tell him about her hidden talents? *Nah*, she decided. 'How did you find out about my MSS history?'

'You're changing the subject again,' Zeven objected.

Taren looked out the windows to view the anomaly in daylight. 'Shouldn't we be able to see our cloud of Starman's stuff on the day side of the planet by now?'

'It just blends with the cloud by day,' Zeven filled her in.

'Have you done a topographical scan?' Taren wandered further off the subject of her Powers. 'Is there anything but ocean under our anomaly?'

'There's a landmass typical of that left in the wake of volcanic activity,' he advised her.

Taren's eyes parted wide, her mind cast back to her history of astronomy class. 'The meteor that hit Oceane a couple of hundred years back must have cracked the crust on the ocean floor.'

'That is Lucian's theory also,' Zeven concurred.

'That could explain why the molecular and electromagnetic readouts in that area are vastly different to the rest of the planet,' Taren posited. But it still didn't explain the strange rainbow light cloud, however.

'Is that a fact?' When Zeven didn't receive a response, he noted that Taren's eyelids were beginning to droop. 'Perhaps it's time to pack it in for the night?'

The thought of sleep brought a broad smile to Taren's face. 'No perhaps about it.'

'Argh!' Taren returned to consciousness to find herself seated bolt upright in bed, gasping for air, her skin cold with the moisture of her own perspiration. Both her hands were wrapped around her throat, as if trying to protect it from attack.

The scare that woke her from slumber was a dream that someone had cut Amie's throat. 'Surely I wasn't lusting after Lucian enough to wish his wife dead?'

In the dream, Taren had assumed the murderer's point of view, but she recalled having distinctly masculine arms. It had been a long time since Taren had had a prophetic dream.

'No, it wasn't prophecy!' She convinced herself that she was only experiencing some side effect of space travel. After all, she hadn't really dreamt in weeks, so it was not surprising during her first few bouts of sleep here on the station that her dreams were a little intense.

There was something else she'd dreamt before the murder of Amie, but the recollection was elusive — a feeling of great desperation and bewilderment was all that remained.

'A shower is sounding real good.' Taren decided she needed to get back to work.

As the overhead jets in her shower-tube massaged her head and shoulders with hot, steamy water, Taren began getting flashes of someone in a bio-suit extracting a sample of Starman's stuff from the lab. The vision was oddly clear for a procedure she'd never seen before.

Could it be future sight?

Precognition was one of the Powers she'd shown the most aptitude for. Taren's heartbeat began to race as she recalled having taken an impromptu nap in the lab yesterday.

I could have seen the thief remotely, while I was sleeping? she considered. *Or, I could have been sleeping with my eyes wide open!*

This brought to mind her little session with Swithin Gervaise and the MSS hypnotherapist. What if she'd freely allowed the spy to take the sample? That would seem to link Swithin Gervaise and the MSS to the spy they'd sent her after. It was possible that what they had told her was a fabrication to allow her to be hypnotised into being, not a stooge, but a double agent!

Taren was out of the shower and dressed before she'd reasoned herself into maintaining an open mind about everything. Her troubling premise was built on a random vision, so it would be silly to get too alarmed at this stage.

It was a scary scenario that she hadn't considered, but Taren would certainly bear it in mind from now on.

In need of sustenance, Taren headed to the mess room, where she bumped into Kassa Madri, the ship's doctor, having a late lunch.

'How are you adjusting to life in space, my dear?' The doc paused in her eating and motioned to a chair at her table to invite Taren to sit. 'Any problems?'

'Space life is great,' Taren stated positively, setting her tray on the table and seating herself in the chair offered. 'It's the sleeping that's proving difficult.' Her smile faded to a frustrated frown as she admitted to having bad dreams.

'That's quite normal,' Kassa assured, her smile comforting as always. 'The pent-up fears of anticipating your stint in space are starting to surface via your subconscious now that you are here.'

Taren bit into her sandwich. She wanted to accept Kassa's assurance, but something did not feel right.

'You're still concerned, however.'

Taren swallowed her mouthful and washed it down with tea while she figured how best to broach her subject. 'Have you ever had a prophetic dream, Kassa?' she inquired of the doctor in a whisper, knowing that Kassa did not wish to advertise her psychic talents.

Kassa shook her head. 'Have you?' Her eyes crinkled with curiosity.

Taren nodded and forced a smile. 'But I found a way to stop them a long time ago.' She took another bite of her sandwich.

'And the dreams you've had since landing on AMIE . . .' Kassa prompted. 'Do you want to talk about them?'

If she mentioned her dream about Amie, Taren felt she'd have to confess her concern that finding Lucian so attractive might have caused it. 'Is there a small vacuum device that is used to sample substances that are being held in bio-molecular quarantine?' Taren held her hands apart to indicate the size of the device. 'Like a transparent tube inside a metal casing that plugs into the BM storage system in my lab?'

Kassa nodded. 'Why, yes, there is.' The doctor imagined this query to be somehow related to Taren's dream.

'Well, that indicates a clairvoyant perception if not a prophetic one,' Taren mumbled, bringing her vision back to mind. *I could have perceived some future instance of legitimate sample extraction? But then, why would my subconscious be eager to bring such a scenario to my attention — it has to be a warning of some kind.*

'Surely the computer monitoring the substance in your lab will indicate whether it's had a loss in mass?' Kassa suggested, having perceived the vision Taren was entertaining. Taren suddenly stared at Kassa, obviously suspicious that she was using telepathy.

Kassa could have been making an educated guess as to her problem, Taren figured, but maybe Kassa's telepathy extended beyond hearing inner dialogue to perceiving mental images as well.

'You're right.' Taren stood, using the suggestion as an excuse to rush off.

'You've barely touched your food,' Kassa pointed out.

Taren gulped down her tea, and grabbed the remains of her sandwiches to eat en route. 'Thanks, Kassa. 'Bye.' Taren made for the door, desperately blocking any thought of Lucian from her mind.

Taren disappeared around the corner and Kassa smiled, now enlightened as to the real reason for the young woman's hasty exit.

'Oh dear.' She shook her head slowly. *If you only knew how much Lucian admires you also.*

Sure enough, when Taren checked with the computer in her lab monitoring the sample in the BM containment facility, it had registered a ten per cent reduction in the molecular concentration of the sample at around the same time in the early morning that Taren had dropped off to sleep.

'Shit!' she cursed under her breath. 'I hate being right all the time.'

Someone had taken a sample and she had allowed

them to do it. Her subconscious recollection of the event was useless when it came to identifying the thief, as he or she was masked by the BM suit they were wearing. If hypnotism had been used to put her to sleep, the thief would most likely have instructed Taren's subconscious not to remember their identity.

'I should never have allowed them to screw with my brain!' Taren was starting to fume, finding the anger helped to subdue her panic. 'But then I wouldn't be here at all,' she reasoned, and she was now somewhat wise to what was going on.

Taren leaned back in her seat and took a deep breath. How had she let this happen? For ten years she had left all her secrets behind her and it had been a hard slog to be taken seriously in her chosen field of endeavour. Now that she had finally achieved her dream posting, why was it all coming back to haunt her? She was so over the spying and lying, and being scoffed at every time she had used her psychic skills to obtain information. Science and reason had worked in her favour, because even if most were still sceptical about her findings, she did have data to back up her claims.

Taren glanced to the handheld FFRD monitor that had been the tool to support many of her theories over the past few years and was shocked to find the needle was at the outer limit of the negative range — a reading Taren thought she'd never ever see.

Her heart leapt into her throat as her logical mind was thrown into panic. *Am I dreaming again?* Taren pinched herself. 'Ouch!'

Nope, definitely not dreaming. Her gaze turned to the sample in her lab and she gasped when she saw the intensity the colourful explosions inside the gassy mass had reached. She looked at the computer monitoring the sample but the readouts didn't indicate any fluctuation at all. The computer wasn't reading the increased activity that was so apparent to the eye and her FFRD.

'Are you the driving force behind this negative quantum flux?' Taren felt a little silly asking the sample a question … until the needle bounced immediately into the positive and then back into the negative.

The blood drained from her face as her brain struggled to digest the phenomenon. It was too much to ask — an intelligent being that did not have solidity!

'Are you distressed?' she asked, as the FFRD reading seemed to support this conclusion.

Again the needle swung briefly into the positive.

'Are you in danger or pain?'

Twice the needle bounced into the positive.

'Is there something I can do to assist?' Taren was concerned. She didn't want to cause another being pain.

Positive.

'Let you go?' Taren guessed, and was surprised when the needle wavered at the negative end of the readout.

Taren closed her eyes to focus her telepathic knowhow on the sample. Telepathy was not one of Taren's strengths; she was sensitive to energy fields, body movements, emotional states and suchlike, but she was not a true telepath. 'I need Kassa,' she decided when she kept sensing the same desperation and bewilderment that she felt every time the vision of the sample being stolen came to mind.

If someone had stolen a sample, they had breached quarantine and Taren needed to reclaim the misplaced substance, as exposure to the gas could be disastrous!

* * *

Outside the mess room door Taren spied Kassa chatting with Leal. Knowing that the co-pilot was rather sweet on the doctor, Taren was loath to interrupt, but couldn't count on their conversation stopping any time soon.

'A thousand apologies,' Taren said to Leal and then looked at Kassa, 'but I urgently need your assistance, Doc.'

'What is it?' Kassa was intrigued by the turbulent energy of Taren's inner panic, which was not apparent enough to the eye for Leal to be concerned by it.

'I'll catch you later.' The man's disappointment at losing Kassa's undivided attention was reflected in the weak smile on his face when he waved and departed into the mess. Kassa must have been aware of how Leal felt. Why was she torturing the poor guy by pretending not to notice?

'I'm not sure it would work,' Kassa whispered as she kept pace beside Taren.

Shocked by just how telepathic Kassa was, Taren paled. 'But you're interested,' Taren ventured, picking up on the whimsical tone in the woman's voice.

'He is a little young for me, and we are very different people.' Kassa shrugged noncommittally. 'How about you tell me what's so urgent?'

'Wait until we get to the lab,' Taren replied.

As soon as they were locked inside, Taren spilled her guts about everything, including her vision regarding Amie, which she was sure Kassa would pick up on before long anyway. She was careful not to even think about anything that occurred before landing on this ship, but told of the dialogue that had passed between herself and the anomaly sample in quarantine via the FFRD. 'And as I can only ask it yes-or-no questions, I need you to see if you can telepathically perceive what this entity's problem is? It might even be able to identify the thief.'

Kassa, although stunned and rather concerned by Taren's claims, was eager to help if she could. 'You ask the questions and I'll tell you if I perceive any answers.'

'Do you mind if I tape this?' Taren suspected this might be a sticking point.

Kassa considered the request a moment. 'On the provision that you consult me before you make anyone else privy to it. I can't hide forever and I'm not sure I want to any more, but it's a big coming out for me, so I want to be consulted should it come to that.'

'I understand completely.' Taren gave a nod in agreement. They both turned as one to confront the anomaly in the lab and Taren instructed the computer to record.

'What can we do to assist you?' The FFRD needle again wavered about in the negative range, but the fluctuation wasn't detected by the computer systems monitoring the sample.

'Ah ...' Kassa gave a slight moan of pain, or perhaps frustration.

'Something?' Taren queried.

Kassa screwed up her face. 'Distorted sound,' she informed. 'It's like it's trying to tune into my frequency.'

'Perhaps it is.' Taren gave the theory some thought before double-checking that Kassa was still keen to do this. 'Does it hurt?'

'I'm good,' she hissed, motioning Taren to silence, as she was perceiving faint words in a voice not specifically male or female, but monotone and distorted. 'Return the missing part. Return all parts to the whole.' She repeated the words she could now hear. The unearthly tone of the being's voice echoing in her mind caused Kassa to shudder as she continued: 'A part is not infinite in energy, as it might at first seem. The part draws from the whole and the whole is weakened. It is damaging to us to be sucked of energy in this manner.'

Taren had stopped breathing during the discourse and drew breath to query. 'What manner? I have only measured the electric charge of this part, which, as you say, seems infinite. But I have not attempted to extract a charge,' Taren explained to the sample and its channel.

'The *missing* part was the energy extraction point,' Kassa conveyed.

'Was?' Taren queried.

'Now it travels,' Kassa relayed, 'to the next star system to be further abused. This will not be tolerated by the whole. We will do whatever we must to protect ourself from attack. Return the parts to the whole, before the whole departs.'

'Departs?' Taren was anxious. 'Where are you going? When do you leave?'

'Fourteen more times around the planet of water and our job here will be done. Home is the next project to which we are drawn across space and time to tend.'

'Wow!' Taren was pleased to be taping this. The way the being referred to itself in the plural and the singular was very interesting, the implication being that the separated parts of this substance were still in contact with each other and with the whole. And the anomaly's use of the word 'tend' seemed to support her theory that this entity had been drawn to this planet to implant the potential for the genesis of life here — much like the role attributed to devas in the ancient legends of her home planet of Maladaan. Perhaps a deva was exactly what this was? Still, Taren had a big problem. 'If you depart in two weeks, there's no way we'll be able to return the missing part to you in time. Our space travel is not fast enough.'

'Release the parts from containment. That is all that is required,' Kassa stated, snapping out of her trance-like daze. 'It has withdrawn,' she informed Taren, feeling a little giddy.

Taren looked at the FFRD to find the needle still at zero point. The colourful electrical activity inside the sample in the containment lab had ebbed to some degree.

How did I get in so much trouble in so little time? Taren quashed her defeatist attitude to determine her next course of investigation. 'Who is in charge of pod launches here on AMIE?'

'That would be Bonar Colbers,' answered Kassa.

'Are you okay? Can I get you anything?' Taren inquired as she looked towards the door.

'I'll come with you.' Kassa stood, but as she was clearly still woozy Taren declined.

'I'll be back soon.' Taren quickly moved off.

'Try the mess room,' Kassa called after her.

Bonar was punching buttons on the menu of the hot breakfast dispenser when Taren caught up with him to inquire whether any pods had departed the ship during his last shift.

'No, nothing,' he informed.

'You're sure?'

Bonar grinned, his cheeks all rosy. 'No one gets in or out of here without my knowledge, and yesterday was dead quiet on that front.'

'Oh.' Taren didn't know what to think. How could the sample possibly be in transit to the next star system if it hadn't gone by pod? 'No deep-space cruisers docked with AMIE yesterday?'

Bonar shook his head. 'I told you ... nothing.'

Was the sample lying? Had Kassa misunderstood the message or messed up the translation? The message had seemed extremely clear.

'There you are, *finally*.'

Taren was startled by Zeven's rather loud entrance into the mess room.

'What do you mean, finally?' Taren protested. 'I was up early.'

'On your second day of sleep,' Zeven informed. 'You slept right through your shift last night.' He had to laugh at the stunned look on Taren's face.

'Tell me you're joking,' she requested before panicking too badly.

'I'm deadly serious. But don't worry, everyone tends to oversleep at first.' Zeven did his best to allay her horror.

'I've really been asleep for two days?' Taren gripped Zeven's shirt, desperate for the truth.

'It's no sweat —'

'Oh, my cosmic forefathers.' Taren ran back to Bonar, who was now seated at a table with the rest of his crew. 'Did a pod leave for Maladaan any time during your last two shifts?'

Bonar seemed a mite bored with her obsession, but as he cast his mind back he recalled, 'Yep, the shift before last. Eleazar Kestler left for Maladaan. He's finished his sabbatical and was headed home with his research results.'

'Kestler?' Taren knew that name. 'The physicist?' Her heart jumped into her throat. She'd attended some of his lectures at the University of Esponisa many years back. His passion was electrodynamics. The man was a legend and she didn't want to be the one to accuse him of stealing a quarantined sample. 'No other craft?'

'Nope,' said Bonar, biting into his sandwich to avoid having to pursue this conversation any further.

'We did have that pod misfire when Kestler's launched,' mentioned the youngest technician at the table, whose name was Raggus, which kind of suited him as he looked like a bag of rags. All his clothes were too big and his blond hair hung past his shoulders in long knotted clumps.

'Really?' Taren looked back to Bonar. 'Did you chase the pod up?'

Bonar shook his head as he slowly chewed up his mouthful.

'It'll show up on Maladaan in a couple of weeks,' Raggus added.

'Does that happen often, pods misfiring?' Taren now directed her questions at Raggus, as he was more eager to oblige her with responses.

'First time for us.' He looked to his companions, who nodded confirmation, and then, noting Bonar's dark expression, he shut up and went back to his food.

'Thanks, guys.' Taren wandered back to the doorway in a daze.

'What's the matter?' Zeven headed her off. 'Why are you so interested in departures?'

'Where is Lucian?' Taren needed to see him yesterday.

'I'm here.' He walked in with Kassa in tow. 'You need to speak with me, I believe.' He motioned to Kassa, who'd passed on the message.

'I haven't told him anything,' she said, letting Taren know Kassa had left that pleasure to her.

'My office.' Lucian led off, and Kassa served Taren a smile of reassurance as they both fell in behind him.

Zeven wanted to follow them and find out what had everyone so excited, but he'd not been invited so he decided to grab a sandwich and see what he could discover about the missing pod.

CHAPTER 5

BEARER OF BAD NEWS

'Okay, Taren, you have my undivided attention.' Lucian reclined comfortably in his desk chair, appearing eager to be enlightened. Kassa had taken a seat on the lounge, but Taren was too full of information and theories to sit.

'When was the last time you saw your wife?' Taren began and Kassa looked at her, stunned that Taren would choose to begin her explanation this way.

'Amie's been analysing data from the recent dive on Oceane for the past few days.' Lucian was frowning. 'So, I guess the pick-up of E module was the last time I saw her ... why?'

'Would you page Amie and ask her to come to your office, please?' This was more of an instruction than a request. Taren had to determine if that part of the vision was true or false and if it had any bearing on anything else that had transpired.

Lucian detached his communicator, punched in Amie's number and at the tone left a message, all the while never taking his eyes from Taren.

'Okay!' Taren slapped her hands together and drew a deep breath in preparation for her confession. She fixed her eyes on Lucian and let him have it. 'How well do you trust Swithin?'

'What do you mean?' Lucian smiled but he was very disturbed by this question. 'He's my brother. What are you driving at?'

'Yes, what indeed?' Kassa echoed, concerned, and as the telepath focused on the other woman she perceived the memory of Swithin that was playing on Taren's mind.

Lucian doesn't know about the problem. He'd have a fit if he knew any of his precious research might be going astray, or that one of his team out there might not be faithful to his project and his people. None of the crew are aware of the spy, nor are they to become aware that you are seeking one.

'I believe I might be a double agent.' Taren further shocked her company. 'I believe I allowed a spy to steal a sample of our quarantined substance, because I was stupid enough to permit your brother and an old acquaintance from my MSS days to hypnotise me before I embarked for my stay on AMIE.'

Lucian was dumbfounded. He didn't know whether to start fuming or laughing. He looked across at Kassa, who appeared equally confused. 'There's more to this than I knew about,' she told him, 'but I believe Taren might be telling the truth about Swithin.'

'What?' Lucian was surprised by this turn of events.

'And I know there's more to that sample in the lab than meets the eye ... best hear her out,' Kassa encouraged.

'All right.' Lucian pressed his fingertips into his forehead in an attempt to maintain his composure. 'How about you start at the beginning?'

Once brought up to date, Lucian only had one question. 'What has all this to do with my wife? And what is keeping her?' Lucian buzzed for Rory and sent her on a mission to find Amie.

'Hopefully, nothing.' Taren was starting to get a bit concerned at Amie's failure to arrive or communicate with Lucian and, clearly, so was Kassa.

Taren had not mentioned anything about Kassa's channelling session, as promised. She had only revealed enough to get Lucian interested in investigating the matter further.

The chime on Lucian's office door alerted them to company.

'At last.' Lucian pressed the intercom key on his desk. 'Enter.'

It was Zeven Gudrun at the door and on sighting him, Taren's and Kassa's moment of relief was snatched away.

'Sorry to interrupt.' Zeven noted that they all seemed disappointed to see him.

'State your business, Zeven,' Lucian said shortly, as his mind was awhirl with other matters. 'We have a bit of a situation unfolding.'

'I understand that you do.' Zeven's eyes turned to Taren. 'I decided to run a trace on that missing pod for you.'

Despite the horrible day she was having, Taren felt warmed that the pilot cared enough to take the initiative in this matter.

'And, guess what?' Zeven handed her a printout. 'It's not headed back to Maladaan at all. It dropped like a stone when it misfired and fell to Oceane's surface ... smack bang in the middle of the area covered by our anomaly.'

Taren was mortified by the news and cast a horrified gaze towards Kassa. They both realised that the misfired pod could not contain the missing sample because the stolen substance was on its way to the next star system. Therefore, Taren could only assume that the missing sample was on the same pod as Eleazar Kestler. Still, she could not tell Lucian of her suspicions without giving away Kassa's secret. 'Can we retrieve the pod?'

'We'd bloody well better,' Lucian objected. 'Our insurance is bad enough without that kind of a claim. What the hell was Bonar thinking, not chasing it up sooner?'

A very good point, thought Taren.

'I plan to give Bonar an earful on the matter,' Zeven assured Lucian. 'I tried to extract the pod from Oceane's surface with the magnetic retrieval system but the electromagnetic disturbance inside the anomaly must be jamming it. I thought I could take a salvage vessel down to the surface and see if I can locate it that way.'

'And risk losing another expensive craft and my chief pilot? I don't think so.' Lucian was most annoyed, although Taren knew it was Amie's failure to turn up that was worrying him more than the thought of financial stress. 'We'll just have to cop the loss of the pod.'

'Maybe not,' Taren proffered, and Kassa stood, knowing what the young woman was thinking. If their sample was still in contact with the whole, then perhaps it could help them to get the pod out.

'Let us try something,' Taren begged Lucian, who was not in the mood for playing games.

'Like?' he queried impatiently.

'Why, an experiment, of course.' Kassa intervened to take some of the heat off her younger colleague. 'Have a little faith, Lucian.' She ushered Taren out the door ahead of her. 'We'll report back presently.'

'Why didn't you tell me about Swithin's suspected involvement in this theft sooner?' Kassa asked on the way to quarantine.

'I'm winging this, Kassa,' Taren confessed, sorry that she had the need to keep secrets. 'I love this project and having admired the work you do here for so long, damned if I will be the one to bring the project into ruin or disrepute. I just want to do whatever is best for AMIE.'

'I know you do,' Kassa assured her. 'I know the inner thoughts of all and you are a good soul, Taren Lennox.'

Taren's curiosity was sparked by the comment. 'What do you feel about Bonar Colbers, Kassa?'

'You don't think *he's* the spy you're looking for?' Kassa was half stunned, half amused by the suggestion.

'Only he has access to all the equipment and technology needed to sneak a sample out of quarantine unnoticed.'

Kassa shrugged; this was true but he had no motive. 'Bonar might be a little obnoxious and simple minded at times, certainly, but he's a simple man. He loves his work and the people he works with. I feel very sure he is loyal to AMIE.'

'But he might not be consciously aware of being party to the crime,' Taren said. 'It's only because I have such extraordinary powers of subconscious recognition that I began to suspect I'd been involved in the burglary.'

Kassa nodded to concede the point. 'That would also explain how a spy on board could conceal their intentions from me.'

'And what of Eleazar Kestler? Could he too have been involved without conscious knowledge?'

Kassa had gone very pale. 'It makes me sick to think that Lucian was diligent in keeping the corrupt away from our work but even all the way out here, covert operators have managed to infiltrate our tightknit crew.'

'Yeah, and I'm the key member of the covert op.' Taren hated that she'd been party to it all.

'No, Taren.' Kassa stopped, stressing her words. 'Our enemies didn't know how badly they would cut their own throat by sending you to us. You're a very brave woman, one of the bravest I've ever known, and you will be this project's saving grace, I know it.'

This was the nicest thing that anyone had ever said to Taren. 'Thanks ... but I don't think Lucian is sharing that viewpoint right now.'

'You're fond of him, aren't you?' Kassa sounded a little sorry for her.

'It's just a schoolgirl crush really,' Taren shrugged it off and punched in the code that opened the lab door. 'I hardly know the man, bar that he is obviously and happily married.'

'Perhaps.' Kassa hated to think that Taren's foreboding about Amie could prove to be valid but she had an awful feeling about it.

'Do you sense something regarding Amie?' Taren wondered aloud.

Kassa merely shook her head. 'I just wish she'd bloody well make an appearance and put us all out of our misery!'

Lucian was clearly distraught when Taren and Kassa returned to his office. 'What prompted you to ask after the whereabouts of my wife?' He demanded an answer from Taren the second she set foot through his door.

'Why?' Taren didn't like the note of panic in his voice.

'No one has seen Amie for at least two shifts. She was headed to see me when she was last spotted this time *yesterday*.' He was full of fear, which was highly out of character. 'She never arrived.'

Taren didn't want to tell Lucian what she'd seen in her vision and looked to Kassa for aid.

'Kassa?' Lucian understood that she'd been made privy to Taren's reasons.

'Taren had a prophetic vision regarding Amie at the same time that she had a vision of the theft,' Kassa began diplomatically.

'What did you see?' Lucian directed the query at Taren, having lost all desire to be diplomatic. He did not doubt Taren's abilities, as precognition had been a large part of Taren's work with the MSS.

'I could be wrong ...' Taren hesitated again.

'I've read your MSS files, Dr Lennox. I know you have never been wrong.'

Lucian's certainty stunned Taren a little; people weren't usually eager believers. 'To tell you what I saw would be to influence the outcome in this affair. Outcomes are influenced by what we all collectively believe, Lucian. I don't want to direct energy into the wrong probability. I have not had the sight in a long time, so my senses may not be as attuned as they once were. Neglected for ten years, any talent is bound to suffer.'

Lucian could see what she was saying but it brought him no peace. 'Your vision regarding the theft seems to be proving true enough.'

'That event was most likely one that I witnessed first-hand, so I'm employing nothing more than subconscious recall to perceive the information. To know what has become of Amie would require ESP, unless I have taken up sleepwalking. In other words, there is a greater chance of me being wrong about Amie's whereabouts.'

'But the very fact that you knew she'd gone missing, when no one else has noticed! Please …' Lucian appealed. 'Your insight cannot be worse than all these terrible scenarios running through my mind.'

'Give energy to the good scenarios you can imagine,' Taren suggested. 'Like, she's bumped her head and passed out somewhere, or overslept like I did last night. I suspect our spy-cum-thief subliminally induced me into a deep slumber. Perhaps the same fate has befallen your wife?'

As Kassa felt some of the weight lift from the captain, she thought Taren's attempt to comfort him was very wise. Kassa also believed that will could affect and even change the future.

'You're right.' He backed away to take a seat at his desk. Every conscious soul on board was looking for his wife; someone was sure to locate her soon. 'Did you find a solution to our pod problem?'

'We believe we might have,' Taren said, 'as it seems that the pod cleared a trail through the anomaly as it fell. A small craft might be able to enter and retrieve it.'

Of course, this was a fabrication of the truth. In fact, Kassa and Taren had persuaded the anomaly to clear a path to the missing pod. Finding the missing craft was vital to solving the mystery surrounding the stolen part of the anomaly's essence. The degree of electromagnetic activity surrounding this path through the anomaly did not allow for remote retrieval of the pod, but they had safe passage for their recovery craft to go to Oceane's surface.

'What!' Lucian wondered how this possibility had escaped Zeven's attention.

'It was just a hunch that checked out.' Taren was pushing her luck and, clearly, Lucian was sceptical.

'You've been chatting with your sample again, haven't you, Dr Lennox?' Lucian still wasn't sure he trusted Taren's method of communication with the sample via the FFRD. 'You expect me to put Zeven's life at risk for what could be nothing more than a fault in your machinery.'

Taren noticed that Kassa was obviously in two minds about mentioning her involvement in Taren's plans. Taren jumped in to save Kassa from having to expose herself just yet. 'I have been in telepathic communication with the anomaly as well,' she blurted out, having had a brainwave. She would simply get the computer to swap Kassa's voice and her own on the recordings, then it would seem like Kassa was merely asking the questions on her behalf and that Taren was doing the channelling.

Lucian almost smiled at this. 'You swore to me that telepathy wasn't one of your attributes.'

'You also knew I was lying,' Taren ventured, and momentarily held her breath, hoping he was convinced.

'All right,' he conceded reluctantly. 'I said I'd support your theories and I shall.'

'I'd like to go with Zeven, if that's okay,' Taren volunteered. 'This was my suggestion and if anything goes wrong — which it won't — I want to be there.' In truth, she was eager to get a look at what the entity was tending beneath its mists.

Lucian briefly dwelt on her request. With his wife missing, accusations flying around about his brother, and this theft from quarantine, Lucian didn't like to risk the loss of Taren — the only link in all these mysteries. Then again, he knew he'd feel safer sending Zeven down if Taren was with him. 'You may go,' he decided in the end.

'You are a total star!' Zeven told Taren as they suited up for the trip. 'Do you know how long I've been trying to persuade Lucian to let me fly into that mass?'

The man was clearly excited. His enthusiasm was catching and it tickled Taren's heavy mood into retreat. 'Starman, you're a maniac, you know that, don't you?'

He nodded proudly. 'But you know what is really encouraging?'

Taren shook her head.

'I've finally found someone who's as big a psycho as I am when it comes to jumping right in.' He bowed to give Taren her due.

'I figured I owed you one for tracing that pod for me,' she retorted, waving off the intended praise.

Zeven looked disappointed. 'Is this trip payback for the trace? Damn, I was hoping that deed was going to score me a date.'

Well, at least he was honest. A flirt, but right upfront about it. Taren knew he was trouble, but it was so long since she'd been pursued that she was rather flattered by the younger man's attention.

'Geez!' She emphasised how ungrateful he was. 'You're getting to take me out, aren't you?'

'I'll have Colbers pack a picnic brunch then, shall I?' His cheeky grin grew.

'Yo,' Leal called, entering the suiting room to hurry them along. 'Your target zone is entering daylight.'

Zeven motioned for Taren to lead the way. 'Time to take one large step for mankind?' He raised his brows, impressed with himself, and served Leal a smug smile on his way out.

The reconnaissance-carrier vessel they were using for this mission was larger than the tandem spacecraft they'd taken on their first flight together. Taren liked being able to sit alongside Zeven, and the front screen window of this transport awarded her a much better view of the planet they were approaching.

'Will you look at that,' Zeven mumbled, beholding a large tubular void disappearing into the cloud mass. The spectacular light show had been dimmed by the brightness of the twin suns above. 'Science couldn't hope to manufacture a better tunnel through an unstable mass!' He looked at Taren and covered the microphone on his headset to speak with her on the quiet. 'I know that passage wasn't there when I scanned the anomaly earlier today.'

Taren didn't bother covering her mouthpiece. She didn't mind who knew what she'd been up to or whether they believed her explanations. She was sick of keeping secrets. 'I have a new friend, it seems.'

Zeven stared in disbelief. 'Are you telling me that the gas did this at your request?'

'I don't believe it is just a gas,' Taren told him bluntly. 'I believe what we have here is an entity that the ancients referred to as an arupa-deva — a formless being whose body is entirely composed of electricity.

These beings were said to be the builders of all things in the universe, the architects of matter, and I believe this particular arupa-deva was drawn to this planet to tend to it after the explosion when that meteor hit Oceane a couple of hundred years back.'

Zeven was so stunned by her response that he simply scoffed, but no words were forthcoming.

'You're not getting all mystical on us, are you, doctor?' Leal queried through the intercom, as this was the first he'd heard of this theory.

'Looks that way,' she retorted dryly, 'and I have a couple of prophecies for you as well.'

'Shoot.' Leal played along.

'I expect that we are about to find life on this lifeless planet,' Taren stated. 'Below this cloud mass, we'll find a different atmosphere to the rest of the planet, maybe even oxygen.'

Leal and Starman both got a good laugh out of that.

'This deva of yours would have to have sped up the evolution process by millions of years, in just a couple of hundred.' Lucian explained his crew's amusement.

'Yes, I do realise that.' Taren tried not to sound insulted. 'However, if I am proven correct and I can establish the existence of such an entity, then that would explain many of the knowledge gaps about the creation of our own planet and its species, wouldn't you say? It would establish the missing link between physics, chemistry and biology.'

There followed a long silence, which Lucian broke. *'You said you had a couple of prophecies?'*

'Ah, yes,' Taren recalled. 'In two weeks, Oceane time, the deva will be moving to its next project.'

'It told you so?' Lucian guessed.

'It did,' Taren agreed, imagining Lucian rolling his eyes. 'At the same time, it told me that we had to return its missing parts by then or face dire consequences.'

'Now you're scaring me,' Starman stated flatly, unsure of what to make of all her statements.

'I scare myself,' she admitted and then shrugged. There wasn't anything she could do about it. 'Believe me, it is not by choice that I got landed in the middle of this shit storm.'

'You're doing a great job of keeping it contained,' said Lucian, with as much conviction as he could muster in his still-frantic state.

While they'd waited for daylight in their target area, Lucian had had the spaceship searched from end to end, and found no trace of his wife. All AMIE's smaller craft had been checked and accounted for; only this misfired pod was outstanding.

He noted Kassa standing in the shadows at the rear of the flight deck and moved to have a quiet word.

'Won't you give me some idea of the gravity of Taren's vision concerning Amie?' Lucian begged. 'Did she foresee an accident, a death?'

'Don't give up hope, Lucian,' Kassa pleaded. 'You were never one for unfounded speculation, don't change now.'

'I feel like a child being kept in the dark for his own protection, which leads me to think the worst!'

Kassa shook her head slowly, which indicated he'd not yet imagined the worst.

'How am I to know that Taren isn't at the bottom of all of this? Perhaps my brother had nothing to do with the stolen sample. Maybe this self-confessed spy is playing us all for sport?' He was suddenly worried that he'd sent Zeven on a mission with her.

'Lucian ...' Kassa grabbed his arm to encourage him to disregard such thoughts. 'If Taren was behind this theft, then why would she be so desperate to return the sample to its source? And why would she have alerted you to Amie's absence if she had anything to do with it? If Taren was part of the problem, she would have been aboard that pod headed back to Maladaan, don't you think?'

Lucian conceded the sense of this and calmed down.

'We're entering the tunnel now.'

Zeven's report drew Lucian's attention back to the flight deck.

'This is just amazing.' Zeven struggled to express the awe he was feeling. *'There are great explosions of colour all through here.'*

'And lightning,' Taren added. *'It's shooting through the anomaly like veins through an animal form. And yet, the electricity is contained beyond the tunnel. It's not threatening our craft, but is lighting the way very nicely.'*

'The passage is arcing down at a low angle and the surface of the tunnel has been perfectly even around its circumference.'

'What I think Starman is trying to say is that this passage is too perfect to be an accidental formation,' Taren said and Zeven wasn't heard to disagree. *'There's excessive turbulence beyond the tunnel, but inside the passage it is quite still ... not a trace of wind, cloud or anything ... just light.'*

'Conditions are beautiful, totally beautiful!' Starman exclaimed, obviously enjoying himself. *'Leal, you should be here, my friend ... this is a pilot's wet dream!'*

'Yeah, don't rub it in ... I'm already a bright shade of green,' Leal retorted.

Zeven chuckled and went quiet for a bit. *'The descent arc of the tunnel is increasing now.'*

'I read that.' Leal cast an eye over the systems that were monitoring the flight path of the reconnaissance vessel. 'You're approaching the lower atmosphere *and ...*' Leal was surprised to note, 'we're picking up some trace elements of oxygen. Atmospheric pressure is much higher than that measured at the same distance from sea level on the rest of the planet. I'm reading methane, hydrogen and ammonia! It's like you've just flown into a gigantic greenhouse!'

'You might have hit the nail right on the head!' Taren's voice had a tinge of victory about it. *'The readouts of the sample were much the same.'*

'The tunnel is expanding,' Zeven related. *'It looks like we've cleared the anomaly and are entering a steamy mist. Lightning is shooting down all around us,'* and he sounded a little concerned about it. *'The anomaly appears much brighter from this side and is casting a good light. The pod is close ... I'm slowing down to skim the surface. There are some shadowy patches below that are moving?'*

'Starman, watch out!' Taren yelled a warning.

'What the —' Zeven's sentence was cut short by static, and every piece of equipment monitoring the craft went dead.

'Starman!' Leal endeavoured to restore contact, even though he suspected the craft was no longer transmitting and that probably meant the craft was destroyed or badly damaged.

'Could it be interference?' Lucian clung to their only hope.

'I fear the disconnection was too quick and neat,' Leal replied honestly. 'An electromagnetic pulse could do it, but that would leave Starman's craft dead in the air. Of course, he could reboot his systems, but we'd know if he got back online. None of AMIE's sensors are picking up evidence of an EMG event and there's nothing else I know of that would take out all the monitoring systems at once. Unless the tunnel through the anomaly collapsed?'

Lucian's jaw clenched as he digested the news.

Kassa had never seen the good professor so close to losing his perspective.

'Damn it!' He turned away so his angry outburst wasn't directed at Leal. 'Damn it,' Lucian repeated in a calmer, more accepting tone. He ran both hands hard through his hair, massaging his thoughts into a more reasonable order. 'Run a trace —'

'On it,' Leal advised.

Only the lost pod was registering on the monitor at present. 'NOT FOUND,' advised AMIE's computer.

Leal turned to Lucian, both of them looking gravely at each other.

Out of the corner of his eye Lucian noted Kassa making haste from the flight deck in the direction of the launch bay and the quarantine labs beyond.

'Keep trying,' he instructed Leal, striding off after Kassa.

As suspected, Lucian found Kassa inside Taren's lab. 'Lennox told you the entry code?' Lucian was surprised, thinking of the theft and how guarded Taren had been about who had access.

'I have my means,' Kassa replied, figuring that Lucian would soon discover the extent of those means.

'How do you plan to consult our friend here without the FFRD or the telepath?' Lucian knew what Kassa was considering as the doctor had been supportive of Taren's claims about the intelligence of the gas.

This was it for Kassa. No way to avoid exposing herself if she wished to save her crewmates. 'Lucian, please just hush and let me concentrate a moment.'

Kassa turned towards the contained anomaly and bowed her head to focus; Lucian's jaw tightened as he suddenly suspected so much, but he remained silent.

'You promised safe passage for our vessel. What went wrong?' Kassa raised her eyes to look at the anomaly. After a moment, she conveyed the information to Lucian. 'The craft encountered one of the developing species on the surface ... a tundrell.'

Lucian opened his mouth to ask what a tundrell was —

'These long tentacles of vegetation extend above the steamy mist on the surface to photosynthesise in our light. We have just discovered that, deprived of our light, as the area underneath our tunnel was during this exercise, tundrells will wave about seeking a better vantage point. We are most apologetic for this oversight.'

Lucian couldn't figure out what was more amazing: Kassa being a channel, or the anomaly's explanation.

'And what of our crew?' he found himself demanding of the gas.

'We are seeking them,' Kassa conveyed, 'and will report their condition to you as soon as it is known.' Kassa then breathed a heavy sigh as the anomaly withdrew from her mind. Feeling faint after conversing with the entity, she staggered back to sit in Taren's chair.

'Are you all right?' Lucian went down on one knee beside her.

Kassa nodded and then dared to look at her old friend. She was not surprised to find a bewildered expression on his face.

'How long have you had this Power, Kassa?'

'All along,' she confessed, forcing a smile.

Lucian's mind and eyes boggled. 'But I've known you for over a hundred years and in all that time you never once even hinted —'

'I've been a coward, Lucian,' she admitted. 'The importance of respect and acceptance was instilled in me from a young age. I doubt very much that I would be where I am if anyone had suspected my hidden talents. Such people are a risk to security ... or at least they were in my younger days, before the MSS got many of us registered, under surveillance and under control.'

'But they never pegged you.' Lucian smiled for the first time in a while. In a way, he was proud of his old friend. 'Well, your hidden talent could prove to be our hidden advantage.' He tried not to think of all the adverse thoughts he might have had about Kassa over the years, which she had probably perceived in the midst of their disagreements.

'You've always meant well, Lucian,' she answered his thought. 'That's why I'm still here on AMIE. I couldn't ask for a better employer or friend.'

His smile broadened. He couldn't hide how extraordinary he thought she was. 'I'm fine with that.' He stood, subconsciously hoping that distance might shield his thoughts. 'I'm not too sure how the rest of the crew will handle the fact.' He was thinking of Leal in particular.

'Must everyone know?' Kassa seemed ashamed to ask.

Lucian frowned in thought. What was the moral thing to do here? 'I feel that in this case, ignorance is bliss. I'll leave it to your discretion who knows and who does not.'

'Thank you, Lucian.'

He had to force a smile now, as all his worries returned to haunt him. 'Stay with our friend and let me know when it reports back.'

'Will do,' she confirmed, sensing how heavily circumstances were weighing on his shoulders. 'They'll be fine,' she reassured him. 'I feel it in my bones.'

'Coming from your bones, Kassa,' Lucian decided, 'I find that encouraging.' He knew she was referring to Taren and Zeven ... Kassa had offered no such assurance about his wife.

CHAPTER 6

PROPAGATION

When Taren awoke with her right temple throbbing, it was painfully obvious that she had hit her head. Her sight was blurred ... then the steamy, wet shield window, against which pelting rain streamed sideways, came into focus. Taren was lying on her side. *We've crashed!*

The last thing she recalled was seeing long, curling tentacles rising below their craft and flaying around violently. 'What the hell were they?'

Her eyes darted across and up to the pilot's seat, where she saw Zeven hunched forward in his harness. Due to the slanted angle of their craft, he was leaning slightly over and above her. 'Zeven!' She raised an arm to try and slap him back to consciousness, but this required greater effort than expected — delayed shock was making her feel weak, shaky, and nauseated. The idea of being stranded on an alien planet without a pilot was an absolutely horrifying notion and she began to panic. Taren's reach fell short of Zeven's face, but she could stretch as far as the pilot's right shoulder, which she proceeded to shake with all the strength she could muster. 'Zeven! Please wake up! Please! Shit!' When he did not stir, Taren decided to take off her harness in order to get to him.

In her dazed state and awkward position, unbuckling was a huge effort. Once released from her safety harness, however, gravity cast Taren face-first against the side shield window. Through the window she could see that their craft was buried in mud topped by a layer of water that was, thankfully, not seeping inside. She crawled around to a kneeling position to wipe away the layer of mist on the inside of the front shield window, but nothing could be seen beyond the steamy, pouring rain.

Taren turned herself around to face Zeven and the craft rocked beneath her in response to the sudden movement. It obviously wanted to tip down onto its belly, but for all Taren knew it could be teetering on a cliff face, or resting on a pile of rocks that might cause even more damage than it had already sustained.

Taren leaned slowly towards Zeven, placing a hand on each of his cheeks. 'Starman?' She carefully positioned herself underneath him to look him in the face. 'I really need you to wake up. You're my *pilot*!' As she inspected the bloody wound on the side of his head, her fears intensified and she began to weep. 'You're really scaring me now.' She leaned in close to support his forehead upon hers. 'Please, please, please, wake up!' Zeven's head remained a dead weight. He was still alive, but how much life he had left would rest upon her ability to take charge of the situation.

'Get it together, girl.' She sucked back her fear and looked at the control panel of the craft, which was blacked out. 'What would Zeven do?' The answer seemed rather obvious. 'Start it up.' She recognised the ignition button, but was that wise with the craft on this angle?

'I have to go outside.' It was the thing she was most

loath to do, but she had to know the full extent of their predicament before she could take any action.

With her suit helmet locked on, Taren climbed into the back of the craft and, using the manual override, she sealed off the rear section and prepared to open the exterior hatch. As she inched forward to pull the lock lever, the craft rocked before settling again. *This is insane!* Taren lost her courage for a moment, but the thought of her injured crewmate inspired her to endure. 'If this doesn't work, we're going to die anyway, so what the hell.' She unfastened the lever and kicked the heavy metal hatch open.

Steam came pouring in at her, which immediately fogged up the exterior of her helmet visor ... she couldn't see a thing! 'Not good.' She felt her way out the door and stood up.

There was light, but the pelting rain and steam prevented her from seeing anything. The read out on the monitor inside her visor was registering a breathable atmosphere, and as the lack of visibility was making her feel claustrophobic and frustrated, Taren bravely took her helmet off. Her head was instantly drenched by the warm, torrential rain.

'Great wonders of the universe, that feels good.' Taren revelled in the relaxing, rejuvenating force of the warm shower. The air, so pure and delightful, made her tingle all over, although at the same time it was like trying to breathe through water — it was a heavy, moisture-laden atmosphere. Ripe for propagation, thought Taren. It felt like spring on Maladaan, but intensified one thousand times. Ringbalin would appreciate some samples, and Taren decided she must oblige him before she left.

If she left?

This thought snapped Taren out of the strange natural high she seemed to be on and she looked around to get her bearings

The craft was in the middle of a rocky marsh, in which grew huge fern-like vegetation. Unfurled, these plants rose way up into the and rain mist that was currently drenching the entire area. The storm itself was alive with the colourful lightning flashes that they had seen while flying to the surface through the cloud of gas. From the ground this phenomena was both exotic and spectacular to the eye.

In the knowledge that the water and mud below weren't deep, Taren climbed of the reconnaissance vessel and landed with a splash. She was grateful to find neither a cliff, nor large rocks, just a huge pool of water skirted by the tall vegetation. The ship was being prevented from righting itself by the collection of rocks that the nose of the craft had crashed into. Still, the damage appeared minimal.

'Well, that's something,' Taren decided. Now all she needed was a forklift to move it off the rocks. With both hands shielding her eyes from the downpour, Taren noted that the remote tracking device for the pod, the monitor of which had swung around to the underside of her wrist, was picking up a signal. 'The missing pod!' Taren looked in the direction that the signal indicated. According to the read out, she was practically on top of it.

'Well, aren't you just full of surprises?'

Taren gasped in relief at hearing Zeven's voice and swung around to find him removing his helmet.

'Look at you, Miss I-don't-like-to-leave-my-lab, wading your way around an alien planet.' He chuckled, delighted by her fearlessness. 'And unprotected, too.'

'Starman!' Taren splashed toward the pilot as fast as she was able and overwhelmed him with a hug. 'I have never been so glad to see anyone!' She pulled back to plant a kiss on Zeven's cheek, but he turned his head and drew her into a much longer and more intimate moment than expected.

Her scruples told her to end the encounter — she was not serious about this lad. But her repressed sensual side just wanted her to rip off her spacesuit and have wild passionate sex in this steamy alien environment. Zeven may have been only slightly taller than her, but he had an amazing body, as her wandering hands were discovering. *I've never felt this impassioned in my life!* She attempted to justify her actions to herself, but her heart and her head were not buying her excuses. *It's just this place.* Her reservation won out and she pulled away, hyperventilating on the excitement that was coursing through her veins.

'I am so sorry,' she blurted. 'I didn't mean that.'

'You could have fooled me,' Starman grinned.

'What I mean is,' Taren took a few deep breaths to clear her head, 'it's the atmosphere here. It's like pure aphrodisiac.'

'All right!' He was inspired, rather than deterred.

As he made a move toward her, Taren held out a hand to hold him at bay. 'Please, Zeven. Listen to reason.'

Very reluctantly, he backed up. 'That wasn't good for you?' It was a rhetorical question, for the answer was already clear to him.

'That is not the point.' Taren attempted to be serious. 'Here we are, stranded in a hostile environment, with our mission in jeopardy. We have a crewmate missing and all we can think about is having sex! Is this how you would normally act under such conditions?'

'No. But then I've never been in these conditions before, with company like *you*,' Zeven emphasised, admiring how her white suit had gone see-through and clung to her skin and underclothes. 'I have never seen a spacesuit look so ... *hot*.'

He moved closer once more and Taren was tempted to give in and match the lust she saw in his beautiful, big brown eyes. 'I think everyone back at base is worrying about us ... and my tracking device is bleeping.' She held her wrist monitor in his face to remind him why they were here.

Taren hated that her commonsense prevailed, for she was allowing a unique and amazing experience to pass her by. Professionally, it was the right thing to do, but personally, she felt she needed to be shot.

'Right.' Zeven felt very put in his place. She was right ... they were here to do a job, they were in a *lot* of trouble, and this was probably not a girl's ideal seduction situation. 'Sorry, lost my head.' He took a deep breath, hoping to regain perspective, but the surge of virgin air through his lungs only made him feel more aroused — he couldn't drag his thoughts away from that kiss.

'According to this ...' Taren moved off in the direction her reading indicated. '... our pod is about twenty paces this way.' Taren picked up the pace as she spotted it sitting in the steamy water.

Zeven was hot on her heels, and they both came to a stop beside the pod. 'That would be it,' he confirmed and moved around to the far side, opened a panel and smiled. 'It still has juice,' Zeven noted, referring to the power supply.

'Can it get us home?' Taren didn't really see how it could, as needed to be launched.

'Hell, no!' Zeven obviously found the question elementary and amusing. 'But I can use the communicator inside to inform base of our whereabouts,' he continued, to Taren's great relief. 'So ... then will you have sex with me?'

'Starman!' Taren whacked his shoulder, pretending to be surprised at his cheek, but she had to love his persistence and he was gorgeous when he was being heroic.

Zeven shrugged nonchalantly and wiped the streaming water from his face as he began punching a code into the control panel of the pod's locking system. 'You don't like that I'm younger than you, do you?'

'It's not that, really. I'm just not up for a relationship right now.'

Zeven laughed and momentarily stopped punching in the code to look at Taren. 'If that is you *not* up for a relationship ... I would sure like to be there when you are.'

He finally hit the last digit and the door opened, although his eyes remained fixed on Taren and she felt uncomfortably aroused by his gaze. She couldn't breathe, she couldn't speak, she couldn't focus on anything but kissing him again.

And so it was that she found herself backed up against the pod, her suit being stripped from her wet body. Zeven's passionate kisses were descending down her neck, and his hands upon her breasts made her gasp in delight — and he had yet to strip her of her singlet and underclothes. Her head rolled to the side and noted with some difficulty that the supposedly empty vessel was occupied.

'Starman.' She shook him off.

'I won't tell anyone, I swear —'

'No, look!' Taren pointed to the cockpit. She could only see the legs of the occupant from where she stood but she was fairly sure she knew who the legs belonged to.

Zeven was quick to investigate. 'Oh, please no.' He was even quicker to turn about once he had seen the corpse. 'It's Amie,' he explained to Taren, an expression of horror across his face. 'Someone has —' He couldn't say it; instead he made haste to find a private place to throw up.

Her prophetic vision had been accurate. Taren knew it before she saw the cut on Amie's throat that ran from ear to ear.

Leal thought he was alone on the flight deck of AMIE when the communication from the lost pod came through. He had been starting to doze in his chair, but as soon as he heard the tone, he was at the com-link in a flash. 'Starman?'

'It's Taren here.'

Leal began to panic. 'Where is Zeven?'

'He's here, he's fine, he's just . . . not very good at being the bearer of bad news. Is Lucian present?'

'No. Shall I fetch him?' Leal offered.

'Best not,' Taren said, *'just yet. Um . . . we've found Amie, and it would seem my nightmare was indeed a prophecy. Kassa will know what I mean.'*

'I understand,' replied Kassa, whose presence both startled and delighted Leal.

'What does she mean?' Leal didn't like being left in the dark.

'She means that I have some grave news to deliver to our captain.' Kassa left to do so.

'How grave?' Leal queried, but Kassa waved off further comment.

'Starman wants to know if you have a fix on our location.'

Taren's request dragged Leal's attention away from the departing doctor. 'Affirmative ... but it's going to take time to formulate an extraction plan. With you down there, I don't know how we are going to communicate with our gas cloud friend and get you out of there.'

Kassa stopped just short of the elevator. She could arrange the extraction with the sample in Taren's lab, but then Leal would learn the truth about her telepathy and he would cease coming to see her with minor ailments and delighting her old ego with his delicious secret fantasies about her.

'Tell Kassa I might be able to communicate with its larger body from down here. I'll give it a go.'

Kassa closed her eyes, grateful for Taren's talent to think up a good cover story. Perhaps she didn't have to lose her young flyboy's attentions just yet. She promised herself that she would confess the truth to him at the first appropriate moment. *'Leal, you pussy. Get your arse into a salvage ship and get us out of here!'* Starman's voice came through the intercom, which made both Kassa and Leal smile.

'I am so relieved you survived,' Leal told him, wiping a tear from his cheek. 'I was afraid that if you died and rotted there, we might end up with an entire evolution spawned from you! A Zevolution —' he joked.

'Leal, my friend, under normal circumstances I would be touched,' Zeven replied flatly, *'but I'm leaning over a*

corpse to speak with you, so whatever you're planning, make it snappy ... I really don't want to spend the night here.'

Leal was left gaping at his friend's speech. 'That's a little graver than I expected ... leave it with me.'

Leal shot up from his chair to chase Kassa. 'Is there anything I can do?'

'Prepare to go down to Oceane,' she replied and then forced a smile to reassure him. 'You may have to take charge on this one, Leal. Lucian is going to be devastated for quite some time, I would think.'

Leal nodded as Kassa entered the lift down to the middle modules, where, the medical chamber was located.

'Do not mention what you know about Amie to anyone,' she advised him as the lift doors began to close. 'Her death was no accident.'

Leal was stunned speechless and by the time he found his voice, it was too late to question the doctor.

Kassa paged Aurora and asked her to have the captain meet her in her consultation rooms as soon as possible. Lucian arrived shortly after she did.

'Please tell me you have good news.'

The captain was looking very tired and Kassa felt her report could well send him spiralling into a nervous breakdown. 'I have *some* good news ... Zeven and Taren have made contact and they are both alive and well.'

'That's fantastic!' Lucian's heavy cloud lifted momentarily, until he noted Kassa remained sombre. 'But?' he asked more wearily.

'They found the missing pod, Lucian, and Amie's body was inside.'

Lucian was alarmed to hear his wife referred to as 'a body'.

'It is as Taren foresaw.' Lucian's eyes widened in horror. Kassa struggled to deliver the crushing blow. 'We have good reason to believe that your wife was murdered.'

Lucian began choking at the shock of this news, his utter desolation so intense that Kassa's heart went out to him in empathy and she began to weep.

Her tears were not for Aime, however. Kassa had never held any love for the woman. Unlike everybody else, Kassa was not fooled by Amie's warm, bubbly, innocent exterior. She had known that Amie Gervaise was a far more treacherous creature than everyone realised. Still, as she was now dead, perhaps Lucian would never need to know what his wife had been up to behind his back. Kassa fully expected it was Amie's underhanded dealings that had led to her death.

'I am so sorry, Lucian.' She took a seat beside her long-time colleague and held the man as he collapsed in tears.

After a while, when the full implications had sunk in, Lucian regained his sensibilities and dried his eyes. 'So there is a murderer on board our craft,' he concluded, his voice filled with venom.

'Leal and I will quietly coordinate this rescue,' Kassa said to prevent Lucian feeling any more overwhelmed than he already was. 'If we can keep our recent discoveries secret until everyone is safely back on board, it could make it easier to seek out and surprise the person responsible for Amie's death.'

Lucian nodded, seeing sense in her words.

'You should lie down —'

'I am not going to lie down,' he insisted, swallowing his grief to rise and get involved. 'I'll fly the salvage —'

'You most definitely will not,' Kassa asserted. 'In your current depleted state you'll kill somebody.'

'How did she die, Kassa?' Lucian demanded to know, hysteria not far from the surface.

Kassa had feared it would come to this and pulled a syringe full of sedative from her pocket. 'Sorry, my friend ...' She injected Lucian and when he began to stagger she assisted him to the lounge where he promptly passed out.

Kassa paged Aurora. 'Our captain is out of commission for a little while. Please advise anyone seeking him that he will be unavailable for the next ten hours.'

'What has happened?' Aurora queried.

'He's getting some much-needed rest.' Kassa felt that was explanation enough.

'So with Amie missing, Leal flying salvage, and Zeven still absent — although found, *yay*! — who is in charge? You?'

'I'm a little tied up right now.' Kassa remembered she had to go and speak with their sample.

'Shall I page Dr Portus up from the Marine Department?'

'No, let's not involve the other departments at this stage,' Kassa recommended. 'You be captain for this shift.'

'Cool. I'm on it!'

Kassa had to smile at the girl's excited enthusiasm. Aurora was blissfully unaware of all the tragedy and treachery unfolding around her, and that was best for now.

'Where will you be?'

'Incommunicado.' Kassa switched off her communicator and made for Taren's quarantine lab with great haste.

When Leal entered the flight deck to find Kassa at the communicator having a hushed conversation, he was immediately intrigued. 'Anything I should know about?'

Kassa was startled and did an about-face. 'You gave me a start.' She held a hand to her chest to calm herself. 'It's Taren,' she advised. 'She has spoken with the entity and the porthole is open for you.'

'We're running out of daylight hours.' Leal was a little suspicious at Kassa's jittery reaction. 'By the time we leave the surface of the planet, we'll be flying in darkness.'

'Actually, you'll be flying in in darkness,' Kassa replied, to Leal's initial horror. 'You see, the tundrells — the plants that caused Taren and Zeven to crash — curl into a passive state at night, and so will not hinder your rescue.'

Leal smiled and frowned at once, intrigued by her as always. 'How very well informed you are. Been here chatting for a while, have you?'

Kassa gave a nod. 'The entity shall light your way through.'

'Tell Taren I dig this whole inter-dimensional extra-terrestrial communication thing she has going on ... but at the first sign of a tentacle, I am opening fire,' Leal said with good humour. 'I'm sending Bonar up to man the control deck.' Leal backed up to admire the good doctor before he turned and made for the launch bay hangar.

'Right you are.' Kassa gave him the thumbs-up and a wave. 'Fly safe.'

As Leal departed he felt something wasn't right with Kassa. She was always so laidback and calm ... perhaps the pressure was getting to her? 'Are you all right?' he turned back to inquire. Her forced smile and insistent nod did nothing to convince him. 'Is there something you want to tell me?'

Kassa looked rather startled by his question and Leal smiled, knowing he'd hit the nail right on the head.

'Now is not the time,' she said quickly.

'When I return, perhaps?' he suggested calmly, inwardly excited to have a reason, apart from an ailment, to see her.

'When the smoke from today has cleared,' she suggested, more aware of the time damage control for the past few days might take.

'At your leisure then.' He tossed the ball into her court and left to be about the business of salvaging their craft and crew.

The salvage mission lasted most of the night, and when everyone arrived back on AMIE they were completely exhausted. Aurora was the only admin person waiting to greet them upon their return.

'Welcome back!' she said in a cheery tone, which quickly faded when she saw the loaded body bag that the crew were pulling from the craft. 'Who is that?' she queried Taren and Leal, the first to exit the craft, fearing it was Zeven.

'It's Amie,' Zeven said as he stepped out of the vehicle.

Aurora was completely blindsided by the news, which hid how ecstatic she was to see the young pilot. He'd never know how worried she'd been about him. 'How? What's going on?'

Zeven held up a hand, in no state to deal with one of Aurora's inquisitions, and bypassed her to speak with Taren, who was handing over a bunch of samples to Ringbalin.

'I even got you a seedling.' Taren held up a sealed jar filled with soil, out of which sprouted a tundrell. 'It's a —'

'Tundrell,' Ringbalin interrupted, smiling broadly. 'I've heard talk of these being discovered elsewhere in the galaxy, but I've never actually seen one up close.' He lowered his glasses down his nose to inspect the specimen. 'I've got a greenhouse in quarantine and finally I'll get to utilise it,' he told her, inspired. 'Thanks for thinking of me. This is beyond expectations.'

'You're most welcome,' Taren assured him. 'As soon as I smelt the air and saw the vegetation, I knew you'd appreciate ...'

Zeven, who was standing back a bit, waiting patiently to have a word, didn't like how friendly Taren seemed to be with the gardener. He'd never had much to do with Ringbalin, but the few women on board AMIE all seemed to adore him. The very gorgeous and mysterious Dr Ayliscia Portus from the Marine Department, for one, was constantly seen coming and going from his greenhouse in Module C. He couldn't understand what women saw in the scruffy, tree-hugging recluse. Zeven decided to tap Taren on the shoulder.

'I'll catch you in the office.' Ringbalin placed the seedling sample in his quarantine trolley with the other soil, air and water samples Taren had collected for him and wheeled the lot away.

'What's up?' Taren turned to Zeven, already knowing what was on his mind, but since leaving the surface of Oceane her passion for the young pilot had cooled, as expected.

'We need to talk,' he said quietly. 'Please.'

'There is nothing to discuss,' she whispered back. 'Like I told you, it was just ... something in the air, and Ringbalin will surely prove that.'

'It's more than that, and you know it,' he challenged playfully.

'No, I do not. Under normal circumstances, I would *never* act like that in a professional situation.' She wanted him to understand that, as it was the truth.

'I accept that.' Zeven was also not feeling quite as obsessed as he had been only hours before. 'But don't write me off just because I let things get a bit out of hand when I shouldn't have.'

Taren found it rather sweet that he was prepared to admit fault, but the truth was she was too tired to discuss this right now.

'You're stuffed, I know that. I am too,' he added, frustrated, 'but can I call you later?'

Taren, too exhausted to argue, nodded agreement.

'Thanks.' His dimple flashed as he grinned. 'Great job today.' His voice resumed normal volume. 'See you in debriefing.'

Taren watched him depart, wondering what the hell she was going to do about him, when her gaze drifted back to their rescue vessel beside which Aurora stood, staring at her with daggers in her eyes. *Oh no.* 'Rory ...' Taren knew she needed to explain before she made an enemy, but Aurora swiftly exited the hangar. It was clear she was not very receptive at present. 'Oh ...' Taren groaned to herself. '*Nuts.*'

Taren was desperately in need of sleep, but she was not going to get it. While waiting to be rescued, Taren had employed her psychic skill to extract the identity of Amie's killer from the corpse.

This skill was a form of psychometry, adepts being able to pick up information from an object about its previous owners, or from a person, animal, plant or even a mineral. However, Taren's grasp of this talent extended only to people, living or recently dead, so her skill in this area was probably related to her clairvoyance rather than being true psychometry but the MSS had found it extremely helpful in solving recent murders. Taren had hated that work. She loved catching the bad guys, making the world a safer place, but she had witnessed many murders, rapes and other violent crimes first-hand. Such scenes never failed to suck the life out of her because she empathised with the victims and, in some cases, the perpetrator.

Witnessing Amie's brutal murder from the victim's point of view had been every bit as draining. Taren knew who was responsible; now all she had to do was stay conscious long enough to prove it. She took a step towards the hangar bay doors that led into the rest of the ship but her legs merely wobbled and collapsed beneath her.

'Dr Lennox?' she heard Leal call to her, right before she hit the ground.

Into consciousness Taren drifted ... it was the voices that woke her.

'My wife had her throat cut!' the captain stressed in a whisper. 'Things began going horribly wrong from the moment Dr Lennox came on board and now you want me to trust some vision that she had!'

'Shhh, she'll hear you,' Kassa insisted, leading him further away from the patient. 'May I remind you that before we found your missing wife, you were pretty eager to believe in her visions.'

'You don't have to trust my vision.' Taren struggled to a seated position on the bed. She was in sick bay with Kassa and Lucian. 'I believe I can get the murderer to confess.'

'Really?' The captain was feeling slightly remorseful at having voiced his apprehension as he realised Taren was his best chance of getting to the bottom of this tragedy. 'How?'

'Hypnotism.'

'No!' Lucian flatly refused. 'I will not have the personal lives of all my crew exposed —'

'I know who did it ... but ...' Taren shook her head to let the captain know she was not going to disclose who she'd seen. 'I have to confirm —'

'You will tell me now.' Lucian, losing his cool, took a step toward Taren.

'Lucian.' Kassa drew his attention to the full syringe she held. 'I know it's difficult, but keep it professional. You are too personally involved —'

'I'm good,' he assured her. 'However, if you stick me with that needle again, I'll be looking for a new medical officer.'

'Don't make me,' Kassa cautioned him lightheartedly. They both knew that she had the power to have him relieved of duty.

Taren swung her legs down and slid off the bed to stand up. 'There is a good possibility that even the murderer doesn't know they did it. If the agent on this ship can be triggered into action by a code name, like I believe I was, the agent in question will only remember their covert operations under hypnosis. Or in a hyper-conscious state.'

'If that's the case,' Lucian reasoned with Taren, 'the first person I want hypnotised is you.'

'Fair enough,' Taren agreed without question, hating that the man she idolised now thought so little of her as to imagine she'd been involved in the murder of his wife! Well, perhaps she had and it was her perception of events that were skewed? 'Who shall hypnotise me?'

'I can do it,' Kassa offered, even though she knew it was a waste of time. Taren was true to the project, unlike the woman whose death they were investigating.

'Then feel free to open me up.' Taren's eyes turned from Kassa to Lucian. 'Everyone else has.' She sat on the bed again.

'It's not that I suspect you are a killer, you understand,' Lucian said, now feeling he'd been too quick in accusing Dr Lennox. 'As you say, you may *subconsciously* know more than you realise.'

'That's okay.' The damage was done as far as Taren was concerned. 'I'm used to being the centre of an interrogation. But I want it taped, so that I can hear the truth from my own mouth.'

'Of course.' Lucian wanted to kick himself. He'd promised to always give Taren the benefit of the doubt. Still, this was not a science project they were talking about but cold-blooded murder.

Zeven — fed, showered and changed — was just crawling across his sleeping pod, on the verge of collapsing into it, when his room buzzer rang. 'This had better be important.' He dragged himself up and staggered slowly to the door. 'I'm off duty,' he grumbled. 'Unlock,' he instructed and his chamber door opened. He was neither surprised nor delighted to find Aurora waiting to speak with him. 'Oh ... not now, Rory, I'm real tired —'

'I know.' She seemed surprisingly subdued. 'Dr Lennox is awake and I thought you might want to know.'

'Well, that's good news,' Zeven confirmed, playing dumb and nodding his head vaguely, while Aurora observed him closely. 'Is there something else?'

It took a moment for her to pluck up the courage to ask, 'What happened down there, Starman?'

'We crashed, we found the pod with Amie's dead body in it and we phoned home.' He summarised the experience as he had in debrief.

'I was worried about you,' she confessed although she knew he wouldn't give a damn.

'There was no need.' He grinned, as he did every time his mind returned to the steamy surface of Oceane.

'But your head?' Rory, concerned, moved to touch the patched-up wound, but Zeven gently blocked her touch and shook his head.

'I'm fine,' he told her coolly, 'just *very, very* tired.'

'Oh, okay.' Aurora had promised herself that no matter what he said or did, she wouldn't cry in front of him or turn nasty. 'I hope you sleep well,' she concluded, as lightheartedly as she was able, turned on her heel and did not look back.

Zeven closed the door, and headed back to bed. He mused on Aurora's agitation as she had left, even though he'd done nothing wrong. Yes, he'd probably just broken her heart, but it wasn't his fault he was attracted to someone else. He'd never really got close to the girl in the first place and he'd made it clear years ago there was no future for them. So why was she making him feel guilty about this?

'Arrgh!' He collapsed backwards onto his sleeping pod and mentally shook off the encounter. 'I refuse to feel guilty about the most sensational sexual encounter I *nearly* had.'

Zeven was grinning again, and rolled over into his pillows to indulge in the arousing memory.

CHAPTER 7

INTERROGATION

'I have acquired a quantity of the original gas sample that was extracted from the anomaly on Oceane, which, from initial observation, Eleazar Kestler suspects to be an infinite source of energy. That being the case, the Master is eager to export the entire sample back to Maladaan, but such a theft will be too obvious. Instead, I extracted only a small amount of the sample to send back to the institute. After all, if each particle of this gas is capable of producing infinite amounts of power, as theorised, the size of the sample is irrelevant.'

'What is she saying? Who is the Master?' Lucian queried Kassa. They had asked Taren to tell them what she'd perceived about Amie's murder and were apparently getting a monologue. 'Is she claiming Amie stole the sample?'

Kassa raised her brow but said nothing, not wanting to disturb Taren, who was on a roll.

'I am making my way to the pod bay with the sample. I plan to have the Puppet stash it in Kestler's pod, which leaves for Maladaan in a few hours — no one aboard AMIE will be any the wiser.'

'The Puppet?' Kassa queried Taren about the term.

'The MSS code name for one of their sleeper agents on board this vessel,' she replied.

'Amie worked for the MSS? This is rubbish! We are being had!' Lucian flatly refused to listen to any more nonsense.

'Lucian, Taren is incapable of lying under hypnosis,' Kassa cautioned him, realising the truth about Amie was going to surface no matter what and Lucian was going to be devastated all over again.

'You are telepathic, Kassa. Did you ever suspect Amie of being a double agent?'

Lucian was putting Kassa in a very uncomfortable position, so she shushed him to be quiet until they got the full story from Taren, who was still caught up in Amie's last moments. 'Did Amie have an MSS code name?'

'The Puppeteer,' Taren replied and then continued her account. 'I meet my contact in his office as arranged. When I first enter, he is curious about my visit, but upon speaking his code name he assumes his true personality, one far more menacing and aware.

'"Did you get the sample?" he asks me and I hand it over.

'"It was much bigger than this," he says, noting the size of the containment cylinder. "The Master requested the entire supply."

'"You can tell the Master to shove it. I am not going to blow my stake in this project to save his arse! And if he doesn't like it, I'll tell Lucian what has been going on, and then the gravy train will stop." I blink and there is a large blade a hair's breadth from my right eye.

'"I may be a puppet, darlin', but you're not the one pulling the strings."'

Taren suddenly jolted in her seat, and gripped her throat.

'Leave that experience behind you, be at peace and relax,' Kassa advised Taren, and then looked at Lucian, whose mouth was hanging open.

'All this time ...' Lucian was finding the accusation hard to digest. '... *Amie* was the leak.' He held a fist to his heart to try to endure the extent of his wife's betrayal. 'Why? Why would she betray us all?' He looked to Kassa for answers. 'Did you ever detect that she might be disloyal to the project?' he asked once again and Kassa shook her head. She didn't want to be accused of protecting a criminal to spare her own career.

'You would have exposed your unacceptable skill had you told me, I realise that,' Lucian said, 'and the last thing I want is to get you in any trouble, Kassa. You're my rock right now. All I seek to know is if you can verify Amie's guilt?'

Kassa took a deep breath and looked up into Lucian's dark stormy eyes. The man did deserve to know the truth, if not the whole truth. She nodded, too ashamed to say anything, and Lucian backed up to take a seat, completely bewildered to discover he'd been sleeping with, was married to, the enemy.

'Yes, Amie had her own agenda.' Kassa finally found her voice. 'I cannot tell you any details. I think she suspected I knew something, and so kept her distance. I was never able to discover much.'

Lucian had lost all expression. He didn't know what to feel now. 'If I had known, Kassa, I would have cut her throat myself. Amie knew how I felt about the MSS constantly interfering and exploiting our research. And she was the leak!' He gripped his head and collapsed forward to contain his sudden fury. 'How could I have been so blind!'

'She was very convincing, Lucian.' Kassa tried to be reassuring, but Lucian wasn't having any of it and recoiled from her.

'I knew our relationship was too good to be true!' He burst into tears again, but was equally quick to recover. 'No ... I refuse to mourn our saboteur.'

'Why don't you let Taren and me handle —'

'No more needles!' He looked at Kassa to ensure that was not what the doctor intended. 'I'm okay. I'm learning so much about my life suddenly that I am afraid to go to sleep in case I miss another revealing chapter.'

'I can let you know if —'

Lucian knew what she was going to say. 'No. I want to find this Puppet and his Master.'

The thud as a very relaxed Taren slid off her chair sent both Kassa and Lucian racing to help her back into her seat.

'I believe you owe this one an apology,' Kassa commented. 'She is one hundred per cent faithful to your convictions and this project.'

'Is that a fact?' Lucian observed Taren in a fresh light. 'Who is the Master?'

Taren frowned and shook her head, not understanding the question.

'I just told her to leave Amie's memories behind,' Kassa explained. 'Do you want me to guide her back in?'

Lucian looked at the pale-faced young doctor and shook his head. 'She has already lived through Amie's death at least three times ... it's enough. Bring her out.' He pressed Aurora's com-link number on his belt.

'Yes, Captain,' she replied with a sniffle.

'Are you all right?' He was concerned that Amie's death may have upset the girl.

'I'm fine ... how are you doing?'

'I'll live,' he replied. His heart felt as if it was dead and it left him feeling more determined to get to the bottom of this web of deceit. 'I want you to send all ground crew from the launch bay to Kassa's consultation chambers right away.'

The launch pod bay in Module F was where the spacegoing craft were launched from, including the interplanetary pods; sub bay in Module E was where all submersibles were launched from.

'Yes, Captain.'

As Amie had been heading to the pod bay to meet her contact, reason dictated that he would be found among the flight crew. Bonar Colbers, as head engineer, was the only one with his own office and was in charge of pod launches. Lucian was fairly sure that Bonar, once hypnotised, would disclose Amie's 'Puppet'.

'What's this all about then, captain?' Bonar was curious when he entered Kassa's consultation office ahead of the rest of his crew, who'd been asked to sit in the waiting room. He looked from the captain to Kassa and back again. 'Has this got something to do with your wife's death?' He took a few steps backward, fearful that he was under suspicion.

'We are going to have to question everyone, and we plan to do so using hypnosis,' the captain said. 'The session will be recorded so that you know exactly what has been said. Do you object for any reason?'

'Well, no, captain.' Bonar did not look at all guilty, just concerned. 'But why start with me?'

'Actually, Dr Lennox went first,' Lucian told him, which relaxed the engineer a little.

'I thought she was passed out?' He took a seat.

'She regained consciousness and has returned to her quarters to rest,' Kassa said, sitting down in front of the engineer. 'Now, I want you to just relax and listen to my voice...'

Once the engineer was under, Lucian and Kassa questioned him about what he was doing at the time of Amie's death. The engineer could not recall and thought he was probably taking a nap.

Lucian sat back in his chair and threw his hands up in frustration. 'He cannot lie, right?'

'I suspect ordinary hypnotism cannot break through MSS conditioning.' Kassa frowned. 'I am wary of —'

Before she had finished voicing a caution, Lucian leant forward in his seat to confront the docile engineer, whose eyes were closed. 'I want to speak with the Puppet.'

Bonar's eyelids sprang open instantly, startling Lucian and Kassa so much that they could not move fast enough before the hefty man gripped both their throats. 'Why am I talking to you two?' he asked. 'Ah, the cat is out of the bag,' he figured and grinned. 'All good things must come to an end.'

'Who is the Master?' Lucian squeaked out the question while struggling with both hands to loosen the engineer's grip on his throat.

'Wouldn't you like to know?' Bonar said, his snide grin infuriating the captain. Before he could summon the strength to hit the man, Bonar's killer grip loosened and he fell to the floor unconscious.

The captain, astonished and gasping for air, looked at Kassa who held an empty syringe high and was breathing heavily in shock. 'I'd say... we've found... our killer.' She conjured up a smile.

'But the Master remains elusive,' the captain said, with some disappointment. 'Any ideas?'

Kassa shook her head, annoyed that he refused to think it through. 'Taren told you who he was days ago.'

'Are you referring to Swithin?' The captain really did not want to believe the worst about his brother and business partner.

'Come on, Lucian, it is blindingly obvious,' Kassa appealed. 'And if that sample is for him, we have to advise him to release it or face the consequences.'

'What consequences?' Lucian wanted specifics.

'We don't know —'

'Then as soon as Dr Lennox wakes, I suggest you find out.' A very dark mood had settled over Lucian and Kassa was not about to argue with a man on the edge. 'Let me know what you discover. Then I can confront Swithin.'

Kassa nodded, looking over at the unconscious engineer. 'What shall we do about him?'

AMIE didn't have any security personnel. Lucian had hand-picked all the crew and the scientists on board and had deemed hired muscle unnecessary. 'I'll have his boys drag him up to bio-containment. We can lock him in there for now.'

'What will you tell the crew?'

'As soon as I figure out the truth,' Lucian advised, 'I'll let everyone else know. Until then ...' He placed a finger to his lips and left the room.

Taren's dreams were disturbed by the horrid images of Amie's last moments, yet as she moved closer to a waking state, she was mentally transported back to Oceane.

She was being ravished by her admirer and she felt

the erotic atmosphere coursing through her, arousing all her senses and dispersing her inhibitions. His lips caressed her neck and shoulders as his hands explored the contours of her body. He pulled back to give her a reassuring smile and Taren's heart skipped a beat when it was not Zeven seducing her.

'Ah!' she gasped, wide-eyed and confused to find herself awake and sitting bolt upright in her sleeping pod. 'Wow.' She felt so hot, and not in an unpleasant way.

The door buzzer startled her and this seemed to explain what had dragged her so rudely from her dream. '*Lucian*,' she murmured under her breath, horrified and delighted to feel his touch all through her. 'Wait a second! I am angry with him, aren't I?'

The buzzer went again and Taren was forced to abandon that train of thought. 'Just a minute,' she called, looking around for her robe.

Taren was still tying her robe on when she checked through the peephole, relieved to see Kassa, looking impatient.

'Open up. We have work to do.'

'Unlock.' The door slid aside to reveal Taren's dishevelled state. 'Did I oversleep?'

'Not really,' Kassa sympathised, as she stepped inside and the door closed behind her. 'I brought you breakfast.'

The doctor handed Taren a bag which she opened and inspected. 'Organic muesli, and fresh juice.' Taren was relieved to discover Kassa had brought her exactly what she wanted. 'How did you know?'

Kassa cocked an eye and gave her a worried look. 'You're not really awake yet, are you?'

'Not really,' Taren yawned. 'I had confusing dreams.'

Taren wanted to retract that statement, for her mind immediately skipped to her vision of Lucian all wet and steamy, which Kassa promptly picked up on.

The doctor smiled broadly. 'Been having sweet dreams about our captain again, have we?' she teased and Taren begged her to hush.

'What do you mean, *again*?' Taren realised Kassa already knew about her crush on Lucian and waved off an answer. 'The man's wife has just been murdered, I don't think this —'

'His *unfaithful, treacherous* wife,' Kassa stated firmly and Taren's jaw dropped.

'What?' She was appalled. 'Amie cheated on Lucian? Was the woman mentally defective?'

'Well, Lucian doesn't know about the unfaithful part yet, and hopefully he never will. Learning that Amie betrayed the project has been enough for him to bid her good riddance,' Kassa summed up her shocking little confession. 'So, I am overjoyed you have a *thing* for Lucian, as I happen to think you would be wonderful for each other.'

'Shh!' Taren urged, although she couldn't wipe the smile off her face. 'For the last time, I am not on AMIE to fall in love.'

'Fine.' Kassa, sceptical, humoured her. 'Let's work.'

'Fine,' Taren concurred, heading for the shower. 'Won't be a tick.'

En route to the bio lab where the sample was being housed, Taren spotted Ringbalin working away in his quarantine lab. Curious about his discoveries, she backtracked, telling Kassa she'd meet her there.

'This is important,' Kassa said, not wanting to be kept waiting.

'*I am aware*,' Taren sang back, as she buzzed to get Ringbalin to let her in. He pushed a button to unlock the door, very glad to see her, and beckoned her inside.

'Wow!' was all he would say as he looked over the data on the screen of his workstation.

'What are you looking at?' Taren queried as the lab doors automatically closed behind her.

'The analysis of the air you brought me and it's intense!' He pushed his glasses up his nose.

'The analysis?' She bent over the back of his chair to see if she could make head or tail of it.

'No, the air itself is intense,' he corrected. 'Everything a thriving planet needs. If I put this stuff in my greenhouse the plants there would outgrow Module C in a week!' he said excitedly. 'I'm surprised you're not pregnant from just breathing it in!'

Taren grinned at the comment, considering how close she'd come.

'I'll have to bonsai the tundrell to keep it alive. If this is the atmosphere that is required to sustain it, it would use all my current greenhouse resources in no time at all! It's a good thing we're heading back to Maladaan. I'll leave it with the labs at the institute. They are going to be —'

'Wait a minute ... we're heading back to Maladaan?' Taren was disappointed at this news.

'The captain gave the order about five hours ago.' He was surprised she hadn't been informed already. 'Don't worry about the time it will take out of your assignment. They'll add any time lost to the end of your stay, so you'll actually gain time aboard AMIE.'

'That's not my concern. We're going to miss the anomaly's departure — a once-in-a-lifetime event.'

'Relax. The captain deployed several satellite probes before we left Oceane,' Ringbalin advised her. 'They'll relay images of the event, so you won't miss it completely.'

'Thanks, Balin. I'll catch you.'

Inside her lab, Taren was greeted by an explosive situation. The gas sample inside the bio-containment room was visibly excited within its transparent tube.

'It's furious,' Kassa explained as she crouched against the back wall of the lab. 'It wants to know why we are moving away.'

'*I* want to know why we are moving away.'

The instrumentation in her lab was going berserk, although normally the being had only communicated through the FFRD — this was a show of strength.

'Captain.' Taren hit his number on her communicator.

'Dr Lennox,' he responded at once.

'There's a situation unfolding in the lab that you should see.'

'How fortunate that I am right ...' He walked in and was stunned by the chaos he witnessed. '... here.'

Kassa gripped her head as the confined being endeavoured to voice itself through her. 'Ahhhh,' she wailed and when Lucian moved to assist her, Taren held him back. Then Kassa threw herself back up to standing to confront them .

'Why do you retreat without returning our parts to the whole?'

The voice speaking through Kassa was clearly not her own. It sounded like numerous voices all speaking at once, and the words were slow and laboured so as to be understood. But its volume was almost deafening.

'Are your crew and machines not safe?' it appealed to Lucian.

Lucian, absolutely speechless, nodded.

'We humour you because you are ignorant and fragile. Release us immediately or we will free ourselves at a fatal cost to you.'

'I will have you released from containment at once,' Lucian assured it, his voice sounding soft and tiny by comparison. 'But the other small portion that is en route to our home planet cannot be released until it arrives at its destination in ten days, time.'

Kassa's eyes narrowed as the entity stewed on the information.

'We will refrain from using force at present, but we will not be responsible for the consequences should you not take action before we must depart. Is it not better to lose one man than to risk the entire population of a planet?' it asked.

Lucian stewed on the question. He greatly respected the mind and work of the man this entity was suggesting he sacrifice, and as far as he knew, Kestler wasn't aware he was carrying the explosive cargo. But he was obviously an MSS sleeper agent if he'd done tests on the sample for Amie and her Master.

'I have already lost one of my chief scientists. I do not wish to lose another.' Lucian made his decision. 'I will ensure that my people on Maladaan release the sample immediately upon its arrival.'

'We hope the timing works for you, as for us it makes no difference. We move on, regardless of the constraints of any given universe.'

Suddenly, Lucian realised the magnitude of experience that the being before him must have had. He had merely crossed a few solar systems, whereas this being jumped universes and dimensions! He didn't feel that now was the right time for a question-and-answer session, however.

'Clear the vacuum trap and jettison the contents,' Lucian ordered Taren.

'Yes, Captain.' She was stunned and a little heartbroken by the sudden turn of events, but moved to the control panel for the bio-containment lab. 'Before you go ...' She looked at Kassa, who turned to give Taren her undivided attention, and the way the being stared at her was a little off-putting. 'Do you have a name?'

'Azazèl-mindos-coomra-dorchi,' it replied.

'My name is Taren Lennox and it has been my greatest honour to meet you.'

Azazèl-mindos-coomra-dorchi observed her a moment. 'We know you. You are special, Taren-lennox. A twelve-tone organism is a very rare find in a physical dimension, so the honour is ours.'

Kassa bowed low, which so overwhelmed Taren that tears streamed down her face. Once Kassa straightened up, she smiled, closed her eyes, and collapsed on the floor.

Lucian ran to her aid. 'Release it!' he commanded. The close encounter had him spooked.

Taren turned to view the contained part of the mighty being one last time, wishing she had the grace to ask it what a twelve-tone organism was. 'Peace go with you, Azazèl-mindos-coomra-dorchi,' she said, hitting the release button on the vacuum trap that kept the sample contained.

The coloured gas drifted out into the bio-containment area, spreading out and shimmering more brightly — clearly it was joyful.

And also with you, Taren-lennox.

Taren's eyes sprang open when she heard the being's voice in her mind. *Telepathy!*

How many Powers are there? the being asked.

But my question was, what did you mean, I am twelve-toned? She attempted to mentally convey this and as an answer was forthcoming, Taren assumed that the being heard her.

I understood your query.

Her delay in jettisoning the sample caused Lucian to spring to his feet and do it for her. Everything inside the containment area was immediately ejected into space and Lucian closed the exit hatch doors. 'Are you all right?' he inquired of Taren.

'Yes,' she replied, shaking like a leaf.

'You don't look all right.' He guided her to a seat.

'Is Kassa hurt?' Taren saw her on the floor and snapped out of her trance-like state.

'By all appearances, no,' Lucian replied. 'But I should get her down to sick bay.'

'I'll help.'

'No, you rest,' Lucian ordered.

'Have *you* had any rest, Captain?' Taren thought to ask, although he didn't look at all weary.

'Given the number of times my world has spun around today, I don't think I'll ever sleep again!' He squatted down next to Kassa.

'I'm so very sorry to have brought all this —'

Lucian held up a hand to stop Taren apologising and stood. 'I made some unfounded accusations earlier and I couldn't have been more off the mark. You didn't bring this trouble upon us. You've weeded out the trouble that was already here and I could not be more grateful.' Lucian nearly broke down, but managed to hold himself together. 'And there is still more to deal with.' He drew a deep breath, boggling at the enormity of the task.

'Anything you need from me, just ask.' Taren's heart went out to him. She suspected Lucian had seen more misfortune and sadness in the past few days than he had in his one-hundred-year career!

Lucian lifted Kassa up. 'I most certainly will do that. Until then, you are on R and R. I'll have Aurora introduce you to the recreation module and —'

'I'm sure she has work to do. I can find it on my own.' Taren recalled that the last time she'd seen Aurora, the woman had not seemed very well disposed towards her.

'I insist,' said Lucian. 'Some of the rec equipment is a little hard to figure out how to operate.'

'Okay.' Taren resigned herself to the confrontation. Perhaps it was for the best. She really liked Rory and didn't want to be off-side with her or anyone on board — a task that seemed to be becoming increasingly difficult. Still, she did seem to be back on-side with Lucian, which was a huge step in the right direction. If she could just figure out how to get Zeven uninterested, she'd be home free.

Taren arrived in the lovely foyer-cum-waiting room area of Module D ahead of Aurora, and was thankful to be able to collapse onto a lounge and take a deep, quiet pause for a moment. There was some wonderful relaxing, watery-sounding music wafting through the room, which was decorated in earth and sea shades: lovely calming blues and greens.

The rollercoaster had finally stopped! The magnificent being who had briefly entered her life was now gone, and she mourned the lost opportunities to learn from the inter-dimensional intelligence. *I thought I had more time*, she rationalised her non-action. *And with the thief, a murder, and getting stranded on an alien planet ... is it any wonder I got sidetracked?*

The double entrance doors to Module D slid open and Aurora thudded in, wearing an attitude and chewing gum very loudly.

'Do you want to eat first?' she queried Taren without looking at her, then headed straight over to the other set of double doors that gave entry into the large recreation area.

'Rory?' Taren appealed. 'Stop.'

Aurora turned around, rolling her eyes in the process.

'You're angry at me because you think something happened down there on Oceane.'

'Well, did it?' Aurora shot back, her anger still evident.

Taren didn't like her tone, as it was really none of her business. 'I'll be happy to give you a full account of what happened, if you will calm down and reserve judgment until I've finished. Deal?'

Rory took a deep breath, not ready to give up her fury. 'If you are just going to tell me how much you love him, then —'

'I'm not,' Taren interrupted.

Rory's clenched jaw finally loosened up a little. 'In that case ... I'll listen,' she growled, plonking herself on the lounge.

Taren started with the crash, with Zeven unconscious and having to brave the outside believing it was up to her to get them home. 'So when Zeven woke, I was just so glad to see him that, *well* ... things got a little out of hand —'

Rory gasped, horrified.

'In a *clothes-on* kind of way,' Taren added, to take the sting out of it. 'And the encounter was brief and, as it turns out it, not entirely our fault.'

'What!' Rory was upset again.

'The atmosphere of Oceane is like breathing a pure aphrodisiac. Ringbalin tested it.' Taren smiled to reassure Rory. 'I am truly not attracted to Zeven. He's a lovely guy and very heroic, but just a little too wild for my taste.'

'Not mine,' Aurora grinned and sulked at the same time. 'He's been making goo-goo eyes at you since you got here,' she grumbled. 'He's got a thing for older women.' She began to blow a bubble with her gum.

'Do you want my advice?' Taren queried, though she thought the girl was probably not going to like it.

Aurora nodded, her bubble growing bigger.

'Well, if you really want him, I suggest you get with the program, Rory, and grow up.'

Aurora's bubble burst.

'He's looking for a sensual woman, not a rebellious chick,' Taren explained.

'It doesn't matter how grown up I try to be, Zeven still sees me like a little sister or something.'

'Rory ...' Taren looked over the girl's hairdo of the day. 'Your hair is bright pink, right?'

'So? Your hair has a couple of purple stripes,' she retorted.

'But if I let my hair down, you can hardly see them at all ... so I can be conservative or a little wilder, depending on circumstances.'

'But I like standing out,' Rory brooded. 'I want him to like me the way I am.'

'I don't think this *is really you*,' Taren replied. 'I think it's a bit of a performance because you are afraid that the real you might be boring, or go unseen.' The look on Aurora's face told Taren she was on the right track. 'The simple truth is, the true you is far more likely to attract your true love.'

'Wow,' Aurora choked out, holding back her tears, 'that's pretty profound, Doctor.'

'Well, often it's easier said than done,' Taren confessed, thinking about the psychic skills she kept hidden because of what society thought.

Aurora pulled out a tissue and wiped her already red nose and then sniffled. 'I've been pouring energy into being *Rory* for so long, I don't know that I'll be able to find the true Aurora ... she's been well buried!' She forced a laugh, and wiped her nose once more. 'Would you help me?'

'Ha! I'm hardly a fashion guru,' Taren said in amusement, but when she saw Aurora's downcast appearance, changed her tune. 'Look, when we get back to Maladaan, we'll go shopping, and maybe we can help each other out?'

Aurora's face lit up at the suggestion. 'That would be wicked.'

Taren could see that Aurora was going to need to change in more ways than just her dress sense. 'That would be wonderful, marvellous, splendid, lovely, or even sensational, but not wicked, rockin', killer or neat.'

'Awesome?' Rory attempted to find the middle ground and Taren cringed a little. 'Superb,' Aurora put on a posh voice and sat up straight.

Taren winked. 'Now that's more like it.'

Lucian was really not looking forward to having this conversation. He had no real proof of his brother's involvement in any of this, only the word of Dr Lennox, who he barely knew but greatly admired. With all he'd seen of her in the past few days, he was inclined to believe Dr Lennox was an innocent victim, but maybe she was far more powerful than she was letting on — their inter-dimensional guest had seemed to think a lot of her?

Swithin, however, was another story altogether. His brother had been something of a wheeler-dealer in his time, but since he'd become interested in exploration and they had started this project together, Swithin appeared to have put his hustling ways behind him — until yesterday. Still, Lucian wasn't going to jump to conclusions. Amie could have been working for the MSS when Lucian had met her, and both he and Swithin may have been deceived by her from the start.

His heart ached a moment as Amie came to mind, although not as it had when he'd first learned of her death and seen her mutilated body. At that time it had felt like he'd taken a dagger straight in the back and through his chest that could not be withdrawn. Now that he knew the truth about his wife, it felt as if his heart had been cut right out, and there was only a heavy, painful emptiness left in the wake of what he'd thought was the love of his life.

As he sat down at his desk to place a request for an audio-visual link-up to base, he thrust his personal feelings and suspicions aside. He had no proof; he could not accuse Swithin, he could only relay some of what had unfolded here and see what kind of a reaction it fetched.

'Lucian, you inconsiderate bastard.' Swithin appeared on the screen at Lucian's workstation, wiping the sleep from his eyes. 'You know it's the middle of the night here, right? You did check the time difference before —'

'Amie has been murdered, Swithin.'

The news served to grab his attention. 'What? Are you kidding?'

'Her throat was cut,' Lucian told him, unwillingly taken back into some of the emotions he'd felt when he first discovered that the woman he adored had been taken from him.

'Damn ... that's bad.' Swithin put his head down, hiding his initial reaction, which could be seen as grief at the loss of a close friend and business partner. When he looked up, his eyes were moist with tears. 'I can't believe it.' His tears overflowed. 'Do you know what happened?'

'She was killed by an MSS sleeper agent,' Lucian informed him coolly, and his brother looked startled.

'Dr Lennox?'

'You know about her MSS history?' Lucian found this most interesting.

'Well, yes, I know it,' Swithin confessed. 'I sent her up there to discover our leak!'

'You know how I feel about the MSS?' Lucian lectured.

'Yes, yes. I also know how you feel about having our research stolen ... so shoot me!' he said, and winced. 'But I didn't expect this!'

'The really bad news is that there is a highly explosive gas sample traveling back to you on Kestler's pod.'

Swithin was stunned again.

'It's a secret delivery for the MSS, who have no idea what they are dealing with. You must get the sample before they do and release it immediately, or the entire planet is in jeopardy.'

'What kind of jeopardy?' He was curious.

'The kind that we *do not* want to be accountable for, understand me?' Lucian wished he'd asked the entity to be more specific about what would happen if they failed, but the encounter had been so intense and unexpected he hadn't been thinking straight. 'We are on our way back to you as we speak, but have no chance of catching the pod within ten days, which is when this sample will become very volatile. So make sure the pod's arrival is not delayed for any reason.'

'I'll take care of it,' Swithin said vehemently.

'I stress again, release it *immediately*.' Lucian emphasised the point, so that whether or not his brother was working with the MSS he knew the score.

'I got it.' Swithin gave Lucian a stare that entreated him to have a little faith.

CHAPTER 8

HOMEWARD-BOUND

During the ten days that followed, Taren managed to get some of her own research done, whilst keeping an eye on the images of Azazèl-mindos-coomra-dorchi that their satellites on Oceane were relaying back to AMIE. At present, the being overshadowing over a third of Oceane's surface area seemed just as it always had, but Taren expected that would change soon, as the entity was due to depart in the next few days.

As far as her own research went, the first series of experiments she intended to run was to see if space and distance affected an individual's ability to alter the past.

Taren had already proven that time was not the one-way forward-moving procession that humans had always believed it to be — debunking the old myth that cause must always precede effect. She had done this in a study of people with incurable tumours, who received remote healing intentions for a six-month period. Their tumours were then compared to those of other patients with similar-sized growths who had not received healing. Taren had discovered that those who received the healing maintained a stronger resistance to their disease, and some subjects had even gone into remission — against all medical probability.

What this had to do with changing the past was that Taren had actually sent the healing to her subjects four years after the final analysis on the patients involved had been completed.

This discovery had gone down like a lead balloon on Maladaan, and although the institute had kept this research under wraps they had not discouraged her from continuing her work.

Taren was not a psychic healer as such, but as a psychic she had proven adept at focusing and sustaining an intention to heal, much as any well-trained mind could. As any psychic kept themselves well hidden on Maladaan, she had been forced to utilise the only psychic she'd known at the time — herself.

Since the day she had left the planet, there were students in her labs on Maladaan who were monitoring subjects that she would be working with from space. And as before, her students were comparing rates of recovery in this group with other test subjects who would not be receiving the healing intentions that Taren would begin sending this week. They were limiting the trial to a one-month period, and she could hardly wait to discover if her patients had shown any improvement yet. Taren had planned to be in distant space while sending her healing intentions, so it would be interesting to see if the decreasing distance between their craft and Maladaan was having any impact on the results.

Taren's assigned students were not as excited about her work as she was — they worked with her under sufferance until they earned their way into the labs of more respected and renowned scientists, but she knew they were conscientious and would be diligent in recording information.

Taren placed a request for an audio-visual link-up from her office to her labs back on Maladaan, and waited to be patched through by Aurora.

After releasing their inter-dimensional guest from the craft, Taren had switched over to the day shift, not that one could really tell the difference in space. It was only day in so far as it was daytime back in their capital city, Esponisa on Maladaan.

This meant Taren had been successful in avoiding Zeven, as they were now on different shifts and inhabiting different parts of the vessel. Taren had also been learning her way around AMIE and found there was no need to go anywhere near the bridge. The pilot left a couple of messages for her, and she had tried to return the calls only to get his message service. With every day that passed, time was putting a greater distance between them and their misadventure on Oceane and this was a relief to Taren. She really didn't need any personal dramas right now.

'Patching you through,' Aurora advised from the monitor of Taren's workstation. Another window appeared in which Taren's senior student was waiting to speak with her.

'Greetings from space,' Taren gloated, knowing how jealous people had been of her assignment to AMIE. 'What's new?'

'What's new!' exclaimed Frank, her normally reserved and sceptical colleague. 'You've cured them all!'

'What do you mean, I cured them all?' He had to be pulling her leg. 'Don't mess with me, Frank, or you can kiss that PhD goodbye.'

'Hey, I'm the cynic, remember! You want me to show you all your terminally ill patients bouncing around like teenagers?'

'Yes,' Taren replied, her excitement mounting.

'No trust!' He rolled his eyes as he picked up his communication station and walked with it into the study rooms.

All her positive-healing test group were up and walking about, smiling, looking healthy. When they noticed Taren on the monitor, they all wanted to speak with her at once.

'I've never believed in psychics,' laughed one of her older male patients, 'but I am a *living* testament to your work, Dr Lennox.'

'Thank you seems so inadequate, doctor,' said another young woman, her eyes filled with tears. 'My children will have a mother, thanks to you.'

'This is a miraculous supernatural phenomenon,' an older lady said. 'Your field truly exists!'

Taren was overwhelmed by their expressions of gratitude and their claims that she'd performed a miracle! Indeed it was, for them, although she felt she was just proving a theory correct.

'Okay, time to say goodbye.' Frank got them to bid farewell, then went back to his office where it was quiet and they could talk.

'Let that be a lesson to you. I always tell the truth.' Frank sat down in front of his monitor once more. 'Either space has a profound effect on one's ability to change the past or your psychic talents have increased about tenfold.'

'And I haven't even done the healing yet.' Taren laughed in a nervous kind of way. What would account for such a resounding success? Was it space itself? Was it her stay on Oceane, or had her brief association with Azazèl-mindos-coomra-dorchi had something to do with it?

'Does anyone else know about this?' Taren wanted a chance to analyse the results herself.

'Well ...' Frank cringed, motioning vaguely in the direction of the hullabaloo in the patients' rooms, 'it has been a little hard to keep quiet. But the institute isn't going public about this, if that's what you mean.'

'Could you send me —'

'My full report is already in your inbox,' Frank assured her.

'Keep —'

'I'll keep monitoring the group and let you know if there is any change.' He grinned.

'Could you be any more efficient?' Taren rolled her eyes and smiled.

'I'll have a follow-up report ready by the time you get back,' he winked.

Taren told him that that could be a little sooner than expected as AMIE was making an unscheduled return to Maladaan.

'I'll see you soon then.' Frank ended the transmission and Taren sat back at her desk and clenched her fists triumphantly. '*Yes!*'

'Success?'

Taren was startled by Zeven's voice and swivelled her chair around to find him leaning in the doorway. He waved, looking a tad unsure about his visit.

'Mr Gudrun?' She checked her watch to be sure she hadn't lost track of the time. 'What are you doing up at this time of day?'

'I got a day off and figured this was the only chance I'd get to actually make contact.' He shrugged in conclusion. 'Do you have time to get something to eat?'

Taren felt really put on the spot — Aurora was at her desk across the room, and was no doubt watching.

'I can't right now. I have an isolation chamber booked for an experiment I'm —'

'Some other time then.' He moved to leave without further ado.

Taren felt really terrible … he'd obviously put his whole sleep cycle out of whack, just to see her. 'It is really important that I do this —'

'I understand, really,' he said, trying to sound convincing. But when he gave her a sad half smile as he slowly moved off, her heart couldn't stand the thought of letting him leave with nothing to show for his effort.

'I'll be free in a few hours,' she mentioned, wanting to kick herself as soon as she said it.

'Cool.' His smile was warm with sincere happiness. 'How about takeaway at my joint?'

That was a more private engagement than Taren was expecting. Obviously, he wanted to talk, and perhaps privacy was for the best. 'I'll come as soon as I'm done.'

'Excellent,' he said, 'see you then.'

Taren waved, and as soon as he was gone she headed to the doorway to see if Aurora was watching. Of course, she was.

As the pilot passed her desk on his way out of the offices, she rose with a pile of papers to file.

'Wow.' Zeven noted Aurora was wearing a classy dress and heels and as he was in such a good mood, he thought he'd pay her a compliment. 'You look hot today, Rory.'

'Thanks,' she replied, and walked into Lucian's office without serving him a second glance.

Her lack of interest took him aback for a second, but he shrugged it off and continued along his merry way.

When he was gone Taren went dashing across to Lucian's office, and knowing he was on R and R for a few days, she entered to speak with Aurora. 'Did you see how Starman looked at you just then?' Taren was delighted. Aurora was not.

'He asked you out, didn't he?' She wasn't hostile, just disheartened.

'Actually he asked me in.' Taren wanted to be up front about it.

'He invited you back to his place!' Now Aurora was devastated. 'You're a goner.'

'No, I'm not,' Taren insisted, 'but it does give me the perfect opportunity to tell him I'm not interested, in private. I really don't want to hurt him, or you, I just want to get past this so we can all move on.'

Aurora drew a deep breath to bury her feelings and smiled. 'He said I look hot.'

'He did.' Taren smiled back.

'Thanks,' Aurora said. 'For someone I've only known a little while, you're a *real* good friend.'

'Ditto, girlfriend.' Taren gave her a squeeze and then noted the time. 'Oh gosh, I'm going to be late.'

'Good luck with the break-up,' Aurora whispered as Taren rushed to her appointment with an isolation chamber.

Taren was feeling wonderful in the wake of her two-hour meditation, throughout which she had been sending her intention to heal the people that she had already healed. Having the effect precede the cause gave her ultimate confidence in her abilities. It was like a composer hearing his musical masterpiece before he writes a single note, leaving no room for doubt that he will finish the composition. Taren was thinking she should have some tests run on herself to see if there had been any change in her physiology since the medical she'd had before boarding the craft. Her experiment had been a huge success. Now she just had to figure out why.

She was in a real dilemma about what to wear on this date of hers — pants were definitely the order of the day, but she didn't want to look like she was dressing up for him, or show up looking like a complete dag either. She found a modest top, a bit of jewellery and just a touch of make-up — which she only ever donned for social occasions.

As she walked out of her living quarters and headed towards next door, Taren saw Lucian walking down the hall towards her.

'Where are you off to looking so fabulous?' he commented on his way past.

I look fabulous? Taren panicked on the inside — it was not the impression she'd been hoping to give — and she found herself completely lost for words. Why did this man always make her feel like a blithering idiot?

The door to Zeven's quarters opened. 'There you are.' She was startled by his sudden presence, and glanced back to catch Lucian's reaction.

The look on his face was one of wry amusement. 'I see ... have a good evening,' he said, and moved on.

Taren badly wanted to tell him it was not how it looked. 'Damn it,' she muttered under her breath and looked at Zeven, who appeared most confused by her reaction.

'What's wrong?' he inquired innocently.

Taren gave him the evil eye, although she did smile to lessen the sting. 'You know damn well what is wrong.' She raised a finger and beckoned him to follow her into his quarters.

'This is not going to be romantic, is it?' He paused before entering, not quite as eager to be alone with her now.

She shook her head and, releasing a huge disappointed breath, Zeven entered and closed the door behind them.

Taren had envisioned a really awkward confrontation, ending with her walking out and Zeven never speaking to her again. Instead, he respected her decision to concentrate on her work while she was here on AMIE.

'But once we are not stuck on this bucket of bolts, you have to let me take you out to dinner,' Zeven proffered.

'If you still want to by then ... sure,' Taren agreed.

So they ate, watched a movie, had a few drinks and quite a few more laughs than Taren had expected. When he wasn't trying to chat her up, Zeven was a seriously interesting and funny guy who had many fascinating stories to tell.

In the end, Taren thanked him for a great night and left with their friendship still intact, and no chance of a relationship on the immediate horizon. She'd managed to maintain the status quo and it was a great relief indeed.

Swithin was waiting in the pod bay to meet Kestler on arrival, just as he had promised his brother. Lucian had made the urgency of releasing this sample very clear, so he ordered the ground crew to give Kestler's pod top priority.

He was waiting in the hangar area observing the pod being lowered to ground level in its cradle, when a large black hovercar pulled up and stopped close beside him. At the same time the handset in his pocket started ringing. Swithin knew it was Lucian calling, so he switched the handset to his message service.

'Gentlemen,' he greeted the unofficial government officials wryly. 'What can we do for the MSS this fine day?'

One of the darkly clad foursome, who carried a briefcase, removed his dark eye-bands, to look Swithin in the eye. 'Ask not what you can do for us, but what we can do for you.' He handed over the keys to the hovercar and the briefcase. 'Your off-world craft awaits you at the Central Bay port. Have a great trip.'

Swithin opened the case and after closely scrutinising the large bundles of notes within he was a little confused. 'Don't you want me to wait around until you secure the sample?'

'No need.' The agent smiled. 'We know the sample is on board and intact. We'll take it from here.'

Swithin was the only person who knew the substance was volatile, but as time was short to escape the consequences his brother had warned him about, he wasn't going to argue.

'Where will you go ... the Maratosh system?' the agent inquired as Swithin made for the vehicle.

'A tropical environment could be real nice for a while.' Swithin didn't commit.

'It's a shame your lovely partner in crime was so unexpected taken out of the equation, Swithin,' the agent commented. 'Who will share paradise with you now?'

Swithin forced a grin at the implication that he'd had Amie killed. 'I'm sure I'll find somebody.' He hopped into the driver's seat and closed the door.

'Don't count on it.' The agent watched the vehicle speed out of the hangar doors.

As soon as he was in the open car park, Swithin stopped the hovercar, grabbed the briefcase of money and bolted for cover inside a neighbouring hangar that was not currently in use. The MSS vehicle exploded behind him, hurling Swithin into his hiding place. He looked back to find that there was nothing left of the luxury hovercar. 'Fucking bastards.' He got himself to a seated position and, pulling a handset from his pocket, called for his own pilot to pick him up at their designated meeting spot in ten minutes.

In a dark corner of the hangar he uncovered a hoverbike, helmet and a backpack containing a change of clothes that he'd organised the night before. A quick change, helmet on, and out the gate on a guest pass — no one was any the wiser that he'd left the premises. After all, how could he have left? Swithin Gervaise was now officially a dead man.

Early the next morning Taren was eating breakfast while skimming through the report Frank had sent through, when Kassa entered the cafeteria. Taren waved to her, wishing to have a word.

The doctor picked out a small breakfast and then headed over with her tray to take a seat at Taren's table.

'How are you doing?' Taren hadn't bumped into Kassa since she'd had her collapse. 'I heard you were out for a couple of days!' Taren had kept a check on her progress, but she'd been asleep at the time Kassa had finally come around.

'I'm fine.' Kassa waved off any concern, and then whispered, 'The biggest problem I had was trying to explain it.'

'Obviously, Lucian now knows,' Taren wondered what had gone on whilst she'd been stuck on Oceane.

Kassa nodded. 'I couldn't leave you stranded there,' she shrugged. 'But Lucian has left it to my discretion who knows and who doesn't.'

'Well, thank you,' Taren said.

Kassa forced a smile. 'He believes I should tell Leal.'

'Lucian said that?' Taren was surprised as he didn't seem the type to interfere in other people's personal affairs.

'He didn't have to,' Kassa said, sounding disappointed in herself for being such a coward about it.

Taren's pager went off, startling them both. It was Lucian, requesting that Taren come to his office as soon as possible.

'I've got to go.' She stood up. 'But I need you to give me a physical today, if possible.'

Kassa nodded. 'Sure, just page me with a time.'

'We'll talk then.' Taren knew Kassa wanted help with her moral dilemma and Kassa nodded gratefully.

'Dr Lennox.' Ringbalin caught Taren on her way out the door.

'Call me Taren, please ... we're practically living together,' she joked.

Ringbalin was very pleased, but it was not her sense of humour that had him so excited. 'I need to speak with you about our tundrell. I think I've discovered something amazing —'

Taren's beeper went off, alerting her to the fact that the monitor satellites on Oceane had detected a change in the anomaly. 'Damn it! Not now, sorry,' Taren hurriedly said to Ringbalin. 'I'm sure it's incredible, but the captain has summoned me and our being is getting ready to depart Oceane.'

'Excellent, I'll get back to my workstation. I want to see this.' He rubbed his hands together.

'Tape it for me, just in case,' Taren requested, as she backed up the corridor.

'Sure,' Ringbalin said. Although obviously bursting to tell someone about his discovery, he accepted the delay with a smile.

'Thanks a million. I'll catch up with you later.'

'Do I need to make an appointment?'

'Not usually.' Taren gave a laugh, thinking she had been exceptionally busy since her arrival on AMIE.

'You haven't seen my greenhouse yet,' Ringbalin chided.

'Today, I swear!' Taren held up a palm to seal her vow, before she waved and turned to resume her course to the captain's office.

In retrospect, she felt she had been rude not to ask Ringbalin what he was so excited about and now wished she had, as he had made her curious. She was just nervous about being summoned to Lucian's office; it usually meant that either she, or the project, was in trouble.

'Good morning, Aurora. You look lovely today.' Taren smiled as she approached, and received a smile in return.

'How did it go?' Aurora whispered.

'We are still friends and nothing more,' Taren was pleased to say and Aurora squealed with delight until they heard Lucian clear his throat.

'Sorry to interrupt, but this is rather urgent.' Lucian beckoned Taren into his office. Intrigued by the serious look on his face she complied with the greatest of haste.

'What has happened?' she asked, remembering that this was the morning that Kestler's pod was due on Maladaan. 'Is something amiss with the sample? The being is preparing to leave, you realise?'

Lucian pointed to a spare monitor displaying the event, and Taren immediately moved in to take a closer look.

The bright mass of coloured electromagnetic gas had detached itself from Oceane and was now floating well apart from the planet it had nurtured. The being had formed into a sphere, leaving a large continent of green amid the oceans of blue on Oceane. The new landmass could only been seen in part, due to the dense cloud forming from large-scale volcanic activity that had erupted on the planet's surface in the wake of the entity's departure.

'Wow,' Taren uttered, spellbound.

'Indeed.' Lucian agreed. 'I'd love to be able to tell you what is happening with the sample in Kestler's pod on Maladaan, but my brother won't answer his phone and it's been too early in the morning to catch anyone in the office.' He glanced at his watch. 'We are attempting to get a living body in front of a monitor as we speak.' Lucian glanced sideways and was shocked to see Taren's horrified face.

'You entrusted Swithin with releasing the sample?' Taren gasped.

'I have no proof of Swithin's involvement in this beyond sending you to us, which he freely confessed to me,' Lucian explained, rather put out that she would question his judgment. 'Swithin's first conclusion was that you had killed Amie.'

Now Taren was insulted, but held her tongue. It seemed Lucian changed his mind about her as often as he changed his clothes. 'Have you spoken with anyone at the pod bay? Has Kestler landed?'

Lucian shook his head, but just then Aurora advised from his workstation screen, 'Patching you through to pod bay seven, homeside, Captain.' Lucian smiled at Taren and took a seat. She strolled around the desk to view the screen.

'Pod bay seven, Cato Paley speaking.' The engineer seemed rather overwhelmed when he discovered who the caller was. 'Professor Gervaise, sir.' He looked around him, obviously searching for a superior he could fetch to speak with the professor.

'I am wanting to confirm that Eleazar Kestler's pod has landed,' Lucian queried.

'Yes, professor, it did land.'

'Was my brother, Swithin, there to meet the capsule?'

'He was here,' the engineer confirmed, while seeming reluctant to continue. 'But ... there was an incident ... I'm going to patch you through to the office —'

'No —' But before Lucian could delay him, the engineer was gone. The next thing they knew, Swithin's secretary was on screen wiping tears from her face.

'Professor Gervaise.' She collected herself to address him. 'I am so sorry to be the one to inform you ... but your brother has reportedly been involved in a freak car accident.'

'What!' Lucian was shocked, Taren was not.

The MSS would not leave anyone alive who had had any contact with the sample they had stolen — if nobody knew about it, then it never existed. That meant her life was probably in danger, and the thought of going to Maladaan was a little daunting. She could only hope that they'd rooted out all the MSS sleeper agents on board AMIE.

'The hovercar Mr Gervaise was driving exploded in the car park outside of pod bay —' The woman collapsed into tears and one of her male colleagues was forced to take over the transmission.

'The authorities are investigating,' the man advised, 'but to tell you the truth, Professor, there is not a whole lot left to investigate.'

The news was awful and Taren wanted to place a friendly hand on Lucian's shoulder, but she felt the gesture would be of little comfort to him if he still suspected that she was in some way involved.

'They are also looking into why Kestler's pod misfired soon after it had docked ... before the occupant was even extracted!' 'A recovery vessel is being launched to fetch the pod, as it has barely enough fuel left to clear the atmosphere.'

Another dead agent with no stories to tell. Taren's heart swelled with sorrow at the thought of such a great scientific mind as Kestler's being allowed to slip into obscurity at the whim of some government agency with a money-making agenda. Her eyes drifted from the monitor link-up with Maladaan, to the one monitoring Oceane and her heart skipped a beat.

'Captain.' Taren warily directed his attention to the monitor displaying images from Oceane. 'We're running out of time.'

The sphere of rainbow electric light had now shed all its colour. Only the bright electrical blue-white activity remained and intensified. In a brilliant flash the sphere of energy vanished from sight completely and their satellite image went static.

Lucian was becoming more disillusioned by the minute, and looked back to the fellow on Maladaan. 'Can you patch me through to the investigating officer?'

'I sure —' The screen went static and then blank.

'Not now!' Lucian whined, as he pushed Aurora's intercom number. 'The line has dropped out. Can you get them back?'

'One moment,' Aurora said.

Lucian looked at Taren, concerned.

'A coincidence?' he asked rhetorically and in a sarcastic tone. 'You think Swithin failed to release the sample in time?' He attempted to think it through to keep from falling to pieces, but it seemed Taren had beaten him to the mark, for she wiped a tear from her cheek and took a seat. 'I am surprised my brother's death would upset you like this?'

'Not your brother,' she explained. 'Kestler.' She forced a grin to stop herself from bursting into tears. 'The man was a legend.'

'He still is,' Lucian was surprised by her needless concern. 'They will retrieve his pod —'

Taren shook her head, just as certain. 'No, they won't.'

Lucian didn't seem to know how to respond, so Taren helped out.

'I am very sorry for your loss, captain. Would you prefer that I leave?'

'I don't know,' Lucian answered honestly. 'What am I supposed to feel right now?' he appealed to her. 'Was my brother loyal to me? Should I grieve his loss, or be thanking the heavens to have another traitor exposed and expunged?'

Taren felt a little awkward as she was not a telepath, nor did she know much of the history of the project beyond what had been documented by the institute. 'I believe Kassa is really the only person who may be able to give you those answers.'

Lucian nodded. 'That has occurred to me. I guess I have been avoiding that conversation ... if you don't want to know the answer, then ...'

'... don't ask the question,' Taren concluded, understanding completely.

Aurora knocked and entered. 'Sorry to barge in, but all the feeds to Maladaan are completely dead.'

'Is it our equipment?' Lucian was wondering if they'd been sabotaged from the inside.

'I can get a line through to the Maratosh colonies, and those on Sermetica, Frujia too. It's just Maladaan,' she advised. 'It's like the entire communications network down there has just been shut down.'

'An event of such magnitude could only have been caused by an unprecedented electromagnetic occurrence.' Lucian looked at Taren.

'Did I mention I don't believe in coincidence? If it was the sample that has caused the telecommunications breakdown, I doubt the sample was also the cause of Swithin's death, as he was reported dead before our entity had altered its state of being.'

'Swithin is dead!' Aurora had never known anyone who had died, and now two colleagues had died in the same month! 'How?'

'A freak accident,' Lucian explained in an attempt to calm her, but Taren scoffed, and the captain didn't need to be a mind-reader to know her mind. 'You think the MSS had him killed, don't you?'

'I don't think they did.' Taren made it perfectly clear. 'I *know* they did.'

* * *

After an hour of trying and failing to re-establish communication with their home planet, Lucian truly felt the weight of the world upon his shoulders. For the sake of everyone on Maladaan he had to know the extent of the covert operation inside his project and he needed answers by the time they arrived home at the institute in Esponisa.

Aurora advised through the intercom that Kassa was waiting to see him, and Lucian asked Aurora to send her in.

The doctor didn't need telepathy to sense the ominous mood that hung heavily around the captain. 'Lucian?' She took a seat, knowing this was going to be the conversation that she'd hoped they would never have.

'You have been telepathic all your life, yes?' Lucian asked and Kassa nodded warily. 'And you have been on this project practically from its inception . . .'

Kassa drew a deep breath for strength, knowing where this line of questioning was leading.

'Were you aware then, or at any time, of my brother having ties to the MSS?' Lucian asked her outright.

'I believe that you should ask Swithin that question. I can only spec—'

'Swithin is dead, Kassa.' Lucian's jaw tensed. 'The car he was driving *blew up!*'

Kassa gasped, her eyes filling with tears.

'We have lost all communication with Maladaan and the colonies have reported the same problem. Dr Lennox and I suspect our sample had something to do with it, and as I trusted Swithin to ensure the release of the substance and he is now *dead*, it has been left to me to find out what the hell might have happened to him and the sample.' Lucian felt compelled to stand. He was angry, and worried that their negligence might have caused a major disaster at home. The mysterious being had warned him that there would be repercussions on a global level if they failed to release it on time, and Lucian didn't even want to imagine what that meant. 'So, now more than ever, I need you to come clean with me, Kassa, were Swithin and Amie working together for the MSS?'

Kassa closed her eyes, and nodded to confirm ... 'Before you even met her.'

Lucian's jaw set hard as he struggled to control his emotions.

'Without your reputation and influence at the institute, they would never have got this project off the ground, Lucian,' Kassa said, her guilt choking her. 'In retrospect, I know that I should have confessed all this to you sooner, but up until recently there had only been a few leaks and there had been no major harm done.'

Lucian collapsed back into his chair, completely devastated by the news.

'You have to realise that it was a few leaks in your project, or my entire career!' Kassa attempted to rationalise her lack of action. 'I felt I had no choice but to keep silent. I am fast realising how selfish I have been. I am so sorry, Lucian.' It hurt her to see her dear friend so completely shattered, and she felt some responsibility. She had helped to break the spirit of one of the greatest men she'd ever known. 'Now I see that I am just as much to blame for the tragedy that has befallen this project. I resign my post as Chief Medical Officer. You can find a replacement for me when we reach Maladaan.'

Lucian could only nod. They had been friends a long time and he felt betrayed by Kassa's secrecy. He knew she had done what she thought was best for all, but he was afraid that if he went any further into any of this sordid history at present, he'd just break down completely. 'Are there any other nasty little secrets that I should know about before you go?' He managed to squeeze out the question before Kassa left the room, and she paused before opening the door.

'These people are dead now, Lucian.' Kassa turned back to look him in the face. 'Are you sure you wouldn't rather let sleeping dogs lie?'

It was beginning to seem that the last ten years of his life had been a lie, and he shook his head. 'The truth might be a refreshing change.'

Kassa supposed it was better that Lucian hear the truth from her than from the MSS or some other investigating authority back on Maladaan. 'Swithin and Amie were lovers, Lucian.'

Of all the bombshells that had dropped on him recently, this perfidy hit the hardest. 'Before I wed her?' Lucian was loath to believe it.

'All along,' Kassa managed to reply, and as Lucian buried his face in his hands, she escaped into reception. Closing the door behind her, she burst into tears.

'Dr Madri, are you all right?' Aurora assumed that it was the news of Swithin's untimely death that had her so upset. 'It is a tragic loss, I know.' She moved to assist the doctor. 'Can I get you some water, or —'

'No, nothing.' Kassa regained her sensibilities, and managed to rouse a weak smile for the girl. 'I am fine. You see to the captain.' She patted Aurora's hand in reassurance, and gathered her wits long enough to retreat to her chambers.

Aurora ventured a knock on the captain's door.

'I'm not in for the rest of today,' he advised via the intercom on her workstation.

She moved to her desk to respond, overwhelmed with sympathy for the captain. 'Is there anything I can do?'

'Close the office. Take the day off. Thanks, Aurora.'

The captain had had more grief and pressure piled upon him in the past few days than any human being should handle alone — she didn't feel that leaving him was the responsible thing to do.

'I'll be fine, Aurora,' he added, sensing her hesitation. *'I just need some time to myself.'*

'Of course,' she said. 'I'll be on call should you need me.' She left it at that. He seemed rational and needed time to grieve, as did everyone. With so much controversy surrounding AMIE now, she could only hope that the entire project was not about to collapse.

Taren was concerned when Kassa wouldn't answer her pager and hadn't returned her calls. She really needed that examination for her research. She dropped by Kassa's office, but was informed she'd been summoned to see the captain. Taren felt a little guilty having suggested that the captain interrogate Kassa regarding his brother, but what else could she do? She certainly had no answers for the man.

As it seemed she was at liberty, Taren decided that she would head over and see what had Ringbalin so excited. She knew her way to Module C. She'd often passed signage for it on her way in and out the cafeteria. She'd never ventured down to the greenhouse, however, as all the rooms she usually frequented lay in the opposite direction.

On her way past the eatery, a whistle forestalled her trek into the unknown and Zeven came running up to meet her.

'Is it true?' He glanced back to his source, Aurora, who was sitting at a table collecting herself over a cup of coffee. There were also a couple of engineers and divers from the marine department about, so he kept his voice low. 'Was Swithin murdered by the MSS?'

'We don't know what happened.' Taren declined to comment, as many of the crew were casting suspicious glances her way. 'The communication lines are down, as you probably know.'

'A fact that is even scarier than the first premise.' He joined her in the corridor, walking with her until they were away from prying eyes. 'Only a full-scale attack on Maladaan could have taken out all the communication systems on the entire planet!'

'I know,' Taren was also concerned, 'but I don't have any great truths to share with you right now. I am as much in the dark as you are.' She began to move away to be about her business.

'Keep me informed?' he asked nicely.

'What are friends for?' Taren didn't feel he mistrusted her, but rather he had intuited that if there was trouble brewing, she was likely to be right in the middle of it.

Taren followed the signage to Module C and upon entering the bio-dome she was awestruck. The ceiling of the module was a high curved screen that displayed an image of the sun slowly moving across the daytime sky; but that image also projected rays of heat and light onto the garden, along the sun's trajectory. Beneath this was a cloud layer that cast a shadow onto the expansive gardens below. It was like a huge version of one of Ringbalin's bonsai incubators. Taren truly felt as if she had just stepped outside into a garden, which was the last thing she expected to encounter in space. The sound of filters, bubbling water and poultry animals were apparent as she began to stroll down the central path. The smell of wet earth, herbs and compost intermingled and made her homesick to the core for the first time since she'd arrived on AMIE.

Amid the din of nature and equipment, Taren heard voices, and turned off the main pathway onto a smaller one in order to track the source.

At the end of this pathway was a lab and inside, a beautiful, tall woman, dressed in a wet suit, was leaning over a bench, speaking with Ringbalin. They were both fascinated with some sealed beakers on the bench, so the scene was quite professional but the body language of the woman suggested that she was quite well disposed towards the young botanist.

When Taren knocked, they were startled and straightened up to put a more respectable working distance between them.

'Dr Lennox,' Ringbalin seemed a little flushed, 'your timing is impeccable.'

'Are you being sarcastic?' Taren chided as she entered.

'Not at all.' He picked up his glasses from the bench and put them on. 'Dr Portus has discovered a tiny algae in one of the water samples she collected from just outside the anomaly zone on Oceane.'

'A single-cell organism! Life is developing fast down there then.' Taren was stunned, but held out her hand to introduce herself to the marine botanist. 'Hi, I'm Taren Lennox.'

'Sorry.' Ringbalin suddenly realised he was being rude. 'Dr Lennox … meet Dr Ayliscia Portus, from our marine department.'

'My honour is great to finally meet the woman who has inspired Ringbalin's work very much.' She smiled warmly.

Dr Portus had a very strong accent, which was almost as striking as her stunning good looks, poise and tall stature. Taren was guessing that she was Phemorian. In ancient times the women of Phemoria had rebelled against eons of repression at the hands of their menfolk and, in one of human history's most famed rebellions, the women seized control of the entire planet and forbade any man citizenship. Since that time, Phemoria had been a haven for women, especially those who sought sanctuary from male brutality.

Taren was more interested in Dr Portus' discovery at present. 'So, tell me about your algae.'

All eyes turned back to the beaker as Ringbalin took up a small torch. 'Check this out.' He shone the torch into the beaker of murky water, which seemed to be filled with deep green plant shavings. He then switched the light source off, whereupon all the tiny free-floating algae began to pulse with bright green light in perfect unison.

'Delayed luminescence!' Taren was delighted by the display.

'I have studied light emissions between luminescent algae in the seawater on Frujia, because although on the evolutionary scale they are classified as a plant, they move like a primitive animal. What I discovered was that the movement of each dinoflagellate perfectly synchronised with that of its neighbours —'

'The algae are using the light to communicate.' Taren jumped two steps ahead in the conversation.

'Exactly. But that is not what is most interesting.' Ringbalin was pleasantly surprised to be able to skip ahead in his tutorial. 'We know from your past research in biophotonics that all living things are antennas and transmitters of light. The more complex a living organism is in the evolutionary scheme of things the less biophotons it emits —'

'That is not a widely accepted fact,' Taren felt she should point out.

'It will be soon, I feel, as my research corroborates your findings,' Ringbalin assured her with a smile.

'Why? What is the biophoton count on this algae?'

'About fifty photons per second at a wavelength of two hundred nanometers,' Ringbalin advised.

Taren was shocked. 'That is well under half the rate of any rudimentary plant or animal I have studied,' she said, and Ringbalin nodded to agree that the results were exceptional.

'Indicating that this is a very advanced strand of algae,' Dr Portus added.

'The biophoton count of our tundrell is also way below what one would expect,' Ringbalin said. 'It also pulses in the dark when the lights are turned off, and although I am yet to confirm this, I will bet my life that the tundrell and these algae pulse in time.'

'A visual means to confirm communication between species via photon emissions!' Taren was absolutely beside herself, and could well appreciate her colleagues' excitement. 'This could go a long way to proving that light photons are the great translators and communicators of creation.'

'I believe the intense atmosphere within the

anomaly region on Oceane has a lot to do with why these plants are more evolved than any we have encountered before. Lights off,' Ringbalin instructed and the lab fell into darkness.

'What are you doing?' Taren wondered why he'd plunged them into darkness until her eyes adjusted and it became apparent that her body was also pulsing with faint bursts of green light and in perfect time with the algae. 'Oh, my stars ...'

'You've breathed in that heavenly atmosphere, too, and your biology is now in sync with it,' Ringbalin reasoned.

'But I'm pulsing light!' Taren found this somewhat distressing.

'We all are,' Ringbalin reminded her, 'you're just absorbing less light and rejecting more of it now and so it is more obvious. Lights on.'

'It also seems to suggest that your biology has undergone an evolutionary advancement,' Dr Portus concluded.

'I want to do a photon count on you asap,' Ringbalin added, 'as I am also guessing that you are emitting much less than the ten photons of light that your average human being emits in the same area, time and frequency.'

'That would explain a whole lot.' Taren's thoughts had turned to her own research. 'Like the unprecedented results I have achieved in healing the test subjects in my current trial.' Ringbalin nodded to agree, and was startled when Taren gasped. 'If I have been affected by the atmosphere of Oceane, then wouldn't Zeven Gudrun also be affected?'

'No doubt.' Ringbalin raised an eyebrow, knowing that the macho pilot would probably be freaked out to discover that his biological structure was now attuned to some higher alien frequency.

Taren found the fact rather amusing. 'Well, let's run some tests on me first. No point in alarming the poor man needlessly.'

'What about Leal Polson?' Ringbalin wondered about the pilot who had rescued them from Oceane.

Taren shrugged. 'He never disembarked or breathed in the atmosphere, so I doubt he will have been affected.'

Zeven had been very open with Taren about his interest in the Powers — from an observer's point of view he found it all very fascinating. However, Taren didn't think he would appreciate the information that his experience on Oceane may well have accelerated his biology to a point where his own dormant Powers might be activated.

Taren drew a deep breath, not wanting to get too far ahead of herself. *Let's just take this one revelation at a time.*

It had been a rather eventful day, Taren considered, as she lay in the large round sleeping pod in her darkened room, staring out into the vastness of space through the floor-to-ceiling windows of her quarters.

She raised a hand to observe the faint green light-pulses of her body which were noticeably lessening in intensity the longer she lay in the dark. *Why always me?*

No matter how much she wished to downplay her psychic Powers, some strange quirk of fate kept landing her in situations where she was forced to promote the unfashionable fact that she was capable of feats that science, on the whole, refused to accept were possible — no matter how many experiments she did to prove them wrong. 'Well, seeing is believing.'

Just as Ringbalin had expected, her biophoton count was way down, strongly indicating that she had undergone a quiet evolutionary leap.

Which should mean I can now perform other psychic feats that I could not previously, she reasoned to herself. *What should I try?*

On her bedside table a small round clock caught her attention and she focused upon it, of a mind to try to make it rise. In her mind's eye she imagined that it lifted off the table, but when nothing happened, Taren gave up ... a single heavy thud from the vicinity of the table startled her. She scampered to the table to inspect the clock. When she tried to lift it off the surface, Taren found that a heavy magnet in the base of it prevented her from lifting it more than a fraction. She let the clock drop and gasped when she recognised the heavy thud.

A buzz at her chamber door gave Taren a start, and she drew a deep breath to calm herself down.

'Coming!' She pulled on some trousers and a shirt, wondering who the hell would be visiting her five hours into downtime. Didn't people realise that she needed to sleep sometimes?

Taren switched the lights on and, checking through the peephole, she was surprised to see no one there. *Did I imagine that?*

The buzzer startled her again but there was still no one in sight through the peephole.

'If someone is playing a practical joke...' Annoyed, she opened the door, to find the good captain in a crumpled heap on the floor hugging a large bottle of spirits that was near empty.

Oh, dear heavens. 'Professor, this is not a good look on you.' Taren squatted in front of him.

'Call me an idiot,' he suggested, 'everybody else has.'

'You're not an idiot.' Taren sympathised with his sad state of dishevelment, and she smiled in reassurance. 'You are a brilliant man. Never let anyone tell you otherwise.'

'Ha!' he said mockingly. 'Sure, brilliant enough to allow everyone to pull the wool over my eyes.' He took another long swig from the bottle, which Taren confiscated. Too late, it was empty.

'So, you're a bad judge of character.' Taren took hold of his arms to haul him to his feet and get him into the privacy of her cabin before anyone on the crew saw him this inebriated. 'Join the club.'

'That's why I'm here ...' He cooperated with her efforts, although he staggered about like a sailor who hadn't found his sea legs. 'I figured that if I had been so wrong about the people I thought were my friends, then I have probably been wrong about those I assumed were my enemies.'

Taren wasn't too sure how to take the comment. 'I'm so flattered,' she chided, as he would never remember this conversation anyway. 'I'm not your enemy, professor.' She was glad to deposit him on a lounge, and called the order for her door to close.

'I realise —'

'To the contrary, I am one of your greatest admirers,' she concluded, placing hands on hips as she looked down upon the man spreadeagled on her couch and wondered what to do with him.

'Admire?' He struggled to sit upright. 'My project is just a front for MSS operations ... I bet they funded the entire thing!'

Taren was disappointed by his attitude, but he could hardly be blamed for being down on himself at present. 'Well, good,' she stated defiant. 'Now that you know, you can have the ultimate pleasure of doing them out of their investment.' Lucian smiled and cocked an eye, impressed by her comeback. Taren shrugged. 'Even in the worst of situations, there is always opportunity.'

Lucian nodded, knowing she was probably right, but he was not feeling very opportunistic. 'Kassa has resigned and I accepted it,' he informed Taren, not happy with himself, but he couldn't imagine how he could trust Kassa again.

Taren was dismayed, and a little angered, by this news. 'She cannot be held accountable for what has happened, any more than I can!'

'By saying nothing, she was an accomplice,' Lucian argued.

'She couldn't prove it, professor,' Taren lectured him. 'Oh yes, even if she had come clean with you, I'm sure you would have believed her!' she finished sarcastically.

'I would have investigated —'

'Rubbish! I saw the way you regarded your wife. Before all this, you were completely infatuated! The only way anyone was going to get you to believe Amie's treachery was over her dead body, and even then you wouldn't —' Taren realised she'd gone too far as Lucian held up a hand to beg her to stop, bowed his head and collapsed into tears.

'I'm so sorry.' Taren fell on her knees in front of him in an unconscious gesture to beg forgiveness. 'I am not a subtle woman, professor, and I —'

'No ...' Lucian wouldn't hear her apology and he brought his emotions back in to check. 'I came to see you because I knew you would set me straight. And you're right, I wouldn't have believed it ... I still can't believe it,' he confessed in utter bewilderment.

Taren's heart exploded in her chest. She had never wanted to take someone else's pain away as much as she did in this moment. 'I know how it feels to be so deeply betrayed, believe me I do. I came to learn from a *very* young age that I am the *only* person I can rely on. Be that as it may, since landing on AMIE I've formed some amazing friendships, with some truly amazing people, all handpicked by you —'

'But how many more of them have been got at by the MSS and not remembered, as you did?'

Taren shook her head. 'Except for Amie, no one on board this vessel has betrayed you of their own free will. These people are completely devoted to you, professor. Your vision made their dreams come true ... that's why the MSS had to use underhanded means to get them to cooperate. So don't you dare let one bad apple ruin all that you have achieved here. I tell you in all sincerity that if you let Kassa go, you'll be losing one of the truest friends you'll ever have.'

Lucian was gazing at her, wide-eyed with wonder at her impassioned words. 'I just —' Too compelled to even finish his sentence, Lucian kissed her, and Taren, hesitant at first, lost her reservations in seconds and returned his kiss with fervour.

In a moment, the intense encounter was over, leaving both of them dumbstruck and awkward.

'That was unexpected.' Taren broke the silence.

'It certainly was.' Lucian was somewhat dazed, although the smile he was suppressing seemed to indicate that he was not remorseful. 'I should go,' he said, although he made no attempt to do so.

'A coffee might be in order first.' Taren rose to make it, her heart doing somersaults in her chest, flushing her face with waves of heat.

'Good call,' he seconded.

He doesn't want to leave! she deduced as she quietly went about making the coffee.

When Taren turned to present the coffee to Lucian, she found him happily snoozing in a horizontal position on her lounge. 'He is not capable of leaving, more like.' She pouted in brief resentment.

The professor would not remember their encounter and as he was drunk, and on the worst of rebounds, perhaps that was for the best.

'Oh, stop this! You're not here to fulfil some silly schoolgirl crush,' Taren told herself sharply. Now, if she could just stop her heart from palpitating every time she looked at the man, she might be able to focus on why she was here.

CHAPTER 9

THE VOID

Consciousness attempted to lure Lucian from his slumber, but the pain that awaited, tormenting him in brief bursts, did nothing to encourage him to emerge fully from his dreams.

These people are completely devoted to you, professor. Your vision made their dreams come true.

An image of Dr Lennox invaded the twilight of his sleep.

You are a brilliant man. Never let anyone tell you otherwise.

Her smile was disarming. Why was she being so sweet to him, when he had been so mistrustful of her?

If you let Kassa go, you'll be losing one of the truest friends you'll ever have.

In his vision, Dr Lennox was the most beautiful, sympathetic, fairminded and forgiving person he'd ever encountered, and he felt an overwhelming urge to kiss her.

Lucian awoke with a start, but recoiled from consciousness as his throbbing head forced his eyes closed and he groaned in agony.

'Captain?'

His eyes shot open. *What the hell is Dr Lennox doing in my quarters first thing in the morning?* He gave a silent prayer that he had not acted on his drunken desires as he rolled over and unexpectedly fell onto the floor. 'What the —' Fully awake now, he looked around and realised that he was not in his chambers, but in Dr Lennox's. He looked at Taren, who was smiling down at him, a cup of coffee in her hand.

'Are you all right?' She suppressed an urge to laugh.

'Fine, I think.' Lucian hauled himself up to take a seat on the lounge. 'Just pride-bruised, hung over and very embarrassed, I expect.' He accepted the coffee from her and was almost too afraid to ask: 'Why am I here?'

'You said that you suspected I was not your enemy,' Taren told him and he cringed.

'I apologise if I caused you any offence.' Lucian sipped at the coffee, infinitely grateful that it was a strong brew.

'Not at all,' she assured him, heading back to her kitchenette to fetch herself some juice.

Lucian frowned as he dwelt on the bits of conversation he'd recalled before coming fully awake. He wondered how much of it was accurate. 'Did we discuss Kassa's resignation?'

Taren nodded. 'I think you decided that you wouldn't have believed her even if she had told you the truth much earlier.'

Lucian cringed again. If that much of his recollection was accurate, what about the rest? Had he kissed Dr Lennox? She had already said that he had not offended her in any way. He felt befuddled enough right now and was not game to inquire any further. He poured the remains of the coffee down his throat and placed the cup on the table. 'Well, I feel sure I have imposed upon you enough.' He stood and headed meekly to the door. He half turned to look at Taren. 'Please allow me to apologise again. I assure you that I do not normally drink to such excess ... I do not normally drink, *period*. I shall never inconvenience you in such a manner again.'

'That's a bit of a shame really ... you are rather charming when you let your guard down.'

Was he still drunk, or was Dr Lennox flirting with him? 'I wish I could remember what you mean by that.' Lucian played ignorant as her comment seemed to indicate that he had sexually harassed one of his crew whilst under the influence — that would look wonderful on his résumé. 'I don't know what I was thinking. I am never drinking again.'

His discomfort was plain so Taren did not try to detain him. She wanted to put his fears to rest. 'It's forgotten.'

'That's easier for me to say than you, unfortunately ... but thank you, Doctor. You've been most gracious.'

Eyes to the ground, he exited Taren's quarters and felt a rush of relief as the door closed behind him.

'Whoo-hoo!' An implicating whistle sounded from up ahead.

Lucian was embarrassed to find a flight crew, Leal and Zeven among them, returning from night shift. Obviously they had seen him exit Dr Lennox's quarters and, as his clothes looked slept in, they'd jumped to the obvious conclusion. 'It's not how it looks, I assure you.' Lucian downplayed their envious jeers and whistles and Zeven's resentful glare. 'Anything to report?' Lucian asked in an endeavour to change the subject.

'I'd say your morning has been more eventful than ours,' Zeven commented rather coolly.

'The inter-system gateway to Maladaan is in view,' Leal jumped in to prevent the young pilot's jealousy getting him in trouble.

The inter-system gateways were built in ancient times to speed the rate of travel between the major star systems within the United Star Systems. Each gateway in the system was a huge superconductor and could connect to any other gateway within the system by attuning to the same sonic frequency to form a bridge through space — the stations were fuelled by a refined form of liquid metal that had the capacity to reach into high-spin states when heated to excess, hence the super-conductive nature of the gateway system. The technology of the stations was so ancient that it was no longer completely understood — the USS knew how to maintain the system, they knew how to build the gateways, but had long since failed to fathom how it worked — who or what had originally built the system was just another universal mystery.

'We'll not reach the station for a few days yet,' Leal finished his report.

'Call me if I'm needed.' Zeven headed straight to his room.

As the rest of the crew headed for the mess the captain detained Leal.

'Have the crew at the station our side of the gate had any word from Maladaan?' Lucian hoped he'd missed something.

'Nothing,' Leal was sorry to say. 'The same goes for the station on the Maladaan end of the gateway.'

'Have they sent a scout to investigate?'

'They have, but it's going to take even their fastest solar-hawk cruiser a few days to reach the capital. I'll keep you informed, of course.'

'Many thanks.' Lucian's head was throbbing, and he massaged his temples to ease the pain so that he could think straight.

'I think you might need to see Dr Madri,' Leal commented. 'You appear positively green.'

'No. I'll go and rest.' Lucian only wanted to retire to his bathroom where he could purge himself of the excess liquor churning in his gut. 'Could you do me a favour?'

'Anything.' Leal knew how much the captain had been through and was eager to help.

Lucian just couldn't let Kassa go on thinking that he hated her, nor let her carry on in fear of his reporting her to the PMD, the Psychic Monitor Database, and so be held in contempt by many on Maladaan. That was the very fate she had lied to him to avoid. Lucian was not ready to speak with her, his feelings still raw, but that was no reason to prolong her torture. 'I need you to deliver a message to Dr Madri for me ... tell her that I refuse to accept her resignation.'

'Resignation!' Leal, predictably, was alarmed to hear this, but Lucian wasn't in any fit state to explain. He was inwardly compelled to turn and make for his quarters, only metres up the hallway, with the greatest haste.

'I'll take care of it at once,' the co-pilot confirmed in his wake.

Lucian gave him a thumbs-up, as the door to his quarters opened and he charged towards the solace he so urgently required.

When Kassa received Leal's request for a meeting, she assumed he was trying to arrange the private chat she'd promised they would have after the Oceane debacle had blown over, and which she had since managed to avoid. Now that she had resigned, Leal was bound to learn the truth and she would much prefer that he heard it from her first.

As she awaited his arrival, Kassa rehearsed her confession, and was unable to avoid feeling a bit like a dirty old woman who had taken advantage of, and used, the younger man's overactive imagination. Still, she needed his forgiveness if she was ever to forgive herself.

So it was that when Leal arrived Kassa would not let him speak first, despite his eagerness to do so.

'Leal, please. I have to get this off my chest or I shall go insane!'

'It sounds serious.' Leal yielded to her request and took a seat. 'Does this have anything to do with you resigning?'

'You know about my resignation?' She was shocked that it was common knowledge already.

'Only that you intend to,' Leal said, 'but —'

'It doesn't matter.' Kassa was on a roll. 'What matters is that I tell you what I must before the powers that be embellish the truth to tarnish me in the minds of all who have known me.'

'My dear Dr Madri,' Leal said immediately, 'I assure you that nothing anyone could ever say about you would tarnish you in my eyes.'

'Shush.' Kassa was nearly in tears, her guilt overwhelming her. 'I have betrayed our captain and this entire project.'

Leal was frowning, but still refused to take her seriously. 'Just what have you done to justify this *outrageous* claim?'

'I kept silent about certain agents attempting to sabotage this project, because I acquired my knowledge of their affairs via psychic means —' Kassa paused, took a deep breath, and came right out and said it. 'I am a telepath.'

'I know,' replied Leal with a cheeky grin.

'What?' Kassa was shocked, relieved and delighted all rolled into one. 'You knew! How could you know?'

He cocked an eye. 'Is the answer not blindingly obvious?'

Kassa calmed herself to a rational state and, indeed, the answer was so obvious it made her gasp. 'You are telepathic!'

Leal nodded and neither of them could wipe the huge grin from their face. 'So, if you are guilty of keeping silent then I am just as guilty.'

Kassa began to blush as she realised that when she had been secretly viewing the young co-pilot's fantasies about her, he had been fully aware of what she was doing. 'So, it seems it is I who have been deceived.' She sat herself on the edge of her desk to process the fact.

'Not deceived,' Leal was quick to defend himself. 'I couldn't tell you about me until you opened up enough to tell me about you.'

'You seduced me into trusting you.' Kassa now suspected that he was not as attracted to her as he'd made out.

'Did I?' he grinned, fishing for compliments.

'You know exactly what you did. And how I felt.' She was starting to be embarrassed, and a little angry too.

'That is true, I did know how you felt,' he replied gently and rose to confront her. 'I've just been waiting for you to realise ... and your need to confess all to me today seems to indicate that you might have finally got in touch with your emotions.'

'Leal,' Kassa considered it made little difference what she felt, 'I am resigning.' She leant back as he entered her personal space.

'That's going to be a little difficult if the captain won't accept your resignation.' Leal moved in for a kiss, but was halted.

'He has accepted it,' she argued.

'No,' Leal shook his head slowly to assure her, 'the captain sent me to tell you that he will not allow you to resign.'

Kassa felt rejuvenated by the joy that poured into her heart and tears of relief began to roll down her face.

'Any other questions or excuses that you need me to address before I consummate this secret fantasy of ours?' he queried, his lips poised at a very intimate distance from hers.

'As a matter of fact, yes, there is something.' Kassa placed both hands on his chest, and leaning forward she urged Leal to back up a little. 'How did you manage to conceal your telepathic gift from me?' She held him at bay, rather enjoying toying with his affections for real.

'But I didn't conceal it from you.' He happily debated the issue. 'Wasn't me being a telepath, like you, part of the fantasy?'

Indeed it was, Kassa quietly conceded.

The fantasy they had been quietly sharing for several years had developed from the romantic, sexual kind of fantasy that Leal had first presented her with, into something altogether more like what really turned her on. Kassa had thought she'd been manipulating his imagination with her own telepathic suggestions, to enhance the fantasy, but now she realised he'd been a fully aware contributing member to what was obviously *their*, and not just *her*, ideal relationship.

Kassa, aware that she was no longer a young woman, knew this might be her only chance to know the true happiness of a life without lies and secrets. The idea of a lover who knew all her secret desires and was not intimidated by her psychic talent was the greatest turn-on for her *ever* and Leal knew it.

'Make no mistake about my intentions. I am in love with you, Kassa,' he looked deep into her eyes, 'and I shall —'

Kassa silenced her enigmatic suitor with a kiss of reckless abandon before he made any promises and complicated the issue — he was her ideal lover and that was all she needed to know.

Toward the end of her shift, Taren sought Zeven out, knowing he'd be scoffing breakfast at about this time. She felt obliged to tell him about Ringbalin's discoveries, because Zeven would definitely want to know why she was dragging him off for a photon count.

The young pilot was not to be found in the cafeteria. However, a few of the engineers directed Taren to the flight bay where Zeven was gearing up to go check for hostiles in the vicinity of the inter-system gate station.

'Word from the station is that things are all cool there,' Raggus advised, 'but Starman always does a flyby, just in case.'

Taren figured that would make a long shift for the pilot. 'But I thought the gateway was still over a day away?'

'For *AMIE* it is, sci-chick,' Raggus emphasised. 'Starman will be there and back by dinner.' The handful of technicians and engineers sitting around became engrossed in telling each other stories about their living legend.

Taren didn't want Zeven going anywhere before he was tested. If his biology had been accelerated, he was now an untrained psychic and that could be worse than an untrained gunman — accidents were bound to happen.

She found the pilot up a ladder, loading supplies into compartments around his cockpit. 'Starman, thank heavens I caught you —'

'You are so full of shit.' He jumped down to ground level to confront her and his hostility took her completely by surprise. 'So much for not mixing business with pleasure!' He blew her off and went back to prepping his ship.

Taren was completely baffled, then it dawned on her. 'You saw Professor Gervaise leaving my quarters,' she assumed, shaking her head to control her rising anger at being so quickly judged.

'Professor Gervaise ... that's rather formal, isn't it? Yeah, I saw Lucian leave *at dawn*, looking like he'd had a real good time.'

Loose objects hanging around the flight bay began to rattle as if the ship was experiencing mild turbulence, which was impossible on a vessel the size of AMIE. Zeven was fuming so hard that he hadn't noticed anything yet. Taren feared that he was the cause of the disturbance.

'If I really don't turn you on, just say so. Don't hand me some crap about being all professional and then go sleep with my superior!'

'Zeven.' Taren held up her hands in truce. 'Please, calm down —'

'I will not calm down!' He shook a fist at Taren, whereupon several loose tools went flying in her direction and although she wrapped both arms around her head for protection, a huge metal wrench hit her right between the eyes.

After several hours of being sick, several more hours of sleep, a shower and something to eat, Lucian had only just found his sense of wellbeing when Aurora arrived at his door to advise him that Taren Lennox was in surgery in a critical condition.

'How did it happen?' Lucian was out the door and heading to the medical chambers before Aurora could turn around.

'She was hit on the head with a wrench.' Aurora burst into tears. Lucian ceased his charge and returned to ease the information out of his assistant with a bit more sensitivity.

'Was it an accident?' He gently placed both hands on her shoulders, as she sniffled and brought herself under control.

'No ...' She shook her head, tears welling for a second coming. 'Zeven Gudrun was the only one with Dr Lennox at the time.'

Lucian was shocked to the core. He'd seen the look of resentment in the pilot's eyes this morning, when Zeven had witnessed his exit from Dr Lennox's chamber. It made Lucian groan in frustration to think that his own drunken foolishness might have played a large part in Taren's current plight. 'I cannot believe Zeven capable of such a malicious act.'

Aurora was relieved to hear him say so, but all she could do was cry.

'I'll get to the bottom of this,' he assured her. 'Where is Zeven now?'

'In your office.' Aurora wiped her tears away with a tissue.

'Let me know the second that Dr Lennox is out of surgery.' Lucian headed for his office to find Zeven looking hollow-eyed and sorry for himself.

'I didn't do it,' he insisted straightaway, staring Lucian square in the eyes. 'I don't know what happened in there, but I swear I didn't touch her.'

'So what did happen?' Lucian folded his arms to listen, neither man taking a seat.

'I don't know.' Zeven threw his arms up in frustration. 'It's like she suddenly turned into a human magnet. All these tools came flying at her from every direction and we were the only ones there!'

Lucian didn't know what to make of this, but with all the psychic phenomena he'd witnessed since Taren arrived on board, he could not discount Zeven's version of events.

He took a more personal tone. 'I saw the daggers in your eyes this morning, Zeven. I don't know what has transpired between you and Dr Lennox, but I do know you jumped to the wrong conclusion this morning when you saw me stagger out of her quarters. All Dr Lennox did was feed me coffee and let me crash on her lounge because I was too inebriated to move anywhere.'

'What an idiot!' Zeven muttered to himself.

'Hey!'

'I meant me,' Zeven said morosely. 'I'm the idiot.'

'Can you honestly tell me that you were *not* angry at Dr Lennox at the time of the accident?' Lucian asked, to clarify whether the pilot might have taken temporary leave of his senses.

Zeven clenched his jaw, angry at himself. 'I admit I was mad at her, but I could never *hit* her ... or any woman! I swear to you, her injuries are not of my doing!'

'Actually, they probably are.'

Zeven and Lucian looked towards the door to find Ringbalin had snuck in unannounced.

'Um, sorry.' He knocked belatedly and entered. 'I came seeking information about Dr Lennox's condition, overheard your dilemma and believe I can be of some assistance.'

'How is that?' Zeven was perturbed by this breach of his privacy.

Ringbalin explained that he'd been working with Dr Lennox for the past few days and of their discoveries. 'Dr Lennox was coming to fetch you for a photon count when the accident occurred.'

'I have the Powers?' Zeven didn't know whether to laugh or scream — this was insane.

'It's a very distinct possibility, but we won't know for sure until you are tested,' Ringbalin said, trying to make a dent in Zeven's scepticism.

'Hold on a moment.' Having taken a seat to hear Ringbalin's story, Zeven was back on his feet. 'You're saying that *I was* responsible for the attack on Dr Lennox!'

Ringbalin shrugged. 'The shoe fits.'

'Why, you ...' Zeven charged Ringbalin and Lucian was forced to step in between them and hold Zeven back.

'You cannot control your emotions,' Ringbalin said, continuing to bait the pilot. 'You wanted to hit her, own it.'

'I will not own it!' Zeven barked. Objects started flying violently in Ringbalin's direction while the scientist batted most of them away with his clipboard.

As Zeven realised Ringbalin had just proven his case, all the objects dropped to the floor.

'It was me,' Zeven moaned and staggered to a seat, utterly devastated.

Lucian finally found his tongue. 'You can hardly be held responsible for a deadly talent that you didn't know you have,' the captain attempted to console the pilot.

'My spiteful intent may have killed her.' Zeven's head fell into his hands and, as anger was no longer a safe outlet for his frustration, he collapsed into tears.

While Ringbalin took Zeven to be tested, Lucian sat back in his office chair, staring out the window, feeling completely drained. It seemed as if his entire reality had gone down the gurgler!

This morning Lucian had felt that he'd finally reached a comfortably numb state, beyond care. He'd had it in his head to resign from his position at the institute ... provided his home planet was not in ruins or under siege by some previously unknown hostile force, of course. He thought perhaps he'd move to the Maratosh system, where he could vanish into obscurity and lie on a beach pondering his misadventures alone, in peace.

The news of Taren's accident, however, brought home another reality. It was beginning to dawn on Lucian that there was still someone who inspired him to remain involved in this life he'd created for himself. It was a wonder to him that in a broken, drunken delirium he'd been more in touch with his true feelings and instincts than he had heretofore. Taren Lennox had sparked a flame in him last night, and although he couldn't remember most of what had been said, he suddenly felt more attached to her than to anyone else in his world. *I don't want to lose her!*

'The immediate threat is over.' Kassa answered his unspoken fear and Lucian spun around in his chair to find her at his office door.

He smiled and rose to welcome her. 'Kassa, old friend, that is good news.'

'I can see that it is,' she mocked affectionately, and Lucian knew at once that she had picked up on his revelations about the previous evening.

'Now, don't you start jumping to conclusions,' Lucian warned her. 'This is all very weird for me just now and I'd rather we didn't go there.'

'It's wonderful.' Kassa gave a little clap, in an attempt to downplay her excitement.

'Look ...' Lucian couldn't believe he was actually grinning and embarrassed; he felt like a schoolboy. 'I was very drunk and she was just being polite —'

'Rubbish,' Kassa insisted. 'She's had a crush on you for years!' The doctor immediately covered her mouth and scolded herself. 'I did not say that.'

Lucian was absolutely gobsmacked. 'Really?'

'No.' Kassa said, trying to back-pedal, but Lucian's smile had widened. 'Damn it. I've spent so many years keeping secrets that now the floodgates have opened, well ...' She shrugged, as if she didn't give two hoots any more. 'By the way, I accept that you don't accept my resignation.'

Lucian was so pleased to hear this that he actually embraced her. 'That is the very best news I've had all month.' He let her go to observe her. 'I don't have so many good friends that I can afford to lose one.'

'It will never happen, kiddo.' She made a fist and gave a soft nudge to his jaw. 'I assure you that from now on, I shall use my talent to this project's greatest advantage, and not my own.'

'Well, now you have that choice,' Lucian proffered.

'Yes, I do,' Kassa responded, looking very grateful for it.

Lucian's concern returned to Taren, and Kassa answered his unspoken thought.

'There wasn't as much damage done to her frontal lobe as I first feared. Just a lot of swelling and clotting, so I had to operate to ease the pressure,' Kassa advised, as if that were the good news.

'But?' Lucian prompted her.

'Physical damage seems to be minor. But because the wrench hit her centre forehead, between the eyebrows, the knock may have impacted on what those, in metaphysical circles at least, would term her third eye.'

Lucian rolled his eyes. 'Kassa, I am a scientist, not a witch doctor —'

'Several ancient cultures,' she spoke over his sceptical protest, 'believed that those of us with the Powers use our third eye to access inner realms of consciousness, which is why clairvoyants like Taren are known as *Seers*, because they see within themselves and beyond this realm of time.'

'Oh, please,' Lucian argued. 'I've toured through every accessible system in our galaxy and I have seen nothing that would lead me to believe that there is some grand inner realm hidden within this universe. Be that as it may, I assume you are implying that Taren's psychic ability could be impaired.'

Kassa nodded. 'It's a possibility. I'm sorry to be spouting ancient belief at you, professor, but when it comes to the realms of the esoteric it is the only doctrine I have to work with apart from the works of Dr Lennox herself.'

'We are all breaking new ground at present, which is what we set out to do ...' He raised his brows at the realisation, and softened his stance. 'Although I hardly imagined it would be like this. I claim to be open-minded but I see I am going to have to be far more so if I am to make sense of any of this mission and its repercussions, whatever they may be.'

Ringbalin led the pilot to his lab. Zeven had gone very quiet since his emotional collapse in Lucian's office.

'I broke down in front of the captain,' Zeven said awkwardly. 'I haven't cried since I was in junior space camp!'

'Shock and remorse tend to make you do that. I cry all the time,' Ringbalin stated unabashedly and shrugged it off as no big deal.

'Really?' Zeven found this odd. 'Why?'

'Beauty,' Ringbalin said as he stopped and faced Zeven. 'The beauty of the natural world never fails to bring tears to my eyes.'

Zeven nodded, kind of relating. 'That's how I feel when I get behind the controls of a powerful vehicle.'

Ringbalin frowned and chuckled. 'You and I are very different creatures, methinks.'

'Oh, yeah,' Zeven agreed, as both their pagers went off.

Aurora had put out a general bulletin advising that Dr Lennox was no longer in a critical condition and was resting comfortably.

'Praise the universe.' Zeven breathed a great sigh of relief. 'I thought I'd killed her.' He was nearly overwhelmed by his emotions once again, but he managed to pull them back into check. 'You have to help me, Malachi. I've never been scared of anything and now I scare myself.'

'Hey, don't freak out, that's the worst thing you can do. Learn to control your emotions, instead of allowing them to control you. If you can do that, then you shall master your Power and you will have the potential to truly be a superhero.' Ringbalin was glad he almost roused a smile from his petrified crewmate.

'You think?' The idea held appeal.

Ringbalin slapped Zeven's shoulder in encouragement. 'Let's just get you into my darkroom and see what the photomultiplier has to say.'

Zeven frowned, having no idea what the scientist was talking about. 'What's the photomulti-what's-it do?'

'It counts light, photon by photon.' Ringbalin led Zeven through the greenhouse towards his labs. 'Hence the need for a darkroom so that the prevailing light conditions don't interfere with the count. Dr Lennox conceived of it several years ago to assist with her experiments.'

'There's a strange irony in there somewhere!' Zeven was amazed to discover just how much Taren's research had impacted on modern science. 'Jeez, I knew she was some hotshot scientist — I mean she has to be, to be on AMIE — but I didn't realise she'd done anything really famous.'

'Are you shitting me!' Ringbalin would have been outraged if the comment hadn't come from someone so uninterested in the world of science. 'Taren Lennox is one of the greatest, if not *the* greatest, visionaries of our time. She is conducting experiments to answer questions that most of us haven't even fathomed yet. Hell, Gudrun, if you're going to hit on a girl — no pun intended — at least go to the trouble of finding out who she is first ... you might get further.'

As they passed one of the labs, Ringbalin waved to Dr Portus who was running some experiments and she smiled at him warmly and waved back.

Zeven gave her a wave also, which she ignored, looking back at her work.

'I thought her labs were down in the marine module?' Zeven was suddenly intrigued by Ringbalin's good rapport with women and saw this as an opportunity to pick his brain on the subject.

'There are too many men in the marine department for Dr Portus' peace of mind, especially now that Amie is out of the picture,' Ringbalin advised. 'So she prefers it here, where she can work in peace.'

'So what are you, gay?' Zeven replied sarcastically, trying to gauge what the story was with these two.

Clearly the pilot was fishing for information, but Ringbalin did not take offence. 'Not at all, just more focused on the job than most.'

He entered the lab containing his darkroom and Zeven followed. 'So ... is that strategy getting you anywhere?'

Ringbalin was amused as he fired up his equipment and took a seat at the workstation. 'Strategy is for the art of war, not love.'

Zeven considered the reply to be avoiding the question. 'But you know she's hot, right?'

'Hot,' Ringbalin considered the word. 'Hot is a word I would use to describe the weather, or a beverage, or food perhaps, but it is not a word that immediately springs to mind when I think of Dr Portus.'

Zeven was amused. 'Oh, I get it ... you're one of those gentleman types, who never tells.'

Ringbalin was desperately trying not to laugh. 'Dr Portus, do come in,' the scientist said.

'You're kidding.' Zeven turned to see her in the doorway and wanted to die.

'Are you hot?' she queried rather coolly. 'I'll check.' She placed a hand on his forehead for a moment. 'No,' she decided, 'I do not think so.' Ayliscia left him to speak with Ringbalin.

Zeven, totally out of sorts now, watched how intimately Dr Portus spoke with the green-thumbed genius and she touched him often, whereas with everyone else she kept her distance. Zeven would have assumed they were lovers already, but as Ringbalin did not respond to her touch in like fashion, his restraint cast doubt on Zeven's assumption. Maybe that was Ringbalin's secret to success with the ladies? He played hard to get.

When Dr Portus departed, Ringbalin showed Zeven into the darkroom and asked him to sit.

'She's totally hot for you. You know that, don't you?' Zeven blurted out, as Ringbalin seemed completely oblivious.

'There's that term again, "hot".' Balin positioned the pilot for the reading and then stood, hands on hips. 'Why don't we just focus on you for the moment? I'm going to leave you in the dark,' he said, turning and heading for the door. 'I'll see you in a bit.'

Zeven nodded, not to agree but because Ringbalin's attitude was showing the pilot a way forward. 'I am beginning to see what you mean when you say I must learn to control my emotions. I could learn a thing or two from you, Malachi.'

Ringbalin chuckled, not sure if he was flattered or not. 'Then heaven help womankind.' He closed the door behind him on the way out, blacked-out the room and waited for the scream.

'Malachi! I'm pulsing green!'

The scientist made quickly for the intercom link to reassure his subject. 'I believe I did mention that earlier.'

'But I look like a fucking deep-space beacon! Why haven't I noticed this before now?'

Ringbalin had to suppress his amusement before responding. 'It's most noticeable in complete darkness. Just sit still, like I asked. This won't hurt a bit.'

'How long does this reading take?'

'About an hour or so.'

'An hour! What am I supposed to do for all that time?'

Ringbalin did not reply. He was watching his readouts.

'Is it true that Dr Portus is Phemorian?'

The scientist rolled his eyes when the conversation returned to women. Zeven had a one-track mind. 'I'm sure I don't know,' he lied.

'They say Phemorian women remain virgins all their lives. That would be a crying shame, especially if they all look like Dr Portus, don't you think?'

'As over fifty per cent of the citizens of Phemoria are not conceived via in-vitro fertilisation, that seems to debunk your planet-of-virgin fantasy ... sorry to spoil any aspirations you might have had to remedy that.'

Zeven was heard to chuckle. *'It's good news for you though.'*

'Can we please change the subject?' Ringbalin was getting annoyed. 'Why the hell are you so interested in my love life anyway?'

'All the chicks seem to dig you, and I want to know what the big attraction is?'

'Mr hotshot pilot wants to know why women are attracted to me? That's rich.' Balin couldn't help laughing.

'No, seriously, Malachi. Are you cooking up some love potion in these labs that I should know about?'

Ringbalin shook his head, surprised to be finding the show-off rather likeable. 'Your sexual fantasies are distracting, disturbing and exhausting, Gudrun. Don't you think about anything else?'

'Like?'

'Like why you're here, in existence at this time?' Ringbalin remarked.

'To have sex.'

The scientist rolled his eyes and tried again. 'Do you ever wonder about where humans, as a species, came from ... how we developed?'

'We came from people having sex,' replied Zeven. *'You're a nature boy. Surely you've observed that the entire meaning of life, so far as your natural world is concerned, is to have sex, so why waste time thinking about anything else?'*

'What a revelation?' Ringbalin mocked. 'Why have I been wasting my time all these years pondering how the molecular structure of the universe communicates?'

'Okay, so there might be one or two other things worth pondering,' Zeven admitted, *'but I am certainly not the one to be pondering them. Right now, I'm the biggest mystery in my universe. So, if we do confirm I have the Powers, what then? I get reported to the PMD, they take away my licence and I never fly again!'*

'Settle, petal,' Ringbalin said, noting Zeven's rising panic. 'Taren seems to be doing just fine —'

'She'd be the only one on that database who has managed to overcome the stigma, and that's probably only because of her MSS connections!'

'We'll think positive,' the scientist suggested. 'Maybe Maladaan has been overrun by aliens and the database has been destroyed.'

'*Thanks, Malachi.*' Zeven was even more depressed. '*I feel so much better now.*'

Once Ringbalin had the photon count, he reported to the captain's office. Zeven was asked to wait in reception and the scientist was shown through to speak with Lucian.

Zeven was not in the mood to chat, and the idea of being stuck in reception with Aurora was not very appealing. He was pleasantly surprised when she returned to her workstation without so much as a word, only a brisk smile to acknowledge his presence. Then it dawned on him that maybe she thought he was guilty of attacking Dr Lennox. 'It was an accident,' he assured her.

'I know,' she said, and returned to her typing.

'How could you know?' He wondered how much confidential information she got access to. Did she know about his psychic skill already and was no longer interested in knowing him?

'I know you, Starman,' she said, looking at him briefly. 'You break hearts, not heads.'

She said this with such detachment that Zeven realised her adoration of him had come to an end. She had given up on him, just as he'd suggested. He marked that the change had done her good. Rory seemed to have toned down her appearance and personality to a point where she wasn't so draining to have around. She appeared far more mature now, but she still lacked some indefinable womanly quality that he found attractive.

'*Aurora, you can send Zeven in,*' Lucian requested via her intercom. She motioned Zeven to the door courteously without saying a word.

'Thanks,' Zeven said to Rory as he rose to face the music.

'What for?' Aurora wondered.

'Not hitting me with twenty questions.'

'What you do is your own business,' she said sincerely. 'Good luck.'

Zeven wandered into the office with a sinking feeling in his gut. Aurora's detachment hurt a little more than expected. He regretted that losing her infatuation meant that their friendship had to go down the gurgler as well.

'Zeven,' Lucian acknowledged, and motioned him to a seat.

'I'd rather stand,' he said, eager to know the results of the test.

'Do you want the good news or the bad news?'

'Better give me the good news,' the pilot replied. 'I could sure use some right now.'

'The good news is that your photon count is only slightly higher than Dr Lennox's.'

'Meaning that you are only slightly less evolved psychically than she is,' Ringbalin clarified.

'That's the good news!' Zeven freaked, shattering a few glass items on Lucian's desk.

'Calm down,' Ringbalin suggested.

Zeven needed no cautioning — with the show of his own power he'd scared himself into a calm state. 'Sorry, Captain. It's just a bit of a shock ... there goes my career!' He threw his hands up in despair.

'Provided Dr Lennox agrees, I do not intend to report this incident, or you, to the PMD.'

'What?' With the captain's reassurance relief swept over Zeven in waves. 'Why not? I'm a security risk like this!'

'That is why you are going to report to Kassa Madri, who is going to help you get a grip on your little ...'

Zeven expected the captain to say 'problem', as Lucian was eyeing the shattered glass over his desk.

'... attribute,' the captain concluded with a grin.

'Why send me to Kassa?' Zeven frowned. 'Do you plan to sedate me?'

'Hardly. Now, here's the bad news. The station on the far side of the inter-system gateway has lost touch with the scouts that were sent to Maladaan. Before losing contact the scouts reported being unable to target their destination due to their instrumentation going haywire.'

The pilot finally opted to take a seat.

'Every other craft that has tried to approach Maladaan has reported the same malfunctions and is now missing,' Lucian continued. 'The United Council of Free Worlds has declared our entire system a no-go zone. Any vessels heading that way, or in the vicinity, are being advised to detour to another system.'

'So, no one has any idea what has transpired on Maladaan.' Zeven glanced out Lucian's window to the inter-system gateway that now loomed in plain view. 'Let me go.'

'No.' Lucian flatly refused.

'With this talent I have, maybe I'll fare better than the pilots they sent in ahead of me,' Zeven argued.

'A talent you cannot control, Zeven. I'm sorry, but I can't let you do it, and, quite apart from me, the USS armed forces are not going to let you in there either.'

'But they are not there yet, are they? We have a

unique window of opportunity to get some answers before the USS and the MSS quarantine the entire system, and spin some story of their own concoction that won't even vaguely resemble the truth of what has happened to our planet!'

Zeven could see by the look in Lucian's eyes that he wanted answers more than anyone, but he was not prepared to put anyone's life at risk to get them. At last he shook his head. 'The answer is no, Zeven. The mission is too perilous. I can't authorise it.'

Zeven nodded to assure Lucian he understood. The captain may have been saying 'no' but he was thinking 'go for it'.

Lucian appeared to be happier than Taren had ever seen him before. Horizontal beside her and draped with a white linen sheet, he smiled broadly as he toyed with her hair. *'You never talk about your parents,'* he said, *'tell me about where you grew up.'* Her heart sank, for she could only recall tiny fragments of her childhood, thanks to her MSS conditioning.

Her consciousness was torn from the warm, intimate moment, and flew through a bright light into clouds, which parted to reveal a city below laid out in tidy street blocks, abuzz with traffic and fairly unremarkable in every way. Then another city, an etheric city, began to materialise before her very eyes. It rose high above the first city, interpenetrating it, and was far more impressive and remarkable than the city that concealed it. In a flash, Taren was propelled into one of the tower rooms of the ghostly city. A beautiful tall woman, elegantly clad all in white, was there. A *Phemorian*, Taren noted, trying to hone in on what the woman was saying to her.

'... you know in your heart it is the truth. Why do you think you have managed to remain immune to the discrimination of the PMD?'

'The MSS service wiped my record,' Taren replied.

'But why did the MSS choose to believe in your Power, whilst they chastise all others with the same abilities?' The woman's questions caused panic to arise in Taren.

Another flash, and Taren was adrift in space, looking down upon Maladaan. The scene was awe-inspiring and peaceful and she was set at ease to look upon her home planet. She could see the capital city, Esponisa, lit brightly on the morning side of the planet, and was alarmed when a blue-white electrical anomaly erupted and spread quickly across the face of the planet, plunging cities on the night side into darkness. The activity of the all-consuming electrical web intensified to a point where the planet's surface could no longer be seen due to the blinding energy engulfing the globe. A great crack — louder than any thunder, earthquake or landslide Taren had ever heard — sent her into a state of utter terror. *It's a space-quake.* She had never heard of such a phenomenon, but she knew in her soul that was what she was witnessing. In a blinding flash the entire planet vanished, along with its orbiting satellites, space stations and off-world resorts, sucked into the gaping black void that was left in the planet's wake where they too vanished.

Taren woke with a start, her headache all-consuming and demanding her attention. Her mouth was drier than the deserts of Sermetica — she was so parched, she couldn't speak.

'Here, drink.'

Taren smiled to hear Kassa's velvety tones, and as a straw was stuck in her mouth, she drank her fill of cool water. She slowly opened her eyes. 'That's so much better. What happened to me?'

'You were hit in the head by a flying wrench,' Kassa informed her. 'It seems Zeven Gudrun has had his Powers enhanced by your little stopover on Oceane.'

It was all coming back to her now. 'Thank heavens. So you know that this wasn't deliberate.' Taren held her head, relieved, and Kassa nodded. 'Can I see him?'

'Ah, no,' Kassa replied, 'he's busy at present.'

'Please tell me he hasn't been sent on a mission.' Taren sat up in a panic.

'No,' said Kassa, having difficulty lying, 'not sent.'

'Zeven *is* in danger.' Taren could sense the truth behind Kassa's silence.

Kassa nodded reluctantly. 'Well, the knock hasn't impaired your psychic senses at all,' she commented. Taren began ripping the monitoring equipment off her body.

'You still need to rest,' Kassa said in an attempt to stop her.

'Tell me he's not headed towards Maladaan,' Taren begged and Kassa could not deny it.

'How could you know?' Kassa was stunned into retreat. 'Have you had a premonition?'

Taren scampered from the bed. 'I sure hope not.' She whipped on some trousers and fled the room, her headache suddenly not so all-consuming.

Taren entered the control deck of the ship to find Leal Polson at the helm and Lucian pacing the floor. There were several of the flight crew hanging back to listen in on the proceedings.

'What do you see?' Leal was querying someone, presumably Zeven, through the intercom.

'You can see what I can see,' answered Zeven.

'We can't see anything,' Leal replied, staring at a blank screen.

'That's because there's nothing to see,' Starman yelled back in frustration. *'There's nothing there! No planet, no debris, nothing! Just a big black void.'*

Taren's heart began pounding in her chest; her nightmare was looking more like precognition now. She pushed her way through the onlookers and ripped the co-pilot from his chair to speak with the wayward pilot. 'There is no such thing as a void in quantum mechanics, Zeven. It's a black hole, get out of there!'

'Taren?' Zeven sounded astonished and happy to hear her voice.

'Yes, it's me!' she assured him, tears welling in her eyes, as she knew better than anyone how much trouble he was in. She was infuriated as she looked at the captain. 'I can't believe you let him do this.'

'My order was to stay put,' Lucian said defensively.

Taren heard the guilt in the captain's response, but this was a pointless debate just now.

'I'm so glad to hear your voice,' said Zeven and her attention was diverted back to the cause of her concern. *'I'm so sorry about what happened —'*

'Forget it, I'm fine. Just listen ... I've had a premonition that when our mysterious being left this universe it took everything, including our planet, with it. The vacuum left in the wake of the planet's disappearance has caused a black hole to form.'

'What!' everyone in the control room said at once.

'She's delusional,' Leal suggested to his gobsmacked superior, who didn't know what to think.

Taren heard the comment and took offence. 'Was I delusional about Amie?' she challenged, and both men held their hands up in truce. She looked around at the crew watching and listening behind her and they all took a step backward.

'Shit, my equipment is starting to go haywire,' Zeven reported, alarmed.

'I need to talk to him,' Leal insisted.

'Do you know anything about psychokinesis?' Taren retorted.

'Not really.' Leal was bewildered by her forceful stance and the question.

'Then back off.' She looked to the excess personnel. 'And get them out of here.'

Leal looked to the captain who nodded to support her order.

Taren turned to focus her full attention on Zeven, suppressing the pain of her injuries, and once the room was cleared, she felt more at liberty to speak to Zeven about his new talent. 'Starman, the Power you have gives you the ability to physically and intentionally direct the atomic structure of matter.'

'What does that mean?'

'I've missed something?' Leal whispered to the captain, who did not comment.

'Exert your will to hold your craft together and get your arse out of there!' Taren didn't think she could put it any plainer.

'It's not working, the interference seems to be getting worse, the ship is shaking like a motherfucking —'

'Zeven, you have to focus harder on your desire,' she urged, tears of empathy welling in her eyes. She could sense his fear, she had to calm him down.

'I'm trying!'

'You *can* do this, but you have to want to survive —'

'*I do want to survive,*' he responded, his voice straining under the pressure of the vibrating craft, '*but I don't know how much willpower I have . . . that's a real big fucking hole that's sucking me in . . .*'

Taren curled up close to the intercom microphone to block out the rest of existence and focus on her intent. She knew Lucian was watching and listening, but right now, she didn't care what he thought of her. Starman's life was more important than her reputation or romantic aspirations. 'I want you to want this with the same kind of passion and vigour you had on Oceane.' She envisioned his craft stabilising. 'You have an abundance of desire, Zeven. Draw on that and channel it into your present intention.'

'*Oh, yeah,*' Zeven's voice had steadied, '*now I'm reading you.*'

'Just keep the pressure on and don't let up,' she advised seductively into the mic, as she envisaged the pilot regaining control of his craft. 'Feel the power of all creation streaming into your body through your heart and injecting you with the vitality to bend your reality to your bidding.'

'*It's working! I'm turning about!*' Zeven reported, amid cheers of relief from Leal and the captain. '*I'm clear of the vacuum . . . I can outrun this thing back to the gate. I totally get it now, Taren. That was awesome!*'

Taren was gratified to know Zeven was out of danger, but her pain would not be ignored any more. She was overwhelmed with giddiness and before she could congratulate him, she was flat-faced on the console.

PART 2

FRUJIA — TROPICAL PLANET

CHAPTER 10

CASTAWAYS

The bliss of unconsciousness was ebbing to an end and the woes of reality came to haunt in short disjointed spurts of awareness. The catastrophes of the past few weeks did nothing to encourage a return to the land of the living, until a conversation with Zeven came to mind and concern for his wellbeing propelled Taren from her slumber.

Her eyes opened to take in the recovery room of Kassa's medical chambers. Taren looked aside to the clock, eager to discover the time, and the sight of Lucian Gervaise asleep in the chair beside her bed filled her heart with delight. *He must have been sitting there for some time, if he actually managed to fall asleep.* The thought tickled her insides and brought a smile to her face.

Her head was not throbbing as it had been and as she reached up to check on her wound, the tube attached to the drip in her arm passed across a trolley of medical instruments and sent several crashing to the floor.

Lucian awoke with a start and his sight turned straight to Taren, who was wincing.

'I didn't want to wake you ... this stupid thing —' She tugged the long thin tube that had caused the calamity away from the trolley.

'I'm glad you did.' Lucian rose to move the trolley and take a seat on the bed, 'I've been waiting for you to wake up. How are you feeling?'

'The head is good.' Taren finally touched the area to find the bandage had been removed and replaced with a large padded sticking plaster. The spot still felt bruised and sore to the touch but, even on dragging herself up to a seated position, it no longer made her entire head throb. 'It's the recollections inside my head that are more disturbing.' Immediately Zeven came to mind. 'Starman?'

'He's back and safe,' Lucian assured her. 'His discoveries have been reported to the United Star Systems, and they have had the inter-system gateway to Maladaan evacuated and shut down.'

Suddenly, the implications of what she had seen in her visions of Maladaan's last moments in this universe overpowered her in all their shocking reality. 'Our planet is *gone*.' She looked at Lucian, who could only nod in sympathy with her rude awakening. 'Everyone and everything I've ever known ... Not that I had anyone I really held dear ...' she confessed, feeling sorry for those on the crew who had family and friends on the planet. 'All the people I healed — What have we done?' She was increasingly distressed. 'This catastrophe is equal to none that the USS have ever seen!'

'Taren ...' Lucian gripped her shoulders and glared into her eyes. 'You did *everything* you could, everything! I should have listened to you.'

When she heard Lucian take the weight of this disaster upon his shoulders she snapped out of it. 'In your place, I would have trusted my brother over some lunatic scientist sent to me by the MSS.'

'That is *not* what I think of you,' he assured, tears flooding his eyes against his will. He endeavoured to look her in the eye so that she might know how sincere he was. 'I have wanted to put a gun to my head many times in the past few weeks, and the only thing that discouraged me from doing so was you.'

Taren burst into a smile and her tears flowed at hearing his words. She'd never thought she'd see a man lay himself open and be so vulnerable — could he possibly be any more perfect? She breathed in deep the relief of feeling free to confess a few things herself. 'I am not having an affair with Zeven Gudrun,' she blurted out.

Lucian tipped his head, confused. 'But something happened down on —' He stopped himself from finishing. 'Sorry, that is none of my business.'

He rose to return to his chair, but Taren grabbed his hand to forestall him. 'I'd like very much for you to make it your business,' she said shyly, her heart doing backflips like it never had. They had lost their planet, their world, and she couldn't contain the joy that was rushing in surges through her entire being.

'In that case.' Lucian backed up to sit down again, and listened to Taren tell the tale of Oceane, including a complete analysis of the scientific data, which proved her temporary attraction to Zeven had not been entirely of her choosing.

'I can't imagine that I have made such a fantastic first impression either.' Lucian wanted to set her at ease about her misadventure. 'I've mistrusted you, accosted you, passed out on —'

'Ah, so you remember the kiss,' Taren grinned and his grin was as good as a confession. 'You're braver when you're drunk,' she teased him.

'Am I?' He cocked an eye to dispute this and in all sobriety moved in close to claim the kiss she was inviting.

A quiet knock on the door averted the event and Kassa entered to find Lucian hopping off the bed. 'I'm sorry,' Kassa said, knowing what she'd interrupted, 'but a spokesman for the United Star Systems is on the phone for you.'

The joy fell from Lucian's face. 'I'll take it in my office,' he advised Kassa and she politely retreated, the door closing behind her.

'Duty calls.' Taren roused a smile, as she witnessed the weight of the world return to settle on Lucian's shoulders.

'I shouldn't keep him waiting,' Lucian hated that he had to rush off, 'but when you are feeling more recovered, we could have dinner perhaps?' he suggested, just coyly enough to seem uncertain.

'That would be wonderful,' Taren told him sincerely and made him smile. 'I'll look forward to it.'

'You and me both.' He gave a reluctant wave and left to take the dreaded call.

Kassa was outside Taren's door directing traffic and as Lucian came out and hurried past, Zeven attempted to get in to see the patient. 'Now is not a good time,' Kassa informed him sharply. 'You'll have to come back later.'

'So who is going to help me get a grip on this thing?' Zeven protested. 'I mean, if I sneeze, is the ship going to explode?'

Kassa rolled her eyes, frustrated. 'Go spend the morning in a meditation chamber. That ought to keep you out of trouble.'

'I've tried that before, but I just sit there in the dark, nothing happens, then I fall asleep.' Zeven shrugged, not understanding all the hype about meditation. 'I really don't see how that will help.'

'You really do need to learn how to meditate,' Kassa said seriously, as she considered who might have the time and patience to instruct him. 'Ringbalin,' she concluded resolutely, and spoke up to stop his protest. 'Ringbalin is very practised at the art and, what's more, he is the only other crew member who knows about your predicament.'

'Actually, after witnessing my escape from a black hole, Leal has figured out that something supernatural is going on with me. He won't gossip though.'

'I don't think Leal is going to be much help with meditation,' Kassa pointed out. She would not betray her lover's secret, not even to his best friend ... when Leal felt compelled to confide in Zeven, he would. 'Ringbalin is your man.'

'But he's —'

'No *buts*.' Kassa turned him away. 'Doctor's orders.' She gave him a shove in the right direction and immediately retreated into Taren's recovery room.

Zeven was disturbed by the doctor's orders and thought about consulting the captain to see if he couldn't have them overturned. What did Kassa, or Ringbalin, or anyone bar Taren, know about his predicament? They didn't know how it felt to be a borderline outcast of society. Only Dr Lennox was going to be able to empathise and help him to master this potentially deadly talent he'd been infected with. Maybe there was an antidote? If the atmosphere on Oceane had enhanced his Power, maybe there was another planet somewhere, where exposure to the atmosphere would restore him to normal?

As Zeven pondered his many woes, he realised he'd bypassed the captain's office and was now in front of the double glass doors that led into Module C. 'What harm can there be in giving it a go?' He trudged into the greenhouse and upon breathing deeply of the moist fresh air, he paused to appreciate the potent scents in the atmosphere and bask in the artificial sunshine from above.

The voice of Dr Portus somewhere in the vicinity made Zeven's ears prick to attention and as she was something of a fascination to him, he moved more stealthily to investigate.

He found the lovely doctor, leaning against a well-developed fruit tree, speaking with Ringbalin who was down on his haunches inspecting an exotic bunch of blooms growing amid the large, partly exposed roots of the tree.

'Where will you go, now your home is gone?' she asked Ringbalin, obviously very concerned for him.

'AMIE is my home,' he replied in all seriousness, his eyes still very much focused on the flower. 'And when the day comes that I have to leave ...' He paused to consider this, as he'd never had to think about where home was before.

'You shall come and live with me,' she insisted, in a very inviting manner.

'Perfect,' he decided, picking the flower and rising. 'This is one of the rarest blooms in the known universe,' he said to Dr Portus to enlighten her.

How many more hints does this poor woman have to drop? Ringbalin's indifference seemed completely insane to Zeven! But then —

'It is exquisite,' Ayliscia said, reciprocating his interest, despite her invitation for him to live with her being ignored.

'Just like you.' Ringbalin spread his legs to stand upon the two exposed roots that Dr Portus was standing between, effectively making himself taller than she was. 'It grows wild in the remote mountain rainforests on Frujia, where they call it *Lotu-rina*, meaning Heaven's bell.'

The 'bell' part of the name was obvious due to the large bell shape of the flower. '*Heaven's* bell?' Ayliscia questioned, enjoying being cornered by him.

Ringbalin smiled. 'The scent of the flower is said to be so euphoric that it sends the senses into a state of complete bliss.'

'May I?' Ayliscia invited him to hold it to her nose.

But he did not. Rather, he teased her with it, gently brushing it across her cheek. He touched it to her chin and as she raised her eyes to look at him, he slowly slid the flower down her long neck and back up the side of her face, never touching her skin with his own, his lips but a breath from the kiss she so desired.

With only a flower connecting the lovers, Zeven was stunned to admit he'd never witnessed such intense passion pass between two people. He had to back away from such a private moment, but it had been a real eye-opener for him.

The pilot tiptoed back to the entrance, of a mind to leave them to their gardening, but in his hurry rounding a corner Zeven kicked a metal bucket and made a hell of a ruckus.

'Hello?' Ringbalin called out from behind him.

Zeven now wanted to kick himself. This just gave Dr Portus another reason to dislike him. 'Malachi, where the fuck are you?' Zeven covered his departure with an entry.

'If it isn't my angry little test subject.' Ringbalin was surprised to see him back again. They'd been on this ship for five years and barely spoken two words to each other before this week. 'What can I do for you?' Ringbalin noted the flower still in his hands. 'One second ...' He held up a finger and ran back through the foliage.

As Zeven was playing dumb, he felt at liberty to follow Ringbalin and watch from a distance as he handed the flower to Ayliscia. She breathed in the scent and with a smouldering gaze returned to her lab.

Zeven decided that Ringbalin was turning out to be something of a legend in the art of romance and seduction — every time they met Zeven seem to have an epiphany of some kind. 'Am I interrupting something?'

'Just my life's work,' Ringbalin said with good humour. 'Your mission to Maladaan will be one for the history books.' Ringbalin felt he owed the pilot some accolades for solving the mystery; many more may have died trying to discover what had happened to the planet. 'What you did was insanely brave.'

'Yeah, well, insanely brave is the only thing I do really well,' Zeven bantered back. 'I think Taren had more to do with my narrow escape than was apparent at the time, but they won't —'

'What makes you say that?' Ringbalin was curious.

Zeven pulled his head in, put off by the question. 'All I know is that I was losing the plot badly and the next minute I'm in control and feeling like I just scored with Miss Universe! I can't even remember what she said to me, all I know is that she brought me home.' Even Zeven was surprised by how solemnly he said this and meant it.

Ringbalin dwelt on this only a moment, as Zeven was looking uncomfortable. 'So, what brings you to Module C again?' He noticed a tree that needed pruning nearby and moved to tend it.

'The doc said that, in order to master my psychic disorder, I have to learn how to meditate.'

Ringbalin was amused to hear Zeven describe his talent as an affliction.

'She doesn't have time right now and said I should come see you.' Zeven shrugged to distance himself from the idea, in case Ringbalin objected.

'Well,' Ringbalin pruned as he spoke. 'There's not that much to it really ... you just get comfortable, focus on your breathing, clear your mind and go within.'

'What does that mean?' Zeven was frowning, bemused. '*Go within?* I just fall asleep. Is that the same thing?'

Ringbalin stopped what he was doing and took a deep breath, accepting that the doctor's order was going to eat into his time. 'I'll tell you what. I'll teach you how to meditate, but for every minute I invest in you, you in turn will help me catch up on my work here. Deal?'

Zeven was of precious little use as a pilot until he mastered his emotions and, secretly, he found Ringbalin to be one of the most intriguing people he'd ever met. 'Sounds fair,' he agreed. 'When —'

An announcement came through the ship's intercom, calling everyone on board AMIE to a crew meeting in the cafeteria.

The two men looked at each other and moved quickly to attend. Everyone on board was eager to find out what the next destination of their castaway vessel was to be.

CHAPTER 11

THE INVITATION

Once all the technicians, divers, pilots, scientists, caterers, office, medical and cleaning staff were assembled in the room the head count was fifty-one.

Lucian began his address with an expression of his deepest sympathy for the majority of crew on board who had lost family and were now homeless — as the captain had endured the same losses, no one doubted that his sentiments were heartfelt. Lucian then moved on to address more practical concerns.

'I have just had a lengthy dialogue with a representative of the USS, who assured me that all the refugees from Maladaan will be awarded citizenship on the planet of their choice and compensated for their losses, in order to start over —'

'Whoo-hoo,' cheered a couple of the technicians. 'Phemoria, here we come!'

'However,' Lucian spoke up over their din, 'Phemoria will only be accepting applications from female refugees —'

'Aw, not fair —' objected the male crew.

'Sermetica will be more than happy to give any male refugees citizenship,' Lucian added, knowing it would not help matters.

'Sermetica is a bloody *wasteland* run by up-themselves bastards!' Raggus bantered back, and Ayliscia applauded his appraisal.

Sermetica was where all the males of Phemoria had fled after being booted off the planet by the female population. The Phemorians had been mining the mineral-rich desert planet, in the adjoining system to theirs, for hundreds of years prior to the uprising. As Sermetica had hosted a primarily male workforce at the time of the uprising, it had been the logical retreat position for the male population. Since that time Sermetica had been ruled with complete male autonomy, and had become the mining capital of the galaxy — far richer and more powerful than the now female-ruled planet they had fled long ago.

'I'll be heading for Frujia,' Raggus decided, and a large majority of the crew nodded to agree that the tropical planet was where they would choose to base themselves. 'Better weed there, anyhow,' the tech concluded and his associates all seemed to agree.

'In that case,' Lucian surmised, 'what I have to tell you is a fortunate coincidence. We have been summoned to Frujia for the inquest and memorial service for our home planet.'

Many in the room gasped in unison, having never been to the tropical paradise. If you were not born on Frujia, it was very expensive to get a visa to even visit there — let alone the cost of becoming a citizen.

'We are all to be guests of the USS for the duration of our stay,' Lucian finished loudly while much excited chatter erupted.

'What is to become of AMIE?' Ringbalin silenced the commotion with his question.

'That is to be decided at the inquest,' Lucian advised in a far more reserved manner. Clearly, he was worried that the project would be terminated. 'That's all I know.' He brought the meeting to a close. 'We should be docking in Kotan-Bathaar ...' Lucian looked at Leal to fill in the information.

'Tomorrow evening,' he announced in a grandiose manner that inspired another eruption of chatter from the beleaguered crew.

Kotan-Bathaar was acclaimed as Frujia's pleasure capital, and as the majority of AMIE's staff were single, they could see that this turn of events was a brilliant opportunity to gain citizenship on the paradise planet.

'Sounds almost too good to be true,' Taren said to Kassa as they watched their elated colleagues.

'Could we be lucky enough that all in the MSS were on our planet at the time it disappeared?' Kassa bantered back.

The notion made Taren smile a moment. 'I think not.'

Across the room Zeven was waving to get Taren's attention and once he secured it he made his way over.

'I meant to tell you that he's been waiting around to speak with you ever since he got back from the mission,' Kassa warned Taren, who mentally prepared herself for the impending conversation.

Taren was in two minds about speaking with Zeven alone, and not just because she'd ended up in surgery the last time they'd met. There were many things she wanted to discuss with him, but there were also topics that she dreaded breaching — Lucian being her primary concern, as he'd been the trigger for their last run-in.

'Taren, I have been wanting to apologise —' Zeven began, until Kassa came to stand between them.

'I am not sure if you are suitably trained, nor my

patient suitably rested, for you to have this discussion,' she cautioned him, having kept Zeven away from Taren for good reason.

'I *really* need to speak with her,' Zeven appealed calmly.

'Kassa, I'm fine.' Taren stood and moved her aside to address Zeven. 'You don't need to apologise —'

'Yes, I do,' Zeven stressed. 'Can we please speak alone for a minute?'

Kassa was alarmed. 'I don't think —'

'Sure,' Taren agreed and with a wave to Kassa, she led him out the cafeteria door.

Lucian noted Taren and Zeven's departure from the meeting, as did Rory, and both struggled to supress their discontent.

Inside the closed office Taren sat down to hear Zeven out, although, now that he had the floor, he was pacing and not saying much. 'Shit, I've been waiting so long to speak with you and there is so much I want to say, I don't know where to start.'

'Well, skip the apology for this,' Taren pointed to the sticking plaster on her forehead. 'I know it wasn't your fault.'

'See. I should have listened to you.' He pointed out that an apology really was in order. 'You were trying to warn me, but —'

Taren shook her head. 'I don't blame you for being mad at me, Zeven. I wasn't being entirely straight with you.'

Zeven stopped his pacing and looked to Taren. 'How do you mean?'

'I've had a crush on Lucian for years.' She felt her cheeks flush as she admitted it and, as much as she didn't want to see Zeven's expression right now, Taren raised her eyes to his. 'I do have a thing for the captain,' she stated, and shrugged.

Zeven was dumbstruck for a second, bewildered and finally a little amused. 'Does *he* know how you feel?'

'I suspect he does,' she said, pleased that the pilot was taking it so well. 'He's invited me to dinner.'

Zeven nodded, keeping his feelings calm — the last thing he wanted was a repeat of their last meeting. He let go of the urge to be angry, and as he reached into the depths of his heart in order to voice his true feelings, tears began to build. 'After what you did for me during that last mission, I will regard you as a friend for life, Taren Lennox.' A tear escaped his eye and he wiped both eyes immediately. 'So, one friend to another, I wish you well.'

'Oh, Zeven.' Taren was so touched she had to hug him and he didn't object. 'A friend for life is something I could really use … but I didn't do anything during your mission besides give you the will to accomplish your objective yourself.'

Zeven pulled away from her shaking his head. 'One of the primary things we know about black holes is that nothing escapes the grasp of one, *nothing*! I was at that event horizon from which there is no return, but something, *you*, pulled me back.'

'No,' Taren insisted. 'Quanta respond to the most influential force in their environment —'

'Well, somehow or other, you were that force,' Zeven insisted right back.

'That is most unlikely, as that would be like bi-location psychokinesis or *quantum teleportation* … feats that have only ever been posited in theory. You are the PK ace. Is it not more likely that you —'

'Nope,' he shook his head. 'I tried and failed ... but then I got an extra boost of influence when you started talking sweet to me.'

Taren bit her lip, a little embarrassed now. 'Well ... when I was speaking with you, I was visualising your deliverance —'

'Whatever you did, you should work on developing it, because it *really works*.'

Taren smiled at his total sincerity. 'Starman, I still think you must have —'

'I know, but I doubt very much that I have more influence than a *black hole* in *any* environment, and as for controlling this — what did you call it ... PK?' Zeven liked that, it sounded less threatening. 'As for controlling my PK, I'm completely shit at it.'

Taren laughed at his agonised expression. 'It's just like flying a spacecraft, I expect. You improve as you train.'

'Ringbalin was going to start teaching me how to meditate, but now it looks as if that might be cut short! What am I to do if the project is cancelled and they let me loose on an unsuspecting public like this?'

'Calm down, Starman, you'll scare yourself,' Taren said, making light of his performance.

'No, seriously, I do scare myself,' he said, distracted. 'Look at what I did to you.'

'If worst comes to worst, and it won't, then I shall train you myself,' Taren assured him, briskly rubbing his arm to snap him out of his low.

'How do you know the project won't be terminated ... a premonition?'

Taren shook her head, and took a seat at her desk. 'I'm just optimistic.'

'Yeah, but you're lovestruck,' Zeven joked as he slumped into a seat beside her, 'so your optimism is bound to be exaggerated.'

'So is your pessimism,' Taren chided him. 'I'm sure you already know that confronting a fear head-on is the only way to demolish it. I know that mastering PK might seem daunting, but with a bit of training, you will surprise yourself. *Truly.*'

Zeven was encouraged and glad to have cleared the air between them. 'What have I got to lose, eh?'

'Nothing you'll ever miss, that's for sure.' She grinned and nudged his shoulder.

He figured he should get out of her hair and stood. 'I don't know about that ...' He backed to the door, gazing at her mournfully for a second. 'I guess I'll be seeing you.'

'You will,' she assured him.

As Zeven closed the door, Taren's heart went out to him. She greatly regretted that he'd been hurt, but was glad to know that their friendship would endure.

As Zeven made his way through Module C, he couldn't decide how he felt. He was infinitely glad to have secured Taren's friendship and future guidance, but the thought of seeing her romanced by the captain made him feel rather down.

'I thought you'd be back,' Ringbalin commented from the seedling room, as he spied the pilot wandering aimlessly through his greenhouse.

Zeven came to lean in the doorway and watched the botanist plant seeds for a bit. 'Unrequited love sucks,' he said, voicing what was on his mind.

Ringbalin was thankful to be forewarned of Zeven's bad mood. 'Yes, it does,' he agreed.

'What would you know about unrequited love?' Zeven scoffed.

'I was abandoned by my parents when I was one year old,' he commented back to Zeven, no remorse or hatred in his voice, just a simple answer.

'Whoa.' Zeven was more surprised by how Ringbalin wore the fact, than by the fact itself. 'You sound so cool with that.'

Ringbalin smiled. 'I am sure they had their reasons, and I am happy with how things turned out for me,' he shrugged, brushing the dirt from his hands.

'You must be pretty concerned about the future of the project. You have more to lose than anyone,' Zeven suddenly realised. 'But I guess someone like you could have a ball on Frujia.'

'Oh, I'm not disembarking at Frujia,' Ringbalin informed Zeven. 'The captain has given me permission to remain on board AMIE and tend to Module C.'

Zeven couldn't understand anyone throwing away such a rare opportunity, until he thought about it a second. 'And would Dr Portus be remaining on board also?'

Ringbalin cracked a smile at being caught out and Zeven was even more bemused.

'I don't get you.' Zeven was so frustrated he had to say something. 'If you dig her and she digs you, then why do you tease her so?'

Ringbalin was taken aback by Zeven's ever-more-candid questions, but clearly the pilot was torturing himself, so Ringbalin put him out of his misery. 'Two reasons,' he said finally. 'Firstly, Phemorian women don't like being manhandled. They like to be the dominant predator.'

Zeven was intrigued. 'And second?'

Ringbalin went to open his mouth, and then decided against it. 'No offence, Gudrun, but I don't know you well enough.'

'What do you mean?' Zeven objected. 'You know my deepest, darkest secret! So where is your trust, Malachi?'

'Well, considering my past, I do have a few trust issues,' Ringbalin replied, justifying his tight-lipped stance.

'Aw, come on,' Zeven pressed, not wanting to let the other man off the hook. 'We're friends, aren't we?' Ringbalin wasn't convinced about that, so Zeven thought up a better reason. 'Well ... I did just save you and your greenhouse from a very large black hole —'

'All right!' Ringbalin couldn't deny he owed the pilot, but it was a dangerous risk he took confiding in Zeven, or anyone. 'The only reason I am telling you is because you have a secret that is equally great.'

Zeven's eyes opened wide in anticipation.

'I need your word you will never tell anyone,' Ringbalin demanded.

Zeven held a hand to his heart. 'I swear on my life.'

Ringbalin motioned him to follow to another bench where there was a potted plant that was a little droopy. 'Watch,' instructed Ringbalin and as he reached out and made contact with the sickly plant it became restored to full health in moments.

'You're a healer.'

'It would appear so, I know, but no.' Ringbalin shook his head. 'I have the ability to manipulate the emotional frequency of living matter and as a by-product of that I can do hands-on healing.'

With this knowledge, Zeven suddenly solved a puzzle. 'That's why you won't touch Dr Portus, because you don't want to influence her emotions.'

'Exactly. And it probably explains why my parents did what they did, as being controlled by a one-year-old was probably a little scary,' Ringbalin observed.

'And no one else knows?' Zeven queried, amazed to learn that some of those with the Powers had managed to slip under the radar of the PMD.

'Very few people I came into contact with ever worked it out. Such a gift as I have is easier to hide than most,' Ringbalin admitted. 'Now that you know the truth about me, perhaps you'll get off my case about Dr Portus.'

'What?' Zeven objected. 'No way! I've seen how she is with you. She wants you *bad*.'

'Don't you have enough of your own problems?' Ringbalin said in exasperation. 'Why don't you worry about what happens if you don't get a grip on your PK? Your own love life could end up something of a disaster.'

'Holy crap!' Zeven turned white as a ghost.

'Cheer up,' Ringbalin said, placing a hand on Zeven's shoulder in comfort. 'Once you're trained though ... just think of all the possibilities then.'

If nothing else, Zeven did have a fantastic imagination and that notion brought a large smile to his face.

Frujia was a glorious sight from space. The city of Kotan-Bathaar was the largest island of an extensive archipelago, located on a long stretch of shallow sandy ocean. Lovely reefs grew between islands. AMIE approached their host city in the afternoon, which gave them a clear view of a sprawling modern metropolis surrounded by tropical forest, shallow aquamarine waters and white sandy beaches. Compared to Maladaan, the atmosphere of this planet was pristine.

Taren dragged her sights from the spectacular view beyond her sleeping quarters to finish packing for surface leave. She was excited that she and Rory would finally be able to go on their shopping spree. It was fortunate timing, as Taren's dinner date with Lucian was this evening and she didn't have a thing to wear.

On the other hand, she couldn't help but worry if she'd be able to return to work on AMIE. Every aspect of her life and career were so up in the air right now that the outcome was way too scary to think about.

Just ... enjoy the moment, and take the rest as it comes, Taren told herself as she drew on her courage. Hanging over everyone on this luxury stopover was the inquest into the Maladaan incident, which Taren was not looking forward to.

'Knock, knock,' said Lucian, as he entered through the open door of her room.

'This is a pleasant surprise.' Taren shoved her smalls into the suitcase and out of sight.

'I wanted to check that we are still on for tonight?' In reality, Lucian just wanted an excuse to see her, and now he felt rather silly for interrupting her for no good reason.

'Absolutely,' Taren confirmed delightedly, and then second-guessed Lucian's motive. 'Unless you are wanting to cancel?'

'No,' he said hastily, 'I just wanted to make sure you hadn't changed your mind.'

'Nothing could change my mind,' Taren assured him, a little confused. Why would Lucian think that she might have reconsidered? Was her attraction not obvious enough?

'I also wanted you to know, um ...' Lucian paused awkwardly. 'That I am not the kind of man who would normally be dating only weeks after his wife's death. I loved Amie, once.' His jaw clenched as he suppressed the ill-will that her memory now evoked in him.

'I know you did,' Taren said to prevent him from drowning in his memories. 'You really don't —'

'What I mean to say is ...' Lucian recaptured his lighter mood. 'I feel it would be a double tragedy to lose the woman who could make me truly happy, whilst mourning a woman who never loved me at all.'

'If this date is too soon for you, I'll take a rain check,' she sympathised. 'People will think —'

'I don't care what people think. What I am trying to say is, as I met Amie about a decade ago by my reckoning, this date is about ten years overdue. So I figure why wait for someone else to sweep you off your feet —'

'Your hurry to woo me wouldn't have anything to do with Zeven?' Taren figured her little conference with the pilot was what had sparked Lucian's concern. And although he shook his head and smiled to deny it, Taren neared Lucian to reassure him. 'Zeven asked for my help to master his PK, and he remains a friend.'

'I believe you,' Lucian said. 'I'm just not sure that's how Zeven sees it.'

'That is exactly how he sees it. I told him about us,' she advised, thinking that 'us' made them sound like a couple and they hadn't even had a first date. 'That you were taking me to dinner, I mean,' she quickly said, downplaying her slip of the tongue.

Her awkward sincerity delighted Lucian. 'And how did Zeven take it?'

'Like a friend.' She was pleased to find Lucian's smile was more confident now.

'In that case ...' He took her face in his hands and leant forward to bequeath a kiss at last.

A gasp, just short of their lips touching, followed by a suppressed squeal of delight, startled Lucian and Taren out of their wits. They turned to find Aurora doing a happy dance at the door.

'I had no idea!' she explained. 'I think it's just fantastic!'

Both Taren and Lucian felt a little odd at being congratulated on a relationship they hadn't been given the chance to quite start yet.

'Aurora and I are going shopping this morning,' Taren told Lucian.

'Well, have fun, ladies. I'll see you this evening, about eight?' he commented to Taren and she nodded.

'Are you going to be all right dealing with the authorities?' Taren knew he would be handing over Bonar Colbers and going through the gruelling task of recounting Amie's death for the record.

'It will be good to be done with it,' he replied, a little downcast, but then recaptured his more positive mood. 'I can finally put it all behind me.' He smiled at Taren, seeing in her a future that was worth wading through all the drama for.

'How will you explain how we discovered her murderer?' She had been quietly concerned about that since she'd exposed the culprit.

'Anything I tell them is going to sound more realistic than the actual truth.' His grin instilled confidence. 'I have a good idea how to get around it.'

'If you get held up, leave a message at the hotel,' Taren suggested.

'I won't be held up,' he stated, waving them both farewell as he headed out the door.

As soon as the captain was out of earshot, Aurora went ballistic. 'When did this happen?'

Taren rolled her eyes as she clipped her luggage closed. 'It hasn't happened ... yet.'

Aurora gasped with horror. 'I'm *so* sorry ... my timing really sucks, huh?'

'Not to worry.' Taren waved off the missed opportunity. 'Tonight will be a very different story.'

'You bet!' Aurora was excited for them both. 'Especially in new threads.' She clapped happily having been in space way too long.

Taren grabbed up her luggage and linked arms with Rory. 'Let's go shopping!' they announced in accord, heading out to explore a whole new world.

Taren was nervous going through customs, but she was processed without a fuss. She had feared the MSS might have an alert out on her, but if that had been the case, she would have been taken into custody immediately.

Could she dare to dream that the Maladaan incident had happened so abruptly that no one in the MSS had had time to inform agencies off-planet about the mysterious power source they had coveted, or Taren's connection with it?

Someone had given Colbers leave to kill Amie, and Taren hoped that someone had been Swithin, now deceased. What if all the MSS had perished, along with their files and the Psychic Monitor Database? That would mean a clean slate — no more of the past coming back to haunt her. Every planet in the USS was said to have a secret service and all these underground government agencies were known to share information and work together at times. By the same token, these agencies were called secret service for good reason and Taren very much doubted that the MSS would share the details of their covert operations with other agencies within the USS. No one truly knew where the chain of command ended, however, bar that unknown Master who was pulling the strings. That person had certainly not been Swithin, who would have been small fry in the MSS scheme of things. Hopefully, he or she had been snatched from this universe along with everyone else on Maladaan.

Taren decided she was going to give energy to that thought and, provided things didn't turn pear-shaped at the inquest into Maladaan's disappearance, she could start a new life with the man of her dreams.

AMIE's crew were supplied with accommodation in a seaside resort hotel. It was near the Parliamentary Centre in Kotan-Bathaar where the USS would be conducting the memorial service for Maladaan and the inquest into the planet's mysterious vanishing. At customs, Taren and Aurora were handed gift tokens that gave them a certain number of goods and services on Frujia, along with an electronic palm pamphlet that explained where their credit could be spent.

'We are deeply sorry for your loss,' concluded the customs officer. 'On behalf of the citizens of Frujia, we hope your stay with us is a pleasant one.'

The girls accepted the commiserations graciously, although neither one of them had lost anyone close. Aurora's only family, her father and brother, were both in mining on Sermetica, and those Aurora considered close friends these days were on board AMIE.

'So, have you had any luck with Starman?' Taren thought she'd catch up on the gossip as the hovercab sped them towards their accommodation.

'Nah, that's a lost cause. I don't feel comfortable having to downplay my personality so much around him. So, screw Starman. I'm on the prowl for a new love interest.'

'Good for you.' Taren was happy for her, as Aurora seemed to have struck a nice balance between Aurora the lady and Rory the rebel — her look reflected a little of both today.

'Look, there's the water,' Rory pointed out through the front windscreen, as the cab was moving way too fast to see anything out the side windows, just the green blur of the tropical forest they were driving through. 'We must be getting close to the hotel.' Aurora could barely contain her excitement. 'This is like a dream come true! And I'm not going to waste a second of it pining over some up-himself ace who'd rather I didn't exist.'

'I don't think that's fair —'

'Ah,' Aurora cautioned, 'don't defend him, he's an asshole!'

'He's also my friend, and yours.' Taren had a soft spot for Zeven, and so did Aurora, even if she wasn't admitting it.

'I've got an idea ... let's just pretend he doesn't exist,' Aurora suggested.

'Good call,' Taren agreed, as the cab slowed to a stop in front of their hotel.

'Just look at this place,' Aurora said, eyeing the huge beachfront complex. It was built far enough away from the beach that it would not overshadow the shore until late in the day. Beside the hotel was a long, largely open-air shopping complex, housing all the goods and services a tourist could possibly need.

As they hurried out of the hovercab they found the intense heat of the day overwhelming. But not even the heat could deplete their high spirits, and they both breathed deeply of the fresh sea air.

Aurora was fit to burst. 'This is going to be great!'

CHAPTER 12

APPEARANCES

Once Taren and Aurora had deposited their belongings into their beautifully appointed suites, they headed out to hit the shops.

As the day was so hot, and the shopping centre was so long, Aurora insisted on hiring one of the small two-seater hoverpods that were a popular local way of getting around in the heat. There were no doors and the pod hardly flew faster than walking pace, but it blew cool air on its passengers and had a moulded canopy overhead to keep the sun off. Taren allowed Aurora to do the driving and for a good part of the afternoon the transport served them well. It was on the way back that they ran into problems when the hovercraft puttered to a stop.

'Oh, darn,' Aurora objected. They had quite a few bags and she didn't fancy having to carry them. 'Do you know anything about engines?'

'Nothing,' Taren replied apologetically.

They sat there, dreading stepping out into the sun, although the temperature inside the pod was already rising as the air-conditioner had cut out too.

'Hey there.' A young woman around Aurora's age approached to speak with them. 'You having trouble?'

She was a tiny, big-breasted, bleached-blonde bombshell, tanned to the extreme, who was being incredibly friendly.

'It would seem so.' Aurora climbed out, eager to make friends with the locals. 'Do you know anything about engines?'

'More than most. You want me to take a look?' she offered, and Taren and Aurora were quick to accept.

There was a covered bench and chair nearby under which Taren sought shelter from the sun. She sat admiring the sea sparkling in the distance across the sands for some time. The idea of throwing her body in an ocean was greatly appealing and she decided she must do exactly that at the first opportunity.

The sound of their vehicle roaring back to life drew Taren's attention back to the two girls.

'You bloody legend,' shouted Rory.

'No problem, really,' said the local girl, flicking her long blonde locks back over her shoulders. She straightened up and closed the bonnet. 'But you could meet me for a drink later?'

'My shout,' Rory responded with great enthusiasm. 'At the club bar at the hotel?'

'It's a date.' The sun-soaked beauty winked and departed, leaving Rory high as a kite to have found a new friend.

Taren might have been reading the situation all wrong, but she thought it only fair to warn Rory, who tended to be a little naive: 'Looks like a new love interest found you,' she commented as they climbed back into the cool pod.

'Are you talking about Kalayna?'

'If that's her name, yeah,' Taren affirmed.

Aurora was shocked by the suggestion. '*No!* You

think?' She grinned, seemingly not fazed by the idea of a lesbian relationship. 'No,' she decided at last. 'I think you're wrong.' Her smile grew broader all the same. 'But wouldn't that put a big bug up Starman's —'

'Aurora,' Taren cut her short, 'he doesn't exist, remember?'

'He sure doesn't,' she grinned, full of mischief, as they hovered down the last leg of the boardwalk that led to the hotel.

The woman in the mirror was barely recognisable and Taren feared she'd be overdressed in the pale lavender cocktail dress she'd bought this afternoon. It did look fabulous on her, but Taren just wasn't a 'look at me' kind of girl. She'd dyed the purple out of her hair and was back to her natural shade of dark golden brown. With make-up, heels and a smattering of jewellery she looked way too elegant for her own comfort. 'Maybe I should just wear jeans?'

She made a step in the direction of the bedroom, when the room intercom service advised her that Lucian was at the door.

Taren clicked her fingers at being thwarted by time and looked back to the mirror. 'Okay, if I am to play the lady this evening, I have to own it.' She stood up tall and found her centre. 'Now just remember to have fun.'

When she opened the door, Lucian's jaw dropped. 'Sorry, I think I have the wrong room,' he joked and pretended to walk off.

'No, it's me, professor.' She accepted his compliment with good humour.

'Wow!' Lucian entered her hotel suite and then backed up to look at her again. 'Has anyone ever told you that you are far too attractive to be a scientist?'

'Actually, no. I've spent most of my professional life hidden away in a science lab.' Taren noticed Lucian was wearing a very chic casual suit and shirt, no tie — a style she found most attractive.

'Why hide your beauty?' he asked.

'I didn't want to be distracted from my work,' Taren gave her standard answer. 'But, at present, I have nothing to be distracted from.' She smiled, semi-happy about that. 'Besides, beauty doesn't mean much once people get wind that you might have the Powers.'

Lucian had pushed that fact to the back of his mind, but there was something that still concerned him. 'So, are you telepathic or not? I suspect not, and that you were covering Kassa's involvement with our universal friend.'

Taren nodded and smiled, confirming his guess. 'I have accessed that Power on one or two rare occasions, but it is not one of the Powers I have mastered.' She saw him relax a little. 'When I worked for the MSS I did mainly clairvoyance, and pre-cog work.'

'Pre-cog?' he queried, as he knew very little about the Powers but was now more eager to learn.

'Precognition, like prophecy,' she explained a little awkwardly.

'That's how you saw Amie's death,' he surmised aloud. 'But let's not go there.'

She nodded agreement and grabbed her bag. 'You polish up rather well yourself, Lucian.'

He smiled to accept her praise, and held his arm out to her. 'Shall we go?'

The anticipation was high as Taren and Lucian left to enjoy their evening — deep down they both suspected that they were in for the night of their life!

The prestigious restaurant that occupied most of the ground and first floors of the hotel was busy this evening, with so many officials staying in the area. Yet Lucian managed to secure them a quiet little table in the furthest corner of the upper level, overlooking the beach.

'Who did you have to bribe to get this table?' Taren queried after they'd been seated and ordered drinks.

Lucian shrugged and grinned. 'Just a happy coincidence.'

'Very nice, indeed,' she agreed, admiring the beautiful view. Looking back to Lucian she found his eyes were fixed on her. 'You like my dress?' she concluded, as he'd never appeared so adoring before.

'I like the woman in the dress very much,' he replied with a grin.

As her heart did little backflips in her chest and set her pulse racing, Taren felt herself blush. She had never been comfortable with personal flattery, but coming from Lucian it actually meant something.

'And, as much as I do not want to talk about my afternoon,' Lucian continued, 'I will. Suffice to say, you did not score a mention and have nothing to worry about in regard to my late wife's demise.'

'Thank you,' Taren said and smiled at him. 'Was it very awful?'

'Yes and no. Enough said.'

The waiter arrived with the drinks and Lucian certainly looked pleased at the interruption.

Taren waited for the waiter to depart to voice her other concern. 'Have you figured out what to tell the inquest?'

'I'll answer whatever questions they ask to the best of my ability.'

'Do you think they know about the sample?' Taren spoke softly, although no one in this area would be likely to know what she was talking about.

Luican shook his head. 'At least, they haven't mentioned it.'

'Have they hinted at what will become of AMIE?'

'If they allow us to keep the vessel, I'll still have to find an institute on whatever planet I choose to adopt to fund our research.' Lucian sounded uncertain at the prospect. 'I was never very good at sales. That was Swithin's job.'

'Not to worry, I've pitched a few projects in my time. I'll give you a hand.' Her offer seemed to bring Lucian to life.

'Really? ... that would be brilliant.'

'We'll discuss my fee when I get back,' she said and winked at him. She rose to go and find the ladies room.

'As you are the one who will have to raise the funds ... just name it!' He raised a glass to her as she gracefully moved off.

Lucian had expected it would be a long, long time before he truly smiled again and yet here he was, doing just that. The evening was balmy, the sun was setting over the ocean, the drinks were cool and he was having dinner with a beautiful woman who seemed genuinely interested in him. He sat there quietly sipping his drink, thinking that, apart from the risk of losing his life's work, there really wasn't much, at present, not to be happy about.

His gaze wandered to the boardwalk below and a sight met his eyes that sent his entire being into alarm. A ghost from his past was standing on the promenade, staring up at him. *It can't be*, he assured himself, as he stood to look over the balcony and get a better view.

'Swithin?' Lucian, shocked, called to his brother, who bolted at the sound of his name. Lucian took off down the stairs to the ground level in hot pursuit.

Swithin held many of the answers to the Maladaan mystery and if his brother truly was alive he was going to be brought to justice and held accountable for his many misdemeanours.

Whilst Taren was refreshing her lipstick in the mirror of the elegant powder room, the doors parted and in walked five extremely tall women wearing long flowing veils that fell around them to their knees, in soft waves. Their faces were completely covered, without any slits in the cloth to see through. The rest of their attire was long and flowing also, falling all the way to the floor so that no one could view their feet. The women walked so gracefully and in sync with each other that they almost appeared to be floating on a common platform. They would be Phemorian officials, thought Taren, here for the inquest and memorial. The women walked in formation — four on the outside protecting the fifth and tallest woman in the centre. Taren became a little concerned when the group turned from their course to come and stand behind her.

'Can I help you ladies?' Taren put her lipstick in her handbag and turned to address the officials directly, hoping they understood her language, as she certainly didn't speak Phemorian.

'Dr Taren Lennox?' asked one of the two women in front.

Taren was stumped ... she was known to them? 'Yes.'

The two women stepped aside and the VIP at the centre of the huddle leaned forward. 'You will be seeking political asylum,' the woman whispered in a mature voice that was calm and confident. 'Phemoria will be sanctuary to you.' She placed a smooth, partly, transparent stone in Taren's hand and straightened up to be shielded once again by her bodyguards.

'What —' Taren looked at the stone, bemused, whereupon all five women brought a finger to rest against their veiled lips.

'*Shhh*,' they cautioned, turned and departed.

Taren was in confusion after the encounter. 'What in the stars was that all about?'

She looked at the stone in her hand. It was extremely eye-catching, shot through with waves of iridescent colour.

Taren was mesmerised by its beauty for a moment.

'Lucian,' she gasped. He was going to think she'd stood him up! She popped the stone in her clutch bag.

On the way back to the table, Taren wondered if the encounter had been the Phemorian way of inviting her to take up residency on their home planet. The official had said that Taren would seek *politica asylum*, which sounded rather more drastic than applying for residency. But how could they know what she would be seeking, when she didn't even know — unless the women of Phemoria were trained in the Powers?

They'd never agreed to maintain a Psychic Monitor Database on their planet and many people with the Powers, even men, from other systems were said to be hiding out in the cities of Phemoria. Although the men did not qualify for citizenship, their visas would be extended so long as they stayed on the right side of the law. On the other hand, perhaps the women had access to confidential information; perhaps they knew Taren would be implicated in the demise of Maladaan! Her heart began thumping, but Taren reined in her fears realising her imagination was running away with her. The Phemorian language was very different to those spoken on Maladaan, so sometimes a message got lost in translation. She could well be panicking over nothing bar a lovely invitation. Perhaps they admired her work? Which led her to wonder if they might be interested in funding AMIE.

As Taren dwelt on that promising scenario, she looked ahead to the dinner table to find Lucian was not where she had left him. She looked around the huge restaurant and then down to the boardwalk, but she couldn't see him anywhere. A tall, fair-skinned man like Lucian was hard to miss here on Frujia, where most of the locals were either black- or red-skinned, or tanned to deep bronze, and generally smaller in stature.

She expected that her date would return presently and so took a seat to sip on her drink and watch the rest of the colour drain from the sky. Sunsets were something you really missed in space and the view across the ocean was an image Taren felt she would never forget. It would have been a lovely romantic moment to be sharing with her date. Where had he disappeared to?

Another glance around, with no sign of Lucian, brought Taren's thoughts back to the stone, which she retrieved from her purse. It dazzled her eyes with its rainbow lustre; she'd never seen anything like it.

The stitch in his side finally forced Lucian to give up the chase. 'I have got to get back in shape,' he gasped, as he found a wall to lean against and catch his breath. Five years in space had taken more of a toll on his physique than he had realised. As Swithin's rough ways often landed him in trouble, his brother had learned to keep fit and light on his feet. 'I must have been insane to think I could run him down on foot.' He'd just keeled forward, hands on knees, to recover when his communicator rang — the readout indicated that the mode was audio only and the caller was unknown. Lucian took the call and took a wild guess. 'Swithin.'

'You always were slower than a shopping pod.'

'What did you do?' Lucian was immediately infuriated.

'I didn't get a chance to do anything! The MSS knocked me off, or didn't you hear?'

Lucian stopped short of exposing everything he'd discovered about his brother. 'How did you escape Maladaan?'

'Plain, pure-arse luck,' Swithin laughed. *'With the MSS wanting to blow me to kingdom come, I figured I needed to get out of the system pronto. So, twice over, I'm a dead man still walking and nobody knows but you.'*

Lucian took a deep breath. He wanted to tear shreds off Swithin, but if he let loose at this point he'd miss his best chance to trap him.

'Luc, bro. Just let me walk and you'll never see me again.'

Lucian was really struggling now, his welling emotions demanding tears or rage. He gritted his teeth instead. 'Why did you come looking for me?'

'I didn't. I came looking for that sweet young thing you're with. I still know her code name, you see.'

Horror struck at Lucian's heart like daggers, tearing open old wounds and inflicting a few new ones.

'I planned to reprogram that clever psychic mind of hers to adore and protect me.'

Lucian had to cover the receiver and take a few breaths. Had Swithin done the same thing to Amie, brainwashing her into being his lover and stooge?

'But if you've got something going on, hey, I'm prepared to leave well enough alone . . . provided you are?'

There was no way Lucian was going to refuse his brother before he had Taren in his sights. 'Of course,' Lucian conceded, already making haste back to the hotel restaurant.

Swithin laughed. *'I know you well enough to know that you would never agree to something so amoral so easily . . . I believe I shall need some insurance.'*

He hung up on Lucian, who hastened his pace up the stairs to the first level of the hotel. The table was as unoccupied as he'd left it.

Zeven could hardly believe that Leal was opting out of going clubbing with him. They'd been in space for *years*. How could 'getting laid' not be his highest priority? His co-pilot had given him some lame excuse about not feeling well and having to rest up for a few days — doctor's orders.

Thus it was that Zeven found himself entering the hotel club alone, also with doctor's orders that, due to his psychic affliction, he was not allowed to drink any alcohol.

The sole purpose of this outing was to find a little companionship for the evening, and the pilot's gaze was immediately drawn to two blondes, both dressed all in white, chatting in close quarters at the bar. As Zeven approached he was delighted to discover that one of the women was Rory. He barely recognised her in a sexy mini-dress and high-heeled ankle boots. Her hair had been bleached white and styled, and her make-up made her look much more sultry and mature than she really was. Zeven was almost sorry he'd broken off with her. Her new friend was something else again ... a real siren. Zeven had to get an introduction.

Before he reached the pair, the siren whispered something to Rory who turned to eyeball him. A quick whispered conversation ensued ahead of his arrival.

'Starman,' she acknowledged coolly. 'So they've let you loose on the poor unsuspecting women of Frujia, unsupervised. Where is Leal?'

Zeven grinned at her dig — he should have suspected she would not give him a sterling reference. 'He's a little under the weather. You, however,' he attempted to butter her up a little, 'look good.'

'She looks awesome.' Rory's new friend corrected his understatement.

'I'd look more awesome with your tan,' Aurora said, returning the compliment.

'No way, my skin is like leather,' her friend insisted, caressing Rory's cheek with the backs of her fingers. 'Your complexion is perfect.'

Zeven felt uncomfortable suddenly. Why did he feel like he was interrupting something? This chick was not the slightest bit interested in him, only in Aurora. He was slightly amused by this, and after being introduced to Kalayna, he stood back and observed for a bit, just to be sure he wasn't mistaken.

When the girls went to the bathroom and Rory returned first, Zeven thought he'd best enlighten her.

'It's probably just some experimental phase she's going through —'

'Zeven!'

The pilot turned at the sound of his captain's voice, and was surprised to see Lucian in a state of distress. 'I need you to help me find Taren.'

'Why? Is she missing?' Zeven was confused. 'Weren't you having din—'

'Swithin is alive,' Lucian advised him abruptly. 'And he still knows Taren's code name. If he manages to get close enough to her to use it, or even gets her on a communicator, he could brainwash her into doing whatever he wants.'

'Are you shitting me?' Zeven owed her his life. 'When was the last time you saw her?'

'She left to powder her nose about an hour ago and as far as I know she did not return.'

Zeven was not entirely opposed to the idea of getting an inside view of the ladies room, and headed off in that direction.

Lucian pulled him up. 'I've already checked. She's not in there.'

'Really!' Zeven was surprised. The captain must be very concerned for Taren's safety if he'd gone barging into the ladies room in search of her. 'Did any of the waiters see her leave?' Zeven asked as they headed back into the hotel.

Lucian shook his head. 'Nobody noticed anything.'

'Well, she can't have just disappeared!' Zeven objected.

'I've had them call her room and no answer, and I was just on my way to check her room when —' Lucian broke off mid-sentence.

Ahead of them, the current chairman of the USS

'I think your girlfriend is interested in being more than just your friend.'

'So what if she is?' Aurora said nonchalantly, and finished off her drink.

Zeven was a little taken aback by Rory's attitude.

'Is there a problem?' she asked bluntly.

'It's not right.' He forced a grin, rather stunned to be having this conversation with Aurora, the sweet little girl next door.

'What's not right?' Kalayna asked as she joined them.

'Girl-on-girl *love*.' Rory mocked Zeven's phobia and sidled closer to Kalayna.

'Yeah, it's wrong unless you get to watch, right?' Kalayna's query brought a smile to Zeven's dial.

'Exactly right.' Was that an invitation?

'In your dreams, flyboy.' Kalayna laughed and looked at Aurora. 'Let's dance.'

Aurora nodded with enthusiasm, and as she was led to the floor, she waved Zeven goodbye and blew him a kiss.

The pilot took a seat at the bar and watched the two women slithering up and down against each other on the dance floor, but when they started kissing, Zeven had to get out of there. More air was needed, and heading upstairs he emerged onto the boardwalk to breathe the night's warm sea breeze.

'Am I insane?'

Watching two women get it on should have been a perfect night's entertainment for him, so why did he feel angry? Was this jealousy? Zeven compared how he felt about Taren having dinner with the captain tonight with how he felt about Rory being seduced by a woman. Weighing up the two scenarios, he was quite startled to discover that Rory's seduction pissed him off more.

Council, Jabez Anselm, who was also the long-standing President of Sermetica, exited the elevator amid a throng of bodyguards.

'Isn't that President Anselm?' Zeven boggled at the small army that the man required just to go to dinner.

'The most powerful and influential man alive,' Lucian advised quietly as they moved out of the path of the crowd.

'Professor Gervaise?' Anselm sidetracked when he noticed Lucian waiting to get past. 'We meet again.' He held out a welcoming hand and shook Lucian's firmly.

'Mr Chairman.' Lucian forced a smile, unhappy at being delayed from his search for Taren. 'May I introduce Zeven Gudrun, AMIE's chief pilot.'

'So you are the hero we will be honouring at tomorrow's memorial service,' he said, shaking Zeven's hand.

The pilot was gobsmacked by this news and looked to Lucian, who smiled and frowned in apology. He'd forgotten to mention to Zeven that he'd been recommended for a medal of honour.

'By tomorrow evening everyone in the USS will know your name, son,' Anselm told him.

Zeven, who normally sought out the limelight, was more apprehensive about notoriety now that he had acquired his little problem. 'That's really not necessary. I'm just pleased to have survived and spared —'

'The few surviving people of Maladaan, and all those who lost loved ones in this disaster, need heroes to look up to at this time ... *heroes* like you two gentlemen.'

Anselm had a strong and commanding presence. He was as tall as Lucian, and might have been as fair-skinned, but life on the desert planet had tanned him a deep shade of brown. He was an extremely fit, confirmed bachelor, who, with his rugged good looks, short dark locks and steely blue eyes, was always sought after by women. Needless to say, the Phemorians usually sought to avoid him at all costs. The men of Sermetica and the women of Phemoria tolerated each other, as required by the USS guidelines, but underneath this public accommodation, the two planets were bitter enemies and rivals.

Lucian and Zeven both felt uncomfortable being praised, knowing more about what had truly happened on Maladaan than the leader of the free world.

'That was a truly *miraculous* mission you flew.' The president's curious emphasis made Zeven very uncomfortable. 'I can hardly wait to hear how you managed to free yourself from the greatest gravitational force in the known universe.'

The conversation was getting difficult and even Lucian noticed that Anselm seemed to be probing.

Zeven was painfully aware that both Frujia and Sermetica had their own Psychic Monitor Databases and were as ruthless in rooting psychics out of their communities as the authorities on Maladaan had been. 'The tracker beam from the inter-system station on the Maladaan side of the gateway aided to pull me about and get my craft away.'

'That assistance was never reported,' Anselm replied.

'How else could it have been done?' Zeven said in all seriousness and the president smiled.

'How indeed?' He raised both brows.

'This all unfolded only moments before everyone at the station were forced to evacuate,' Zeven said hastily. 'If anyone deserves a medal, it's those guys.'

'The crew of ISG-6 didn't manage to make it through the gate before it was sucked into the anomaly and destroyed,' Anselm advised solemnly. 'So I guess we'll just have to take your word for what unfolded in the Maladaan system in those final moments. Even if you do not feel you are a hero, Mr Gudrun, you would most certainly concede that you are the luckiest man alive.'

'Yes, sir,' Zeven agreed, having no desire to extend their discourse.

'I look forward to our next meeting, gentlemen. Have a good evening.'

Both men breathed a sigh of relief as Anselm and his crowd of people moved on and the focus was taken away from them.

'That was intense,' Zeven commented, his eyes still firmly planted on the departing diplomat. 'Do you get the feeling he knows something we don't?'

'One does get that impression. Well done.' Lucian slapped his pilot's back and got them moving in the direction of the hotel elevators.

They searched all night and found no trace of Taren, and by dawn the two men were starting to fear the worst.

Lucian contacted Ringbalin, who was still on board AMIE, and asked him to search the vessel and see if there was any sign that Taren had returned there. The captain then contacted his key crew — Kassa, Leal and Aurora — and called a staff meeting in his hotel room, not mentioning his reasons for doing so.

Aurora arrived with a very evident 'high on life' attitude. 'Good morning all, fabulous day, isn't it?'

'I've seen better,' Zeven commented, half falling asleep in an armchair.

Aurora was not fazed by his indifference. 'Aw, what's wrong, Starman, didn't you get lucky last night?'

Zeven finally looked at her. 'Actually, no, last night was extremely unlucky.'

Aurora would have bantered and teased him more, but she detected that something was seriously wrong. 'What's happened now? Are we losing the project?' She switched her gaze to Lucian, just as the room intercom advised that Leal and Kassa were at the door.

'No, we haven't lost the project, not yet, anyway.' Lucian answered the door to admit the last of his most trusted colleagues into their midst. 'But I do have a couple of other problems I could use a little help brainstorming.' He closed the door behind them.

Having recounted what had happened the night before, Lucian put it to his crew: 'So, do I call the authorities?'

'This situation is getting more and more complicated. I know we want to expose Swithin, but how do we do that without exposing our own misguided involvement in Maladaan's disappearance?' Kassa asked.

'We were involved in the disappearance of Maladaan?' This was news to Aurora.

'We can't be certain of anything until we get our hands on Swithin.' Lucian was unsure what his next move should be. He was so tired he could no longer think clearly.

'You would think,' Leal offered, 'that if Swithin had successfully managed to abduct Dr Lennox, he would have called to intimidate and prevent you from reporting anything to the authorities.'

Lucian felt this was a good point, but was prevented from saying so as he accepted a call from Ringbalin.

Lucian held up his communicator to view the scientist onscreen. 'Have you found something?'

'*Does this look familiar?*' Ringbalin held up a clutch bag.

'Taren had that with her last night,' Lucian confirmed. 'Where did you find it?'

'*In her quarters here on AMIE. I rang her communicator and followed the ring tone . . . there is no sign of Dr Lennox, however.*'

'I'm on my way,' Lucian advised.

Zeven snapped to attention as he overheard this. 'But the memorial is in an hour or so. How are we going to —'

'We are not going anywhere. You all attend the memorial as planned and give anyone who might ask my sincere apologies.' Lucian headed out the door alone before anyone could argue.

It felt good to be back on board his vessel. Lucian felt at home here. In the past few weeks he had considered how much simpler his life would be if the USS did shut down the AMIE project, but having been exposed to the politics and society of life planet-side for just one day, he was already eager to get back into space.

Lucian entered Taren's quarters to find Ringbalin and Dr Portus quietly speaking.

'Captain.' Ringbalin acknowledged his presence and approached him, Dr Portus trailing behind.

'Still no luck?' Lucian queried, and the young man shook his head. 'We are going to have a second look around the other modules.'

Lucian gave them a nod and a smile of appreciation as they exited the room.

Bleary-eyed, the captain gazed out the huge window that awarded a beautiful view of their host city, but he did not see the magnificent scenery. His thoughts were preoccupied with the memory of the last time he'd seen Taren. How beautiful she was, both inside and out. Hopes of finding her safe somewhere were fading and he needed sleep desperately, but he refused to close his eyes until he knew that Taren was safe and he could bring his brother to justice.

As Lucian began to sway with exhaustion, he staggered back to take a seat on Taren's sleeping pod. His butt hit the bed and he was startled to feel a large object at his back. When he turned, he found nothing, and so nudged the invisible weight again, whereupon a beautiful stone appeared on the white bedcover. Lucian went to reach for the object when Taren's sleeping form appeared beside him and Lucian near choked on his shock and joy. He checked that she was breathing and gave a great sigh of relief that she was. Her shapely form was still swathed in the stunning cocktail dress she had worn to dinner and the lady was a vision to behold. Lucian felt the spark that Taren had ignited in his heart roar into full flame. He hadn't realised how much she had come to mean to him until faced with the prospect of losing her.

'Never again,' he uttered, referring to a great many things. Never again would he allow his brother to abuse, for his own selfish ends, the lives, talents and work of others. Never again would he protect Swithin, or trust him. He had ruined Lucian's life with Amie; he was not going to have the opportunity to repeat the offence.

Lucian brushed back a curl that had fallen across

Taren's face. She stirred and opening her eyes she seemed pleasantly surprised to find him beside her.

'Wow, that must have been some pre-dinner cocktail. I don't remember anything after that.' She looked down and smiled when she noted that she was still dressed. 'What a gentleman you are.' She had a long, seductive stretch.

Lucian was amused by her conclusion, however misguided.

'Why are we back on board AMIE?' Taren propped herself up on her elbows to look around. When her gaze returned to Lucian, she found him grinning deliriously, his eyelids wavering. 'You look *really* tired.' She placed a hand on his cheek, concerned for him.

'Funny about that,' he forced himself to stay conscious. 'Promise me you won't go anywhere —'

'I won't,' Taren vowed.

'And screen all your calls ... Swithin is alive ...' Lucian collapsed onto the round sleeping pod beside Taren and fell into a fitful slumber.

'Swithin is alive!' Taren gasped and her eyes narrowed as a desire to bring him to account for his part in AMIE's downfall and the loss of Maladaan manifested within her. 'Lucian?' Taren thought the professor might have been playing with her, as his loss of consciousness had been so abrupt, but she realised his exhaustion was quite sincere when she was unable to wake him. 'Interesting date?' She smiled down at him, admiring his good looks at close quarters.

What ordeal had he endured to leave him so exhausted? 'I'll be right here when you wake ...' she told him, taking advantage of his unconscious state to run her fingers through the strands of his long, dark hair '... and we'll talk then.' She kissed his cheek and made a move to make herself a wake-up beverage. As she did, her hand swept up the stone that the Phemorians had given her the previous night. As Taren gazed at the eye-catching treasure, it suddenly dawned on her that the blank in her memory started at around the time she'd been given that stone and with that revelation Taren quickly placed it on her bedside table.

CHAPTER 13

UNGUARDED MOMENTS

It was very hard to keep from falling asleep during the long memorial service. Even with air-conditioning the huge, crowded auditorium was overheating, which didn't help Zeven to stay conscious.

'Tomorrow, the USS will begin an extensive investigation into this mysterious tragedy,' President Anselm was advising from the pulpit. 'Our aim is to provide those of us left behind with an explanation for why this anomaly occurred, whether the event will affect any of the other planets within the USS network, and if indeed we might expect to see this unprecedented tragedy repeated elsewhere ...'

'Starman,' Aurora nudged him off her shoulder and whispered to him. 'It doesn't look good when the hero of the day is falling asleep at his own decoration service.'

'Go on without me,' he mumbled, rolling forward in his chair, of a mind to hit the carpeted floor at their feet in the front row where the crew of AMIE had been assigned seats.

'Zeven,' she hissed quietly, hauling him back up to a

seated position. 'Get it together ... you're going to embarrass the project.'

'Please just let me close my eyes for a couple of minutes.' He nuzzled into her shoulder.

Aurora looked to Kalayna, who she had invited to sit with her at the memorial, as AMIE had a couple of spare seats thanks to a few crew being absent.

Aurora would have conscripted Leal to deal with Zeven, but he was sitting further along the row next to Kassa, and getting his attention was bound to attract notice to their dilemma. 'What am I going to do with him? He'll never make it up the stairs ... heaven forbid if he's expected to make a speech!'

'Would he save your butt in the same situation?' Kalayna asked, already knowing that the pilot had hurt Aurora personally in the past.

Aurora thought about this only a second before nodding. 'Starman is a natural-born hero. He couldn't help but save the day.'

'Then I guess you and I are playing trophy girls,' Kalayna advised and Aurora frowned. 'I'll help you escort him up there, but an acceptance speech is up to you.'

'No problem.' Aurora had written a million of them.

When the time came for Zeven to rise and accept his medal of honour, the girls positioned themselves either side of him and hauled him to standing.

'We're going to get your medal now,' Aurora whispered in his ear.

Zeven was not thrilled to be hurtled back into consciousness to learn this. 'Oh, please universe, no,' he groaned, only wanting to collapse back in his seat and return to the land of nod.

'Don't worry. We've got your back.' Rory gave him a friendly grin. He looked from her, to Kalayna under his other arm, and then back again, his expression one of great relief and appreciation.

'You total legends,' Zeven said in praise of their initiative.

'It takes one to support one, I guess,' Kalayna commented, to assure him it was Aurora's idea.

President Anselm, having met the pilot last night, was a mite concerned by his shambling appearance, but everyone else present just assumed the hero of the day was injured.

The girls supported Zeven as Anselm pinned the medal on his chest, but when Zeven was motioned toward the speaking platform, the look of utter terror on his face said it all.

Aurora patted his shoulder, as she handed over the job of supporting his full weight to Kalayna and smiled as she took the stand to speak on Zeven's behalf. 'Esteemed guests, ladies and gentlemen, friends and colleagues ... Airman Gudrun has been left a little shaken by his adventures and other recent events, but he has asked that I convey his humble gratitude for this honour and his deep regret that his recognition came at such a great cost to humanity ...'

Zeven was spellbound as he listened to her portray his sentiments to one of the biggest gatherings of people in modern history, with eloquence, poise and great sincerity. Maybe it was just the emotion of the moment or the fact that he hadn't slept in days but her address was so stirring that tears were welling in his eyes. It meant so much to him that Rory would do something so daunting to save him from humiliation.

'I think I'm in love,' he mumbled, trying to swallow the lump that ached in his throat.

'Too late, flyboy, you had your chance,' Kalayna responded with cheerful challenge. Their arms were around each other as they admired the girl they both desired. 'She's my girlfriend now.'

'Until we leave,' Zeven concluded with a smile.

'Which may be never if the inquest gets in the way.'

They stared at each other in challenge for a moment, until they both smiled and looked back to Aurora.

When the memorial was over, all were dismissed from the stifling reception and released into the scorching heat of midday. Zeven approached and thanked Aurora and Kalayna before they got into their cab.

'I did it for Aurora, but you're welcome.' Kalayna slipped into the cab.

'I really owe you, Rory, big-time.' He approached to kiss her, but she only offered him a cheek to plant his lips upon.

'You don't owe me anything, truly,' she said, stepping back to put some distance between them, her expression faintly mournful.

'Can I at least buy you dinner some time or ...'

Rory was shaking her head and glaring at him now. 'I know what you are trying to do, Zeven, and you're not going to ruin this for me.'

'I don't want to ruin anything,' he insisted. 'You're entitled to have a girlfriend if that's —'

'She's not just my girlfriend, Zeven. She's my partner,' she informed him in no uncertain terms.

'Wow ... that was quick.' He took a reluctant step backwards.

Rory shrugged. 'I guess women don't have to procrastinate as long as men do. When we are onto a good thing we know it.'

'Well then ...' Zeven fumbled for words, 'um, congratulations, I am truly happy for you.' He tried to make it sound heartfelt, but he was lying and wouldn't hide it.

'You're so sincere.' Rory rolled her eyes and climbed into the cab. 'From now on, you're on your own.' She slammed the door closed and the cab took off back towards the hotel.

'Of course I'm not happy for you,' he called out in the hovercab's gusty wake and then gave a great sigh. 'I am such an idiot.'

Fed, showered and changed, Taren stood in her quarters on AMIE, admiring the distant glistening waters of Frujia that she had yet to cast herself into. She had promised Lucian she would not go anywhere until he woke, but the aqua-green ocean beckoned her indulgence.

'Taren!'

She jumped out of her skin as she turned to find Ringbalin gawking at her.

Then he spied Lucian asleep and figured the emergency was over. 'Thank heavens you've been found. We've been searching for you all night.'

'Really?' This was news to Taren, but it did seem to account for Lucian's depleted state.

Ringbalin didn't understand Taren's oblivious response. 'Didn't the captain tell you?'

A gasp from Dr Portus alerted Taren to the other woman, who was staring at the Phemorian stone on Taren's bedside table. 'A banishing stone,' she said, approaching the treasure reverently, but she did not move to touch it. 'These are a tool of the Phemoray.' Dr Portus served Taren a curious glare. 'Where did you get this?'

Taren was pleased that Dr Portus knew something about her mysterious gift. 'Five Phemorian diplomats gave it to me in the powder room of the hotel restaurant last night. I think it mysteriously made my entire evening disappear!'

Dr Portus was amused by Taren's perception of events. 'It was not the evening that disappeared, but you.'

'Pardon,' said Taren, sensing that communication barrier getting in the way again. 'I vanished?'

Dr Portus nodded. 'And the Phemoray are not diplomats. They are a ...' She sought the right word '... mythical order, who are said to have existed on Phemoria since the time of the sexual revolution.'

'How can they be mythical if they gave me this?' Taren wasn't sure she was following. 'Mythical generally means something that no longer exists.'

'Oh?' Dr Portus' eyes opened wide as she realised her error. 'Is mystical what I mean?'

'Mystical, as in a mysterious spiritual order, or do you mean that the Phemoray are not of the physical world?' Taren questioned.

Dr Portus considered the query and shrugged. 'Both, I think. The Phemoray have access to the inner world, where amazing tools like banishing stones abound.'

'And how does the banishing stone work, exactly?' Taren asked, as she noticed Lucian had stirred and was listening intently to their verbal exchange.

'These stones resonate to a higher realm of existing ...' Dr Portus struggled with the language.

'... existence?' Taren helped out and Dr Portus nodded.

'If a human holds this stone long enough, it will raise their noise ... no —'

'Sonic? Frequency?' Taren had a couple of guesses.

'Yes, yes,' Dr Portus concurred. 'Your sonic rises to a point where you vanish, for you have passed into the realm between realms and only a transparent imprint of you is left behind.'

'I spent last night in another dimension, is that what you are telling me?' Dr Portus nodded. 'This stone could be like a free pass through the Zero Point Field!' Then Taren's excitement ebbed. 'Damn, I don't remember any of it.'

'Subconsciously, perhaps,' Dr Portus suggested with a smile.

'Something to meditate upon,' Taren replied thoughtfully.

'That would seem to explain why no one could find you,' Ringbalin commented.

'If the Phemoray gave you this gift, they want you hidden from something, or someone,' Dr Portus advised Taren in all seriousness.

Taren's eyes opened wide, recalling her brief conversation with the Phemoray. 'They said I would need to seek political asylum and that Phemoria would be a sanctuary for me. But why should I have such a need? How do they know? Unless the Phemoray have mastered the Powers?'

'Officially, the Phemoray do not exist and so can hardly have such talents,' Dr Portus replied and then grinned. 'But just in case they do exist, the Psychic Monitor Databases were set up to try and catch them, but they caught many more psychics in the process.'

Taren took the answer to mean that yes, the Phemoray did have the Powers. 'That is how they defeated the male population of Phemoria.' Taren was beginning to have a much clearer idea of the events of the past. 'And how does one find the Phemoray?' She wondered, thinking they could advance her research considerably.

Dr Portus gave a little chuckle. 'As you have discovered, no one finds the Phemoray. They find you.'

'Whatever their motive,' Lucian said, as he hauled himself up to a seated position, 'I completely agree ... we should keep you hidden on board this vessel.'

'What?' Taren looked at the beautiful ocean view longingly.

'I'll get Kassa to retrieve your belongings from the hotel,' he advised, and before Taren could argue, Ringbalin interrupted.

'If the emergency is over, we'll go and inform the others,' he suggested

'Just tell them all is well, and nothing more. I do not want Taren's name mentioned on any communication device,' Lucian advised as he got to his feet.

Ringbalin agreed and left ahead of Dr Portus, who wanted a last word with Taren. 'You can carry the sacred gift in your clothing without activating it. Only if you hold it in your palm will it trigger the banishing.'

'Thank you so much for your insights,' Taren told her gratefully.

'It was an honour.' Dr Portus bowed her head to Taren and walked off down the corridor.

Taren turned to Lucian. 'So, captain. You plan to imprison me here, do you?'

'Swithin still knows your code name. He has threatened to use it to manipulate you if we breathe a word of his continued existence to the authorities,' Lucian explained.

'And you spent all night looking for me?' Taren could plainly see how worried he had been and went over to hug him for his troubles. 'I am so sorry I gave you all such a scare.'

'I'm just thankful you're safe.' His embrace tightened.

'Meantime, we still didn't get our date,' Taren mused, although the embrace she was now revelling in was well worth the wait. She didn't want to let go and neither did Lucian, so they remained as they were for quite some time. 'I am a little disappointed that I won't get the opportunity to throw my body in that ocean while we're here,' she observed, indicating the glistening water from her snuggled stance.

Struck by an idea, Lucian suddenly released her, took hold of her hand and led her towards the door.

'Where are we going?' Taren was amused by his sudden playful mood.

'I never did finish showing you around, did I?' he replied and Taren couldn't help but be excited as she suspected they were heading towards the marine module.

The space port in Kotan-Bathaar was partly built over the shallow ocean of the atoll to accommodate astromarine vehicles, although AMIE was certainly the biggest vessel of this type ever built. AMIE was attached to a dry dock — built to service marine vessels — that allowed the lower part of the vessel to be partly submerged in water. Thus the main control deck of the marine section had a splendid view of life beneath the ocean of Frujia.

'Oh, my goodness.' Taren wandered into the control deck behind Lucian and gaped at all the spectacular colours of the marine creatures in view. She approached the windows to get a better look. 'Are there any big predators out there?' she asked, imagining how wonderful it would be to get in amongst it.

'Thousands,' Lucian replied to her chagrin, 'but nothing we humans need fear too much. Care for a swim?'

Excitement welled in her gut and the smile returned to Taren's face. 'You know it.'

Lucian beckoned with a finger for her to follow him into the suiting room just outside of the sub-bay area.

Geared up and briefed, Taren followed Lucian into the pool from which they usually launched their smaller marine submersibles. As sub-bay was a pressurised cabin — preventing the launch pool from flooding the chamber — the watery recess dropped straight into the ocean, which was simply teeming with life.

The water was incredibly warm and clear, allowing a view of some distance through the shallow sun-soaked sea garden of reefs, multi-coloured weed and coral formations.

From underwater AMIE appeared even more massive than she had in space and Taren's heart welled in her chest with pride. She was part of an amazing project, and neither the USS, the MSS, nor anyone else was going to shut AMIE down — not if she had anything to do with it.

Although Taren was certified to dive, it had been a long, long time since she had. She felt very confident in Lucian's company, however, as he appeared as at home in the water as he did on land and in space.

It was mating season and all sea life was in a frenzy of activity and flaunting their brightest colours in order to attract a mate. Taren felt spoilt for choice for what to admire, but stayed close to Lucian, as there were quite a few large fish cruising the floor of the reef that she imagined would have no trouble in swallowing her whole.

Lucian swung Taren around in the water suddenly to witness one of Frujia's great wonders.

The aquatic-reptibat, reported to grow to the size of a human being, was the only animal known that could move as fast through the water as it could through the air. Its wings had large, long fingers with a waterproof membrane spread between them that also attached to its body. These skin-like wings and the creature's long agile tail both aided in propelling the large animal through the water and in launching it back into the air. Its deep jade-coloured body was scaled to protect against water and sun.

The huge creature, having targeted its prey, had dived into the water and went soaring past Taren and Lucian at lightning speed. It gracefully darted in and around obstacles to reach its prey, and clutching hold of a huge fish in its back talons it swooped up and into the sky with it.

'That was absolutely amazing,' Taren exclaimed once she was free of her breathing apparatus in the suiting room. 'I thought that thing was coming at us for us a second! I mean, *wow*.'

Lucian was grinning broadly as he listened to her ramble on and inspired by her excitement he kissed her.

This long-awaited event was overwhelming for Taren, and she was glad that the water hid her tears of anticipation and relief. She was also very thankful for the easy-zip removal of the AMIE wet suits, as their romantic encounter intensified into a desperate need to get naked very quickly. As they kissed and shed their suits, Lucian led Taren out of the suiting room and down the corridor where he opened a door to one of the sleeping quarters with the same underwater view as the lower control deck.

'You certainly know how to impress a girl,' Taren murmured, acknowledging the beautiful setting for a moment, although they could have been in the loading bay and it wouldn't have bothered her.

He caressed her naked back with the tips of his fingers, then paused to assess that this was what they both really wanted. 'I hadn't expected to ever have the need again,' he said, nuzzling his forehead against hers. 'My feelings for you are an unexpected and very pleasant surprise.'

'Really?' His confession made her brave, and she smiled mischievously. 'I've been lusting after you since I first started studying science at the academy.' She had no problem admitting this, knowing his wife's betrayal would have damaged his confidence, and Taren wanted Lucian to know that she thought him very desirable — and always had.

Her sultry avowal sent Lucian's desire and ego soaring and he kissed her again with renewed enthusiasm. He swept Taren up to carry her to the sleeping pod and she giggled, as the captain ordered the door behind them to 'close and lock'.

* * *

Many hours later, Lucian was happier and more relaxed than Taren had seen him in quite some time and she felt like a new woman. They had shed all their cares along with their wet suits and were draped across each other, exhausted, viewing the ocean through the large portal to one side of them. They were both quite content never to move again.

'I just know there was something I was supposed to be doing today,' Taren commented, not too worried, as she felt no occasion could be more compelling than her current engagement.

Lucian glanced at his watch. 'We were both supposed to be at the memorial service about —'

Taren gasped, 'Oh my stars, that was today, wasn't it?' She knew the service was for all the victims of the recent disaster, including Amie. 'I am so sorry to have —'

Lucian held up a hand to silence her apology. 'I was still undecided as to whether or not I wanted to go, and as it turned out events decided for me,' he concluded. 'I am not letting you out of my sight, and as you are confined to this vessel, well ...' he shrugged. 'Why celebrate a bad ending, when you can celebrate a new beginning.'

'Indeed.' Taren snuggled into Lucian. Obviously this affair they had begun was not just a fling for him either.

'What to do about my brother is a more pressing concern,' he commented, inviting Taren's thoughts on the matter.

'Without proof that he was working for the MSS, or that he was in some way responsible for the disappearance of Maladaan, then what can we really report him for? Surviving?' Taren reasoned and Lucian nodded in accord.

'If he was responsible for any of this, he is still not admitting it. The only thing he confessed to willingly was sending you to us, and I can hardly complain about that.'

'But he threatened to kidnap me?'

'He said he needed some insurance,' Lucian outlined. 'I just assumed that insurance was you.'

'What did you ever do to him?' Taren couldn't understand why, when Swithin was on such a good thing with AMIE, that he would betray his brother and partner so completely.

'I let him walk all over me, because I wanted to believe that he could be one of the good guys.' Lucian shook his head at his self-delusion.

'Well, you can't choose your family,' Taren said lightly.

'Speaking of family ...' He rolled onto his side to look at Taren and play with her hair. 'You never talk about your parents. Tell me about where you grew up.'

Taren's heart sank as the MSS had stolen most of her childhood recollections, and a strong sense of déjà-vu drowned out her regret.

'Taren?' Lucian asked, as she seemed to be speechless.

She recalled seeing this moment in time before, along with the demise of Maladaan, a huge city of ghostly buildings and a Phemorian woman.

'But why did the MSS choose to believe in your power, whilst they chastise all others with the same abilities?'

As Taren remembered the vision her eyes opened wide, rolled back in her head and she fell into a deep trance state.

CHAPTER 14

PRECOGNITION

Lucian had Kassa report to AMIE immediately and was absolutely frantic as he accompanied the ship's physician down to the marine module.

'Wait here,' Kassa said when they arrived outside the room where Taren lay unconscious, but picking up on Lucian's recent activities, she reconsidered. 'On second thoughts, that won't be necessary.'

Lucian desperately tried to wipe the grin off his face with little success. 'Kassa, please stay out of my head ... I'd really like to think that my private life is my own.'

The telepath humorously denied his implication that she would pry on purpose. 'If you don't want me to pick up on your private life, then stop thinking about the great time you've had this afternoon.'

Lucian sighed at the thought of his own betrayal, while Kassa moved quickly to check Taren's vital signs.

'Is she going to be all right?' Lucian wanted to be patient, but was finding it nigh on impossible.

'I should think so,' Kassa said. 'She seems perfectly well ... glowing, in fact.'

'Then why is she unconscious?'

'I don't think she is unconscious exactly,' Kassa informed him. 'From what I can tell, she seems to be in some sort of deep trance state. I'll have to get her upstairs and hook her up to an EEG to be certain.'

Lucian breathed a little easier at the news. He approached to lift Taren, still draped in a sheet, and get her up to Kassa's medical chambers in Module A. 'Just my luck that I find a wonderful woman and she spends most of her time in an altered state of consciousness.'

'Ha! Welcome to the world of living with someone with the Powers,' she quipped, as she led off to the elevator.

'Speaking of which, you seem to be spending a lot of time in Leal's company lately,' Lucian said, hoping to get her back for sticking her nose in his private life. 'Zeven tells me he's not been well. Is it serious?'

Kassa knew her smile would give her away, but she couldn't help but grin every time she thought of her new love interest. 'Nothing to worry about,' she replied, trying to sound unflustered and casual. 'I'm on top of it.'

'Have you ...' Lucian seemed a little shy to ask further.

'Have I what?' Kassa's heart skipped a beat. Her affair with a younger man was still making her feel a little uncomfortable to admit to at this early stage.

'Have you confided in Leal about your ... you know?'

'Oh ...' Kassa breathed a sigh of relief. 'Yes, I have actually and he is very understanding ... and thankful for my honesty.'

Lucian, although he was pleased to hear this, was curious. 'What did you think I was going to ask?'

Kassa was stumped for a response, her smile growing ever more impish.

'What has happened?' Dr Portus hurried to inquire, as she was passing by on their way down the main corridor through Module A.

Kassa quietly thanked her lucky stars to be spared from her embarrassment. 'She'll be fine,' she assured the doctor, keeping them moving forward.

'But where is the stone?' Dr Portus asked, noting that Taren was naked beneath the sheet.

'What stone?' Kassa wondered, but Lucian could only answer one query at a time.

'I believe Taren left it in her quarters,' Lucian replied to Dr Portus.

'Understand,' she impressed on the captain, 'that if the Phemoray gave her this gift, she is in grave danger and should have the stone with her always, in case she must *disappear*.'

Lucian couldn't see Taren making any such moves in the condition she was in, but to appease the doctor he requested that she fetch the stone and bring it to Kassa's chambers.

'I will now do this,' she assured him and hurried away.

While Kassa attached EEG sensors to Taren's head, Lucian told Kassa about the stone in question. He wondered if it might have something to do with Taren's current altered state of being.

'She could be having some sort of flashback to her recent trans-dimensional experience,' Kassa warranted.

Lucian's communicator alerted him to a call which he guessed was his brother — audio only, caller unknown — and moved into the next room. 'Hello.'

'*It's Swithin.*' He sounded short of breath and possibly in pain.

'What do you want?' Lucian was not in the mood to be sympathetic.

'*I'm calling to warn you that the MSS are alive and well . . .*'

'How would you know that?'

'*Because,*' Swithin paused to suppress his urge to moan, '*I just escaped an MSS-led interrogation. They know everything, Lucian.*'

'What do you mean, everything? What did you tell them?'

'*I didn't tell them anything. They already knew about the sample and our connection to it. They are going to pin Maladaan's disappearance on AMIE and then the MSS will fuck off with our vessel and use her as a base for their operations. You've got to get out of here . . . now.*'

'And be arrested for flying the coop before the inquest? I think not.'

'*How easy do you think it's going to be to pin Amie's death on your new squeeze?*'

'I've already handed in Bonar Colbers to the authorities here and filed a report —'

'*The same authorities now working in cooperation with the USS and the remaining MSS on the Maladaan investigation. Those authorities? Bonar Colbers does not exist, he's an agent! Get it?*'

'So was Amie,' Lucian countered.

'*I'd like to see you prove that outside of the MSS. They are going to pin this on your girlfriend, whose PMD file will miraculously appear out of the ether and it will be trial by public paranoia.*'

'Swithin, you are so full of shit.' Lucian couldn't stand the lies any more. 'You've been working with the MSS all along and so was Amie. My guess is that they own this vessel anyway!'

'*Oh, fuck. So you know . . .*'

'What, that my wife was your lover and spy for the enemy? Yeah, I found out. Tell me, Swithin, did you brainwash her, or was she unfaithful willingly?'

'Nope, I didn't brainwash her . . . she was just a bad girl, pure and simple. Wish I could have warned you about her, but I was already in over my head when she came into the picture.'

Lucian was really struggling to keep from collapsing into tears as the pain of Amie's total betrayal stabbed at his heart. 'Tell me Taren's code name.' It was the only thing he wanted from his brother now.

'I'm real sorry about the past, Luc, but I swear to you on our parents' grave that if you don't believe me now, the future of AMIE is going to be a whole lot more fucked. The powers that be are very interested in your new girlfriend. They want Dr Lennox in their lawful custody, and they'll stage anything to make that happen. This time you can't say I didn't warn you.' Swithin hung up.

Joy and contentment had been short-lived. Lucian sat alone in his office trying to fathom how he would explain their involvement in the Maladaan incident. Obviously, if the MSS were still operational then knowledge of Taren's psychic attributes had not vanished with the planet. Was that why they were so interested in taking her into custody? What lies had Swithin spun the MSS to get himself off the hook?

'Why concern myself with Swithin's lies at all?' Lucian debated himself, as he'd been doing for the several hours since his brother had called. 'Just because I cannot see his motive for contacting me doesn't mean he doesn't have one. We should get out of here now.' He repeated his brother's advice, gave a laugh and shook his head. 'And go where? It's not like we are the fastest vessel in the galaxy!'

He was torn. If it was only a matter of losing AMIE, he could live with that. It was the threat to Taren that had his gut churning. He could really use her advice right about now.

'Captain.' Aurora had knocked and entered with Kalayna in tow. 'This is my friend, Kalayna.'

Kalayna waved from the doorway.

'I just wanted to show her around, if that's okay?'

'Ah ...' Lucian's mind was elsewhere, 'sure.'

'Ta.' Aurora headed back to reception where she nearly collided with Zeven, who was carrying a large bunch of flowers.

'For you.' He handed them to her. 'I really did appreciate your help this morning and I am really sorry for being such a jerk,' he blurted out in a rush. 'I was just pissed off because you found a date better-looking than me.' He glanced in Kalayna's direction and served her a cheeky grin.

Kalayna nodded to him, impressed by the apology. Delighted, Aurora accepted the magnificent bouquet. 'I suppose I could find it in my heart to for—'

'Sorry again.' Zeven made haste into the captain's office.

Curious, Aurora followed him.

'I've got some bad news,' Zeven began before the captain even realised he'd entered. 'United Star System's forces are on their way here to *escort* our crew to the Maladaan inquest. Leal has already been *escorted* there, which is rather curious when the official inquest is not scheduled to commence until tomorrow morning.'

Lucian paled. *I cannot let them find Taren.*

When the captain suddenly rose and fled the room, the pilot was confused and so followed him. 'Where are you going? They are practically on the doorstep.'

The captain did not respond and Aurora was concerned as she watched Lucian break into a sprint down the corridor. 'You should go,' she urged Kalayna.

'Nah, this is far too interesting,' she stated with a grin. 'It will take them a while to work out I'm not one of the crew, and until then we can hang out.'

Aurora loved Kalayna's adventurous and brave spirit. 'Come on then. Let me show you my quarters.'

Zeven trailed the captain to the medical rooms, but on approach to the entrance USS troops rounded the bend ahead and called to the captain by name.

Lucian sped up, determined to beat them to Kassa's surgery, until they raised their weapons and asked that both he and Zeven halt.

Lucian cursed under his breath when the soldiers approached and requested the door to the surgery 'Open'. Fortunately, the door was locked to external access.

'This is Special Agent Nikkos of the United Star System's Task Force. Open this door immediately,' he barked into the intercom.

'This is a surgery, gentlemen,' Kassa advised through the intercom. *'I have a woman indisposed at present, so I'll need a few minutes.'*

'I don't care if you've got President Anselm indisposed in there. Open the damn door!' the soldier demanded.

The door slid aside to reveal Dr Portus arising from the consultation bed that Taren had been occupying. Watching the tall, comely doctor button up her blouse kept the soldiers occupied for a few moments.

Zeven had to wonder why both Dr Madri and Dr Portus were grinning at Lucian. What were they all up to? Lucian, however, was relieved to realise that the women had thought to do exactly what he had hoped. They'd placed the banishing stone in Taren's hand.

'Will you please accompany us, ladies?' the soldier said in a softer tone, motioning the two women to join them in the corridor. 'How many others are on board?'

Lucian did a quick head count to discount Taren. 'Two,' he replied, forgetting all about Kalayna.

'My count indicates that there should be three more,' the soldier brusquely stated. 'Let's go find them, shall we?'

They rounded up Ringbalin from Module C, who objected profusely to being dragged from his greenhouse. 'Is this going to take long? I've got years' worth of research invested in that — Captain,' he appealed when he spotted Lucian in the crowd. 'Could you please explain to these gentlemen that I cannot leave Module C unattended.'

The captain raised both brows in apology. 'I am not the authority here any more.'

'Well, who is in charge?' he demanded to know.

'I am,' stated a mature, nuggetty man, who introduced himself as Special Agent Nikkos.

'Could I please have a quiet word? It won't take a second.'

Lucian observed Ringbalin lead the burly officer aside and place an arm about the solder's shoulder in a brotherly fashion. They spoke quietly for a short time.

The soldier chuckled, and then chuckled again as they reached an agreement. Nikkos turned back to address his men. 'He's just the gardener. Leave him with his plants,' and then chuckled again as he looked at Ringbalin.

Kassa, Dr Portus and Lucian were amazed, but Zeven suspected that Ringbalin had used his Power to influence the soldier's decision-making. Zeven wondered why Ringbalin couldn't get them all off the hook. He couldn't use his own Power, save for exposing himself. And Ringbalin's Power was easier to conceal.

'Here are the other two.' A group of soldiers reported to their commander with Aurora and Kalayna.

'Which one of you is Aurora DeCadie?' Nikkos demanded, and Aurora raised a finger. He turned to the other woman. 'So you are Dr Taren Lennox?'

Kalayna was enjoying the adventure and if she joined the head count then surely one of the crew would escape this round-up. 'Sure, that's me.'

Nikkos was surprised at how young and flippant she was.

Lucian, although it meant bringing Taren's absence to light, couldn't allow this young girl to be dragged along. 'She is not Taren Lennox,' he objected.

Nikkos turned and looked at Lucian. 'You wouldn't be trying to protect her because you are dating her, would you, professor?'

Kalayna was wide-eyed and amused at this exchange.

'She is rather a lush little thing,' the soldier observed, making both Lucian and Kalayna uncomfortable.

'She's young enough to be my great-granddaughter,' Lucian said in desperation, trying to make the soldier see reason.

'Aren't you the lucky one then, eh?' Nikkos turned back to Kalayna. 'You are under arrest for the suspected murder of Amie Gervaise —'

'Excuse me?' She objected to being manhandled as the soldiers took her into custody. 'Hey, no way. This joke has gone far enough. I'm not the girl you are looking for.'

'She isn't,' shouted Aurora, now wishing that she had made her new lover go home.

'I'm going to let the inquest sort it out,' Nikkos advised them all, 'so, everyone, bar the greenie, move.'

Lucian, although very curious as to how Ringbalin had got himself exempted, was also very grateful. 'Keep an eye on things,' he advised the botanist, before a soldier encouraged him to get moving by means of a shove.

AMIE's crew were transported to the interrogation centre in Kotan-Bathaar, where they were split up and led into individual interrogation rooms to be drilled about their movements prior to the Maladaan incident. The rooms were mirrored on all walls and were an odd shape. They were each one-sixth of a hexagon, cut short at the narrow end by a mirrored wall — the door was located in the wall at the opposing and wider end of the room.

The master control room for the interrogation complex lay at the heart of the hexagon and it was from here that Jabez Anselm observed the interrogations.

He had sent a team back to AMIE to retrieve the 'gardener' and had given them strict instructions not to come into physical contact with him.

'Get in touch with the Task Force on their way back to AMIE,' Anselm said as he observed one of the interrogations. 'This is not Dr Lennox. Tell them to find *Taren Lennox*. And release this girl. She is no one of consequence.'

Anselm moved to the next window, where Aurora was being questioned. 'This one is as innocent as she looks.' He kept moving and stopped at Kassa's window. 'However, this one is a seasoned telepath.'

'How can you tell?' his aide queried with interest.

'She cannot prevent her eyes from wandering our way,' Anselm pointed out. Inside the interrogation room, Kassa immediately looked away from the mirror and back to the man interviewing her. 'Even though she cannot see us, she knows we're here. Same goes for this fellow ...' Anselm moved on to Leal, who was blatantly staring past the agent interrogating him into the mirror behind which Anselm and his associates stood.

'No mistake there,' replied his aide.

Anselm moved on and stopped to observe Lucian Gervaise.

'The dear professor is very circumspect indeed and that alone tells us that he probably doesn't possess any true Power, nor pose any real threat.'

'The perfect scapegoat then,' his aide concluded, punching notes into his memo-pod.

'Now, our hero, Mr Gudrun, is a very different kettle of fish. I don't know what he does, but he sure does something! From his heroic little display in the Maladaan system, my guess would be PK or at least TK. He could be well worth recruiting at some point.'

Back where he started, Anselm noticed that the agent interrogating their impostor was getting a little intimate with the female subject, much to her vehement protest.

'Should I call him off?' the aide proffered.

'No,' Anselm smiled. 'Let's see what our hero, Mr Gudrun, is really made of. Link the audio from interrogation room one into Gudrun's room.'

The command was carried out at once, but something went awry with the patch and the audio from interrogation room one was piped into all the interrogation rooms.

'*Get your hands off me, you pig!*' Kalayna was heard to roar.

'*Or you'll what?*' the agent jeered nastily. '*I just got word from my superiors that you're not the girl they're looking for. You're* nobody, *sweet cheeks —*'

'*Ah,*' Kalayna shrieked, repulsed, and the sounds of a terrible struggle ensued.

Anselm, although not impressed that their experiment was being broadcast to everyone, kept his focus concentrated on Zeven Gudrun. True to his hero form, the pilot jumped up at the sound of a damsel in distress.

'Kalayna?' He looked at his interrogator in horror. 'Where is that audio coming from?' He raised the agent from the chair by the man's shirtfront.

'I don't know ... next door?' He took a guess when Zeven stared him down with daggers in his eyes.

'Kalayna?' he called again, releasing the agent.

Anselm gave the nod to his aide to have them patch the audio in Zeven's room through to Kalayna's.

'Kalayna, are you in there?' he yelled, thumping against the mirrored wall.

'*Zeven!*' The way she cried out his name let him know that he was her final hope in a very desperate situation.

He began kicking at the wall in an attempt to smash through it.

'Hey, you can't do that.' The agent moved towards Zeven, but was deflected with great force into the opposing wall.

Zeven didn't notice. He hadn't flinched from his assault on the wall. 'Ah, fuck this,' he muttered angrily, and backing up to the other side of the room, he got really determined.

'*Starman, please . . . help!*'

I'm going through, he told himself as he charged the solid barrier and passed right through the mirror wall into the room where Kalayna was being assaulted.

When it registered in Zeven's brain that he'd passed right through a solid wall, he realised he'd exposed his Power and now that it was out in the open, there was no point holding back.

Zeven grabbed the agent from on top of Kalayna and smashed him in the face several times before casting him into the mirror, behind which Anselm flinched and then watched as his unconscious agent slid down the wall.

Kalayna was crumpled in a corner, trying to straighten her clothes, and Zeven noted her trembling despite a brave face.

'Need a hug?' He held out a hand, which, after a moment's hesitation, she took and launched herself at the pilot and held him tight. 'It's okay. It's over.'

'Thank you, *thank you*. I was just about to kick his butt,' she said, wiping her tears and finding refuge in humour, 'but you saved me the trouble.' She looked about to see where Zeven had entered. She moved to the door and realised it was still locked. 'How did you get in here, Starman?'

'A *very good question*,' Anselm commented through the intercom. At his order, all the walls between the interrogation rooms vanished and the crew were reunited under the watchful eyes of their captors.

Leal made haste to join Kassa, and Aurora overpowered Kalayna with a hug. 'Now we're more than even,' Rory told Zeven with sincere appreciation, and quietly took Kalayna aside to comfort her.

Zeven walked over to join the captain, who was proud of his pilot's heroism, but sorry for him too. 'That was professional suicide, you realise?'

Zeven shrugged off what he had thought would be his most devastating moment. 'What's life without a few challenges, hey?'

One of the exterior doors opened and President Anselm entered, counting off their illegal crew on his fingers. 'Two telepaths, a PK specialist —'

'I wouldn't say specialist,' Starman stated in his own defence.

'*Two* missing scientists —' Anselm attempted to continue.

'Two?' Lucian frowned.

'Taren Lennox and Eleazar Kestler,' he replied.

'But Eleazar Kestler's pod misfired after it landed on Maladaan?' Lucian said.

'Right after a canister of mysterious gas was unloaded from the pod that was launched from *your* vessel,' Anselm accused Lucian, 'and that unquarantined canister is now suspected of being the cause of the entire planet's disappearance!'

'How could you know that?' Lucian flung back without admitting to anything, at the same time realising that Swithin had probably been the source.

'It doesn't matter how I know. All that matters is that I have enough dirt on your project to have your vessel repossessed and your key crew incarcerated for life!' Anselm made his position perfectly clear. 'Now ... I don't want that. I can make this entire inquest nightmare disappear. Sermetica will even fund your project for the next ten years. All you have to do is tell me where Taren Lennox is hiding.'

One of the exterior doors opened and Ringbalin was escorted into the room at gunpoint.

'Well, if it isn't the suggestive sympathetic,' Anselm announced upon his entry.

'Sympathetic?' Kassa had never heard this term used in such a context before. 'Do you mean empathetic?'

'No. An empath feels the emotions of others. This fellow influences the emotions of others, making him something of an emotional enchanter, actually.'

'Where is Dr Portus?' Ringbalin asked, and it was only then that the rest of the crew realised she was absent.

'Dr Portus is a Phemorian spy and is to be extradited to Sermetica for trial and sentencing.'

'What!' Ringbalin nearly jumped out of his skin and would have taken a flying leap at the president if Zeven and the captain had not restrained him.

'Dr Portus is not a spy, she is a serious scientist!' Lucian objected.

Anselm smiled. 'That's what you thought about your wife.'

Now it was Ringbalin and Zeven holding the captain back. 'Taren Lennox did not kill my wife,' Lucian barked.

'I know that, you know that, but nobody else knows or cares,' Anselm taunted. 'It's just a means to an end.'

'What do you want with Taren?' Zeven was beginning to get riled himself.

'Sedate him, the sympathetic and the telepaths,' Anselm ordered one of his agents, pointing to Zeven, Ringbalin, Kassa and Leal, who dropped to the floor as soon as the agent fired his darts in quick succession.

'Leal is a telepath?' was the stunned conclusion Lucian reached.

'You really don't know your crew very well, professor,' Anselm replied. 'You know even less about your lover.'

Lucian's eyes narrowed in defiance, but the chairman appeared very confident.

'I can state that with certainty because I know more about Taren Lennox than even the good doctor knows about herself, for I am the guardian of her memories.'

'You run the MSS?' Lucian asked.

Anselm shied away from the accusation. 'I advise many agencies. Therefore, I know a great many things.'

'But not the whereabouts of Taren Lennox?' Lucian challenged.

Anselm smiled in a determined manner, then strolled over to where the two young girls were huddled together. 'But I know that you know where Dr Lennox is ...'

Aurora flinched slightly as Anselm toyed with one of her short golden locks.

'... and I am fairly confident that you *will* tell me where to find her.'

CHAPTER 15

DISCLOSURE

Voices brought Taren back to the land of the living. She recognised one voice as belonging to Lucian — he was asking Kassa if the banishing stone might have had something to do with Taren's current altered state of being?

'She could be having some sort of flashback to her recent trans-dimensional experience,' Kassa said.

Taren gasped as she realised that she had heard this conversation before, and sat bolt upright.

'Taren!' Kassa recovered from the shock and moved to comfort her patient as Lucian's communicator alerted him to a call.

'Damn it.' Upon viewing the screen he decided the call was urgent enough to take. 'Hello ... what do you want?' Lucian moved into the next room.

'Everything is fine,' Kassa offered Taren a drink. 'You just tranced out on —'

'No.' Taren was running over the details of what she'd perceived during her trance state. 'Everything is not okay,' she stressed. 'That's Swithin talking to Lucian on the phone right now, warning him that the MSS still exists and plans to make AMIE the scapegoat for Maladaan's disappearance. The MSS will expose all those with the Powers amongst our crew, and attempt to pin Amie Gervaise's death on me!'

Kassa was mortified. Under normal circumstances she would assume her patient had lost her tiny little mind, but not this patient.

Lucian returned to the room appearing a little upset.

'Who was that on the phone?' Kassa inquired, to put Taren's claim to the test.

'No one of importance,' he said, wanting to quell his rising panic.

'It was Swithin, warning you that the USS and MSS are coming for AMIE,' Taren told him and Lucian went white with shock. 'Believe it or not, he *is* telling the truth and we have about two hours to escape custody.'

'That's impossible ... we're too big, too slow!' Lucian baulked at the task.

'Not with our crew,' Taren smiled, having being made aware of several others in their midst who also wielded a Power.

'And where shall we go?' Lucian queried, and when Taren smiled he realised the solution and they both replied, 'Phemoria'.

Taren gave a nervous laugh. 'Now I *am* seeking political asylum.'

Leal and Zeven were immediately recalled to AMIE. All the others who would be adversely affected by the events Taren had foreseen were already on board their craft. None of AMIE's other staff were intimately involved in this debacle and would be better off finding new lives on Frujia. Aurora was the only crew member Lucian was undecided about. He knew she would be hurt he if didn't at least tell her they were going. But Aurora was not really in any trouble and Lucian had no desire to lead her into any. In the end, he decided to call her, but was diverted to her message bank, where he bade her farewell.

Once Leal and Zeven arrived, Lucian, Kassa, Ayliscia and Ringbalin joined them in the cafeteria to hear Taren's concerns.

'I have had a vision of our future,' she began a little awkwardly, 'and in that vision many secrets about the people in this room were made known to me.'

Everyone present looked uncomfortable.

Taren went on to outline the intention of the USS and MSS to frame AMIE. 'Everyone here will be arrested, exposed for who they really are, AMIE will be repossessed by the MSS and I am to be charged with the murder of Amie Gervaise.'

Her audience's discomfort snowballed to disbelief!

Zeven whistled as he considered his own situation. 'Hero of the USS one day, intergalactic terrorist the next.'

'That's politics for you,' Kassa sympathised with a grin.

'I believe I have a plan to escape the clutches of the inquest. Phemoria has already offered me sanctuary. But first we must get AMIE to Phemoria and in order to accomplish this, most of us would have to come clean about our hidden *resources*, so that we can work together and avert this disaster. So I guess my question to you all is this: Is there anyone here who strongly objects to being exposed at this time?'

Everyone present had a long hard think about this, and it was only Ringbalin who shyly lifted a finger.

'Would you mind if I just have a quiet word with Dr Portus?' he requested. Dr Portus was intrigued and Zeven frustrated.

'In the name of the universe, Balin, haven't you told her yet?' the pilot grumbled.

'There're been a few interruptions!' Ringbalin retorted as he walked out ahead of Dr Portus, who joined him out of sight of the others in the corridor.

'What have you not told me?' she asked, delightedly curious until Ringbalin explained his mysterious Power and how it worked. This had Dr Portus frowning and appearing hurt.

'So, what I feel for you, this is not real?' She panicked, hating to think she had been tricked into loving a man.

'I can only influence a subject when I am touching them, and I never laid a finger on you,' he pointed out in his own defence and Ayliscia was more than aware that this was true.

'That's why?' She was visibly moved by his amazing restraint and when Ringbalin nodded, she took hold of his hands and placed them on her body. 'No more prudence, *please*.' She kissed him passionately and, being bombarded by his unbridled feelings of joyous desire, she felt compelled to fulfil their long-suffering lust for each other, right there and then.

A whistle from the doorway brought the botanists crashing back to earth. 'It's the end of the world as we know it,' Starman reminded them, 'and while I can well appreciate your sentiment there, we really need to focus on being outlaws right now.' Zeven disappeared back into the cafeteria.

'Right.' Ringbalin found his sensibilities. 'Thank you for forgiving me for my secrecy.'

Ayliscia grinned. 'My pleasure. I understand, as ... I'm a Phemorian spy,' she said, direct and forthright.

'Really?' Ringbalin was stunned and, finding the news an incredible turn-on, he kissed her again.

'Guys!' Zeven called, to move them along.

When Lucian learned the secrets of all of his crew, he felt a little bewildered. 'Am I the only one among us who does not wield a Power then?'

'Dr Portus doesn't,' Zeven pointed out, feeling far more at home now that he wasn't part of the minority any more — even his best mate, Leal, was in the same boat, and he'd never even suspected.

Ayliscia broke into a guilty smile. 'Not entirely true,' she admitted. 'My queen chose me for this mission because of my scientific qualifications, yes, but also because I am a channel ... I can connect directly to the Phemoray from any region of space.'

Taren smiled as she heard this, not only because it would prove very useful to her plan, but because, in that other reality she had foreseen, where Dr Portus had been arrested as a spy, her incarceration would have served to further enlighten the Phemoray. 'Just out of interest, what was your directive, doctor?'

'I was to observe you,' Ayliscia replied.

'But we have barely crossed paths more than a few times.' Either the good Doctor had been distracted from her mission by Ringbalin, or she was harbouring more talents than she cared to mention.

'I can also remote-view,' she confessed.

'Whoa,' Zeven said, 'it's always the quiet ones that surprise you.'

'Why me in particular?' Taren remained focused on the topic and the doctor shook her head.

'I do not know.'

Not entirely believing her, Taren looked to Kassa and Leal.

'She's telling the truth,' Kassa said warily, 'but suspects —'

An alarm tone sounded from Lucian's control belt, and at a glance he knew. 'We've got company ... someone is trying to enter through the dry dock door.'

The entire crew made for the closest monitors in the office area.

'Correction,' Lucian stated, as he consulted AMIE's security systems on the monitor on Aurora's desk. 'They have entered ...' He waited for a visual. 'It's Aurora,' he said, whereupon everyone breathed a sigh of relief.

'I'll go fetch her,' Leal volunteered and headed off.

'Whatever your plan is, we'd better get onto it pronto,' Starman suggested. 'I don't want to be sitting here when the USS forces come calling. Can I at least get us out of dry dock?' he requested of Lucian, who looked at Taren and she gave a nod.

'You get us into space, and I'll prep the others,' she suggested.

'To do what? What is the plan?' Starman begged.

'We are going to teleport this vessel straight to the Phemorian system,' she smiled.

'But none of us have that ability. Do we?' If they were doing a runner from the USS, he wanted to ensure they had some hope of doing it, or they'd be caught and various other charges added to their list of supposed offences.

'Teleportation is an extension of PK —'

'Oh no,' he backed off, fearful of anyone pinning their hopes on his abilities just yet. 'I was wrong when I said I was more afraid of myself than anything ... you scare me more.'

'Don't worry, you'll have lots of help,' Taren winked.

Zeven shook off his horror and made for the elevator to the flight deck. 'I think you are the one who needs help.' He pointed a finger to his temple and rotated it a few times to imply she was nuts.

'Insane is as insane does,' Taren replied, which baffled Zeven. He was spared more bafflement by the elevator doors opening and he immediately stepped inside and pushed the button.

'The Phemoray can assist,' Ayliscia assured Taren.

She smiled, appreciative of the aid. 'I was banking on that.'

Aurora was led straight to Lucian's office by Leal, who then left to assist Zeven with lift-off.

'What's going on? Why are you fleeing Frujia?' Aurora demanded, rather angered that if she hadn't come as soon as she'd got Lucian's missive, they would have departed without her.

Lucian immediately turned Aurora about and began guiding her back towards the hatch. 'AMIE is in a lot of trouble, Aurora, the extent of which I do not have time to explain right now, but as you are not yet involved I insist you remain here on Frujia.'

'No!' She dug her heels in and stopped them in their tracks. 'I've worked long and hard to secure my place on this vessel. AMIE is my home. You guys are my family!'

'We will be *outlaws*, Aurora.' Lucian grabbed her arm and began hauling her towards the exit hatch even faster. 'I don't have time to debate the issue.'

As they turned a corner and the dry dock hatch came into view, Aurora broke away and ran back in the opposite direction.

'Aurora!' Lucian gave chase.

'I can't go without Kalayna,' she wailed, beginning to yell out her girlfriend's name, having no idea where she had chosen to hide.

'Who the hell is Kalayna?' Lucian demanded to know. 'And how the hell did you sneak her on board?'

'I told her to wait inside the hatch, under the security camera, until I had you all distracted,' Aurora confessed. 'Our plan obviously worked!'

The sound of Zeven preparing to detach from dry dock caused them both to freeze.

Lucian punched Zeven's number into his communicator. 'Not yet. Aurora is still on board.'

'We're out of time, Captain,' the pilot explained. *'USS forces are in the terminal.'*

'Continue, by all means.' Lucian shook his head as he looked at his young assistant. 'You had better find your friend and let her know how much trouble you're both in. And then report to Dr Lennox and see what help you can be to her.'

Aurora nodded, very subdued. 'Yes, captain.' She moved off and then turned back. 'I'm sorry —'

Lucian held up a hand. 'You've harmed yourself and your friend, not me. I am the one who should apologise, for embroiling you in this mess.'

'I embroiled myself.' She took full responsibility and departed on her search.

Aurora had searched through all four of the mid-deck modules and the lower marine module, without finding Kalayna. She still had the upper flight area to search, and so decided to head up to check out the pod and launch bays at the rear of the flight deck.

The elevator doors opened and Aurora saw all the crew gathered on the bridge listening to the orders of the Frujian authorities via the com-link.

'This is Special Agent Nikkos of the United Star System's Task Force ordering you to return to dock. If you do not bring your craft around and confirm this order within the next five minutes, you will be fired upon.'

'Oh shit,' Aurora uttered, not realising their situation was quite *that* serious. She decided to give up on her search for her girlfriend. Maybe Kalayna had got cold feet about life in space and stayed behind on Frujia, although she had certainly seemed more than excited about the prospect this afternoon.

'Shut down communication with Frujia,' Taren advised, 'or we'll never be able to focus on our objective.'

Zeven did as suggested, happy not to have the arresting agent's annoying voice in his ear. 'There's no way we can get out of here that fast.'

'Sure we can,' Taren assured him.

'Shut off all the external lights and close all the window shields,' Lucian ordered Leal. This tactic switched the ship into camouflage mode right as it passed to the night side of the planet.

Once this was done, Taren asked those not involved in the next part of the plan to leave the flight deck and Zeven rose quickly. 'Not you, Starman.' Taren pushed him back into his seat. 'You're still our pilot for this next leg.'

'I really don't think I'm capable of this,' he appealed in all honesty. 'Don't you have a plan B?'

Taren swung his chair around so that she could speak with him directly. 'In my vision, when I was seeing our alternative fate, I saw you deflect men into walls without even being conscious of it. You also passed right through a solid security wall to save Aurora's new friend from being raped. That's how you exposed your Power to the USS and the MSS.'

'Really ... he did that?' Aurora came forth to smile very winningly at the pilot who she'd been so mad at earlier in the afternoon.

Zeven seemed just as surprised and proud of himself, but then he frowned. 'Ah, correct me if I am wrong, but neither of those feats entail teleportation.'

'Either you teleported through that wall or you cleared a path through quantum space,' Taren argued confidently. 'Either talent will serve our purpose here today.'

Zeven noticed that Ringbalin had not made a move. 'Why is he here?'

'I'll be going in a second,' he explained. 'I just have a small task to perform first.' Ringbalin, Kassa and Ayliscia stepped in close to Zeven.

'What's happening, guys?' Zeven asked nervously. Ringbalin had moved behind the pilot to place his hands on Zeven's shoulders, and Kassa stood alongside him with Ayliscia Portus at her side.

'Ayliscia has been in contact with the Phemoray,' said Taren. 'They have given her a vision of where they want us to land after our quantum leap. It is a location on the outskirts of their system, beyond the tracking capabilities of the regular Phemorian government. The Phemoray do not wish to attract attention to us by having our craft suddenly appear in their orbit —'

'I can see that might panic the locals a little,' Zeven concurred.

'So, Ringbalin here is going to inject you with as much positivity as he can muster, and then Dr Portus is going to visualise our destination and, via Kassa, we will transfer this image to you. All you need to do is direct all the desire Ringbalin inspires in you into reaching the location Kassa is conveying, and, with a little of my verbal coaxing, hopefully we'll have enough combined willpower to make the jump.'

Zeven was overwhelmed. He didn't want to let everyone down, but his reasoning mind told him that the feat was impossible.

'The Phemoray are empowering our intention from their end, so it isn't all up to you,' Taren assured him. 'Let's just give it a whirl, before you have time to sabotage yourself. Okay?'

He nodded dumbly. He'd blindly trusted in Taren's way before and survived — with any luck today would prove no different.

'This won't hurt a bit.' Ringbalin closed his eyes to focus all his desire and willpower into Zeven.

'Wow, man, what are you doing to me?' Zeven was quite turned on by the energy flowing into him and, as it was coming from another man, it was disconcerting to say the least.

'Your primary motivating force is not willpower but desire, Zeven. You said it yourself,' Ringbalin explained and Zeven felt put on the spot with women present.

'I feel very sure Ringbalin is not thinking about you in terms of desire, if that makes you feel better,' Taren whispered to Zeven, having figured out what his problem was.

'You assume right,' Ringbalin said without breaking his concentration.

These intense feelings are those Ringbalin holds for Dr Portus, Zeven assumed on the quiet. 'Boy, if this gets much more intense, it could really get embarrassing.'

'Okay.' Taren gave Kassa and Dr Portus the all clear to proceed with their transmission. Ayliscia closed her eyes to visualise their target area and when Kassa picked up telepathically on the image, she placed a hand over Zeven's third eye area to transmit the vision to him.

When Zeven perceived a clear image he was visibly startled. 'I see a large pale green planet, and distant twin suns.'

'The planet is Attica, an uninhabited ice planet on the rim of the Phemorian binary star system,' Ayliscia told him, pleased that the transfer had worked.

'Hold that image, Zeven.' Taren gave a nod to excuse everyone. Kassa took Aurora with them into the corridor that led to the quarantine rooms and the flight bays.

'Now what happens?' Aurora wondered, wide-eyed. Zeven was observing her very differently today, and she couldn't deny his amorous glances stirred that same old desire to be close to him.

'Never mind,' Kassa replied insistently.

As soon as the room had cleared, Taren began to verbally coax Zeven toward their goal, just as she had on his last mission, but after a couple of moments Zeven had to admit it wasn't working.

'Don't give up so easily,' she implored him.

'No, I mean, you're the captain's girl now and I feel like I am betraying him or something, which is not turning me on at all.' Zeven gave half a smile. 'No offence.'

'None taken.' Taren bit her lip. 'That does pose a problem though, because the same thing would apply to most of the women here.'

'Except Aurora,' he suggested shyly.

Taren was quietly delighted by the suggestion, but hid it beautifully. 'Don't move.'

Taren headed through the door into the corridor where everyone was bracing themselves for a paranormal event.

'Is something wrong?' Lucian asked.

Taren grinned. 'I cannot inspire Zeven's desire, as neither one of our hearts is in it any more.' Taren looked at Aurora with a grin. 'He asked for you.'

'What?' Aurora was stunned, delighted, bemused and a little sceptical. 'He wants me to talk him through this?'

A loud blast shook their vessel violently and sent everyone off-balance.

'The USS are attacking,' Leal concluded.

'What do I have to do?' Aurora got to her feet. She was determined to prove her worth to her crewmates.

'Firstly, and most importantly, make sure Zeven remains gripping his seat, or he may well teleport himself to a remote location in space ... leaving the rest of us here.' There were some nervous chuckles from the gathering.

'Understood.'

'Zeven has the capacity to rearrange the universe if he wants to ... he just lacks focus and willpower, so you need to keep his mind focused on the region of the universe we wish to reach, whilst gently encouraging him to feel his personal power and have faith in himself.'

'You want me to turn him on and when he's really hot, get him to pour all his desire into reaching our destination,' she summarised.

'That seems to be the ticket, yeah,' Taren conceded, 'but if your intention to help him is fake ...'

Aurora gave a cheeky grin and leaned in close to Taren. 'I never fake it.' She winked in reassurance while another blast, higher up the craft, set them all to staggering again.

'You might also ask Zeven to imagine our craft surrounded by white light,' Kassa suggested. 'If he can deflect men without a second thought, why not missiles?'

Aurora nodded and quickly returned to the bridge where Starman was in his seat, eyes closed, until he heard someone enter and turned his seat about to see who it was.

'You don't have to do this,' he was quick to say. 'I'm feeling fairly confident to try this on my own.'

'If you lose focus, we could end up anywhere,' she reasoned, straddling his legs to sit on his lap facing him. 'And I don't mind, really.' She made him close his eyes and leaned forward so that she might whisper in his ear.

Zeven was delighted by her resolve and his natural reaction was to place both hands on Aurora's behind to manoeuvre her into a comfortable position upon the erection trapped in his trousers.

'Oh no,' Aurora slapped his hands away, placing them on the armrests of his chair. 'You don't get to touch, lest we end up floating alone in space without life support. You get to focus on what I tell you to focus upon, and only I get to touch. Clear?'

'Aye, aye, captain.' He smiled at this sweet turn of events. 'You do know you are only required to talk me through this?'

'I'm a more *hands-on* kind of girl,' she said tartly. 'Any objection?'

Zeven shook his head.

Another blast rocked the ship and the sudden movement proved to be an unexpected pleasure for them both. Aurora repositioned herself so that her lips were close to his ear.

'First, please imagine AMIE surrounded by a force field of light that *nothing* can penetrate.' She gently gyrated her pelvis to excite his desire and a quiet moan escaped his lips.

The following blast sounded further afield and did not rock the craft or disturb Aurora's seductive movement. She was inspired. 'That's fantastic, Starman ... we're good at this.' She pushed against him gently in reward, and he was definitely very aroused.

'A bit too good ... I'd better focus on our destination rather quickly,' he groaned with a cheeky grin.

'Yes,' she urged him, her enthusiasm for the job rather more intense than even she had first suspected. 'Do you see the visual the Phemoray gave you?' she asked in a seductive whisper.

'Oh yes,' he assured, panting as Aurora moved slightly, languorously. Zeven wanted so badly to touch her, and yet the fact he was restrained in both body and mind was even more of a turn-on.

'Take me there,' she sighed in his ear. 'I know you can do it,' she gasped at her own pleasure, 'please, *focus*.'

With all the will Zeven possessed he clung to his chair and held in his mind the vision of space he desired to reach, and when the moment of climax came Zeven felt himself ejected right out of his physical body and through a massive expanse of light at the speed of thought.

When the light faded and Zeven felt conscious enough to open his eyes, all he saw was complete darkness. Before coherent thought set in, a pang of panic shot through Zeven's body. He might be adrift in space! But his senses slowly set him at ease when he realised he could still feel the pilot seat beneath him and Aurora spread over him like a blanket. *So why is the ship in darkness?* He didn't bother answering the question, but felt around for the reboot key and all AMIE's systems came back online, along with the lights.

Zeven then attempted to rouse Aurora. 'Are you all right?' he asked, pinned to his chair by her body and unable to raise himself.

Aurora stirred and peeled herself off him. 'That was amazing ... there was a big blast of light! Did you see it?'

'Did I see the light?' Zeven rephrased the question, his eyes still ablaze with desire. 'I certainly did! You're amazing, Aurora, and I am an idiot for not seeing it sooner.'

She rather wanted to thump him for taking so long to come around, but the door to the bridge opened and the rest of the crew meandered in.

'Please don't move,' Zeven clutched Aurora to him. 'It could be frightfully embarrassing for me.'

'So ... it is up to me to cover up one of your messes yet again?' She made light of his predicament, and leaned forward to kiss him.

When the crew saw the impassioned scene, they were a little uncomfortable about interrupting.

Lucian cleared his throat and failed to secure their attention. 'Are you both all right?' he ventured to ask, maintaining his distance.

'They certainly look all right,' Leal commented quietly to the captain.

'We need to check our coordinates.' Lucian attempted to regain control of his bridge, but Aurora and Starman didn't stir from their mutual interests.

'Or, we could use one of the monitors in the office,' Taren suggested and everyone agreed that was a good idea.

PART 3

PHEMORIA — PLANET OF WOMEN

CHAPTER 16

STOWAWAY

According to the ship's systems, their craft had been dead in the air for a few hours following the electromagnetic disturbance that had shut everything down.

'My greenhouse!' Ringbalin freaked and rushed off to tend to Module C, before discovering whether or not the plan to reach the Phemorian system had been successful.

'Did we shift location?' Dr Portus delayed her departure to ask.

'AMIE's still finding her bearings,' Lucian advised, pushing the button on his belt to open the shield windows.

Everyone moved into the captain's office as a huge pale aquamarine planet came was revealed.

'I don't believe it,' Lucian uttered solemnly.

'Attica,' Dr Portus confirmed with a smile.

For the first time in her life Taren was truly amazed. 'Now I know that nothing is impossible,' she said, 'because I have witnessed *this*.'

'Teamwork, kiddo.' Kassa gave Taren the old chug on the shoulder. 'Those of us with the Powers have never been able to come out of the shadows before, so we've never been able to join forces either. Only the universe knows what we are ultimately capable of if we work together.'

Lucian was still absolutely gobsmacked, his rational mind doing overtime trying to fathom the implications of what he'd just witnessed. 'I believe I have a crew that would be the envy of any captain,' he said, pleased to be rid of their pursuers.

'You'd better believe it,' Leal butted in. 'I'd like to see the USS even work out where we are, let alone catch us.' This proposition brought a smile to everyone's face.

'In a week, I'll be home. My queen, Qusay-Sabah Clarona, is awaiting our arrival with great anticipation.' Dr Portus dragged her sight from the distant twin suns and made a move to the door. 'I should help with Module C,' she requested and Lucian gave her a nod.

'Wait.' Taren pursued Dr Portus into the reception area. 'Kassa said you suspected why the Phemoray are so interested in me.'

Ayliscia was uneasy. 'I cannot say for sure, but … you may have Phemorian in you.' She was not prepared to comment further and departed.

Taren had a lot of food for thought. She had never considered that her parents might have come from somewhere other than Maladaan. She wandered back to the office in a daze.

'As we don't seem to have sustained much damage, I guess the rest of us are on R and R for a bit,' Lucian advised Leal and Kassa as he marked Taren's return.

'We'd best get on with it then,' Leal suggested to Kassa. They both sensed the captain's need to be alone with Taren and closed the door on their way out.

Lucian walked straight up to the object of his desire and kissed her, for he'd been wanting to do so ever since the last time he'd done so.

'Wow,' Taren beamed, overwhelmed by his verve.

'*You rock my world*,' he told her and although the statement was quite out of character for the professor he meant it sincerely.

'And you mine,' she assured him with a seductive smile.

'My eyes have been opened to a whole new universe of possibility.' He turned his head to eyeball the ice planet that had replaced the view of Frujia beyond their craft. 'I am in complete and utter *awe*.'

Taren nodded as she also admired the alien space scape.

Somewhere down near those two stars twinkling in the distance was the planet of the Phemoray. Taren hoped it held a few insights into the mysteries of her past and the disappearance of Maladaan. In her vision of their alternative future, President Anselm had claimed to be the keeper of her memories. Perhaps the Phemoray could confirm if his claim was true. If it proved to be authentic, Taren planned to claim her history back.

Zeven had departed to take a shower and left Aurora lounging in the pilot's seat. She had mixed feelings in the wake of her quantum sexual encounter with the man she'd lusted after for years. Every time she thought about that climax Aurora's joy near suffocated her. Yet when she thought about Kalayna, her heart pined for her too, and she was deeply saddened at the prospect of never seeing her again.

Aurora was ninety-five per cent certain that Kalayna had remained on Frujia, but before she gave up hope altogether, she felt she should check the launch bay area and she rose to do so.

As she wandered down the corridor past all the bio-containment rooms, Aurora really couldn't decide whether she wanted to find Kalayna or not. If it turned out that she had stayed on board, Aurora would have a lot of explaining to do, and a really big decision to make.

She entered the huge hangar area, where all their smaller flight craft were sitting idle. 'Kalayna,' she called, not really expecting an answer.

'Well, it's about *fucking time* you showed up!'

A chill ran down Aurora's spine, for it was not Kalayna who answered her. '*Swithin?*' She looked in the direction the voice had come from and waited for him to emerge from the shadows.

Swithin did so, with a USS phaser to Kalayna's head. 'I've just been chatting to your new friend,' Swithin advised. 'Fancy, little Rory, a homo.'

'That's none of your business,' Aurora fumed.

'Oh, but it is,' Swithin corrected. 'I find people will tend to go a lot further out on a limb for a lover than a friend.'

'Please, let her go,' Aurora appealed more nicely. 'She has nothing to do with any of this. If you need a hostage then take me.'

'But I need you to launch my escape pod for me,' he informed bluntly.

'I don't know how to do that!' Aurora said in distress.

'Well, you had better learn in a hurry or your girlfriend's head is going to look like porridge!' He pressed his weapon harder into Kalayna's temple.

'I know how to launch a pod.' Kalayna winced in pain. 'I'll do it.'

'If you are trying to dick me around —' Swithin warned.

'I'm not! I don't know who you are and I really don't want to know, but if you desire to leave this vessel, I'll be more than happy to assist, I assure you.'

'Fucking smartarse,' Swithin grinned. He kind of liked this chick's spunk; a shame she was so obviously heterophobic. 'Then you get over here,' he said, motioning to Aurora, and once she was close enough Swithin shoved Kalayna aside. He took hold of Aurora and swung her around in front of him to face Kalayna. 'Get to the controls, ready a two-man pod —' He held the weapon to Aurora's temple.

'To go where?' Aurora wanted to know.

'I've made my own arrangements,' he snarled, 'so —'

'You've made arrangements in the Frujian system maybe,' Aurora commented, terrified of his obvious intention to take her hostage. 'But our craft is no longer there! We've made a quantum jump into the Phemorian system —'

'Don't try and *screw with me*, DeCadie.' He burrowed the weapon's muzzle into her temple and she cried out in pain. 'Not even the United Star Systems has that kind of capability ... so just *shut the fuck up* and don't *piss me off!*'

'Okay,' she whimpered, her right temple throbbing from the bruising.

'If you hurt her, you ain't ever getting out of here,' Kalayna warned, now that she was beyond his reach.

'Really?' Swithin challenged, as, having Aurora at such close quarters, he noted an unusual scent upon her that would divide these allies rather quickly. 'Aurora, if you are a lesbian now, then why do you reek of men's aftershave?'

Aurora didn't answer, blindsided by the question.

'What?' Kalayna's eyes narrowed.

'Smell for yourself,' Swithin offered.

Kalayna, sure that he was lying, thought she'd use the opportunity to see if she could get close enough to grab the weapon. The look of remorse on Aurora's face as she approached, however, made Kalayna uneasy, but she focused on disarming their attacker. Just as Kalayna was preparing to make her move she got a whiff of an aftershave that she had endured the smell of earlier that same day. 'Starman,' she said surely and Swithin laughed.

'Hey, good for you, Rory,' Swithin teased his hostage as he backed away with her, having made his point. 'You always did have a bit of a thing for him, didn't you?'

'You slept with Starman?' Kalayna was gutted beyond belief.

'No, it wasn't like that,' Aurora appealed, and then boggled at the task of trying to explain why she had been intimate with Zeven. Who in the universe was going to believe she'd seduced the pilot to save the project? It was useless ... these two had no idea what had just gone down and she wasn't even sure she really understood it.

'You bitch!' Kalayna shouted, disgusted. 'I left my home, my job, and endured hours in a hostage situation with this maniac ... for you!'

'Make her pay, babe.' Swithin found the lovers' dispute most amusing.

Kalayna made her way up the stairs to the launch bay control centre.

'Please, Kalayna,' Aurora appealed, tears streaming from her eyes. She never wanted to hurt anyone, especially not Kalayna. 'Don't do what he asks. Launching us off in a pod from here will sentence us both to certain death!'

'Fine with me.' Kalayna opened the control deck door, went inside, took a seat and put on the communication headset.

'That's the spirit,' Swithin egged her on.

Aurora watched in horror as a two-seater pod lowered in its cradle and was placed on the launch area. Once secured in place, the top of the pod rose up to allow the passengers to embark.

'Come on.' Swithin hauled her towards their transport.

'We don't have suits,' she said, resisting.

'Trust me, we won't be in space that long.' He hauled her over to the pod.

'There's nothing out there!' Aurora yelled, to try and get it through his thick skull. 'Just a huge boulder of ice, and nothing else for —'

Swithin cracked her over the back of the head with the butt of his weapon, and caught her up over his shoulder as she fell. 'That's much easier.' He piled her into the front seat of the pod and took up the rear position himself.

'*Closing you up for launch,*' Kalayna advised Swithin via the headset. '*Prepare for stasis —*'

'Forget stasis. Just launch,' Swithin ordered.

'*Destination?*'

'Just launch,' he repeated, 'which word don't you understand?'

'*It's your funeral,*' Kalayna retorted.

'How do you know all this technical shit anyway?' Swithin asked, as the pod sealed up, and began manoeuvring into the launch tube.

'*Just be glad I do, arsehole,*' Kalayna replied.

'Oh, I am, sweet thing,' he laughed.

The pod locked into the launch position. Kalayna was absolutely fuming and it was all she could do to prevent herself from collapsing into a hysterical state of rejection. Then she had a moment of clarity, dwelling on the past couple of days and how happy and excited she'd been to have finally found love. The sweet memories made her think twice about exacting revenge in this manner. She knew in her gut it was the wrong thing to do. But when she thought about Aurora with Zeven, her heartache overruled her gut. *'Good riddance.'* Kalayna hit the launch key, ripped the headset off and collapsed into tears.

Showered and changed, Zeven felt reborn in the wake of his intergalactic teleportation effort, not because he'd succeeded in saving his crewmates and their vessel, but because of the warm ball of excited emotion that welled in his chest every time he thought about Aurora.

Instead of making him feel like an out-of-control freak, she made him feel focused and proud of what he might be capable of. Much like Taren, but it staggered his imagination how much more intense Aurora's and his chemistry seemed to be. How he'd failed to see her beauty, bravery and intellect before now was completely beyond him. But then, it was only recently that Aurora had seemed to become confident in her own skin, and now that she had, she was truly magnificent. His brief flirtation with Taren on Oceane didn't even come close to comparing with what he was feeling right now. He didn't care how much of an idiot he might look ... he had to find Aurora and tell her that he was in love with her.

The pilot headed out of his rooms, then stopped,

feeling suddenly ill-prepared for his confession. 'I need flowers,' he decided. 'I need Ringbalin.' Zeven made a beeline for Module C.

'Balin! Balin!' Zeven called to the botanist as he wandered through the greenhouse looking for flowers in bloom — he didn't dare prune anything without Ringbalin's permission.

When Zeven spied Ringbalin hopping through the greenhouse, pulling on his clothes and fumbling to get his glasses on his nose at the same time, the pilot realised that he might have ill-timed this visit.

'Sorry.' Zeven suppressed a smile. 'I hope I'm not interrupting anything —'

'Zeven!' Ringbalin was surprised to see him, or anyone. 'Is there a problem? I thought we were all on R and R?'

'I need flowers.' Zeven explained.

'Flowers!'

'To give Aurora,' he elaborated. 'That would please her, wouldn't it?'

'Oh ...' Ringbalin was enlightened, and could plainly see that Zeven was a changed man. 'Your desire is transforming into love. That's excellent, as will is far more responsive to the latter,' Ringbalin commented as he waved Zeven to follow him. 'I know which flowers Rory likes best.'

'Can I have some of those Bells of Heaven things?'

Ringbalin glanced back at the love-struck pilot. 'You won't need those.'

'No, I don't,' Zeven agreed, 'but what if she doesn't feel like I do, then I might?'

Ringbalin laughed. He knew all about Aurora's long-time infatuation with the pilot. 'We are talking about Miss DeCadie here, right?'

'Yeah,' Zeven concurred.

'Then I have something much better.'

The reason Ringbalin knew so much about Aurora's love life was that she often popped in to admire his garden and chat. And she admired one section of the garden in particular.

Ringbalin led Zeven to a huge clump of evergreen plants with large leaves that fanned out from the central stalks. The stalks rose four metres into the air and, halfway up, the green stems turned deep purple. The flowers, which emerged from the spathe at the top, consisted of several brilliant purple sepals and many more hot pink petals.

'Whoa,' Zeven said, well aware that purple and pink were Rory's favourite colours.

'I've never cut one,' Ringbalin informed him, moving into the foliage with a hand sickle. 'Even with water, it will die in just two days.' He slashed at one of the flowering stalks and caught the treasure to prevent any damage to the bloom. 'So, get it to her quickly,' Ringbalin advised, handing it over.

'She is going to really love this. Thanks, Balin.'

'Thanks for getting the USS off our arse.' Ringbalin was equally thankful.

The pilot grinned. 'It was my pleasure entirely.'

'I can see that it was.' Ringbalin gave the pilot a wave as he departed. He had his own erotic encounter to be getting back to. 'Buzz me about that meditation training. We should get started.'

Zeven caught the important part of the request. 'I will be sure and *call first* next time.' He hurried off to be about his mission.

* * *

Zeven searched high and low for Aurora. He tried paging her and calling her through the intercom a few times. He would have asked someone if they'd seen her, but he appeared to be the only soul wandering about.

Leal had been spending so much time in Kassa Madri's company that Zeven — following Ringbalin's gentlemanly example of not asking directly — could only assume that his co-pilot's secret desires had finally been reciprocated. There was no doubting how Lucian and Taren felt about each other, and clearly Ringbalin and Ayliscia Portus were finally consummating their feelings for one another also.

'End of our world as we know it, and what's everyone on board doing? Getting laid,' Zeven muttered as he wandered out of the elevator and into the flight deck, where he had seen Rory last. 'Whilst the object of my desire has just vanished.' He swung around in the empty pilot seat, annoyed, not because he was missing out, but because he was getting worried.

A flashing light on Leal's console caught his eye and Zeven approached to note the co-pilot's monitor was indicating that a pod had been launched.

'Please, no.' Zeven dropped the flower as his heart sank into the pit of his stomach. A vision of finding Amie with her throat cut in a misfired pod sent the pilot bolting towards the launch bay.

Kalayna was slouched in the corner of the launch bay control room when Zeven found her. She was in a semi-catatonic state; her shaking seemed to indicate that she was traumatised. 'How did *you* get here?' He wasn't at all pleased to see her, but felt compelled to check her vital signs. As he crouched before her,

Kalayna snapped out of her trance and began hitting him.

'You!' she seethed through gritted teeth. 'Get the fuck away from me.' She kicked out at him. 'I hate you! You self-centred, egotistical, chauvinistic, fickle, arrogant, shallow, ungrateful prick!'

Zeven didn't attempt to reason with the girl as she was clearly hysterical. He exited quickly, locked the control room door from the outside and called for Dr Madri.

When Kassa and Leal arrived to hear Kalayna still hollering Starman's faults, Leal had to comment: 'Wow, she really seems to have you pegged.'

'Thanks a lot.' Zeven forced a smile, feeling worse because much of Kalayna's impression of him would have come from Aurora. 'I'm glad you're here though. Aurora is missing and so is one of our pods.'

'Not again,' Kassa said despairingly. 'Does this girl know anything about the launch?'

'She's in there, but I can't stop her swearing at me long enough to find out.' He threw his hands up in frustration.

'Not to worry,' Kassa said, giving him a reassuring smile. 'I'll sedate her and see what I can find out.'

'I'll retrieve the pod.' Leal made a move to his station on the bridge.

'I'll help Kassa tame the savage beast here and then I'll be right there,' Zeven responded.

'I'll rouse the captain and let him know,' Leal decided.

Kalayna was no joy to sedate, but once they had her under, Zeven carried her down to the medical chambers — he was oblivious to how long he remained gazing at the girl once he'd laid her down on the bed, until ...

'She's very beautiful,' Kassa said, in such a way as to empathise with Zeven's obsessive attention. 'I saw you together at the memorial. I thought she was a friend of yours.'

'*No*. She's a friend of Aurora's ... a lover, you might say.'

'Oh ... *Oh*,' Kassa commented, wide-eyed with surprise and then concern when she recalled Zeven and Aurora in the throes of a heated moment in the pilot's seat earlier. 'Oh dear.'

'Indeed,' Zeven agreed gravely.

'You think that she might have found out about you and Aurora and then taken revenge?' Kassa said, knowing what Zeven was thinking.

'I'm hoping you can tell me that.' Zeven threw the ball back in her court.

'Okay.' Kassa took hold of the subject's hand. 'Often it is difficult to read the mind of someone who is sedated, but I —'

Zeven's communicator gave an alert.

'Zeven, there're some problems with retrieving the pod,' Leal advised via the speaker.

'I'm on my way up,' he answered, already on the move and saying to Kassa. 'Let me know the second you have anything.'

She assured that him she would.

CHAPTER 17

DAMAGE CONTROL

Up on the bridge, Lucian and Taren had joined Leal at his console.

'What's wrong?' Zeven asked.

'The tracking device on the pod is inactive,' Leal told him, and shook his head to imply that retrieval would be impossible.

'It's been picked up then.' Zeven came to the most positive conclusion first.

'Or, the tracking system might not have been activated upon launch,' Leal suggested.

'Or it could have crashed.' Zeven voiced the most dire scenario, his eyes turning to the large ice planet they were passing.

'Whatever has become of the pod, it is no longer on our scopes,' Leal concluded solemnly, as there was very little he could do to help the situation.

Zeven was quietly fuming inside, but he breathed deeply to calm his anger and focus on a solution. 'If I can will this entire ship into another part of the galaxy, then surely I can transport myself to Aurora, wherever she is.'

Everyone present was shaking their head.

Lucian began the objections. 'Too dangerous.'

'You could find yourself stranded on an ice planet,' Leal chimed in, 'or drifting in open space —'

'Then put me in a spacesuit!' Zeven insisted. 'If I manifest in the middle of a disaster then I can just come back!'

'You are still untrained,' Taren challenged. 'Without guidance to focus, how can you be sure that you won't just get yourself killed?'

'It was Swithin!' Kassa burst out of the elevator and made haste towards them. 'He must have already been hiding on board when he phoned you, Lucian, to warn us about our impending arrest.'

'That's what was in it for him ...' Lucian was finally enlightened. 'A means to escape.'

'What are you talking about?' Zeven was perplexed.

'Swithin ambushed Kalayna and used her to get Aurora to co-operate in aiding him in his escape,' Kassa clarified.

'That explains the two-man pod,' Leal said.

'But Aurora doesn't know how to launch a pod.' Zeven was lost again.

'Yes, but apparently Kalayna does,' Kassa informed him. 'Once Swithin pointed out to Kalayna that Aurora reeked of your aftershave, he didn't have much trouble getting the emotionally distraught girl to cooperate.'

'Shit!' Zeven wanted to hit something; loose objects began flying and everyone present ducked down low.

'Zeven,' Taren appealed very nicely, '*please* focus on being constructive.'

The pilot began breathing deeply in a desperate attempt to calm himself and the objects all dropped to the ground. 'I have to do something!'

'Not before you calm down,' Taren instructed, grabbing up her communicator. 'Ringbalin, could you come to the bridge, please?'

'I don't need Balin to control my emotions for me,' Zeven insisted, as loose objects began shaking and seemed ready to take flight again.

'You are welcome to prove that,' Taren invited his composure, and the objects around them stilled themselves.

'We don't have a lot of time to figure out a rescue plan,' Kassa continued. 'Swithin didn't bother putting them in suits or setting a destination.'

'Then he was expecting to be picked up,' Leal concluded.

'In the Frujian system, yes,' Kassa explained.

'But we are no longer there,' Zeven concluded, horrified. 'Without suits to charge the system, the pod will only last a couple of days in open space before it will shut down completely.' His sight fell upon the exotic flower intended for Aurora, which was already starting to wilt. 'If you won't let me use my Power to find her,' Zeven said to the captain, 'then at least let me take the recon vessel and follow the pod's trajectory.'

Lucian wanted to see Aurora safely back on board as much as this young pilot did. Finally, with a firm nod, he gave him clearance to depart.

'Someone should go with you.' Taren was about to volunteer herself.

'I'll go with him,' Ringbalin said, stepping into the conversation.

Everyone was shocked speechless, and Zeven most of all.

'But what about Module C?' The pilot could hardly believe the botanist would leave his beloved sanctuary to aid him in this.

'Dr Portus knows what to do,' he replied.

'But why would —'

'You can't go alone, untrained, so it's just a simple process of elimination,' Ringbalin outlined. 'Taren has to stay in hiding, the captain cannot go, we need Leal here in case anything happens to you and Kassa is certainly not dispensable.'

'Thanks for the vote of confidence,' Zeven said flatly, although he admired Ringbalin's bravery.

'Who better than me to keep you calm and focused?'

'Who indeed?' Zeven appreciated the offer, but cocked an eye, unsure. 'Have you ever even been in a small spacecraft before, Balin?'

'Ah, no, but I don't see this as a problem. You have and you're still here so ... it can't be that bad.' The look of doubt on everyone's face did nothing to reassure him. 'Can it?'

As Aurora stirred from her slumped position in the front of the pod, it took a second to recollect her situation. The back of her head was throbbing and her eyes wouldn't open due to all the light. *The interior of a pod is not this bright.* She struggled against her own eyelids to perceive the brightly lit hangar bay roof — but it was not AMIE's loading bay that the pod was now resting in. She heard voices and stilled herself to listen.

'I have no idea how they did it,' Swithin was saying. 'But the tracking beacon is obviously still working so, no sweat, we haven't lost Anselm's precious daughter.'

Anselm's daughter?

Aurora was stunned to learn the Chairman of the USS had a daughter, much less that she was on board AMIE.

'She's being nailed by my brother, but probably best to keep that out of the president's brief, I reckon,' Swithin added with dark humour.

Aurora gasped when she realised he could only be referring to Taren Lennox. *That's why the USS and the MSS want her back so badly.*

'And now she is headed for Phemoria, which is exactly what we were hoping to avoid.'

Aurora did not know this voice and peeked her head over the pod rim to see if she could get a glimpse. Her eyes parted wide when she beheld Anselm's viceroy, Khalid Mansur.

This man had not reached his high station by being charismatic, as Anselm had, but rather with his dark looks, dress and moods he had intimidated his way to the top. Despite his slight build and height, there wasn't a man in the USS who would choose to get on his bad side for those who did vanished without a trace.

The only man Khalid had ever served, besides himself, was Anselm — no one knew why they had such a bond, but the United Star System's press machine was always rife with unfounded rumours and theories. Aurora had never given the question a second thought, until this second.

'Your little friend is awake.' The viceroy's eyes shot straight to Aurora.

She ducked back down in reflex, but as they knew she was present now she thought she may as well stand and state her mind. 'Swithin, you backstabbing, double-crossing snitch!'

'Ha, ha.' Swithin was glad to see her awake, 'It seems you were telling the truth about the quantum leap AMIE took. I like that ... so I think I'll let you live *for now*.'

'That's not a good idea,' commented the viceroy openly, and his candour in ordering her execution made Aurora's blood run cold. He wasn't just trying to scare her, he meant what he said.

Swithin winced, as he didn't quite agree. 'My brother and his crew are very fond of this young lady, and she has no Powers, so she's a low-maintenance hostage as well.'

'No woman is low maintenance,' Khalid Mansur chided, as he eyed Aurora with distaste. 'If you must keep her, keep her on a leash ... you know where detention is.'

Aurora was offended, but didn't dare let loose at the man who was famed to be both morally and mentally reprehensible.

'I need to report.' He turned on his heel and departed.

Swithin turned back to Aurora and grinned. 'See, I told you there was nothing to worry about.'

'How could you do this to us?' Aurora climbed out of the pod.

'Do what?' he said rather aggressively. 'These are the good guys.'

'What?' Aurora couldn't believe it. She was lucky to be alive. 'Have you gone completely insane?'

'You don't know *what the fuck* you're talking about, Aurora. Women and politics just don't mix. You'll just have to trust that I'm doing you and AMIE a favour. Believe me, you don't want to be taking sides with the Phemorians. Anselm and the USS might be sneaky, underhanded bastards, but at least they are open about it. The Phemorians will blindside you with love and kindness, and you'll be their prisoner and slave without even knowing it!'

Aurora didn't really know enough about Phemorians to dispute his claim, but the one Phemorian she did know was lovely. 'Dr Portus —'

'— is *a fucking spy*, Aurora. Wake up!' Swithin hollered at her. 'Why am I bothering to reason with you?'

Aurora felt bewildered, naive and very put in her place. Swithin grabbed her by the arm and hauled her out of the launch bay to a detention cell.

'What's going to become of me?' she asked as she was tossed into the cell.

'Let's just wait and see how this all pans out, shall we?' Swithin closed and locked the door.

The second she was alone, Aurora began shaking violently. Shock and fear took her in waves and she broke into tears. Head bowed low, she caught a whiff of Zeven's aftershave on herself and she gripped her shirt and held it close to her nose to breathe in deep. Just the smell of him made her feel safer. How she wished she'd never left the pilot's seat. If she had just waited there as he'd asked, she imagined she'd be making love to him right now, which caused her tears to flood anew.

'No,' she told herself, finding her courage and raising herself upright. *I have discovered information that I never would have if I had not been dragged away from AMIE . . . now I just have to figure out how best to get the information and myself back to base. I know Zeven will come for me.* There was no doubt in her mind about that. She had witnessed first-hand his amazing new Powers that no one in the USS knew about, and when she imagined her rescue it brought a confident smile to her face.

* * *

'This isn't so bad,' Ringbalin grimaced. His knuckles were white as he gripped the seat. In truth Balin hated anything artificial — his Power only gave him influence over the natural world — and looking around the cockpit the botanist could not imagine a more artificial environment.

'You're doing great,' Zeven encouraged, not game to pull any stunts, as Ringbalin was clearly on edge.

Ringbalin looked at Zeven, envying how very relaxed he was. 'To conquer my fear, I rehearsed in my mind how this rescue would go ... that's a very powerful technique for influencing outcomes that Taren discovered,' Ringbalin informed Zeven. 'Athletes who ran a race in their minds before the fact, performed outstandingly and the more detail you include in your imagined pre-run the more profound your effect on causality can be once you are actually in the situation.'

Zeven was intrigued by this. Although he might not have been very good when it came to meditating, he wasn't bad at visualising — precisely the technique he'd used to move AMIE. The idea of rehearsing his plans before he actually executed them was very appealing.

'I convinced myself I would feel safe and secure throughout the rescue.'

'And is it working?' This was a rhetorical question for the answer was plain to see.

'Maybe ...' Ringbalin was feeling calmer suddenly, but then their craft began to vibrate quite violently. '... not! What's happening?'

'Feels like we're caught in a tracker beam,' Zeven advised, perplexed to find no vessels registering on his screens. 'In which case, it has to be a USS base cruiser hauling us in. They're the only transport with complete cloaking capability.' The pilot smiled, happy to be hauled closer to his destination. 'That explains who picked up the pod.'

The violent vibrating of their craft was starting to get to Ringbalin. 'I think I'm going to be sick.'

'Oh no, you don't.' Zeven placed both hands on Ringbalin and concentrated all his will on returning them to AMIE's flight deck.

With a rush of energy, Zeven felt himself freed from the confines of his craft as he was pulled back through space to the bridge on AMIE, where he deposited Ringbalin safely. 'There you go ... safe and secure.'

'Thank heavens!' The botanist, badly shaken, lost his legs and landed in a heap on the floor.

'No time to explain.' Zeven backed up a few paces. 'I've found my focus ... I'll do this alone. The USS has Aurora, and I'm going to get her back.' The pilot was gone before anyone could argue with him.

'What, in the name of heroism, do you think you're doing?' Leal demanded through the recon vessel's intercom as Zeven returned to the seat of his flailing craft.

'Ask Balin for an update of the situation. Communications are now off.' The pilot sat back to focus on using his Power to a different end. 'Reel me in, baby.'

With Aurora as his heart's motivation, Zeven felt his will had strengthened and that his psychic skill was far more responsive. Just as Ringbalin had claimed, love was more powerful than desire. His concern for Aurora's safety had made his own fears dissolve. Zeven was now prepared to embrace his power and use his supernatural gifts to fight those who would try to oppress him and those he cared about.

'Okay then,' Zeven prepped himself, 'if I am a master of matter, I shouldn't have any trouble doing *this* ...'

He imagined himself completely transparent and was shocked when he looked down to see straight through to the seat in which he sat. Zeven's surprise caused him to lose focus and his shape, colour, tone and texture returned. This amused him greatly and he laughed out loud. Now that he had some idea what he was capable of on his own, he was inspired. '*This* is going to be a hoot!' He cast his mind forward to the rescue to rehearse in his mind how the situation would unfold — he would not lose his focus again.

The back of Aurora's neck, where she'd been struck unconscious, was throbbing more now than it had when she first awoke. Her head was splitting from the harsh lighting in the cell, and she was hungry. Her tears had been flowing in steady streams for hours, so she was dehydrating rapidly. It wasn't that she was scared, but the pain in her head that made her weep. If she'd had a weapon in the cell, Aurora felt she would have shot herself by now to be rid of the torture.

The door to the cell vanished and Aurora nearly keeled over from relief. '*Finally* ... I need a medic, I —'

Swithin entered, scowling. 'Sorry, we've got other plans.' He pulled her to her feet, and she nearly toppled over. 'You *are* a bit woozy on it.' He steadied her against himself and hauled her back into the flight bay.

'Are we going somewhere?' Aurora was feeling drowsy until she spied the craft at the centre of everyone's attention. It was AMIE's recon vessel and despite her pain, the young woman smiled.

Swithin, at her back, placed his weapon to her head. 'Looks like your new boyfriend came after you.'

'He did.' Her heart welled with the romance and relief of it all. 'You're in *so* much trouble.' She didn't attempt to keep her amusement from her voice.

'Unless the little upstart is fireproof, I don't think I have anything to worry about,' Swithin assured her, and despite the threat, Aurora's hope did not waver.

She knew from the little she had learned from Taren about the quantum world that whether or not she'd tapped into her psychic power her will could still support Zeven. So, she refused to believe that this was anything but her will to be rescued become manifest.

'Open it up,' Swithin ordered the USS soldiers, who did not follow his order directly, but waited for their commander to give the nod.

They opened the vessel and entered and after a few moments of quiet confusion, they all got out.

'Why don't I hear any firing?' Swithin demanded.

'There's nothing to fire at.' The USS commander strode past Swithin, his men behind him.

'But we picked up a communication that originated from this vessel.' Swithin questioned the thoroughness of the search.

'What can I tell you?' The commander motioned to the vessel. 'Look for yourself?' and the company departed the hangar.

Swithin's attention turned to Aurora, who was eyeballing the hangar bay with a huge smile on her face. 'What are you grinning at?' He raised his weapon to smack her, but was rudely interrupted when he was belted in the face and his weapon knocked from his hand. He went reeling backwards to land flat on his back.

Aurora was dazed and confused, and doubly so when an invisible force grabbed her hand and began hauling her towards AMIE's recon vessel. 'What the ...? Starman?' she asked quietly, her eyes drooping against her will.

'Your love made me brave,' he whispered, now supporting her as they fled.

'You love me,' she said with a broad smile, as her eyes rolled backwards and her body became a dead weight in his arms.

'Aurora?' He picked her up to make greater haste.

'What the ...?' Swithin observed Aurora begin floating towards the recon vessel, and he rose quickly to try and prevent his unconscious hostage escaping. He took a running dive at the space below Aurora's floating body and was not surprised to collide with a solid object.

Zeven fell through the back door of his craft, landing Aurora safely on the floor inside. He turned and smacked his assailant in the jaw with his unseen boot.

Swithin backed up, as he was way too close to his invisible attacker. His best bet was to get on board the craft and use Aurora as a shield. 'Is that you, Lennox?' Swithin asked. She was the only person on the AMIE project with the Powers that he knew of.

Zeven realised it would be a very wise move to keep his mouth shut. He waited for Swithin to try and barge his way into the craft, and served him another great smack in the jaw before kicking him clear and closing the exit door. Zeven crouched down to place one hand on Aurora and the other on the floor of the craft, whereby he focused on moving them all to the flight bay on AMIE.

'You'll never get out of this flight bay!' Swithin ran at the craft and slammed his hands against it, whereupon the vessel exploded in his face in a great blast of light.

Taren paced the floor of the flight deck awaiting word of their missing team members with the rest of the crew. She was trying to maintain a positive outlook but with every minute that passed it became increasingly difficult.

'We're in the flight bay.' Zeven's voice came through all the crew's personal communicators and startled everyone into action.

In the launch bay dock, they were shocked to find their recon vessel ... and Swithin Gervaise lying unconscious on the floor alongside it.

The side hatch opened and the stairs dropped down, hitting Swithin's torso which startled him awake.

'Kassa, Aurora needs you.' Zeven jogged down the stairs, further squashing Swithin between the metal stairs and the concrete ground and he moaned accordingly.

'Get my bag,' Kassa instructed Ayliscia, and rushed into the vessel to check on Aurora with Ringbalin hot on her heels. The leggy Phemorian ran for the stairway rather than wait for the elevator.

Zeven dragged Swithin out from under the stairs.

His captive looked around and discovering, that he was back on board AMIE all he had to say was, 'Fuck!' His sight fell upon Taren and he smiled. 'Hello.'

Yes, Swithin knew her MSS code name, but he wouldn't attempt to use it on her whilst in the company of others, as that would blow his advantage. She glared back at him defiantly, as she had nothing to fear from him at the moment.

'So, it wasn't you who came to Aurora's rescue,' he deduced, as Zeven was the only person to exit the craft.

Lucian gripped his brother's jaw and directed his attention to him. 'You don't get to talk to her, or anyone on board this ship!'

'Let's just stick him in bio-containment and jettison him into outer space,' Zeven suggested, pulling Swithin's arms back hard for greater manoeuvrability.

'Jettison *him*,' Swithin said, motioning with his head to Zeven. 'He's the freak, you can't trust —'

'Don't speak to me about trust.' Outraged, Lucian cut Swithin off. 'Bio-containment is an excellent idea,' he agreed, as Leal came over to assist with Swithin's removal.

'You're not serious, Luc. Come on!' Swithin protested, as he'd never seen his brother so detached from him before. 'I was trying to do you a favour! The Phemorians will screw you, just as surely as the USS and the MSS will,' he yelled back in warning.

Unfortunately for Swithin, Ayliscia Portus caught the comment as she entered and slapped him hard across the face.

'Sermetic-sympathiser scum,' she hissed, without a backward glance at her victim, and as Zeven and Leal dragged Swithin out of the dock, Ayliscia rushed the medical bag to Kassa.

Taren approached to see what was going on with Aurora, but Kassa came backing out with Ringbalin behind her carrying the unconscious young woman. 'Is she going to be okay?'

'She's had a bad knock. I'll need to operate and relieve the pressure, then we'll see.' Kassa rushed off in front of Ringbalin, with Dr Portus in tow and ready to assist.

The launch bay fell into silence. Taren looked at Lucian blankly and he at her. 'Do you really plan to jettison your brother into space?'

'Yes,' he replied coldly, then softened his stance and shrugged. 'Although I will probably stick him in a pod first,' he admitted as Taren moved to give him a squeeze.

She held no love for Swithin, but was pleased to hear there would be no blood on their hands.

'He's got a few questions to answer before then, including your code name.' Lucian was determined to rid Taren of that threat. 'And he's not going anywhere before he divulges it.'

She was reassured by his promises but what they all craved now was some rest, to take a pause and reassess. With a USS base station looming somewhere between them and Phemoria, Taren didn't expect they were going to be awarded much grace.

CHAPTER 18

NAKED ON THE INSIDE

Lucian left to deal with his brother. Taren headed down to Kassa's consultation rooms to await word on Aurora's condition.

She arrived to find Kalayna sitting on a chair in the corner. The young woman's eyes were puffy from crying and silent tears were streaming down her face by default.

Taren wasn't sure what to say to the girl, as she had yet to determine her state of mind. 'Hello. Can I get you anything? Some food, a room to sleep in, or —'

'Why are you being nice to me?' she asked in a very hostile fashion. 'I have probably killed a dear friend of yours.'

Taren saw through to her heart at once — Kalayna was angry at herself and she was fearful that everyone on board this craft must now hate her. 'You are not the first person to be tricked into doing something stupid by Swithin Gervaise,' Taren replied, holding high one hand to confess. 'I too have been his puppet, much to the detriment of this project, yet no one on the AMIE crew has held that against me.'

Kalayna sniffled, encouraged. 'Really?'

'Really,' Taren assured her, smiling, and Kalayna forced a smile in response. But then Zeven came charging into the waiting room and Kalayna's frown and fear returned.

'You ...' Zeven pointed a finger at her.

'Zeven, that won't help.' Taren grabbed his finger to deflect his anger.

He brushed Taren off, remaining focused on his foe. 'Who do you work for?'

'What?' Taren was surprised by the question.

Kalayna was baffled. 'What do you mean? I'm a stowaway. I used to work for the resort you were all staying at, but Aurora made me a better offer, so I took it.'

'*That's crap.*' Zeven took a step closer to stare Kalayna down. 'You didn't learn how to launch a pod working in a *fricking* hotel! So answer the question. *Who do you work for?*'

'My dad taught me,' Kalayna said, bursting into tears all over again. 'He was a techie for the Frujian pod link system.'

'Crap!' Zeven insisted.

'It's true!' Kalayna hollered back, distraught. 'He was teaching me his trade until he died, then I was forced to find alternative employment.'

'A great story that we have no chance of checking!' Zeven scoffed.

'You're a systems engineer,' Taren said happily.

'Ninth year,' she replied, which meant she only fell short of being fully qualified by one year of her apprenticeship.

'Hey, we need one of those,' Taren commented to Zeven, desperately trying to clear the air.

'You lay your hands on any of my vehicles,' Zeven

warned Kalayna venomously, 'and I'll personally rip them off.'

'Zeven!' Taren was unnerved by his inceasing hostility, but his focus did not waver.

'And heaven help you if Aurora does not come through this one hundred per cent intact!' Zeven turned around to storm from the room.

'You don't love her,' Kalayna stood to yell back. 'She'll just be another conquest to you and then you'll toss her aside.'

Zeven halted, his jaw clenched. 'Don't you pretend to know anything about how I feel about Aurora, or she me. I've known her for five years, you've known her for five minutes!'

'So what took you so long?' Kalayna challenged him.

Zeven had to catch his breath to answer that question for the answer was buried deep within him. 'I am well aware of the kind of a guy I am, and I have had plenty of opportunities to do just as you claim I will. But I have only ever wanted the best for Rory, and I never, but *never* would have endangered her life out of jealousy. *Never*,' he went on, relaxing as Kalayna hung her head in shame. 'So don't speak to me about love ... when you obviously have no concept of what it means.'

Taren was mystified at his cutting eloquence, honesty, self-control and insight. 'You've changed,' she said as he looked to her.

'Sorry you had to see that,' he commented, heading for the exit door. 'Let me know the second you hear anything.'

'I will.' Taren looked at Kalayna, now sunk in a seat sobbing, her fingers buried deep in the hair at her scalp, holding back her long blonde locks.

'I can't fix this,' she gasped, overwhelmed by what she'd done. 'He's right, I am to blame —'

'Kalayna, Zeven *will* calm down, and come to see that you were manipulated —'

'No!' She looked up to set Taren straight. 'I could have trapped them both in that pod and sought help,' she confessed. 'I was not under any physical duress to launch.'

'But you were under emotional and mental duress, and they are just as powerful —'

'No. I own my mistake ... what I need to know now is how I can make some amends for it.'

'In that case, I believe you need to see the captain,' Taren said, holding out a hand, and, although Kalayna did not accept it, she did not object to Taren placing a comforting arm around her shoulders as they made their way to Lucian's office.

'Luc! *Thank fuck,*' Swithin exclaimed as Lucian entered the bio-containment observation room and stood, arms folded, glaring at his brother in the containment area. 'You can't be seriously thinking of keeping me in here. Where the fuck am I supposed to pee?' He motioned to the barren cell.

'I never expected to have to contain any criminals on board AMIE,' Lucian informed him coolly, 'but not to worry, I won't be keeping you long. I just need you to tell me Taren's code name and you'll be out of there.'

Lucian was so calm that Swithin was unnerved. 'How dumb do you think I am?'

'Oh, very, I assure you,' Lucian emphasised.

'Look,' Swithin shook his head, frustrated, 'you don't know the half of what is really going on with your girlfriend —'

'But you're here to enlighten me.' Lucian took a seat to listen and Swithin forced a laugh.

'I'm not telling you a thing, little bro ... the less you know the better. Anything you do to torture information out of me would be nothing compared to what the secret services will do to me if I spill the beans. So ...' Swithin shrugged.

'You think the secret services know your deepest fears like I do?' Lucian was not fazed, and Swithin observed his brother warily, having never seen this dark side to him.

What Swithin feared most was anything paranormal or supernatural — hence his hatred for anyone who wielded a Power. People with a Power had always been freaks, to be hunted down and restrained as far as Swithin and billions of others like him were concerned.

Swithin scowled. 'Well, aren't you turning out to be a chip off the old block, hey?'

Lucian ignored his brother's attempt to take the focus away from himself. 'Have I told you that I have discovered a substance that will accelerate your personal psychic power by unfathomable amounts?' Lucian asked and Swithin turned very pale.

'That's what happened to Gudrun.' Swithin almost sounded like he pitied the young pilot.

Lucian did not confirm or deny the comment. 'I have quite a large store of this substance,' he lied. The sample they had of Oceane air was actually minute. 'I will pump that chamber full —'

'All right. You little shit!' Swithin was very frustrated at being bulldozed by his baby brother. 'You want the truth, here's the truth. I only know one of Taren's code names, the one that I use, but she has another, higher-level security code name that I don't know, so you're never going to be able to protect her from everybody!'

'Right now, I only need protect her from you,' Lucian said.

'Her code name is Sci-chick Puppet,' Swithin advised and Lucian wanted to smack himself in the head. Bonar Colbers had already revealed half of Taren's code name as soon as she'd come on board as he had called her sci-chick often. They could almost have guessed the rest from the code names they already knew.

'You are the Puppet Master, yes?' Lucian wanted that verified.

'Yes,' Swithin confirmed.

'You ordered Amie's death,' Lucian concluded.

'She was a dangerous bitch, Luc! I did you a favour!' Swithin growled.

'*Stop doing me favours!*' Lucian stood to roar. 'Enough already!'

Lucian's communicator went off and seeing that it was Taren paging, he left the room to speak with her.

When the captain entered his office to meet with Kalayna and Taren, he was in a rather cool, odd mood. He attempted to hide his deep frustration, but Taren could sense there was something wrong. 'Did things not go well with Swithin?'

'Things went very well,' he assured her with a smile. 'It just drives me to distraction trying to reason with someone so completely self-absorbed.'

Lucian took a seat behind his desk and looked at Kalayna, who gulped as she considered that her offence against this crew had also been rather selfish.

'What can I do for you?' he asked, looking from Kalayna, who appeared nervous, to Taren wearing a soft smile.

'Kalayna has a confession to make.'

'I have committed a crime,' Kalayna began, 'and I seek a punishment befitting my offence.'

Lucian nodded and gave her leave to give her statement.

Once Kalayna had recounted the events that had led to her misdemeanour, Lucian sat in quiet thought before he delivered his judgment.

'Until such time as we know Aurora's condition, we have no idea how serious the effects of your actions are. But should Aurora recover and not wish to press charges, then I would consider this case closed.'

Kalayna was not happy. 'But I could have killed her! I wished to do her *harm* —'

'If I had known what my late wife had been up to behind my back,' Lucian said, 'I dare say I would have killed her. Not because I am a violent man or a bad person, but because my shock and emotional derangement might have driven me to it.' Listening to himself, Lucian smiled grimly, for it seemed he did sympathise with his brother's motivation for ordering Amie's death after all.

'You are sympathising with me?' Kalayna was astonished. 'But Aurora is your personal assistant! Surely —'

'I'm not taking sides here,' Lucian said clearly. 'I am just saying that I understand your motivation, and that you were not entirely sane at the time you committed the offence. But in Aurora's defence you should know that, when she was unable to find you, she believed that you had reconsidered stowing away and remained on Frujia.'

'I would also like to bring another perspective to this if I may,' Taren said, and when Lucian gave her the nod, she looked at Kalayna. 'I am a pre-cog. Do you know what that is?'

Kalayna was wide-eyed at this news, but not fearful. 'You can see into the future and then change it.'

'We were all to be taken into the custody of the USS before we departed Frujia, you included,' Taren informed the astonished girl.

'But why would I have been arrested?'

'In that alternative reality they mistook you for me. During the ensuing interrogation you were accosted by a United Star Systems commander, and it was only when Zeven came to your assistance, to his own detriment, that you were not raped and promptly disposed of by the USS.'

'Really?' she squeaked, her spite choking her.

'It seems to me that what we have here is several misunderstandings and one huge case of very bad timing,' Lucian summarised.

'You see, we actually beseeched Aurora to, not so much seduce Zeven, as just boost his ego a little,' Taren said, without going into detail. 'I just think their past finally caught up with them and things got a little carried away.'

'But why ask her to do that?' Kalayna frowned — what kind of sick operation were they running here?

'That's classified information at present.' Lucian put the matter to rest. 'Perhaps once we know you better, you will be made aware of what we know, but for now you're just going to have to trust that we are on the up and up.'

Kalayna was still frowning, but she had a grin also. 'So what am I to do with myself, captain? Surely you must have some penance for me.'

Lucian thought about this. 'You're a tech, you said?'

'Ninth year,' Taren boasted on Kalayna's behalf.

Kalayna shook her head. 'Starman has already threatened to rip my hands off if I touch any of his craft.'

Lucian was taken aback to hear this, but thought it best to humour the pilot for now. She could be a spy for all they knew. 'Can you cook?'

Kalayna stuck her bottom lip out and nodded her head. 'Sure,' she said. 'Starman might starve, as I doubt he'll trust anything I've prepared.'

'His own cooking skills will drive him to your table, trust me,' Lucian chuckled. 'There will be washing and cleaning chores about the place that I expect you can take care of also.'

'I've got real good at all that stuff since I lost my apprenticeship,' Kalayna assured him.

Lucian was curious. 'With you only having a year to go before you qualified, I am very surprised pod-link did not keep you on.'

Kalayna grimaced. This was a sore point. 'I was the only female apprentice in the program. I wouldn't have been there had my dad not fought to get me in,' she explained. 'They'd been looking for an excuse to dismiss me from the start. Dad's death gave them the perfect opportunity, as none of the other male techs would take me on.'

Taren was infuriated to learn this, and folded her arms in silent protest.

'But Dad taught me a lot outside of work,' she continued. 'I've worked on all kinds of craft and I am licensed to fly. I was more qualified than any of the male techs. If you ask me, none of them had the guts to sit their final exam against me.'

'All good to know,' Lucian nodded with a sympathetic smile. 'Taren, would you mind showing Kalayna where the kitchen is and assign her some quarters.'

'Of course.' Taren was rather thankful to be given a mundane task.

'You'll also need to introduce her to Ringbalin. Our horticulturalist,' he explained for Kalayna's benefit.

'You have fresh produce?' Kalayna asked in amazement.

'And so much more,' Taren assured her. 'Follow me.'

It was on the way down to Module C that the news reached Taren and Kalayna that Aurora was out of surgery. The good news was that she was alive; the bad news was that she had drifted into a coma.

Kalayna did not take the news well. 'I have to see her. She has to know I didn't mean this, and that I'm not mad at her any more and ...' She burst into tears.

'It's okay.' Taren hugged her. 'We'll go now.' She swung them around to head back to the medical chambers.

Kassa was inside the recovery room adjusting the apparatus that was going to help keep Aurora alive. 'She's breathing on her own. Everything seems good. With any luck she'll come out of it of her own accord within a few days.'

Kalayna approached and, taking up Aurora's hand, she sat down beside her to whisper the words that she needed to say.

'Did Swithin do this to her?' Taren queried.

'Who else?' Kassa replied, having telepathically scanned her patient to learn the exact cause of injury. 'He struck her on the back of the head with a weapon, which knocked her out. She regained consciousness for a bit ...' Kassa paused as she recollected the conversation between Swithin Gervaise and Khalid Mansur that Aurora had overheard.

'And ...' Taren prompted.

'The swelling at the back of her head finally caused her to black out and fall into a coma.' Kassa decided not to disclose the private and somewhat explosive claims that Swithin and Mansur had made about Taren.

'Are you here to try and finish her off?' Zeven didn't like walking in to find Kalayna at Aurora's bedside.

'Careful, Zeven,' Taren piped up. 'It was not so long ago that it was you waiting for me to awake, so that you could apologise.'

The parallel took Zeven aback. 'That was an accident —'

'In the quantum world there are no accidents, only action and reaction,' Taren replied. 'But that didn't stop me forgiving you.'

'Aurora is fine, Zeven,' Kassa said to calm him. 'Now it's up to her ... she needs to want to come out of this. And I dare say hearing the two of you ripping shreds off each other will not inspire her to return.'

Zeven immediately backed off. 'I'll come back later.'

'No.' Kalayna stood and forced a grin as she passed him. 'That's okay. I was just leaving.'

'Promise?' Zeven asked, ever so nicely, but his stern expression did not change.

'At the first opportunity,' she assured as she left the room.

'Ask yourself, do I feel better now or worse?' Taren queried, and followed Kalayna out the door.

'I feel better, actually,' he scoffed.

'Liar.' Kassa retreated past him and closed the door on her way out.

Zeven looked at Aurora, knowing Kassa spoke the truth. 'I know it's my fault that she's here at all! If I'd just asked you out that night, you'd never have met and we'd be together, *no complications* ... shit!' He wanted to kick himself. 'Now I may have lost you in more ways than one.' He sat down at her side, and taking up her hand he rested it against his forehead. 'Just give me one more shot at this, Rory, and I promise you I won't ever let you forget that we are *meant* to be together. Please, wake up.' Tears flooded his eyes. 'I have.'

Kalayna had never felt so wretched. She was very thankful to have Taren to show her around, but she felt that her guide could not truly favour her as well as she appeared to.

Taren had assigned Kalayna quarters, near other of the crew, that were more spacious and luxurious than any accommodation she'd ever had in her young life. The canteen in the mess room, where she was to be basing herself, was better equipped than the gourmet restaurant in the five-star hotel she'd been working for on Frujia. Kalayna had nothing to complain about in her work conditions, nor did she have a problem with the crew she was to be serving. They had all been more than fair with her — even Starman, in her opinion.

The sting of it was that Kalayna was bitterly disappointed in herself — for the first time that she could remember, there was no one else that she could blame or be angry at for the hurt she felt inside. If she had only saved Aurora instead of seeking revenge, she would still be in her dream relationship and have scored a dream job to boot! Now, when she had finally found the ideal situation where she might eventually be able to fulfil her technical aspirations, she felt completely undeserving.

'I'm going to leave you in Ringbalin's very capable hands,' Taren advised as she moved to depart. 'If you need anything, just page me.'

'I'm good,' Kalayna assured her and forced a smile of appreciation before looking back to the botanist she'd just been introduced to.

He seemed a very pleasant, gentle fellow who had a rather effeminate quality about him which Kalayna found rather attractive and comfortable. She wondered if he might be gay.

'Let's start with the herb room, shall we?' Ringbalin suggested, leading off down a side path to a string of greenhouse rooms. These were near the labs and offices around the periphery of the huge circular garden area in the centre of the module.

Kalayna was already blown away by the set-up in Module C, but her eyes nearly popped out when she saw the fresh produce rooms. 'Whoa, RB, this is *so* impressive. There are fruits in here that I couldn't dream about affording to eat in my lifetime!'

Her admiration was pleasing to Ringbalin and the way she referred to him as RB amused him too. 'A fellow nature enthusiast, then.'

'Not really. I've always been better with machinery ... but,' she was quick to add when she saw his disappointment, 'I do *love* to eat.'

'Can you cook?' He raised his brow, curious.

'With this array of produce, I'm sure I'll manage,' she told him confidently, as she eyed the choices.

'Well then,' Ringbalin picked up a set of hand shears, 'let's go shopping.'

As Ringbalin gave her the guided tour of his pride and joy, helping her to collect a good range of foods with which to stock the kitchen, Kalayna's mood lightened considerably, and she found herself inspired by Ringbalin's advice and his insight into the natural world.

She just couldn't work him out — he seemed way too charming towards her to be gay, but way too sensitive not to be. For the first time in her life she was finding a man attractive, and as he walked her to the exit door to Module C, she just couldn't wipe the smile from her face.

'I can hardly wait to get started now, thanks, RB.'

'Come shopping any time,' he said, rubbing his hands together. 'I can hardly wait to have a decent meal.'

The exit doors opened and a tall, elegant woman entered the greenhouse. Kalayna's guess was that she was a Phemorian.

'Ah, Dr Portus.' Ringbalin made ready to introduce the woman to Kalayna, but the woman strode up to Ringbalin shaking her head.

'My love, you can call me Ayliscia now we've been intimate.' She bowed down, kissed Ringbalin passionately and then looked at Kalayna. 'Hello,' she smiled, not caring who Kalayna was so long as she got the message that Ringbalin was spoken for. The Phemorian then strode off through the greenhouse.

'Ah ... that was Dr Ayliscia Portus,' Ringbalin explained a little uncomfortably.

'Your lover,' Kalayna verified with a grin.

'Yes,' Ringbalin was proud to say as his eyes drifted after the woman.

'To seduce a Phemorian woman is said to be impossible,' Kalayna said. 'Definitely not gay then.'

'Who, me?' Ringbalin was startled. 'Ah, no. But it seems to be a common misconception. You are ... gay?'

Kalayna nodded. 'Yeah, I was.'

'Past tense?' Ringbalin queried, and Kalayna grinned as she backed up toward the exit doors.

They opened and Kalayna stepped into the corridor that led to the mess. 'Yeah ...' she told him finally. 'I have to admit that you've caused me a bit of confusion this day.' She looked thoughtful, not at all awkward about making this revelation.

Ringbalin chuckled, more embarrassed than she was. 'I take that as a very great compliment indeed.'

'*It is,*' she assured him, rather surprised herself, 'believe me!'

CHAPTER 19

BEST-KEPT SECRET

When Taren returned to Lucian's office he was standing by his large windows, gazing out at the twin suns in the distance.

'Our stowaway has been settled in and set to work,' Taren said as she approached to wrap her arms around the captain. Although he smiled to greet her, she could tell that his mind was elsewhere, and wherever that was it was very disturbing to him. 'What did Swithin say that has you so distracted?'

'It's nothing.' Lucian shook his head to dispel his melancholy. 'But we need to get Kassa up here, to aid with deprogramming your code name ... once that is done, I'll feel a whole lot better.' He kissed Taren's forehead and reaching for his communicator he paged for Kassa to come his office.

'I don't believe for a moment that that is all that has you worried,' Taren told him with a smile, hoping she might seduce the truth out of him.

'You're right.' He held up both hands in his own defence and backed up to take a seat. 'I have a list of things to worry about that's a star-field long!'

Taren slid to a seat upon his desktop, facing him. 'So share the burden.'

Kassa knocked on the wall outside the open office

door to announce her arrival and then entered at Lucian's request.

For what Taren imagined to be the last time, she was hypnotised and advised that she would no longer respond to the code name 'Sci-chick Puppet', and upon being snapped out of her trance she felt liberated. 'Thanks so much, Kassa. I feel lightened of a great load.'

'You're welcome.' Kassa forced a smile in return.

Taren's eyes darted from the doctor to Lucian, who was still frowning. 'What is amiss with you two? Are you keeping something from me?'

The captain and Kassa looked genuinely stunned as they glanced at each other and shook their heads in denial.

'So you each have separate concerns regarding me,' Taren concluded, and her instincts proved right on the mark as usual.

'I do have something to tell you,' Kassa confirmed. 'It's very personal and as far as I know, Lucian has no knowledge of the intelligence I have obtained.'

'Shall I leave?' Lucian offered.

'No,' Taren insisted. 'If I have any secrets you have a perfect right to know.'

Lucian was pleasantly surprised by her resolve.

'Go on,' Taren said to Kassa.

'Could you close the door,' Kassa asked Lucian, which intrigued the captain and Taren all the more. 'What I have to say, if true, has to be one of the best-kept secrets in the USS ... so it might pay to be a little cautious.'

Lucian closed and locked the door from the controls at his desk. 'What have you discovered?'

'What I know, I perceived from Aurora when I was scanning her memory for the cause of her injury.' Kassa turned her full attention to Taren. 'I told you that Aurora awoke for a time whilst in the custody of her captors,' she prompted and Taren nodded.

'Yes, what of it?'

'Aurora overheard a conversation between Swithin and Khalid Mansur —'

'Anselm's viceroy?' Lucian said in disbelief. Kassa confirmed it and he boggled at his brother's high political connections.

'During that conversation Swithin claimed to have a tracking device on board this ship —' Kassa gasped, realising she'd forgotten that piece of information up until now.

Lucian was on his feet. 'I'll get Leal and Zeven on it right away,' but Kassa forestalled him.

'Wait, that's not the important part. What's important is why they are tracking us.' Kassa regained the captain's fullest attention. 'They are tracking us because Anselm's daughter is on board this vessel.'

'What?' Lucian freaked, thinking it must have been their stowaway.

'I didn't know the president had a daughter!' Taren added.

'No one knows,' Kassa stressed. '*That's* the secret.'

'And you think they mean Kalayna?' Lucian voiced his assumption.

'I don't think so,' Kassa's knowledge made her grin, despite everything. 'Swithin implied that the woman in question was your lover.'

All eyes turned Taren's way and she caught her breath at the shock of the news. Taren's mind rushed back to her impressions of Anselm during her perception of that alternative future. *I am the keeper of her memories*, he had claimed regarding Taren. 'Could this be why he was seeking me so desperately?' she said, bewildered that she could be the daughter of the most powerful man alive.

'Taren, you must be horrified.' Lucian approached to see if he could be of comfort. 'And Anselm wanted to frame you for my wife's murder!'

Her heart remained steady. 'It was just a means to an end ...' Taren recalled Anselm saying so and now she understood what he'd meant. 'If he is my father, I know for a fact that he is in league with the MSS and every secret service in the USS. Therefore he's known where I was all this time,' she said angrily, and stepped away from Lucian so as not to take it out on him. 'He probably even had me recruited into the secret servics! Damn it!' She became frustrated by the huge blanks in her memory. 'What does it matter anyway? Anyone could claim anything about my past and I cannot confirm it.' She burst into tears, overwhelmed by her deepest, darkest fears, but her hatred soon enabled her to regain control. 'As far as I am concerned, *I have no parents*. They both died the day my memory was taken from me.' Taren's sights turned to Lucian. 'Did you know any of this?'

'No,' he assured her. 'I truly thought Kassa was referring to Kalayna.'

Taren calmed a little, although anger and confusion still held her in their clutch. 'So what is it that you are keeping from me? Surely your concern cannot be any more shocking to me than what I have just heard.'

'I should go,' Kassa decided, having said her piece. 'I hope I was not wrong to tell you.'

'No, of course not. You are a true friend,' Taren assured her, giving Kassa a hug. 'Thank you for being discreet.'

'I owe you big-time in that regard,' Kassa replied with a smile, and took her leave.

'Please tell Leal and Zeven I need their assistance,' Lucian said as he let Kassa out, and then closed and locked his office door once again. 'I believe part of my concern may have just been answered for me,' he said, finally replying to Taren's query.

'How do you mean?' Taren, still shell-shocked, frowned, not following.

'Swithin claims you have another, more highly classified MSS code name,' he divulged. 'I pressed Swithin about who might know this other code name and he swore he didn't know, which infuriated me. But thanks to Kassa, and Rory's bit of detective work, I believe we now have a very good candidate.'

'Anselm.' Taren's eyes narrowed as she uttered his name with spite. Now she had twice as many reasons to seek the man out.

Lucian was on a mission as he stormed up the corridor toward the lab where his brother was quarantined. The news of a tracking device on board AMIE was alarming, but he hoped to turn the betrayal to their advantage. 'Are we all clear on how to play this?' The captain paused outside the lab to query Leal and Zeven who were trailing him. 'Don't give anything away,' he cautioned.

Leal and Zeven nodded in accord as they all burst into the lab.

'Hey, boys, what's happening?' Swithin noted their irritation as they stormed straight through the observation room and into the security passage that led to his containment area. 'All right ... what have I done now?'

The final security door opened and Zeven came rushing through to hit Swithin on the jaw so hard that his target was spun around to land face-first on the ground. 'Where's the tracking device?'

Leal hoisted Swithin up and turned him around to face Zeven and the captain — so they could question Swithin and hold his focus.

As Swithin spat blood and regained his composure, Zeven decided he was taking too long and belted his ex-employer in the gut. 'The tracking device.' Zeven raised Swithin's bowed head to make him focus. 'Where is it?'

'Give me a fucking chance to answer.' Swithin spat out a tooth and a lot more blood.

'Well ...' Lucian demanded, motioning for Zeven to back off. 'Where is it?'

Swithin smiled a defiant smile. 'I don't remember.'

Zeven looked at Leal who gave a nod. Zeven lined Swithin's face up to take a final punch. '*This* is for Rory.' He punched Swithin with his full force and the blow knocked the consciousness right out of him.

Leal allowed the traitor to drop to the floor.

'Let's go.' Lucian led the way out of the lab, and when they returned to the corridor, he turned to Leal. 'Did you get it?'

Leal grinned. 'I know exactly where it is.' He led off toward the elevators, for the device had been planted inside one of the smaller submersibles in the Marine Module.

Once the offending item was in their possession, the men headed back up to the hangar and launch bay area. Lucian was of a mind to launch the tracking device in a pod, in the opposite direction to their destination. He hoped this would throw the USS carrier vessel that was somewhere in the vicinity off their scent.

'We'll have to shut most of the ship down for a few days and only run the essential life-support systems,' Lucian said. 'With any luck, the USS will continue to pursue their device and miss us altogether.'

'If we are not already on their scopes.' Zeven chewed his lip, not wanting to be the pessimist, but this was a big ship.

'If we are, you'll just have to quantum-jump us somewhere else,' Leal suggested.

'Better hope this works then, as I sure don't want to find out if I can pull that off *without* Aurora's sweet inspiration.' Zeven gave AMIE clearance to launch the pod.

As Kalayna cooked up a storm in the kitchen, her mind kept drifting back to the botanist. He'd made her feel so much better. Besides her father, and more recently the captain, no man had ever attempted to make her feel good about herself. They seemed a rare breed of men on this vessel.

Kalayna thought back to what Taren had said: that in another future, Zeven had saved her from being sexually assaulted. It would not have been the first time that a man had tried to force himself upon her, but in the past there had not been anyone to come to her rescue, nor had she dreamt that there ever would be. Still, it wasn't hard to imagine Starman playing the hero, and as the little flight of fantasy played out in her mind Kalayna found herself smiling and her heavy heart lightened for the duration.

'So, you must be our stowaway?'

Kalayna turned to find a tall, lean fellow heading for the cool room. 'I'm Leal Polson, co-pilot-slash-navigator.' He sidetracked from his path to shake her hand, but as both Kalayna's hands were covered in pastry, he simply raised an open palm in greeting.

'Sorry,' she apologised, 'but I am very pleased to meet you. Navigator, *wow*.' Kalayna was impressed. 'Nice career move.'

'A little birdie told me that you're a ninth-year systems tech.' He whistled, impressed also.

Kalayna laughed. 'Did the same little birdie tell you that I'm forbidden to practise any of said craft whilst on board this vessel?'

'I did get that impression, yes,' Leal granted, ducking into the cool room and emerging with a piece of fruit. 'I wouldn't worry too much ... the little birdie will change its tune when something shorts out and he finds himself unable to fly.'

Kalayna couldn't help but smile, but she was not so optimistic. 'He'd rather crash and burn than ask me for help.'

'Well, be that as it may,' Leal said airily, '*I* can ask you for help, and I am.'

Kalayna gasped with excitement and, thinking that she'd heard him wrong she met his eyes and surmised that he seemed deadly serious.

'Ever done any spacewalking?' he asked with a grimace.

'*No way!*' She couldn't believe what she was hearing, as it was very appealing to her sense of adventure. 'Are you serious? I thought you hadn't sustained any major damage during the escape.'

'The damage isn't major,' he replied, glad to see her enthusiasm. 'When we got blasted leaving Frujia the wiring on the exterior launch bay door was damaged, and until it's fixed we can't use any of our larger craft.'

'Starman wouldn't be happy about that,' Kalayna mused, thinking this could go some way toward getting back into his good books.

'I figure we'll just tell him *after* you fix it,' Leal explained. 'How about after the breakfast shift tomorrow?'

'Are you kidding?' Kalayna couldn't believe he even had to ask. '*That's completely wicked* ... I'll be all over it.'

'That's good, right?' Leal wasn't up on the current adolescent lingo.

'*Very good*,' she assured him.

'See you at dinner.' He waved and left Kalayna high as a kite.

'Another nice guy,' she muttered to herself. 'Do they have a secret breeding program here *or what?*'

No wonder Aurora had chosen to become an outlaw rather than lose her place on this crew — they were all so interesting, professional and caring. Kalayna, wanting to earn her place among them, continued to work feverishly, determined to make her first meal for the crew of AMIE one that would not fail to impress.

At the appropriate time, Kalayna advised everyone via the ship's intercom system that dinner would be served in the cafeteria in ten minutes' time.

The crew dragged their weary bodies down to the mess — having had no sleep for over twenty-four hours most of them had only stayed awake in order to have a decent meal before they finally got some shut-eye.

The wafting, delicious smell of fresh-cooked pie and vegetables engulfed Taren's senses as she approached the mess hall alongside Lucian. Her stomach rumbled, reminding her of how desperate she was to consume something that wasn't out of a packet. When she laid eyes on the dinner table, Taren was almost moved to tears.

Several of the tables in the cafeteria had been pulled together to form one long table. As they were in minimal-power-usage mode, Kalayna had turned all the lights off, bar a small light in the kitchen itself, and the dinner table was candlelit.

'Very nice,' Lucian commented as they entered, greatly approving of the set-up. 'This will be the first time in the history of the project that all the crew have gathered for a meal at the same time.'

Now that there were so few crew, and only one cook on board, it was much more practical to have one set mealtime and not eat in shifts.

'I like the idea of us all eating at the same table,' he said to Kalayna, who was standing by with a decanter of wine.

'More like family ... yes,' Kalayna commented, motioning Lucian to the spot at the head of the table.

'Indeed,' Lucian quietly confirmed, 'and we haven't felt that sentiment on board for quite some time.'

'Smells like our little stowaway has outdone herself,' Leal commented as he walked in with Kassa on his arm. Ringbalin and Ayliscia were right behind them, and they all expressed their delight and thanks as they were seated by Kalayna.

'Should I wait for Starman?' Kalayna consulted the captain, for she suspected the pilot would not be coming.

'First in, best fed, I always say.' Lucian was too hungry to wait, and Kalayna was happy to comply and moved to serve the food to them all.

With wineglasses filled, and people beginning to tuck in, Kalayna requested the captain's permission to make a toast.

'Permission granted,' he allowed, much happier for having a few mouthfuls of pie in his belly.

Kalayna rose, with glass in hand, to say her piece.

If he wasn't *so* hungry — *if he'd only learned to cook* — Zeven would not be heading to the mess hall, against his will and instinct. He really didn't want to see Kalayna, much less eat anything she'd cooked. On the other hand, even a deadly poison would be welcome in his gut at present, as he just couldn't bring himself to eat one more cheesy puff.

He slowed as the smell of real food reached him out in the corridor. That's when he heard Kalayna's voice and stopped short of the door to hear what she was saying.

'To the captain and crew of AMIE, who are the most *gracious*, *generous* and *forgiving* bunch of people that I have ever had the curse of disappointing.' She caught her breath, and some on the crew tried to dispute her impression, but she spoke up to silence them. 'I really haven't had too many second chances in my lifetime, and even though I know I am *so very* undeserving, I am also *infinitely* grateful for the opportunity you are giving me to make amends.'

'Cheers to that,' the captain concurred, and the crew clinked glasses.

Kalayna's words seemed so heartfelt that Zeven felt a lump form in his throat. Yet a thought for Aurora's sad state of affairs made his resolve harden once more. *She's a vixen ... leading us all down the garden path with her sincere sweetness.* He swallowed hard to banish his sympathy and hold onto his prejudice.

Zeven walked into the room and noted a spare place set for him with food already on the plate. He headed straight there, picked up the plate of food and moved to leave.

'Zeven,' the captain called, 'will you not eat with us?'

He looked around the table, at all his dear friends. 'Aurora should be here.' His voice went hoarse and he cleared his throat, to get the rest out. 'I'm going to eat with her.'

Nobody argued.

The pilot backed up a few paces and looked at Kalayna's expression of utter devastation. 'Nice speech.' He left them to their feast.

He got halfway up the corridor before Taren was at his heels. 'Zeven,' she called and he stopped to allow her to speak.

'Hatred and fear will make you sick —' Taren wasn't given the chance to finish.

'— and trust and kindness will get you killed!' he spat back and moved off, but Taren threw herself in front of him.

'What's more important is that *your* hatred in particular has the capacity to injure others *very* badly, without you even realising it!' Taren said firmly. 'Before you kill this girl out of spite, bear in mind that we have two telepaths on this vessel, neither of whom have detected any secret agenda about her.'

That was a good point, Zeven conceded ... and yet? 'Nobody detected a secret agenda about you either.'

'Which only proves that we all deserve a second chance. I got one, and you did too —'

'Taren ...' Zeven spoke up over her. 'You aim to see the best in people, and if I expect the worst that just makes for a nice balanced perspective, don't you think?'

Taren shook her head. He still didn't get it. 'I need you to understand the extent of your own Power.' She paused to think about how she was going to get through to him, and had a revelation. 'Meet me in Module C tomorrow after breakfast.'

Zeven rolled his eyes. He just wasn't ready to give his anger up. 'If I must.'

'You asked me to train you ...' He nodded in submission. 'And *this is important*,' Taren told him in a deadly serious fashion. 'In the meantime, I want you to put Kalayna completely out of your mind.'

'That won't be easy. Every time I look at Rory —'

'— you should find a happy place,' Taren advised. 'Think about the good times you've had and will have again. That is the most constructive thing you can do for her. Dwell on the negative and she'll just go on sleeping. As I keep telling you, intention has great power.' Taren backed up towards the cafeteria. 'I'll see you tomorrow morning.'

'Can hardly wait.' He forced a smile and resumed his course to Aurora's recovery room. 'Find a happy place,' he grumbled, 'and how in the universe does she expect me to do that?' What did he have to be happy about exactly? His career was in tatters, he was wanted by the USS, and if anyone found out about his Powers he'd be a complete social outcast. He felt like he could cope with all that, if only Aurora was still around adding sunshine to his life.

'That's it!' Zeven figured out how he could comply with Taren's request. Every time he got mad about Aurora's situation, he would just imagine how his world would be right now if Aurora's abduction had not happened and Kalayna had stayed on Frujia.

Zeven entered Aurora's recovery room. Seeing her motionless form, he suppressed his urge to direct anger at Kalayna, and instead imagined eating dinner with Aurora. 'In my quarters, perhaps,' he said, speaking his fantasy out loud, 'where we could be alone and be ourselves …' Zeven smiled with delight at the notion. His imagination was on a roll.

The set-up was a very simple form of an experiment that Taren had carried out many times. Usually the effects of the experiment took a few weeks to become obvious, but as Zeven's psychic skill was so advanced, she believed the results would be instantly noticeable.

Ringbalin had donated the three plants they planned to use as test subjects and each had been placed in a separate lab apart from one another. Alongside each of the plants was a vial of fresh spring water. The labs had large windows in the dividing walls, through which you could see all the labs from inside any one of them.

Zeven had undergone his first meditation session with Ringbalin that morning and so was calm, relaxed and focused.

The pilot was led into the first lab where he observed the plant, a healthy specimen whose flowers were yet to bloom. Ringbalin then invited Zeven to look at the vial of spring water that sat alongside this plant. It looked just like normal water.

'What's the water for?' Zeven queried.

The botanist poured half the contents on the plant. 'You will note there is no noticeable reaction in the plant after being watered,' he said to Zeven, who nodded in agreement. 'This represents the normal state of reality before you become wilfully involved,' Ringbalin explained.

As Zeven seemed to be in a good mood, Taren decided to start with the positive test first. She requested that Zeven focus all the loving energy he could muster on the plant in the second test room for just one minute.

Zeven found this easy. He just thought about Rory and the force of his loving intention caused the plant to instantaneously burst into bloom, which stunned him beyond belief. 'Did I do that?'

'You certainly did,' Ringbalin confirmed, 'and check this out.' He poured half the water in the vial onto the plant and its colour vibrancy intensified threefold.

'Whoa!' Zeven had to rub his eyes, thinking he might be seeing things. 'The colour is even more vibrant.'

Taren nodded. 'Such can be the state of matter when you become involved with a positive intent.' With a finger she beckoned him to follow her into the third lab.

Zeven didn't have to be a genius to work out what the third part of the test was. 'You want me to try and kill this one, don't you?'

Taren nodded. 'But I need you to do that *without* using Kalayna as inspiration.'

Zeven let out a long, heavy exhalation. 'I'll do my best.'

'Lives depend on you being able to master your focus,' Taren cautioned him. 'You asked me to help train you, but your base desires will never aid you to be constructive. It is therefore imperative that you learn to put them aside, or better still, release them altogether.'

Zeven nodded more decisively, so Taren hit the release on the stopwatch.

'Go.'

Zeven looked at his victim. *Die, you little weed*, he thought, finding it incredibly hard to feel angry without Kalayna slipping into his thoughts. *I hate and despise your very existence. You make me sick!* At the same time, he instructed himself to focus only on the words, on the objective, and not to let anything from his own life enter into it.

The plant began to wilt and die; the water in the vial became murky and began to turn brown.

'Stop!' Taren and Ringbalin chimed together.

Zeven had been so focused on not screwing up that his conscious mind hadn't even noted what he'd done to the plant. 'Well, bugger me,' Zeven commented as he viewed the devastation that one minute of his hate-focused intention could do.

Ringbalin poured half the putrid water onto the wilted plant and it burned through the remains like acid. 'Would you like to try a few drops on your skin?' he asked the pilot.

'No, thanks, I get the picture.'

'Do you?' Taren turned him about to view the plants in the previous two labs. The perfectly healthy specimens had also wilted. 'The human body is ninety per cent water.' She wondered if he was able to take this in yet.

'Holy smoke!' Zeven panicked, as did Ringbalin, who scurried out into the main greenhouse to find that everything in Module C had suffered.

'Damn, Zeven. Your hatred is intense! I would never have held the experiment here had I known the result would be so catastrophic.'

When Zeven saw the damage even he wanted to cry. 'I'm so sorry, Ringbalin. I feel terrible.'

'Ah,' the botanist said, as he held up a finger, 'that is a point worth noting.'

'I can fix it,' Zeven vowed.

'I know ...' Ringbalin gave a weak smile of faith.

'So, you also see that it is not just the target of your bad intention who suffers,' Taren added to get the message across.

Zeven backed up, feeling overwhelmed. 'We need to get Kalayna away from here. I'm going to kill her and everyone!'

'Or you can choose to send her your love and heal her —' Taren began, but Zeven shook his head. He believed it was beyond his capability right now.

'Zeven, you can't do both!' Taren reasoned. 'You cannot hate and love at the same time and expect to be in control. Either you love unconditionally and choose not to judge people, knowing that those who are truly evil cause exactly this sort of devastation within themselves. Or, you choose to become one of those people who perpetuate evil, so that your hate inflicts this kind of damage on others ... at the same time damaging yourself. I've shown you the evidence and now the choice is yours.' Taren threw her hands up. 'Here ends the lesson.'

After his eye-opening experience in the lab Zeven was feeling very numb. It was as if his emotions could not decide which path to take, and thus had settled in a place of complete indifference. Ringbalin's magic touch had helped Zeven to regain a positive and loving perspective, long enough for them to move through the greenhouse and right the damage his bad intentions had caused in Module C.

Now the pilot was almost afraid to engage any emotion for fear of what it might do. He had work to do in any case — if he felt nothing, maybe he could focus and not cause any damage?

On the way past the cafeteria, Zeven spied the captain and Leal reading through some printouts over lunch. Kalayna was nowhere to be seen, so the pilot decided it was safe to speak with them. 'Are those the schematic readouts for the launch bay I asked for?'

'The very ones,' Leal confirmed, and Zeven took a seat to look them over. 'But you don't have to get a headache trying to read them, as the launch bay doors were fixed this morning.'

'Sure they were,' he laughed. 'You couldn't possibly have done the job on your own.' Zeven realised what Leal was implying and his mood darkened. 'You let Kalayna work on my ship.'

'Actually, Zeven, I believe AMIE is technically my ship,' Lucian corrected him. 'Kalayna was the only one qualified to do the job.'

'But she's not qualified!' the pilot argued.

'Then why is the launch bay door now working?' Lucian asked and Zeven lost the argument.

'She did an excellent job,' Leal reported, 'and knew exactly what she was doing. The spacewalk made her a little woozy, but then it scared the shit out of me the first time I had to —'

'Kalayna got sick?' Zeven was a little disturbed by the news. 'How long ago?'

'About an hour,' Leal replied, confused by Zeven's sudden concern.

Zeven stood and stepped away from the table, rather mortified by the news. 'No,' he protested, quite resolutely. 'I don't want to be responsible for this. You think I would have learned after what I went through with Taren —'

'You're not responsible. We sent her out there.' Lucian didn't understand the pilot's rambling.

Leal was confused too, and concentrated to assess his crewmate's state of mind. 'Kalayna will be fine —'

'You are absolutely right about that,' Zeven stated, all fired up, and made a hasty exit.

Lucian looked at Leal in the wake of the confrontation. 'Do you think I should be worried about that lad? He seems a little ... confused.'

'On the contrary, captain.' Leal grinned and raised his eyebrows. 'I do believe our young friend just had an epiphany.'

Zeven buzzed at Kalayna's door, but when there came no answer and he found the door was not locked, he entered.

The main apartment was in darkness, the only light coming from the bathroom. 'Kalayna?' He turned on the lights, and seeing her nowhere in sight, he made quickly for the illuminated room.

The young woman was in her underwear on the bathroom floor, lying unconscious in a pool of vomit. Her skin tone was looking decidedly yellow, all too reflective of the water he'd contaminated only an hour before.

'Kalayna,' he cried, scooping her up and shaking her. She coughed up more bile and skimmed the edge of consciousness. 'Zeven ...' she mumbled, surprised to see him. 'Help me.' Her head rolled to one side and she passed out again.

'No. Stay awake,' he urged, already dragging her to the shower tube. 'I'm so sorry ...' He turned on the cold water and, holding her up, he launched them both into the freezing stream.

'Ah!' Kalayna awoke with a start, and attempted to pull back from the ice water. She nearly escaped him, but he gripped her tightly.

'It's okay.' Zeven triggered the hot water flow to stop her shivering, and she relaxed into his embrace. 'Shhh.'

'I feel like I'm dying,' she moaned. 'Please, take me to the doctor.'

'No,' he assured her calmly, 'a doctor won't help.'

She choked, unsure of his intentions. Perhaps he wanted to see her dead?

'I caused your disease and I can cure it,' he claimed. 'If you can trust me?'

Kalayna managed a nod and Zeven pulled her near-naked form close to him once more and held her as tenderly as he might his dearest love. 'I am so sorry I made you feel bad,' he whispered to her through the water pouring down upon their heads and he noticed her body tremble. Was it fear, repulsion? Regardless, he conjured all the love Aurora had recently inspired in him and poured it into Kalayna. 'You are beautiful, talented, intelligent and as deserving of love and trust as any.'

Kalayna stopped shaking and started crying, whereupon she began to hug him back.

'I had no right to judge you in the first place,' Zeven added. 'I want you to thrive, prosper and be happy. I forgive you, Kalayna ... please, forgive me.'

When she looked up at him, her skin tone had returned to normal. In fact, she looked positively radiant. 'There is nothing to forgive you for,' she said, smiling broadly through her tears. 'I don't understand how you did this.' She stood firmly on her own two feet. 'I suddenly feel rather ... amazing!'

She laughed nervously at the miracle and gazed up into Zeven's eyes, her breasts heaving with elation as excitement and joy coursed through her being.

There was a sudden pang of desire in his heart that was both exhilarating and disconcerting. 'I should go.' Zeven steadied Kalayna and stepped out of the shower. He really did try not to notice that the water had rendered her underwear see-through, nor how it clung to her tanned, athletic form.

'You saved my life,' she said, as the realisation only just hit home. 'How did you do that, Starman?'

'You don't want to know.' Zeven flatly refused to comment.

'Yes, I do,' she replied most sincerely, and they were held spellbound in each other's gaze for a moment.

'Sorry,' Zeven blurted out. The attraction was intense and confusing. 'Are you going to be okay?' He noticed a towel on the wall, and without looking back passed it to her. 'Do you want me to call Kassa?'

'I can do it.' Kalayna accepted the towel, sounding awkward as she had only that second realised her near naked state.

'Be sure that you do.' He headed for the door, needing to put some distance between them. 'I'll check up on you later.'

'Starman ...' She wanted to say so many things to him, but with such heightened emotions running rampant through her being, she was lucky to string two words together. 'Thank you.'

The feeling in her voice thrummed on his heartstrings, just as it had last night during her toast. 'Just restoring the balance,' he replied.

'It felt to me that you just gave back far more than you ever took.'

Zeven wasn't looking at her. He didn't have to. The image of her all wet, trembling and smiling at him in adoration, was now burned into his memory. He felt it would be dangerous to loiter a second longer and hastened to leave the apartment.

In the corridor, he gave a gigantic gasp of relief. It horrified him to now realise that he still found Kalayna as attractive as when he'd first seen her sitting at that bar. It was easier when he'd disliked her; the attraction could be ignored. And yet, Aurora made him feel better than any other woman ever had, so how could he find himself attracted to another?

It seemed the path of love was just as precarious as the path of hatred.

Zeven wiped all the water from his face and wanted to shout with frustration, but bearing in mind what Ringbalin had taught him only this morning, he took three deep breaths and managed to maintain his composure. 'Damned if I'm negative, double-damned if I'm not. I'm completely *screwed*,' he summarised.

CHAPTER 20

FEM-LIBERTINE

It was concluded that the pod diversion had worked, when in the space-time equivalent of a week AMIE found herself approaching the outer moons of Phemoria without having experienced any USS interference.

Aurora had yet to stir from her coma, but, unfortunately, Swithin had regained consciousness in the wake of his interrogation and was now being housed and sedated in a separate recovery room. Whilst he was in Kassa's care, she took the liberty of quietly probing Swithin's mind, and she was able to confirm that, as far as Swithin was aware, Anselm was indeed Taren's father. It was also true that Swithin did not have the top-level security clearance that was required to have the knowledge of Taren's secret code name within the secret services — but Anselm certainly did. Lucian had decided not to set his brother adrift in space, but in light of Swithin's dislike of the Phemorians and his Sermetic sympathies Lucian had decided to hand Swithin over to the authorities on Phemoria for judgment.

The captain and Taren had been locked away for days thrashing out a proposal for the Phemorians in the hope they would supply the funds and support needed for AMIE's deep-space research to continue. Their time together had not been all work — Lucian and Taren were falling in love and had been making plans for their future life together. They did not envisage an extended stay on Phemoria, but hoped to gain political asylum and patronage swiftly.

Their greatest wish was to return to space exploration as soon as possible so that they might seek the answers to Maladaan's fate. Taren hoped to secure an audience with the guild of mystical women known as the Phemoray whilst on Phemoria, which would be a first for anyone as far as she knew.

Most people maintained that the guild was just a myth promulgated by the Phemorians to incite fear in their enemies, but from the way Dr Portus spoke of the Phemoray they were still very much in existence. They were said to take physical form rarely, as they were a celestial breed in the main. That being the case, Taren imagined they might be able to tell her more about the entity she knew as Azazèl-mindos-coomra-dorchi.

Module C had made a full recovery and Ringbalin had been doing guided meditation with Zeven every morning for a week. The pilot gave his total focus over to Ringbalin during the sessions and found the meditations to be a welcome distraction from his otherwise confused and tortured thoughts regarding Kalayna and Aurora.

The pilot had still to eat a meal with the rest of the crew; he used the excuse of spending time with Rory to retreat from the gathering every evening. Despite his vigilance in avoiding the cause of his discontent, with every day that passed — and that Aurora remained asleep — his lustful thoughts about Kalayna intensified. Every evening he poured all the loving energy he could muster into willing Aurora to recover and wakeup, but still her condition did not change.

What if she never woke up? That question had been plaguing him all week. What if he continued to ignore his feelings for Kalayna, waiting for a lover who would never wake up?

Zeven shook off his fear and attempted to block both women out of his mind. AMIE was approaching Phemoria and he needed to service and fuel the smaller craft in the hangar bay in case they were required.

When the pilot walked into the hangar bay to find Kalayna up a ladder with her head in the back end of the recon vessel he'd taken to rescue Aurora, he didn't know how to react. His instincts told him to turn around and leave quietly, but his mind wished to object to Kalayna being so presumptuous. 'Hey! Just because I made peace with you does not automatically give you the right to start mucking about with my stuff.'

'Sorry. Were you planning on replacing and rewiring your entire propulsion system?' she inquired sweetly.

'No,' Zeven replied, perplexed. 'Why would I want to do that?'

Kalayna's jaw dropped in disbelief. 'What ... you didn't notice when you landed this vessel that the propulsion system is completely *burnt out*?'

'How could that have happened?' Zeven climbed the ladder to stand beside her and take a closer look. 'Holy shit,' he cursed, as the damage was plain to see.

'The only time I've seen this kind of damage to a craft was when a pilot forgot to shut off his system when caught in a tracker beam,' Kalayna said. 'I don't understand how you could have failed to notice the lack of acceleration before you landed.'

Zeven could give no explanation, as he'd used PK to return the vessel to AMIE, and he wasn't about to tell Kalayna that. 'Can you fix it?'

Kalayna gave a sigh. 'It will take a few days, but far as I can tell all the parts I need are in the hold. Although I may need a hand to move some of them.'

'I'll help,' Zeven volunteered with a grin. Sensing a pleasant sentiment forming between them, he retreated down the ladder.

'Okay!' Kalayna jumped to the ground and returned his grin. 'Let's get started.' She bounced off towards parts and storage.

The grin fell from Zeven's face ... after doing his best to avoid the girl, he'd just agreed to work closely with her for several days. *Idiot!* But what choice did he have? He needed this fixed and he certainly wasn't so technically savvy as to imagine he could do the job himself. Grease and fuel, sure, but high-level mechanics he'd always left to the experts.

'Come on.' Kalayna waved to him, her smile beaming.

Clearly she was pleased that they seemed to be getting along and they now had a common goal to work towards. Zeven took a deep breath to suppress his doubts about working in close quarters with her and pursued Kalayna into the hold.

By the time Kalayna had to depart to fix dinner for the crew, they had just about gutted the dead propulsion system, and Zeven worked on in her absence — as far as deconstruction went, he was perfectly qualified.

Kalayna returned, bearing dinner for them both, which they sat about and ate whilst they discussed the initial steps of the reconstruction. This was the first night that Zeven had missed dinner with Aurora; not that he really noticed, as he was learning a great deal. Kalayna's personality was very bloke-like — they'd been working away together all day without any hint of the situation getting emotionally out of control. In fact, Zeven hadn't enjoyed himself so much — when he wasn't having sex — in ages!

After another six hours of hard labour, their enthusiasm for the job began to lessen. They started dropping things and bursting into fits of laughter for no good reason.

'We gotta pack it in for the day, Starman ... before I start welding the wrong wires together.' She wiped tears of exhausted laughter from her eyes, so that she could see what she was doing.

'Good call,' Zeven said, taking the welder out of her hand before she hurt herself.

She took the hint. 'I'll pick it up in the morning,' she said, shoving one hand deep into her filthy overalls and wandering toward the exit doors. She spun about and gave him a wave with her free hand. 'Catch you then?'

'Yeah,' he replied, smiling and wiping his hands on a rag. 'I'll be here.'

'Cool. I'm beginning to see what Aurora saw in you ... you're pretty cool for a guy.'

Zeven's heart shot into his throat, as he was cast into panic. He didn't want to encourage her affection, but he didn't want to hurt her either. 'Thanks. You're pretty cool for ...'

'... a queer?'

Zeven shook his head to assure her that that was not what he was going to say. '... for someone who is trying to steal my girl.'

'Technically she wasn't yours at the time,' she reminded him, regaining her humour. 'And if I'm not mistaken, when we met that night at the bar you were trying to hit on me ...'

She had him there and it made him really uncomfortable. 'What do you want ... an apology? Why bring that up?'

'You're right, that was uncalled for,' Kalayna said, coming nearer to explain. 'What I was really seeking to know was ... do you still find me attractive, Starman?'

Now Zeven was even more annoyed. 'Don't tease me, Kalayna —'

'I'm not teasing you,' she confessed as her eyes filled with tears. 'I've never felt this way about a man before and I don't know what to do about it.'

'Claiming to feel as you do about Aurora, how can you ask me about us?' Zeven made it sound as if he was surprised at her, but in truth he'd been wondering if she harboured any secret feelings for him.

'I know it makes me sound fickle and shallow, but when you're around me, I feel like ... there's electricity between us,' she blurted out, leaving herself wide open to rejection. 'Tell me you don't feel it and I'll just drop the subject and never bring it up again.'

'I think that is exactly what you should do,' Zeven told her. She looked a little shattered and he felt like a coward when she'd been brave enough to put herself on the line. 'Yes, I find you attractive. What man wouldn't ...'

Her spirits soared with his confession.

'... but I could not bring myself to betray Aurora in such a fashion.' He stepped further away from her, and the look on her face was one of complete empathy. 'I would only prove you right about me, and I'm not that kind of guy any more. I'm sorry, Kalayna, but it seems I have found my conscience.'

Kalayna nodded and forced a grin. 'I wonder if *I* have one sometimes. I wish I hadn't brought it up at all. We've just started getting along and now it's going to be ... weird.'

'Nah. We'll get over it.' And just to prove how wrong she was, he gave her a chummy hug. What he wouldn't admit, not even to himself, was how good it felt to feel her in his arms. The electric connection Kalayna had spoken of was clear to him and had been ever since he'd healed her. 'We make a good team.' He let her go knowing he'd already savoured the embrace way too long.

'We surely do.' She sniffled back her emotion and smiled her genuine smile. 'See you in the morning then.'

He waited for the doors to close behind her before he covered his face with his hands and fell to his knees. 'You numbskull!' He wasn't sure if he was cursing himself because Kalayna now knew how he felt about her, or because he'd let such a lush opportunity slip through his fingers! 'Damn it, Aurora, *wake up*,' he muttered under his breath. He needed a little reassurance that he was being a saint for good reason.

On the way down to his quarters, he got the page from Kassa he'd been waiting for, and so quickly raced around to her medical chambers.

'What's happened?' He burst into the recovery room to find Kassa adjusting the feeds that were running into Aurora's still-unconscious form.

'She stirred just a moment ago,' Kassa informed him with a smile, 'and she was calling for you.'

She heard me. Zeven boggled at the news, a little disappointed that he'd missed her brief awakening.

'It's a very good sign that she is starting to emerge,' Kassa said. 'Coma patients rarely come immediately awake. They tend to drift in and out for a while ... as you would when stirring from such a long sleep.'

'Like coming out of stasis.' Zeven was encouraged and took a seat at Aurora's bedside.

'She may not stir again tonight,' Kassa told him.

'I want to be here if she does.' He gripped Aurora's hand so that she might know he was there. 'Could you do me a favour?'

Kassa delayed her departure.

'Could you ask Leal to give Kalayna a hand in the launch bay tomorrow morning?' He knew Kalayna would think he was avoiding her, but perhaps that was for the best.

'Sure thing, kiddo.' She winked conspiratorially, and Starman had to wonder if she was reading his mind. 'You get some sleep,' she said as she departed.

Zeven was being kissed over and over on the head and thought he was dreaming, until his sleep-time visions retreated into his subconscious and the kisses continued to flow.

'Starman?'

The sound of Aurora's voice sent a wave of shocked relief through his being. He found himself lying across her chest, his head being stroked into wakefulness. He turned to see her smiling down at him, tears of joy in her eyes. 'You came for me.'

'I sure did.' He hoisted himself up to kiss her forehead.

'You saved me.'

'I love you,' he said, and could not hold back his tears of gladness at being able to finally say so.

Aurora took hold of his face in both hands and kissed him with several years of pent-up passion.

Zeven was so relieved not to have given in to his desires regarding Kalayna the night previous. He felt he was now sure where his heart truly lay and there would be no more confusion.

Later that day, after Aurora had rested and been briefed on some of what had transpired during her coma, she felt compelled to speak with Kalayna.

Her girlfriend entered in a rather more filthy state than Aurora had ever seen her.

'Sorry,' Kalayna shrugged, as she flashed her grease-covered hands, 'but I've been working my butt off trying to make amends for what I did to you.' She frowned in a plea for mercy.

Aurora had been informed of Kalayna's remorse and of her work for the project over the last week. Kalayna's deep regret was evident in her humbled manner, which Aurora could hardly bear to watch.

'No,' Aurora said, shaking her head, tears in her eyes. 'It is I who should apologise. I can't say that I never would have got with Starman had I known you were on board, because I do love him —'

'I know,' Kalayna said sympathetically, as she moved to take a seat next to Rory.

'I truly thought you had changed your mind when I couldn't find you anywhere.' Aurora took hold of her friend's hands and squeezed them tight. 'I'm *so sorry* I hurt you. What we had was *very* special to me ... you inspired me with confidence in myself, and I cannot thank you enough for that.'

'It's okay.' Kalayna hugged her, and they both burst into tears. 'I was totally wrong about Starman. He's a really amazing guy.'

Aurora's heart gave a little jolt. Had Zeven seduced Kalayna in her absence? 'I thought you said all men were bastards and you'd never think otherwise?'

Kalayna detected Aurora's fear and sat back to reassure her. 'I'd never met this crew then.' She laughed at her own change of heart. 'They're all wonderful human beings ... go figure. I got to do my dream job for a bit. I am really in your debt for that.' Kalayna smiled, but Aurora had a feeling it was not completely sincere.

'Although my place is now with Zeven, I hope we will remain good friends.'

Kalayna nodded agreement, having a little trouble squeezing her words out. 'Of course ... I am really happy for the both of you.' Kalayna stood to make an exit, seemingly afraid that her emotions might get the better of her. 'I'd better get back. Leal's waiting for me.'

Rory was disconcerted ... Kalayna seemed very accepting of their breakup, but that was good, right? 'Cool.'

'See you.' Kalayna departed without further ado, leaving Aurora with an odd feeling that there was something she wasn't being told.

The Phemorian authorities, on detecting the ship in their airspace, made contact with AMIE and invited the vessel to dock in their capital port of Tonissia —

which in Phemorian meant 'twofold' or 'twin'. It was said that this related to the fact that the capital had a twin city on the other side of the planet, but this explanation made little sense to Taren as Tonissia had been constructed first.

They would be docking the next day, so Taren finally returned to her quarters to pack clothes for planet leave.

That's where Zeven sought her out. 'I need to talk to you,' he said, closing the door after entering.

'What's the problem?' Taren asked, taking in his bemused appearance.

'I'm confused,' he announced, as he collapsed onto the lounge.

'About what?' Taren went on with her packing.

'How can I have fallen deeply in love with two different women at the same time?'

His answer got Taren's full attention and she moved to take a seat on the lounge opposite him. 'Spill it,' she invited, and Zeven was happy to oblige.

When all was said, it was Taren looking bemused.

'So, ever since Aurora woke I've been avoiding her because I fear making Kalayna feel bad, and avoiding Kalayna, for fear Aurora will get the wrong impression! I'm going insane trying to choose, and what's most frustrating is that I have two women in love with me and I'm *still* not getting laid!'

His dramatics made Taren laugh, but she toned down her amusement when he gave her the evil eye. 'Sorry. If you want my advice, and I assume you do ... Just be honest with them both. Send them your love and goodwill —'

'But that's what got me in this mess in the first place!' Zeven wasn't satisfied, and stood up in protest.

'If I'd just stayed mad at Kalayna, I wouldn't be in this predicament.'

'No, you wouldn't,' Taren agreed. 'Kalayna would be dead and you'd have to tell Aurora how your hatred killed her.'

Zeven frowned. 'You're right, that would be worse.' He took a seat once more.

'Besides, from what you've told me, your hatred of Kalayna was your way of denying and hiding your attraction, just as you did with Aurora for some time.'

Zeven stared at Taren, hating it that she could read him like a book. 'So who do I choose? The girl who taught me how to love and be selfless, or the girl with whom I have so much in common and feel an almost electric connection to?'

Taren could not answer that and she knew it. 'When in doubt, trust in the universal process.'

Zeven was clearly still very anxious.

'You haven't done anything wrong, Zeven. You cannot help how you feel. All you can do is be honest and forthright —'

'Stalemate,' he concluded with a heavy sigh.

'Nothing stays the same forever,' Taren pointed out, sorry that she couldn't be of more help. 'You've been so constructive in the way you've handled the challenges that have been thrown your way, that the universe is bound to reward you sooner or later.'

With a smile of appreciation, he nodded. 'Thanks for listening anyway.' Zeven departed, seemingly no closer to a solution that would make him happy.

Taren bit her lip, a little remorseful that her advice had led him into such a dilemma. It was still her best advice — positive intention always produced the desired result. She'd proven it over and over! 'Dear

Universe, help that boy out,' she appealed to the cosmos. He was such a good soul, deep down, surely he deserved a little happiness.

When Aurora hadn't seen Zeven for over twenty-four hours and he failed to answer a ship-wide page, she knew for certain that he was avoiding her.

'I am so *sick* of these games. Why tell me that he loves me, and then go out of his way *not* to see me?'

She needed to get to the bottom of this mystery, and she had an idea that Kalayna had something to do with it.

Kalayna had finished her work on the recon vessel's propulsion system the previous day, and at this early hour of the morning Aurora knew she would find her in the cafeteria kitchen preparing breakfast.

Aurora entered the all-but-empty eatery quietly, and as she approached the kitchen, she heard Kalayna weeping. 'I thought you enjoyed your work here?'

Kalayna gasped in fright, and quickly wiped the tears from her face. 'Onions,' she rattled off.

'But you're cutting bread.' Aurora pointed out.

'But I *was* cutting onions … before,' she said, forcing a grin, and knowing full well that her tale was anything but convincing.

'What's going on with you and Starman?' Aurora asked directly, so there was no avoiding the topic.

'Nothing!' Kalayna was clearly panicked by the question. 'Why would you ask that?'

'Because you're both acting so *strangely*.'

'Well,' Kalayna shrugged, and went on with her slicing, 'life's been a little strange lately.'

'Oh, really?' Aurora was curious to hear more. 'Do tell.'

Kalayna drew a deep breath as if to steady welling emotions. 'There's nothing to tell.'

Aurora was losing patience, so she decided to state what she suspected. 'You seduced him, didn't you?'

'What?' Kalayna clearly felt the suggestion was ludicrous. 'No! We weren't even talking until a couple of days ago.'

'And then?' Aurora challenged.

'And then ... *nothing.*' Kalayna kept her eyes focused on what she was doing, although she was now hacking the bread to bits. 'He loves you, Aurora. Any idiot can see that.'

'Then why haven't I seen him in the past twenty-four hours?'

'You haven't?' Kalayna sounded almost heartened to hear this.

'No, I haven't.' Aurora folded her arms, even more suspicious. 'I know —'

'Aurora. There you are,' Zeven called from the cafeteria door. 'Can we talk?'

Aurora could have dropped dead where she stood. Zeven never wanted to talk. 'Sure,' she replied sweetly, turning back to catch Kalayna's reaction.

Her friend appeared uninterested and with a shrug urged Aurora to go.

Aurora felt bad for her friend ... not only had she broken Kalayna's heart, she had made unfounded allegations about Kalayna as well. However, Aurora sensed a vibe that something was going on, and she headed out the door without an apology.

'What's on your mind?' Aurora asked amiably as Zeven led her back to his quarters.

'A *whole* lot,' he emphasised, opening the door to his private space and motioning with both hands for her to enter.

'Do you really want to talk?' Aurora stopped halfway through the door to grin at him, believing 'a talk' was just an excuse to get her alone in his room.

'I certainly do,' he was sorry to say, but not as sorry as Aurora was ... her dreams of a tender, passionate encounter were shattered. If Zeven wanted to talk, something was seriously wrong.

'You don't love me.' As much as it hurt her to suggest it, she wanted to cut right to the chase.

'Oh, I do,' he assured her. 'I love you more than I ever imagined I could love anyone.'

Aurora was truly confused by his openness. 'Then why the long face?'

'Your love opened a floodgate,' he said, once the door was closed. 'I have done things in the past week that I never thought possible. I have changed at a core level —'

'I can see that!' Aurora was overwhelmed by his passion and candour.

'And it was your love that did it. I want to tell you everything. No,' he corrected himself, 'I *have* to tell you everything, *right now*, or I'm going to burst!'

'Better get on with it, before you blow something up,' she said encouragingly as they sat down on the lounge together.

Aurora experienced many different emotions during Zeven's confession — all of them good. She boggled at his heroic feats and insights, and cried like a baby in empathy for all he'd been through on her behalf and Kalayna's. She loved him more now for his frankness, honesty, and for all he'd done for love from the time he'd saved her life till this very moment. She'd never considered in her wildest dreams that Zeven would prove to have such emotional depth, nor the moral fibre to explore his emotional dilemma *before* he had betrayed or hurt someone.

'I didn't want to lie or cause any more hurt, so you see, I had to tell you ... I'm sorry,' he concluded.

Aurora blew her nose and wiped her eyes, hoping to compose herself. Zeven was very red-eyed himself and was fidgeting nervously as he awaited her reaction. 'I do believe this is the bravest I've ever seen you —'

Her strong emotions made her catch her breath and, inspired by his example she figured that it was time for honesty all round. 'The truth of the matter is, I still love her too,' Aurora said, standing up to pace about. She recalled finding her friend weeping in the kitchen earlier and it broke her heart. 'Kalayna should know all this,' she determined and Zeven nodded in agreement. Aurora sent a page to Kalayna, and was surprised to hear the tone of Kalayna's communicator just outside Zeven's chambers. Aurora and Zeven grinned at each other as he got up and opened the door.

'Shit!' Kalayna finally managed to hit the off switch. She turned in a fluster to find Zeven and Aurora with eyebrows raised watching her. 'I was just on my way past, um, when I got your page. So, what's up?'

Once they had Kalayna behind closed doors, Zeven started the conversation. 'I've told Rory everything.'

'What! *Everything?*' Kalayna jumped to the conclusion that Zeven was wanting to make her look the bad guy. 'Look, I don't know what he's told you, but —'

'He told me that he has very strong feelings for you, and you for him. Is that true?' Aurora asked so amiably that Kalayna was confused by hope and delight.

'Maybe?' Kalayna shrugged, still not sure what was happening here. 'But then, I still love you and I've *missed* you, so maybe my feelings are just being misplaced.'

Zeven clicked his fingers. 'That's what I thought, at first. But then, when Aurora awoke I felt there should be no more confusion ...'

'... but there is,' Kalayna realised, enlightened, and then sank back into confusion.

'Look ... I love both you guys. I don't want to give either of you up,' Aurora confessed openly, with joyful tears in her eyes. 'You love each other and you love me, *so* ... as far as I can see, *we don't have* a problem.' A mischievous smile formed as she looked from Kalayna, who gazed back astounded and grinning, to Zeven, who looked like he'd just won the intergalactic jackpot. 'Okay then ...' Aurora slinked over to Zeven and, with a glance and a smile in Kalayna's direction, she shoved him backwards onto his sleeping pod. 'Let's dance.'

When their pilot reported to the bridge to dock AMIE at the Tonissian spaceport, he was in a very good mood indeed.

The only time Taren had ever seen Zeven look that happy was on the surface of Oceane. She could only assume that Zeven had finally got himself laid! Taren was dying to ask who the lucky girl was, but was spared the trouble when the pilot left for shore leave on Phemoria with a girl under each arm.

'What a handful,' Lucian commented as they trailed the happy threesome.

'He certainly is.' Taren shook her head in disbelief. *The universe helped him out all right.*

'I meant the girls,' Lucian corrected with a chuckle in his voice. 'But I dare say that being held in such high regard by two gay women will have Zeven in the residents' good books in no time.'

'Looks like we're frightfully out of fashion, then.' Taren hugged her man around his waist.

'Only me, really,' replied Lucian, 'as the only thing more admired on Phemoria than a gay female is a gifted psychic.'

'I don't really like to advertise that fact. I'm quite happy to be completely un-chic with you.'

All the crew were going ashore, even Ringbalin. He'd promised Ayliscia Portus that she could show him around her town, although he planned to return to the ship periodically. Kassa and Leal were keen to spend a few days alone together, away from their working lives and the accompanying interference.

At customs their party was met by a tall, elegantly dressed Phemorian official. The majority of Phemorians tended to be olive-to dark-skinned, very tall, and their hair and eyes were usually darker shades. Dr Portus was more blonde and blue-eyed, although her skin did have that healthy olive hue. The official sent to meet them was dark-skinned and her long jet-black hair fell back from an ornate jewel clasp on the crown of her head. Her eyes, however, were a very striking shade of indigo; as were Taren's, although slightly lighter.

Lucian recognised the official as the Phemorian viceroy and uttered as much in an aside to Taren, adding: 'Our visit must be considered *very* important.'

She was not at all like the Phemorian officials Taren had met on Frujia — no veil, no floating about.

Perhaps Dr Portus had been right in saying that they had been no ordinary government officials, but were, in fact, the mystical Phemoray.

'Greetings, Captain Gervaise,' the viceroy said, knowing Lucian by sight, and bowed her head to him in respect. 'My name is Jalila Lamus and I am here to welcome you and your crew ...' Her eyes came to rest upon Taren. '... to Phemoria, where you will be given sanctuary. On the instruction of our illustrious queen, the Honourable Qusay-Sabah Clarona, I am to extend to you every courtesy and luxury our planet has to offer.' Jalila smiled warmly at Taren, who was a little discomfortted by the attention.

'On behalf of my crew, I thank you,' Lucian replied, regaining the viceroy's attention. 'Your queen is most gracious.'

'The Sermetic sympathiser under sedation in your ship's medical quarters will be transferred to our maximum security detention facility here in Tonissia.' At the viceroy's nod, several of the customs officers and security police entered AMIE to collect Swithin.

Lucian, as much as he despised his brother for his betrayals, regretted being the one to finally have him incarcerated. But if he didn't see Swithin safely behind bars, one of the secret services would happily see him to his grave and Phemoria was the only planet where the intergalactic secret service agencies held little sway. In fact, they were despised by the Phemorians.

'I have been instructed to see you to your accommodation.' Jalila dispersed the sober mood with her lovely smile. 'I have transport waiting, if you will kindly follow me.'

The crew were shown to the larger of the two luxury transporters, complete with government chauffeur.

Taren and Lucian were invited to ride in the other with the viceroy. It was there that Taren finally introduced herself to Jalila, who smiled broadly. 'Your reputation precedes you, Dr Lennox. Our queen is most eager to meet with you at your earliest convenience.'

'That is fantastic news,' Lucian said, pleased. 'We are eager to speak with your queen about funding —'

'I do apologise, captain,' Jalila said, sounding almost insulted by his assumption, 'but the Qusay-Sabah Clarona extended the invitation to Dr Lennox alone.'

Pangs of panic shot through Taren. Why was she so important? Did this honour have something to do with the Phemoray and their banishing stone? Why did they wish to keep her hidden from Anselm, if he was her father? Did they know that? Dr Portus had said she suspected that Taren was part-Phemorian. Was Anselm's blood enough to make her Phemorian — as he was Sermetic his ancestry was also Phemorian.

'Oh ... I see.' Lucian tried not to sound belittled, although Taren knew he was. 'I do apologise.' He turned his gaze to the window, although he could only view blurred streaks of light inside the tunnel they were speeding through.

Taren was surprised by her first taste of male discrimination and reached across to squeeze Lucian's hand, and he squeezed hers in return without looking at her. 'I would be honoured to meet Queen Clarona. Would this evening be convenient?'

'That would be most pleasing,' Jalila confirmed.

The mood in their transport got a mite uncomfortable after that and Taren was glad the journey was not prolonged.

The express tunnel ended in front of a huge domed construction with security doors and guards. A government pass was obviously the only way someone could enter. Inside the dome was an expansive, round esplanade, the walls of which were composed of adjoining terrace apartments, five storeys high. These protected sandstone dwellings were in immaculate condition and sunlight streamed in through large elongated windows set in the cement-like material of the domed ceiling. A single-lane roadway, with parking areas at the side, ran the full circuit of the indoor complex, and then out through the security doors at the front and into the tunnel to the spaceport. The central area of the esplanade was ornately paved, and was dotted with lush leather seating, tables and potted plants to give it a very sparse but elegant ambience.

It was only as they disembarked from their ride that Taren and Lucian realised that the other crew transport was no longer in front of them.

'The rest of your crew have been accommodated in the civilian centre of Tonissia for their own enjoyment. Our queen felt that for political and security reasons, you and your partner would be safer here, on government ground,' Jalila informed Taren when she queried the absence.

Lucian was suspicious and his brother's warning regarding the Phemorians came to mind. *The Phemorians will screw you, just as surely as the USS and the MSS will.* 'I would prefer that my crew stay with me,' Lucian replied in a not-so-friendly fashion.

'Then I can arrange to have you accommodated with them,' the official replied amiably.

Lucian was satisfied, until Jalila added: 'But our queen insists that Dr Lennox remain in the government sector.'

Lucian was livid at the suggestion. Taren felt his annoyance and intervened. 'We'll remain here for now, thank you.' She didn't want to lose their last chance of support for their project just yet.

The viceroy handed over an electronic key to the apartment they were standing in front of. 'The apartment has everything you should require ... housekeeping and catering are contactable via the intercom system in the kitchen, they service the entire establishment,' Jalila advised them, as she returned to the transport. 'I'll send someone to collect you this evening.'

'Please tell Queen Clarona that I greatly look forward to our meeting.' Taren waved, grateful to see the official get inside the car and leave.

'I don't trust this entire set-up.' Lucian finally let the brake off his tongue.

Taren had to admit that 'a set-up' was exactly what this felt like. But to what end? Only by walking straight into this trap did she have any chance of finding her answers.

The penthouse apartment of the hotel gave a grand view of Tonissia. For a capital city, it had a very low-lying skyline; none of the buildings stood much over ten storeys tall and were nearly all historic. The Phemorians preferred to maintain their old structures rather than tear them down and build huge new skyscrapers, as was the practice on Sermetica, and on Maladaan — when there was a Maladaan. Still, there was more creative freedom of expression here than on any other planet under the USS banner. The Phemorians were passionate about beauty and the creative process, and were great supporters of artists — painters, poets, actors, musicians, writers and designers of all stripes. That was why people flocked here. The night life, entertainment, galleries and libraries on Phemoria were said to be the best to be found anywhere in the known universe, and this was the case in Tonissia most of all.

'I'm going to go down and have a look around,' Zeven decided, as both girls were still lying around half naked, reading magazines and watching the intergalactic network on the huge multi-screen wall in the bedroom. 'I'll see if I can find some place interesting to take you ladies later.'

'I vote we stay here,' Aurora said cheekily, snuggling deeper into the huge pillows.

'Oh, come on.' Kalayna tossed a pillow at her. 'This is Tonissia, the most exciting city anywhere!'

'That's two against one.' Zeven headed for the door. 'Be back soon.'

'If you guys think you are dragging me to that spaceship expo downtown, you're seriously mistaken.' Aurora knew that Zeven and Kalayna had similar interests which she did not share in the least.

'Really! There's a spaceship expo?' Kalayna grabbed the magazine Aurora was reading from her hands.

'Later, girls!' Zeven blew kisses and left them to argue it out.

'This looks great!' Kalayna found the article and became very excited. 'Please can we go,' she whined, putting on her pouting, seductive face.

'Aw ...' Aurora groaned at the very thought. 'Wouldn't you rather go to the theatre, or a movie, or —'

'No way! They've got the new hyper-lite DS-700 on display!'

'Wow ...' Aurora stared back blankly. 'Whatever a hyper D thingie is.'

'You're *such* a girl.' Kalayna rolled her eyes. 'Starman will be excited, I assure you.'

A chime toned to let them know someone was at the door. 'Speak of the devil.' Kalayna figured Starman had left something behind and rose to let him back in.

'I'm going to take a bath,' Aurora decided, and kicked her way out of the bedding.

Kalayna waited for Aurora to enter the bathroom and close the door — just in case their caller wasn't Zeven.

The door slid aside to reveal a tall cloaked man, which freaked Kalayna! She would have closed the door in his dark hooded face had he not barged his way in.

'Miss Zuri.' He grabbed hold of one of her wrists and held it tight as he backed her into the apartment and the door closed automatically.

'Who are you?' Kalayna was fearful that he knew her name, and she tried to catch a glimpse of the face beneath the hood with no success.

'Where are your friends?' he asked in a strained whisper.

'They went out,' she blurted, and thought to add, 'But they'll be back *very* soon.'

His attention turned to the sound of a bath running.

'That's for me,' Kalayna explained, to set him at ease. 'I should go turn it off.' She moved to do so, wanting to warn Aurora, but he held onto her wrist and swung her back into his clutches. 'What do you want?' she said loudly, hoping that Aurora might be alerted.

'I want to talk,' he taunted. 'I want to talk to *Fem-Libertine*.'

Kalayna froze in his hands and, like a haze lifting from her mind the reason for this stranger's visit became perfectly clear to her. Indeed, he was no stranger to her at all.

'What do you want!'

Aurora heard Kalayna cry out, so she immediately put on her robe and moved to investigate. As Kalayna had sounded panicked, Aurora cautiously slid the bathroom door open to give the smallest gap to peer out through the bedroom and into the living area.

She smothered a gasp when she saw the dark hooded figure standing over Kalayna. The sound of the running water covered the sound of her movement, as she slipped out of the bathroom and made for the far wall of the bedroom, where she sank to the ground and peered into the lounge.

'I want to talk to *Fem-Libertine*,' the hooded man told Kalayna, who froze like a zombie for a second and her attacker let her go and removed his hood.

Again, Aurora was forced to suppress a gasp. *President Anselm!* She recognised him at once. *What was he doing here? And what business could he possibly have with Kalayna?*

When Kalayna emerged from her short trance, she bowed her head at once. 'Mr President.'

'Hello, little siren.' He smiled at her warmly. 'What have you to report?'

She's a sleeper agent! Zeven was right about her! Aurora's heart began beating so loudly that she could barely hear a word being said.

'They have all been very tight-lipped around me,' Kalayna told him, 'insofar as their Powers are concerned. Except Dr Lennox, who freely told me she was a pre-cog.'

'I know that already,' he bantered, in good humour. 'Did she say anything about PK ability?'

'No. Why do you ask?'

'Because someone from AMIE made themselves invisible to rescue Miss DeCadie from one of our deep-space cruisers and then made the entire recon vessel we'd captured disappear.' Anselm explained.

Starman! Aurora's mind screamed in anguish.

'Zeven Gudrun would be my guess,' Kalayna piped in.

'Why?' Anselm was intensely interested to learn this.

'Because *he* rescued Aurora. That would also explain why he failed to notice that he'd burned out his entire propulsion system being dragged in by your tracker beam. Zeven claimed that his bad intentions made me ill, and I was *very* ill — he could have killed me — but he chose to miraculously cure me instead.'

Anselm smiled, well pleased. 'I must have him.'

'I already have,' Kalayna grinned, proud of her work.

'You certainly do live up to your call sign.' Anselm touched her cheek fondly.

'I greatly enjoy my work.' She kissed the palm of his hand before he withdrew his touch.

'Do you know where they are keeping my daughter?' Anselm got back to business.

'In the government sector, of course.'

'I have no chance of getting to her there. We have to draw her out.'

'Well ... she is very fond of Zeven Gudrun,' Kalayna ventured. 'If anything were to happen to him, she would surely go to the ends of the earth to find him.'

Aurora was practically hyperventilating now, hoping with all her might that Kalayna would not expose her before she had the chance to expose Kalayna. *Why hasn't she exposed me?* she wondered. Perhaps their love ran deeper than even MSS conditioning could thwart? She had exposed Zeven to the enemy, however, and in Aurora's mind that was completely unforgivable.

'Kill two birds with one stone, you think,' the president said, very happy with the notion.

'Leave it to me,' Kalayna suggested. 'You should go, as Zeven *will* be back soon.'

Anselm nodded in accord and came close to look Kalayna in the eyes. 'When I walk out that door, you will consciously forget I was ever here, but the *Fem-Libertine* shall not.'

Kalayna smiled as she watched him leave. Aurora gulped as she realised she was about to be confronted. Feeling unprepared she dashed back into the bathroom and closed the door.

When Aurora heard Zeven come back through the door, she emerged gingerly from the bathroom.

'I thought you were never coming out of there,' Kalayna said in relief as she rose to take up occupation in her stead. 'What's wrong?'

Aurora wiped the mortified look off her face and smiled. 'It's the thought of going to that space con.'

'It'll be fun,' Kalayna insisted, kissing her cheek, before vanishing into the wet room.

Aurora made a beeline for Zeven.

'Hey, sweetness,' he smiled, wrongly thinking she was rushing to greet him. Instead, she planted both hands on his chest and pushed him to the furthest corner of the living room, where she burst into tears. 'What is it? What's wrong?'

'You were right about Kalayna. She's a sleeper agent,' she whispered, petrified.

'What?' Zeven couldn't imagine what had led Aurora to this conclusion in the short time he'd been gone.

'It's true! Anselm was here —'

'President Anselm?'

'Shh!' Aurora begged him to keep his voice down. 'Kalayna told him about your PK ability and now he wants you as an agent.'

'What ... no,' Zeven said in disbelief. 'She doesn't know about my PK. I never told her.'

'She worked it out when she saw your fried propulsion system. And you miraculously cured her, remember? They plan to use you to get to Taren.'

This piece of news turned Zeven's whole attitude around. 'Where is Kalayna now?'

'In the bath,' Aurora informed. 'Anselm said she wouldn't consciously recall him being here, but the sleeper agent inside her would.'

'Did you hear him use her code name?'

Aurora when into a fluster. 'He called her by a couple of different names. *Little siren* and ... the other one was kind of foreign-sounding.'

'Think, Aurora, think,' he urged. 'It's really important.'

'Yes, Aurora, *think*.'

They turned to find Kalayna standing in the bedroom doorway, fully dressed and ready for action with an explosive device in her hand.

'I thought she wasn't going to remember anything?' Zeven protested.

'Unless my mission is threatened, whereupon I remember *everything*.' She held the device up, showing a light on the side was blinking. 'You know what this is?'

'You don't want to use that.' Zeven moved slowly towards her. Aurora gasped and tried to stop him, but he gently brushed her hand aside, staying focused on Kalayna.

'I have a mission,' Kalayna stated, 'and I will succeed in delivering you into USS hands, or we all die. I daresay your deaths would draw Dr Lennox into the civilian sector of the city and that will be mission accomplished for me.'

'You're on our side, remember?' Zeven said. 'Whatever you've done before, we don't care!'

'I am *not* who you think I am.' She became angered by his support.

'You are whoever *you want* to be,' he insisted. 'Personal choice is the one thing no one can take from you.'

'Oh, yes, they can,' she said, beginning to tremble as her eyes welled with tears. 'When you're alone in the world, anything can be taken from you.'

Aurora feared that Kalayna would accidentally hit the trigger on the device if Starman did not take it from her soon.

He wanted to avoid exposing his PK to a known enemy — at present, she only suspected his Power and he thought it wise not to confirm her guess. Instead he poured all the love he could summon in her direction and she moaned as she felt the healing force bombarding her being.

But the secret agent in her resisted his advances and compassion. 'You do not control me!' Her finger was poised upon the button, when Aurora suddenly remembered the code name.

'*You are not the Fem-Libertine!* That bitch has no control over you, Kalayna!' Aurora yelled. Kalayna froze and Zeven seized the device from her, and then held her tight as she burst into tears.

'I nearly killed you,' she gasped in shock and despair. 'I … I … who *the fuck* am I? What just happened?' She looked at Aurora, who was shaking her head as she breathed a sigh of relief. 'No, wait a second.' Kalayna scanned her own memory and found an excess of MSS experience she'd never consciously known she had. 'It's all starting to come back to me.'

CHAPTER 21

THE TWO-FOLD CITY

Lucian was very wary of Taren going to dinner with the Queen of Phemoria. 'What if they're not taking you there at all? Why should we trust these people?'

Taren suspected Lucian's concerns were driven by his anger at being so obviously discriminated against. 'I need some answers, Lucian.' She didn't appreciate him trying to strike fear into her about this. 'And we need funding, supplies and crew or we won't last another week in space. Can't you please envisage a more constructive outcome? You know my beliefs, and channelling energy into a bad scenario will not help anyone. Maybe the queen will not speak with a man? From what I hear she rarely meets with anyone.'

This was true enough. Qusay-Sabah Clarona never left Phemoria and gave her envoys responsibility for political dealings on her behalf. This behaviour gave her an air of mystique and protected her from political violence, and assassination, for no one was really sure what she looked like.

'Personally, I don't think the Phemorians are interested in the project at all. It's you they're after.'

'Then let me find out why,' Taren appealed.

As the apartment door chimed, Taren turned to give her appearance the once-over in the mirror and then looked back to her lover's worried face. 'I have a communicator. If anything happens I'll buzz you.' She kissed him. 'Wish me luck.'

'Be careful,' Lucian said with a smile.

'I promise.' Taren kissed him again, feeling a great lack of urgency to go anywhere, but the buzzer on the door downstairs urged her to get this meeting over with.

Taren was not thrilled to discover Jalila Lamus waiting to escort her to the engagement with the queen. The way she had spoken down to the man Taren loved and respected had really rubbed Taren the wrong way.

'Why was Professor Gervaise not invited to this dinner with me?' she asked. The viceroy sat directly opposite her in the back of the car.

'Is he your keeper?' was Jalila's curt reply.

'We are each other's keeper.'

Jalila looked aside, seemingly impervious to Taren's sentiment, and uttered, 'Not for long.'

'I beg to differ.' Taren was shocked by the comment.

The viceroy's attention darted back to Taren to engage with her. 'You don't have to beg for anything. Tonight your life will change *forever*.'

Taren was dumbstruck. She didn't know whether to be afraid, angry or offended!

'You have nothing to fear, Doctor, and everything to gain. Be patient ... the answers you seek are coming.'

Shit, she's a telepath, Taren surmised on the quiet, whereupon Jalila smiled confidently and turned her gaze back out the window.

The queen's estate and residence were high on a forested hilltop overlooking the city. It was a sheer-walled circular dwelling, several storeys in height, rendering it virtually unscaleable and giving it a very modern appearance.

Queen Qusay-Sabah Clarona was protected by a fierce group of female guards, rumoured to be ten thousand in number. These were the 'Valoureans', the elite of the Phemorian army. True to name, they were supremely fit, focused, beauteous and well armed. Silver-spiked armour, worn over a red leather uniform, made them look formidable, but with a seductive twist.

Jalila led Taren past the guard to the door and then halted to take her leave. 'Do have an extraordinary evening, Doctor.' The viceroy bowed her head briefly.

'I feel confident of that,' Taren replied coolly, as her escort retreated to the transport and departed the residence.

Taren breathed deeply of the cool night air to compose herself. She truly hoped that Queen Clarona was not as arrogant and elitist as her viceroy. Taren really didn't like Jalila Lamus very much, and was not keen on being associated with the Phemorians if all the women here were of the same ilk.

An older female steward answered the door. 'Dr Lennox, welcome.' She bowed deeply to Taren as she invited her inside. 'Our majesty is awaiting your presence in her council chamber. If you would please follow me.'

At least I have definitely been delivered to the queen's palace, she thought. Whether that was a good thing or not remained to be seen.

The walls of the residence were adorned with huge frescos depicting the heroines of Phemoria's past. Looking up at the ceiling, Taren beheld a breathtaking depiction of many elegant veiled women overseeing the scenes unfolding on the walls below. *The Phemoray*, Taren guessed as she and her guide reached the top of a staircase and the steward opened the double doors at the top. 'Dr Lennox, majesty.'

A tall woman stood with her back to the door, gazing through panoramic picture windows at the city below. She was dressed all in white: a sparkling veil fell to her waist over a slim-fitting floor-length gown. The underside of the queen's long sleeves reached the floor also.

'Very good, Salantea. Thank you.' She waited for the doors to close behind her steward before she turned to view Taren.

'Your majesty.' Taren bowed her head briefly, in a show of respect. 'Thank you for seeing me.'

'It is I who am grateful for this audience,' she replied. 'I have dreamt of this meeting for some fifty years.'

'Fifty years?' Taren smiled politely, confused. Her work had only brought her recognition over recent years. 'But I was barely born fifty ...' The revelation hit her like a brick wall. '... years ... ago ...'

'I know,' the veiled woman said, her voice filled with warm sentiment. 'I was there.'

Taren didn't know what to make of this and did not jump to any immediate conclusions. 'Are you saying you knew my mother?'

'Yes, I know her,' she replied, waving Taren forward. 'Come closer, child. Let me look at you.'

Overcome by the prospect of learning something about her mother, Taren began to shiver as she acquiesced to the stately woman's request. 'My mother *lives*?' The subject of her parents never failed to set her on edge, since they had both chosen to abandon her. Or so she'd always assumed.

'Yes, she does. However, she did not abandon you as you imagine.' The queen reached out to touch Taren's cheek and turn her face to the light. 'You look *so much* like her,' she claimed, her voice betraying strong emotion.

'If my mother didn't abandon me, then why have I not heard from her in all these years?' Taren asked defiantly.

'You were stolen and up until your recent involvement in the disappearance of Maladaan, we have been unable to find you.'

Taren stepped away, bewildered and becoming angry. 'Who stole me? Why?' Her eyes narrowed, determined to get her answer. '*Who am I?*'

'You are *my* daughter, Princess of Phemoria and heir to the throne.' The queen removed her veil to show Taren the striking resemblance they bore to one another.

'No.' Taren was beyond shocked at seeing a clear family likeness.

'Yes. My agent stole one of your blood samples from AMIE and your DNA is a perfect match with both myself and your father.'

Taren frowned, still shaking her head. 'But others claim my father is President Anselm, and I know that can't be. The two of you are mortal enemies.'

The queen nodded. 'We are mortal enemies, because he is the one who stole you from me.'

'What!' Taren could barely breathe any more.

The queen placed a hand over Taren's third eye area and it had an immediately calming affect.

'Thank you.' Taren pulled away once she was breathing normally. 'This is all a bit difficult to digest.'

'I understand that it is.'

Taren dared to look into the woman's face, to find

her looking joyous ... sincerely so. But Taren could not honestly say she was thrilled at the prospect of being the heir to this planet.

The queen led Taren to the windows to view the city, its tidy street blocks abuzz with traffic and fairly unremarkable in every way. 'I know our capital does not look as grand as the cities on Maladaan, as beautiful as those on Frujia, or as rich as the cities of Sermetica, but this city has a secret that only true Phemorians know about and can utilise.'

'How do you mean?' Taren was intrigued. She loved nothing more than a good secret.

'Do you know how to raise your vibratory rate to employ your third-eye vision?' the queen asked.

'It's not something I've had call to do very often,' Taren said with a laugh, 'so, no, it is not my forte.'

The queen shrugged. 'Not to worry, you shall learn, but for now ... allow me.' She moved around behind Taren and placed one hand over her eyes and the other over her third eye.

There was a tingling sensation on her forehead, an effervescence, that brought a smile to Taren's face.

'Behold your true inheritance.'

Another city, an etheric city, had materialised and it rose high above the existing city, but also interpenetrating it. The ghostly metropolis was far more impressive and remarkable than the city that concealed it and even the room in which she stood had completely altered. Where there had once been a solid wall of windows in front of them, there now extended a long walkway that led into one of the huge buildings of the mega-city.

'The twofold city,' Taren said with a beaming smile of wonder as she comprehended the true meaning behind this city's name. The image mentally propelled her back in time to a vision she'd had of this very moment, and the recognition gave her a start.

'You know in your heart it is the truth. Why do you think you have managed to remain immune to the discrimination of the Psychic Monitor Database?'

'My MSS service wiped my record,' Taren stated in reply.

'But why did the MSS choose to accept your Power, while they denigrate, and worse, all others with the same abilities?' The queen's questions caused panic to churn in Taren's gut. 'Because your father used the MSS and their database to protect you from being found, at the same time subduing any psychic who might threaten your Power or expose you. That is how Anselm has kept you hidden from me all this time.' The queen reached out and fondly stroked Taren's hair. 'I know this must all be a little overwhelming, but given time you'll see that you belong here —'

Taren withdrew from her touch, unsure of how she felt, or whether or not she even believed her. 'I belong in space on the AMIE project.'

The queen did not look sympathetic as she shook her head. 'Surely you can see how impossible that vocation is now.'

The horrifying truth sank into her bemused brain. Whether or not *Taren* believed what the queen was saying, the queen certainly believed it. She had ultimate power here and was probably more psychically gifted than Taren had ever dreamt of being. What hope did she have of resisting the will of such a woman?

'I want to return to Lucian, please.' Taren felt the trap closing on her.

The queen was displeased with this suggestion, but stopped short of shaking her head in refusal. 'It is my understanding that you wish to meet with the Phemoray. They are certainly eager to speak with you.'

Taren's eyes opened wide. She was intrigued and found the courage to swallow her fears and continue her quest. 'I would like to, very much.'

'Then I am afraid you shall have to make do with my company, at least until dawn,' the queen smiled. 'The Phemoray are easier to contact at dusk and dawn when the veil between our worlds is thinnest.'

Taren looked back to the ghost city, wrongly believing that the Phemoray were its occupants. 'But I assumed —'

'Heavens no.' The queen was amused. 'The Phemoray detest cities. We'll have to venture into the forest to make their acquaintance. Tonissia is the dwelling place of all true Phemorian citizens.'

'No men then,' Taren chided.

The queen detected her daughter's cynical undertone. 'Nor will there ever be.'

The deep prejudice in the woman only increased Taren's fears that she might never see her lover again, but she suppressed her worry for the moment. Her meeting with the Phemoray was of the utmost importance.

'Allow me to show you what women can create without any masculine hindrance.' The queen proceeded up the long walkway towards the ethereal city.

Taren didn't want to believe that this queen and her planet had any claim on her, but nevertheless she warily trailed behind, of a mind to humour the queen as long as it served AMIE's interests. Taren was rather attached to the males in her life and was not prepared to consider a life without them. If she went missing, the Phemorians would find themselves confronted with a few masculine hindrances they hadn't banked on.

It was not long after Taren left that Lucian got a call from Zeven, requesting that Lucian meet them in town at the spacecraft expo, the DS-700 exhibit. Zeven wouldn't say why he needed to meet with his captain, only that their meeting was of the utmost importance.

As chance would have it, the invitation was a stroke of luck ... as Lucian's cab rounded the esplanade, heading for the security exit, he saw a large vehicle pull up in front of the apartment and ten armed Valoureans converge on the place he'd just vacated.

This only confirmed what Lucian already suspected — Taren was in trouble and so was he.

When the cab passed through the security exit and onto the expressway, Lucian breathed a sigh of relief. As soon as the tunnel ended and he saw he was in the city centre, he requested to be dropped off.

Lucian made haste towards the rendezvous point, his concern for Taren mounting. All he could think was that his brother had been right about the Phemorians, and they now had a member of the AMIE organisation in their custody who they would grill for information. Thankfully, Swithin didn't know much about the revelations Lucian had been exposed to recently in regard to AMIE's operations and crew. But Swithin *could* connect the AMIE project to the MSS and other intergalactic secret service agencies and that alone was enough to have them all put away for life by the Phemorian justice system.

AMIE needed to depart Phemoria as soon as possible, but Lucian was not going anywhere without Taren, or his brother. With the crew he had, he'd learned nothing was impossible. Possibly not even penetrating the high-security complexes guarded by Valoureans.

The spacecraft expo was massive and filled to capacity with people from all the planets in the USS territories. To Lucian's way of thinking, this was the perfect place to meet ... they could lose themselves in the crowd should the need arise. Zeven may have been right out there when it came to heroics, but he was smart enough to keep a low profile if need be.

Having found the DS-700 exhibit, Lucian couldn't see any sign of his crew, and began to worry that they might have been picked up before they could meet him.

'Captain!'

Lucian turned to find his pilot waving at him from the launch pad where the DS-700 hyper-lite was parked. *And here I was thinking Starman could keep a low profile.* The captain rolled his eyes at his own naivety.

'I've convinced this fine gentleman here to allow me to take you for a test drive,' Zeven announced as Lucian joined him, the salesman and the two girls.

'This is an honour, Captain Gervaise.' The salesman shook his hand eagerly. 'I believe the DS-700 would be a fine addition to your project.'

'We'll see,' Lucian demurred, playing along with Zeven's arrangements.

'I really envy you,' Kalayna called out as she watched the pilot board the latest supercraft.

Aurora had no interest in throwing up her dinner, and was happy to wave from the safety barrier.

'Get the rest of the crew here *now*,' the captain said quietly to Aurora as he handed her his bag. 'Except Ringbalin,' he advised. He had no inkling as to where Dr Portus' loyalties truly lay and he didn't want her around. With any luck, Ringbalin had pined for his greenhouse and had already returned to AMIE.

Aurora gave a steady nod, affirming that she realised the urgency, and Lucian joined Zeven for a joyride that he suspected would be anything but.

'Sorry I had to drop your name,' Zeven apologised as Lucian slid into the passenger seat alongside his pilot. 'I couldn't find anywhere else in this entire arena where we could have a private chat.'

'Sure,' Lucian said, even though he thought it more likely that Starman just wanted a test drive, 'but we'd best make this snappy, as I believe I have Valoureans after me.'

Zeven looked to the captain with a grin of envy. 'Aren't you the lucky one …' He hit the ignition switch and their craft roared into life. 'I've got the Sermetican Secret Service on my arse.'

'They're here?' Lucian's jaw dropped, as the DS-700 rose into the air.

'And we're outta here.' Zeven hit the gas and shot them into orbit, through an open section in the stadium roof.

It was difficult to hold a serious discussion while Starman was at the helm of the newest sportscraft — as dire as their situation was, he was having the ride of his life! Still, he did manage to recount Kalayna's activities and encounters to the captain.

'So it's true then. Anselm believes Taren is his daughter.' Lucian had hoped that the rumour was just that.

'And it sounds as though he'll go to great lengths to get her back,' Starman confirmed.

'So why is the Phemorian queen so eager to meet with Taren? Do you think she knows she's Anselm's daughter? Perhaps they intend to use Taren for political blackmail,' Lucian mused, his imagination in overdrive. 'What have I got myself into with this woman?'

'I'm happy to take her off your hands,' Starman offered.

'It seems everyone is,' Lucian chided. 'How could I have allowed her to walk into such an obvious trap!'

'Yeah, right, like you could have stopped her!' Starman gave the captain a wake-up call. 'Not even I have a hope of stopping Taren Lennox once she's set her mind on something. I mean ... shit ... the woman can change the future. How the hell are you going to control that?'

'What hope do we mere physical beings have?' Lucian had never felt so powerless and insignificant before, and he didn't like it very much.

'That's not what I meant,' Zeven assured the captain, who he had the utmost respect for. 'I was just trying to make you feel better about giving Taren over to the Phemorians.'

'Well, you failed miserably,' Lucian retorted, knowing that Zeven wasn't being insulting on purpose. The pilot just had a knack for putting his foot in his mouth.

'I vote we grab the crew, get back to AMIE, I zap myself over to Taren, and bring her back into our fold.

Then I zap the whole ship back to the Oceane system, where no motherfucker is looking for us!'

'That's a lot of zapping, Zeven,' the captain said, thinking it was a fine plan. 'Are you sure you're up to it?'

'I'm fuelled,' Zeven assured him, as he aimed their speeding vessel towards the arena they'd started from.

'Good,' Lucian was glad to hear it, 'as we need to break Swithin out of prison too.'

Zeven considered what motive the captain might have for such a move. 'I guess he did prove right about the Phemorians. Maybe he is on our side after all.'

'Make no mistake ...' Lucian warned. 'Swithin is on Swithin's side, which is why it pays to have him with you. He has miraculous survival instincts.'

'What about Kalayna?' Zeven broached the subject of their latest double agent. Despite Kalayna's past shortcomings he still cared for her deeply, as did Aurora.

Lucian could tell by Zeven's sheepish tone that he still wanted her on the crew. 'I didn't dismiss Taren for her unknowing involvement with the secret service. I shall hardly abandon Kalayna for the same.'

'And she's a damn fine tech,' Zeven added, happy with the captain's decision, as he hit the brakes and brought the DS-700 down to a perfect landing. 'Sounds like we have a plan.'

They both nodded in agreement.

No sooner had they disembarked, than their plan fell apart. Kalayna and Aurora were not where they had left them.

Lucian queried the salesman about the girls.

'They left with a tall cloaked fellow,' he advised, 'just after you took off.'

'This is not good.' Zeven headed out into the crowd, with Lucian hot on his heels.

'But what did you think of my spacecraft?' the salesman yelled after them, unhappy at witnessing his most promising sale rushing away from him.

'We'll get back to you,' Lucian assured him, watching Starman spin around in circles as he looked for the girls.

'Anselm has them,' Zeven quietly uttered in an aside to Lucian and they stopped dead as they each felt a weapon head boring into their neck. Although they did not turn, they felt themselves surrounded by several large persons.

'Just keep walking towards the exit up ahead. And if you,' one of the agents pressed the weapon into Zeven's back, 'try any heroic stunts you'll never see *any* of AMIE's crew again.'

Outside, Lucian and Zeven were shoved into a transporter, blindfolded, bound and sped to an unknown destination.

They were soon guided into a building — which sounded like a dance club — were led down several flights of stairs, taken further down in a lift, and led through a complex abuzz with technology and the reserved chatter of people working.

When they passed into a quiet corridor Lucian noticed that it sounded like their party had shrunk.

Finally, the captain was cast into a room, but only his body hit the floor; Starman had been taken elsewhere.

'Captain!' Aurora rushed to unbind him and remove his blindfold.

'Where is Zeven?' Kalayna asked as she gave a helping hand.

'He's here somewhere.' Lucian pulled himself up to sitting, frustrated by this whole mess.

'They'll brainwash him, just like they did me!' Kalayna was fretting because of what she had told Anselm about the pilot having PK.

'Yeah, good luck with that. Zeven can hold his own. It's us I'm worried about.' Lucian had never before wished he wielded a Power, but it was becoming increasingly obvious that to survive in Taren's world it was a prerequisite.

Ayliscia was glad Ringbalin had returned to the ship to tend his greenhouse, because she had been summoned to report to Jalila Lamus, who could not tolerate men at any price. The viceroy would not be pleased if she discovered how deeply Ayliscia had fallen in love with AMIE's botanist. She must do her utmost to put him from her mind, for Jalila was an excellent telepath, if not the best Phemoria had to offer. As long as Ayliscia did not think of her love for Ringbalin in Jalila's presence, Jalila would not detect it.

Ayliscia was led into the viceroy's office by several Valoureans, who departed at Jalila's word. 'Congratulations, Dr Portus. Her majesty is very pleased with your work. Mission accomplished.'

'So Dr Lennox was the person her majesty was seeking?'

'That is no longer your affair,' Jalila said, putting the doctor back in her place very abruptly.

'Is my work with AMIE to continue?' Ayliscia stuck to the pertinent questions.

'That depends ...' Jalila motioned for Ayliscia to take a seat, and she did so. 'Our majesty will fund AMIE's research provided you can convince Captain

Gervaise to leave this planet *without* Dr Lennox and never again attempt to contact her.'

Ayliscia felt a dagger plunge into her own heart at the very thought of being given the option herself. 'But they are —'

'If you say "in love" I will shoot you myself!' Jalila snarled. 'You are beautiful, you are an agent of Phemoria. Our majesty demands that you persuade the captain to this course.'

'And if I fail?' Ayliscia questioned, needing to learn what options were on the table.

'AMIE and her crew will cease to exist,' Jalila informed her with a sly smile. 'Lucian Gervaise will be severed from Dr Lennox's life for good, one way or another.'

'I understand.' Ayliscia rose to leave, hoping the meeting was at an end.

'You are dismissed,' Jalila said with a shooing gesture. As Ayliscia exited the office, the viceroy waved in several of her Valoureans and the door again closed.

'Follow her, kill her,' Jalila instructed her task force quietly. 'The Phemoray have foretold that she will betray us for her lover, the botanist. They command his death also.'

The guards nodded and left to complete their mission, closing the door behind them.

The uncaring smile fell from Jalila's face. She despised her position at times. She needed to feel some semblance of real emotion to dispel the chill in her heart; she needed satisfaction right away. Her lover had made a rare visit to Phemoria and was awaiting her in their secret meeting place, the door to which was hidden by an ornate screen behind her desk.

She hurried down the stairway of the secret passage, her expectation building, and she was pleased to find her lover already naked in the bed.

'Jalila, my goddess. I thought you'd never get here.'

'Khalid,' she gasped, breathless at the thought of mounting him.

'Look what you left behind this morning.' He held up the amulet he'd given her with a scolding expression.

Jalila gasped when she realised she was not wearing it.

'A slip-up like that could expose us to those bloody witches.'

Khalid slipped the amulet's chain around her neck as Jalila slithered onto the bed alongside him.

'I'll never take it off again,' Jalila assured him, drawing him into a kiss.

Ayliscia was frantic.

She had focused her remote sight upon Jalila's office when she saw the guards enter and perceived the viceroy ordering her death, and then Ringbalin's. The upset nearly broke her concentration, but Ayliscia continued to observe Jalila as, curiously, the viceroy left her office via a secret door and rushed down a staircase into the arms of her lover. The shock had Ayliscia gasping, 'She is a traitor!'

All she could think about was getting to Ringbalin before the Valoureans did and she stole a transport to accomplish her goal. She could call Ringbalin, but she knew her communicator was monitored. As there was no speed limit on the freeway to the spaceport, Ayliscia took advantage and drove like a maniac.

At best, the Valoureans would only be minutes behind her. Ayliscia considered locking the access door to AMIE, but she feared the queen's soldiers would destroy the vital exterior entry hatch, and all hope of escape would be lost to AMIE. Her only advantage was that she knew the layout of the ship better than those who pursued her. Ayliscia bolted directly to Module C hoping to hide her lover until she had dealt with the task force sent to kill them.

'This is a pleasant surprise,' Ringbalin said as Ayliscia entered, but then he saw how distressed she was. 'What has happened?'

'Come!' She grabbed his arm and began to run with him.

Ringbalin heard a blast and Ayliscia hit the ground with a huge bloodied mark on her back.

'No!' he protested and, not caring to even look to see who'd fired the shot, he dropped to the ground beside her. 'Ayliscia?'

'Balin, my love ... run,' she uttered weakly.

'Never,' he declared and breathed a sigh of relief ... as long as Ayliscia still drew breath, he had some chance of saving her. 'Hold still,' he instructed, laying his hands upon her wound.

He summoned to him the vital force that was the lifeblood of the natural world, planning to channel this flow through his hands into Ayliscia to repair her damage, just as he might with a wounded plant. But he couldn't block the sound of the soldiers' boots stomping towards him and under such duress it was difficult to retain enough goodwill and focus for his intention to have the necessary effect.

'She's dead, weed boy,' one of the guards commented, as she and another Valourean dragged him away from Ayliscia and onto his feet.

'No, I can heal her,' he insisted, resisting their restraint to no avail. The Valoureans held him with only one arm each, and in their free hands were their weapons. The two guards aimed at his lover's head and fired.

'Heal that,' one of them scoffed.

Ringbalin's world slipped into slow motion as he stared, utterly devastated, at his love bleeding a river all over the floor of his greenhouse. Never before had he witnessed anything that enraged him senseless like this and Ringbalin permitted his horror and anger to fully bombard him. He gripped tightly to the arms of both his captors and let his agony burst forth in a long, all-embracing scream. He screamed and screamed, completely oblivious to anything but the pain coursing through his body, his hate, his want to retaliate — it consumed him to the point that he was unaware of himself at all. His emotion spent, he was aware only of a cold blackness.

Everywhere black.

Leal and Kassa had wisely accommodated themselves away from the rest of the crew; it was their intention not to be found easily.

In a little cabin in the mountains, miles above the city, the couple slumbered, blissfully unaware that their crewmates were in peril.

Kassa. Kassa Madri!

Kassa stirred to her name being called, but did not awaken.

Kassa!

'What?' she mumbled, in her mind's eye realising she was speaking with Dr Portus.

Get back to AMIE. Her crew are in grave danger.

A vision of Dr Portus and Ringbalin lying in a pool of blood in Module C sent horror coursing through Kassa's veins.

Wake up! Ayliscia's face filled Kassa's vision to demand.

Kassa awoke with a start, gasping in distress and covered in the sweat of her panic. She looked aside and was not surprised to find Leal sitting up with a stunned expression.

'Let's move,' he prompted, and they both sped into action, throwing on their clothes, shoving their few essential possessions in their bags as they ran out the door.

'What are we going to do?' Kassa appealed, punching up Balin's number on her communicator. 'Why would anyone want to hurt Balin?'

'The love interest of a Phemorian spy?' Leal felt it was easy enough to figure out.

Kassa's mind was racing with questions, but there was no point in airing them to Leal. He was as much in the dark as she was. 'There's no answer.'

'Try the captain,' Leal suggested, but everyone's communicator returned a 'service out of order' message.

'So we're not just imagining things,' Kassa stated, more fearful now.

'Something's definitely not right.' Leal felt sure that they hadn't dragged themselves away from their private paradise for some fictitious nightmare they'd shared and mistaken for a psychic vision.

At the spaceport the atmosphere was almost too serene. There was no one in the terminal to check their pass. They just walked right on in. 'Where the hell is security?' Leal mumbled, annoyed. 'Even at this hour of the night there should be someone here. Any damn pilot could walk straight in here and —'

Kassa placed a finger to his lips as she heard someone coming down the interior corridor towards the hatch, and they both stood off to the side, pressed flat to their vessel.

Out of the hatchway stumbled the security guard, who made a beeline to the closest bin to throw up.

Leal and Kassa quietly snuck in the door and headed quickly to Module C. As they ran, Kassa hoped with all her might that her vision had been a premonition and they would not be too late to save their crewmates. Leal had a small phaser and it had been a long time since he'd found cause to draw it, but the weapon was clenched in his hand now as they paused for a moment outside the module's door to see if they could telepathically detect anyone close by.

'Nothing,' said Kassa, and as Leal nodded in agreement, they entered.

There were four bodies inside the central area of the greenhouse, all spreadeagled where they fell.

'Valoureans,' Leal commented as they passed by the royal guards warily to get to their crewmates. He turned to keep an eye on the downed soldiers, while Kassa approached the bloodied area to check for vital signs in Ringbalin.

Ayliscia Portus was quite obviously a lost cause as the back of her head had been blown clean away. Kassa really didn't expect to feel a pulse as she pressed her fingers against Ringbalin's neck. 'He's alive!' She pulled out a torch to take a look in his eyes. 'Completely catatonic.' She rose, interested to see if the soldiers were still alive.

'Careful,' Leal warned her. He rolled the first

Valourean onto her back with his foot and then jumped back in horror. 'What in the dark universe happened to her?'

It appeared as if the woman had imploded; her eyeballs had both burst and blood trickled from her nose, mouth and ears. The other Valourean was in exactly the same state.

'Heavens preserve us!' Kassa's eyes darted back to Balin. 'Could he have done this?'

Leal was stumped for an answer. 'Whatever the case, we have two dead Valoureans, one dead Phemorian agent and missing crew.' Leal considered their options, and there weren't many. 'I need to get this vessel into orbit. It will be harder to take in space.' He headed for the control room. 'Are you right to move Balin?'

'I'll move him with a stretcher,' Kassa said.

Zeven was unbound and cast into a room. The door locked behind him. He removed his blindfold to perceive a dimly lit black room with no windows and no two-way mirrors or cameras to be seen. He sensed another presence and turned to find a tall hooded figure standing in a dark corner.

'I don't suppose locks make that much difference to you,' Anselm commented as he lowered his hood.

'Where there's a will, there's a way ... as Taren would say,' Zeven retorted.

'You're never going to see her again,' Anselm informed him matter-of-factly. 'The Phemorians will see to that, whether she likes it or not.'

'Are you saying that Taren Lennox has been kidnapped?' Zeven inquired.

'She has been *claimed*, so her incarceration will be perfectly legal,' Anselm clarified. 'Taren is the daughter of Qusay-Sabah Clarona and the heir to the Phemorian throne.'

'What!' Zeven was bowled over. 'I thought she was your daughter!'

'She *is* my daughter!' Anselm stressed. 'Not that I had any say in the matter,' he grumbled under his breath. 'Who needs sex when you can steal DNA?'

Zeven's mind boggled — he wasn't too sure what Anselm was implying. 'Do you mean to tell me that the Queen of Phemoria raped you?'

'Genetically, *yes*, she raped me,' Anselm stated. 'You see, what they call "true Phemorians", those women who aspire to be Phemoray, aren't like other human beings. They detest physical contact with men so much that they have developed their own reproduction technique ... the ability to absorb genetic material from the man they choose to father a child, or children, without any sexual act — *or consent* — taking place. Unfortunately, I discovered this after the fact! Believe me, the queen of Phemoria would not have been my choice of mother to my child. I wouldn't want my daughter growing up to despise half the population of the USS, nor to be forced to govern a nation of prissy, repressed, prejudice-filled spinsters!'

Zeven was starting to feel sympathetic towards Anselm at this point. 'But maybe Taren would change all that?'

'Not if the Phemoray bewitch her. To prevent them finding her I stole Taren's memory every few years, so that she could not remember her beginnings, her parents, and could not betray herself unwittingly to Phemorian telepaths.' Anselm looked back to Zeven. 'No soul alive knows all of what I am telling you and I don't want any of this leaking out. That would only expose Taren to more danger.'

Zeven nodded.

'To ensure that that remains the case, this room is completely secure. Anything that takes place in here, or is said, will only ever be known to us,' Anselm said, but Zeven was not so fast to nod this time. Anselm wanted to know Zeven's secret.

'Why should I trust you?'

Anselm smiled as if it were a foregone conclusion. 'You and I are the same ... different talents, but extraordinary, nonetheless.'

'Oh, yeah?' Zeven folded his arms in challenge. 'What do you do?'

'I see auras,' Anselm said, and grinned, 'so I can identify a gifted psychic upon sight. The only aura I've seen that is as expansive as yours surrounds my daughter ... which is why I didn't believe your escape from the black hole in the Maladaan system was just a lucky break. Damn it all,' Anselm continued in an inspired tone, 'how amazing it must have felt to discover you could defy the quantum world.'

Zeven gave a goofy grin, but still did not confess.

'But quite apart from the fact that we share a secret,' Anselm said confidently, 'you are surely going to want to rescue Taren. Sermetica is the only nation that will be able to shield you and AMIE from the Phemorians' wrath.'

Zeven went quiet in thought; he found himself wanting to help Anselm, something he would never have considered doing before this conversation. But could he be trusted? Or would Zeven find himself in Swithin's sad situation, despised by those he cared for because of his decision?

'I apologise for the shock tactics to get you to this meeting, but you are the only man in the known universe who can help me get my daughter back,' Anselm appealed, sensing Zeven's reluctance. 'I do have one other PK expert on my staff, but I cannot trust him with —'

'On your *staff*?' Zeven blurted in surprise. 'But I thought that —'

Anselm held up a palm to interrupt. 'It's better that the general population believe that all psychics are under government restraint. The secret services do not hate those with "the Powers". They secretly recruit them and protect their identities from those who would rather see them exterminated. Only the few who pose a threat to society are detained and restrained.'

'Is that a threat?' Zeven wondered.

'With your heroic tendencies,' Anselm laughed, 'I think not. No friend of my daughter's is an enemy of mine. Help me get her back and I shall *never* forget it.'

Anselm's favour was a great prize indeed, but only as long as it served his cause. Still, Zeven mused, at this stage of the game, it did seem that they were on the same side. 'If I help you, I'll do so under my own steam. You must let the captain and the girls go, and see them safely back to AMIE ... including Kalayna.'

'She has paid any dues she owed me,' Anselm said with an affectionate smile.

'Was she recruited for having a Power?' Zeven was curious as to how Kalayna had got involved with the MSS, but Anselm shook his head.

'She was recruited for her technical expertise and her obvious physical attributes.' He raised his brows, knowing Zeven had fallen for her charms. 'Or so I was informed, as I was not the one who recruited her. But I agree to your terms.' Anselm looked Zeven squarely in the eyes and nodded his head firmly.

'I also want AMIE fully serviced and stocked once we reach Sermetica.'

'It will be done.' Anselm held out a hand to shake on it.

Zeven was still hesitant to commit. 'And what of Taren?'

'Her fate is hers to decide, as it always has been, even though she does not remember.' Anselm seemed saddened at thinking of the position he'd placed her in. 'I guess there is really no point in keeping her past from her any longer. Qusay-Sabah has found her now, so she may as well have her memories back.'

'You still have Taren's childhood memories?' Zeven asked on Taren's behalf.

Anselm nodded. 'A copy of them, anyway.'

'A copy!' Zeven was appalled. 'A copy could have been screwed with.'

'The original data is stored in the MSS mainframe computer on Maladaan,' Anselm said apologetically, 'wherever that may be now.'

'So you are as much in the dark about Maladaan's disappearance as we are?'

'I'm afraid so,' the politician confessed.

'In my humble opinion, the MSS were largely responsible, however unwittingly,' Zeven told him. 'If that sample had not been stolen from our project by your agents, our planet would still be where it belongs.'

Anselm laughed at his perception. 'They were not my agents as I am not head of the MSS —'

'But Swithin was your agent,' Zeven rebuked.

'Only so far as getting Taren onto the AMIE project, as that was her greatest aspiration. I thought that, in space, she'd be safer than anywhere. Apart from that, Swithin never answered to me.'

'I know for a fact Swithin has recently been answering to your viceroy, Khalid Mansur,' Zeven said.

'Has he? Well, that's very interesting.' Anselm's eyes narrowed as he dwelt upon that piece of information. 'So Maladaan's disappearance did have something to do with that gas sample,' Anselm said, going back to the other part of the conversation that was of interest to him.

'It was not a gas sample,' Zeven set him straight. 'It was a small part of a larger being, infinitely more powerful and advanced than we are. Swithin Gervaise had been ordered by our captain to release the sample as soon as it reached Maladaan, but MSS agents intercepted it.'

'I would very much like to speak with Swithin Gervaise,' Anselm decided.

Zeven knew it was his captain's desire to rescue his brother from the Phemorians and the pilot smiled, holding out his hand to shake Anselm's at last. 'If it will help clear AMIE of being implicated in Maladaan's disappearance, I think I can arrange that.'

CHAPTER 22

ANGELS IN FAST MOTION

The Phemorians' secret city was beautiful, an accomplishment of the imagination and psychic ingenuity.

Qusay-Sabah Clarona explained that the physical world also had many subtle planes of awareness that were worlds unto themselves — just as the physical body served as a vehicle for the spirit in the physical world, so everyone had an emotional body in the astral plane of awareness, a mental body on the mental plane, and a causal body on the lower causal plane of awareness; beyond this level of existence the spirit, no longer needing individual expression, was formless, as it prepared to merge with the collective consciousness of all there is. Taren imagined that the higher causal realm was the level of consciousness where the being Azazèl-mindos-coomra-dorchi was currently operating from. The secret to accessing these other realms of existence lay in being able to employ one's own subtle bodies. The way to do this was to attune one's sonic vibratory rate to oscillate in harmony with the consciousness you had on the plane of demonstration, or awareness, that you wished to experience.

Taren was sceptical, as the world she was passing through seemed very real, vibrant and solid, as did the form she was walking around in — possibly even slightly more so than usual: she was hyper-aware of colour, smell, movement and all sensations. 'Are you saying that I am not employing my physical body right now?'

The queen nodded. 'You left your physical form back in my council chamber.'

Taren gasped and smiled at once. 'This is an OBE!' She suddenly felt the hyper-state she was moving about in; Taren had documented cases of patients having out-of-body experiences, but she had never had one.

'We prefer to call it astral projection' the queen advised, 'being that one is employing an astral form to move through the astral realm.'

Taren observed the goings-on in the city below from the queen's enclosed, private walkway that sprawled around the secret city. 'Then where are all the physical bodies of these citizens?'

'We have a secure facility beneath the government sector of the city, where their bodies reside in a state of stasis, perfectly aware of their life within this city. These women and girls have freely chosen to renounce life in the physical world and live a life of spiritual discovery and seclusion here.'

'But what of all the experiences they are missing?' Taren thought some of these girls too young to make such a decision about their lives.

'They are free to return to their physical bodies at any time, and are in fact required to at least a few times a year,' the queen informed.

As a scientist, Taren was most intrigued. 'But don't their physical forms atrophy?'

'As above then so below,' said the queen. 'When we exercise and nourish ourselves here in the astral realm, our physical bodies benefit. Much like your studies on athletes who run a race, or otherwise exercise, in their mind. Don't their bodies reap the benefit?'

It was true. 'But they only receive fifty per cent of the benefit of doing the exercise physically,' Taren said.

'Ah ... but if your test subjects were as psychic as we Phemorians, then it would be one hundred per cent! Physical wellbeing is all in the mind,' the monarch stated, 'just as you have been trying to prove for years.

'This ethereal city, everything you see around you, has been constructed from the imagination and willpower of Phemorian women who have learned to mould etheric matter as a potter moulds clay.'

'Etheric matter?' Taren queried.

'You might know it better as atomic mass,' the queen conceded with a smile, 'although the etheric matter of the astral world is more subtle and open to manipulation than the atomic structure of the physical world, you understand. But soon we shall be as efficient at controlling one as the other.'

'*Whoa*,' Taren was impressed. 'They can control matter at an atomic level?'

'As we all do,' the queen concurred, 'some with more intention than others.'

The etheric city was beauteous, harmonious, spotless, luxurious and sweet-smelling. It was all that women love and cherish. Every female here, from the old to the babes, seemed to have mastery over one Power or another. In the open city square, there were performances, demonstrations and lessons in psychic skill taking place.

Taren had never really kept the company of women — her life choices and interests had steered her into situations that were dominated by men. As difficult as men were to deal with at times, she couldn't imagine cutting them off altogether! As she observed a group of young girls, Taren had to ask: 'What happens to the male babies born here?'

'A *true* Phemorian's will is such that there is seldom a male child,' the queen replied winningly, 'but on the rare occasion a male child is conceived, the mother may choose to move to this city's twin in the physical world to raise him. She may then return to her Phemorian sister city once her son has left her care.'

'I bet not many of those women return here,' Taren mused, thinking that raising a child was a lifelong commitment.

'No, they don't,' said the queen with pity. 'They grow old and wither in the service of their men.'

'But you must have loved a man at one time, or I would not be here,' Taren reasoned, sensing that the queen was not happy with the line of questioning.

'I am sorry to shatter any romantic illusions you may have, but an attraction is all that is required,' she stated coldly. 'Anselm means as much to me as I do to him.'

Clearly, this was not a welcome topic, so Taren returned to a more general one. 'What if a mother does not choose to raise her boy herself?'

'The child will be adopted. There are couples on other planets who might cherish a son,' the queen concluded bluntly, hoping that was the end of the matter.

'But surely the sons of Phemoria are as psychically gifted as the daughters?'

The queen laughed. 'Without Phemoray training they will never realise their full potential. They are no threat to us.'

'But I managed,' Taren said meekly.

'You have royal Phemorian blood in your veins. My daughter was always destined to be one of the greatest psychics that ever lived, and you have nowhere near discovered your full potential. Forced to survive in a man's world, your true Power has been repressed, but here ... here, the opportunities for you are endless.'

Taren could see the truth of that. She had never thought to be trained in the psychic arts as they were outlawed everywhere, but here — where she was from! Taren knew she had been repressing her skills to date, but even so there were several others of her acquaintance — most of them male — who she believed to be equally, if not more, gifted than herself. Her heart began beating rapidly as she considered the loaded question she had to ask ... 'Do I have a brother?'

The queen looked affronted, but her anger was quickly hidden by her regal smile. 'Not from my quarter, I assure you.'

'A cousin perhaps, or —'

'Why do you ask?' The queen looked at her curiously. 'Does that man of yours have psychic ability?'

'Lucian?' Taren found the thought amusing. 'Ah, *no* ... but he is very open-minded.'

'Damn shame,' the queen said brusquely. 'He might have proved useful for mating.'

'What?' Taren could hardly believe what she was hearing. 'Lucian Gervaise is one of the finest scientific minds and visionaries of our lifetime. He does not exist for me to *use*.'

The queen merely raised her brows at this. 'You're right, maybe his genes do have some merit.'

The reply was frustrating. Taren wasn't getting through to the monarch at all. 'What I meant was —'

'No matter. We need to leave to be in time for our meeting with the Phemoray. Are you ready?' The queen held out both her hands for Taren to take hold. 'Trust me ... I am your mother, after all.'

Taren was hesitant. She knew she was in way over her head with the Phemorians ... let alone the super-beings they called the Phemoray! *This is even more dangerous than allowing the MSS to screw with my head* — she strongly suspected that the secret services were amateurs in psychic control compared with these women! She had no real knowledge of the spirit realm, nor a means to protect herself from the forces therein. Still, there was one being she knew who was more evolved in the cosmic scheme than she was. If etheric substance was the vital, unifying, all-pervading life force of creation then it followed that it spanned the vast reaches of existence, distributing cosmic light and consciousness throughout. So, surely Taren could use this unified field to find any being in creation?

Taren placed her hands upon those of the queen, but inwardly her focus turned to her celestial friend. *Azazèl-mindos-coomra-dorchi, please hear me, please help me.* She willed the message forth through the etheric web as the celestial city began to be obscured by light and shadows. *Be compassionate and watch over me ... protect me from harm and delusion ...*

From Taren's physical being, through the spherical order of matter to the molecular level, her request for protection connected and spread through the etheric matrix of the spiralling universes, up through the astral, mental and lower-causal dimensions, to beyond ...

In a small galaxy of a distant universe, Taren's request for assistance registered in the condensed memory of the monad Azazèl-mindos-coomra-dorchi.

This being was very aware of the distress caused to the physical manifestation that now sought help, when her planet had been swept through into this universe. The monad was also aware that the Inter-dimensional Council of Watchers had a plan to aid the displaced planet. This soul appealing for help was a very big part of that plan, but she was calling to the part of her monad that was *way* beyond being of personal service to her.

Azazèl-mindos-coomra-dorchi was a causal being and, as such, could no longer become involved in the struggles of those soul-minds still existent on the lower planes of demonstration. But the monad had progressed through semi-causal incarnations of experience to reach its present Arupa state of consciousness. Those many individual manifestations of the monad had semi-causal bodies and were known as the grigori — the Dwellers on the Threshold between physical and spiritual planes of awareness. The grigori were in the service of the Council of Watchers who were in the service of the monad.

The dwellers would be directed to respond to the call of the soul-mind who was the best hope of restoring the imbalance caused by the displacement of her planet ...

Azazèl floated toward the antechamber of the Council of Watchers for debriefing, flanked by Armaros and

Sammael, who were fellow grigori. Their last crusade into the physical realms of existence had been a great success and they were to be reinstated to cosmic service. No more split-soul missions into the physical realms for them; they were completely over any lust for earthly pleasures. Their vocation was guidance, inspiration, support and compassion from now on.

Further down the celestial corridor the rest of Azazèl's grigori brothers waited to greet his return. They called each other brothers although, in truth, the grigori were androgynous beings.

On their last mission, they had been required to split into male and female human soul-minds. They had been assigned this daunting task to make amends to a small pocket of humankind developing on an isolated planet on the outer rim of a galaxy in one tiny universe of this multi-universal evolutionary scheme.

The grigori had fallen from grace when, instead of merely guiding the development of humanity on the planet in their charge, they had been enmoured of humans, and assumed physical form in order to mate with them. As punishment the grigori were cast down by the Watchers and forced to endure human hardship and the burden of leadership until the evolution that the grigori corrupted was, through eons of lifetimes, finally set to rights.

Inside his mind Azazèl heard the voice of his female self incarnate appealing to him, and he stopped still to focus inward.

Azazèl-mindos-coomra-dorchi, please hear me, please help me. Be compassionate and watch over me . . . protect me from harm and delusion.

Tory? he queried the inner voice, and then shook his head to the negative, feeling he wasn't quite hitting the mark. *What physical incarnation of ours, in all of the multiverse, would know our Arupa soul by its full name?*

Did he say Tory? Sammael was stunned and stopped beside their leader.

That's certainly what it sounded like. Armaros stopped still also, for the scholar was concerned they may have overlooked some vital detail of their last mission.

Your female half in the earth scheme? Sammael queried.

No, another manifestation of her. Azazèl zoned out of their questioning to hone in on the source.

In a blinding flash of awareness, Taren's entire situation was known to him. *I have to go.*

But our pardon awaits! Sammael motioned towards the antechamber ahead, a despairing look on his face.

Yes, my lord. Please let's not defy the council again — Armaros appealed for restraint, but Azazèl didn't know the meaning of the word when it came to his female incarnation being in distress.

I have council permission, he assured his brothers. *It is a matter of great import.*

Well, we've waited a few million earth years for our pardon. We are with you. Sammael volunteered both himself and Armaros.

When Armaros smiled to confirm his involvement, Azazèl nodded in gratitude and evaporated into the ether.

Sammael and Armaros hooked into their leader's chain of thought and pursued his spirit into the etheric sub spheres leading into the physical multiverse.

Their destination was to the only time and the only universe where the humans of their soul group had made direct contact with their Arupa self.

Sammael and Armaros honed in on their incarnations — the physical beings presently embroiled in the circumstances of concern to their leader — and it was clear how they could aid with his quest.

I'll ensure the body of your female self is secured. Sammael parted from his brothers.

I'll see if I can rouse the botanist. Armaros vanished, leaving Azazèl to stay his course.

And I shall protect my charge from being engulfed by the evil of a million women scorned.

Lucian had given up hope of ever being released. They hadn't heard a word from anyone since they'd been locked up, and the girls had fallen asleep — one on either of his shoulders. He was starting to doze himself, so when he heard the door open, he felt sure he was dreaming it.

'Getting cosy with my girls, hey?'

'Starman!' Both Aurora and Kalayna sprang to their feet to hug Zeven and cover him in kisses.

'Time to get you out of here,' he stated. The girls backed off a little.

'How did you accomplish this?' Kalayna was cautious; this was not one of his magic man rescues. It seemed that the triple-S were allowing them to walk free.

'I made a deal with Anselm —' he began.

'What!' all three of his crewmates echoed. 'You're going to trust Anselm?' Lucian finished on everyone's behalf.

'They've brainwashed him!' Kalayna threw her hands in the air, one of which Zeven grabbed to get her attention.

'He didn't brainwash me,' Zeven assured her. 'And it's my risk to take,' he said as Anselm's agents filed into the room. 'AMIE has lifted off and is in orbit. You are being given a shuttle transport, and you ...' He looked at Kalayna. '... will fly our captain and Aurora back to AMIE, so that no triple-S agent enters our craft. Are you cool with that?'

Kalayna was wide-eyed — honoured, shocked, excited and scared — but nodded to confirm she could do as he asked.

'I'm a pilot,' Lucian pointed out, but seeing how deflated Kalayna appeared, he confessed, 'although I am a little rusty.'

Aurora directed Zeven to look her way. 'What about you?'

'I'll join you there soon.' He kissed her to stop the questions and then moved to leave.

The captain waylaid him. 'What about Taren?'

'I'm taking care of it,' he insisted, knowing the captain would want to be involved. 'There's nothing you can do here, but the crew need you.'

Lucian had other concerns about leaving. 'Swithin is in a Phemorian detention centre —'

'He's no longer there,' Zeven informed him and Lucian was speechless. 'He's being questioned by Anselm's people in regard to the disappearance of Maladaan and is not in any immediate danger.'

Zeven had always been so paranoid about his Power, that Lucian couldn't fathom what Anselm could possibly have said to lead him to expose his talent and use it in Sermetica's service. 'Why do you trust Anselm?'

'Because the alternative is looking pretty fucking bad,' Zeven said bluntly, needing to move on. 'You'll just have to trust my gut instinct this time.'

Lucian sucked back his pride and concern. 'Your gut instinct has always proved fairly on the mark.'

'When you get on board AMIE, you should head straight for Sermetica. Taren and I will join you as soon as superhumanly possible.' Zeven tried to make a joke of it, but Lucian wasn't appreciating the humour so, on that low note, Zeven departed.

'This way to our launch bay,' their escort instructed, and directed them down the corridor.

Seconds after Taren had oriented herself, she felt the foreboding energy of the place to which Queen Qusay-Sabah Clarona had led her and knew instantly that this meeting was a bad idea. Even in the darkness of the pre-dawn shadows, Taren could perceive the wilting vegetation of the forest around her. 'This is where the Phemoray choose to base themselves?'

'You obviously feel the ill-will here,' the queen said, sounding proud. 'This site is sacred to the Phemoray ... it was once known as the Abyss of the Obstinate. In the times before the revolution, many women were unjustly put to death here and flung into a deep hole to rot. It is from the combined force of those anguished souls that the Phemoray draw their power.' The queen made it sound like a beautiful undertaking.

It was little wonder that everything in the vicinity was dying; the place was steeped in negativity. 'How does one transmute such a negative frequency into a beneficial intention without harm to the self?' Taren asked. According to her research, a negative intention could never produce a positive result, nor benefit the sender.

You shall be proven wrong about that, little scientist.

Taren heard the voices of several women in her mind, speaking in unison.

'Greetings, great mothers of the Phemoray.' The queen immediately bowed low to the ground.

But Taren did not, as she was curious to see those who addressed her.

Five veiled women, floating in formation, just as they had on Frujia, came out of the dead forest and into the barren clearing where the fading moonlight made their forms apparent.

Even more intriguing was the great undulating mass of energy that hovered over them in full technicolour. Taren had not seen or sensed this mass at their last meeting, but she had not been viewing the Phemoray through her third-eye vision at the time either. She had never perceived anything like this anomaly on the Earth plane — the seething body of energy was clearly charged with violent emotions and thoughts and these ancient impressions played out upon the moving fluidic surface of the mass. The horrific scenes of women being raped, tortured and butchered by their men made it very hard to focus on the women who hovered beneath the heavy cloud of sadness and terror.

Your experiments are incomplete, claimed the Phemoray. *Over a vast distance an intent to harm is far stronger than an intent to heal, but healing is best done when in close contact ... hence the saying, keep your friends close and your enemies —*

'Closer,' Taren concluded, intrigued by the premise. She could hardly wait to get into a lab and test the theory.

And a medium can use either force at no personal detriment, provided they believe with every fibre of their being that they are doing the right thing.

This information was not quite as exciting, as Taren had always held the somewhat romantic belief that love was a more powerful force than hatred. But if what the Phemoray claimed was true, it seemed to shatter that ideal. However, Taren had not come here to debate cosmic law; she had but one purpose for seeking the Phemoray and came straight to the point. 'Do you know what has become of Maladaan?'

We concern ourselves with the affairs of Phemoria and so should you. That planet disappearing was the catalyst that brought you back to our fold.

'So you know nothing,' Taren assumed, greatly disappointed. 'Then I thank you for seeing me. I shall not take up any more of your time.' Taren had no idea how to escape this forest and return to her physical form, but she knew she had to leave.

The queen stood up. 'That part of your life is over now,' she announced, in a not-too-friendly fashion.

'Look, I'm sorry,' Taren turned back to confront the monarch, 'but I could never rule Phemoria the way you wish me to. You draw your power from hating men and I *don't*,' she said honestly. 'I *love* the men in my life and I would not relinquish their company for *all* the ancient doctrine in Phemoria.'

'When you are enlightened to the horrors of the past, you will hate men just as much as we do,' the queen said with finality, and Taren felt the trap they'd set for her snap closed.

Time to educate our future queen, the Phemoray advised, whereby Queen Qusay-Sabah backed away.

Taren suspected she knew where that education was to come from and she turned her sights to the horrific mass of malignant memory as it launched itself in her direction. 'No!' She crouched down and willed with all her might to deflect the psychic attack.

Zeven had no intention of returning Taren to Anselm's fold; he had every intention of returning her to AMIE.

After watching the launch of the craft containing AMIE's captain and crew, Zeven accompanied Anselm to the secure room from where he could vanish without exposing his Power to anybody except Anselm.

'So ... now we get down to the serious side of our business.' Anselm removed his hood once they were behind a locked door and addressed Zeven directly. 'There is an explosive device on board that craft —'

'What!' Zeven was immediately on the offensive. 'Why did I trust you?'

'You don't trust me,' Anselm rebutted, 'and I don't trust you. I can plainly see you are of fine character and as such you will be loyal to your captain. So what choice did I have but to give you an incentive to comply with our arrangement?'

Zeven was exasperated — the man had just betrayed him and yet he still liked and admired the guy. Anselm was smart, like Taren. 'You're just like her!' Zeven turned to pace out his frustration.

Anselm was privately delighted by Zeven's words.

'How do I know you will not use that bomb to dispose of us all, once I deliver Taren to you?'

'Because if you do not return Taren to me *before* that vessel reaches AMIE, I shall detonate anyway, and your captain and girlfriends will die.'

'What!' That didn't give Zeven very much time. 'You son of a —'

'I won't risk any harm to AMIE, as that vessel is my link to whatever has become of Maladaan, which is where Taren's original memory data is stored. It was never my intenton for her to forget me altogether! I mean you no harm, Mr Gudrun. I just want my daughter back.'

'She doesn't remember you. If I must bring her back to you, then I am not leaving her side before she is comfortable with that arrangement.'

'I am her protector,' Anselm stressed, as Zeven didn't seem to understand. 'I have been all her life!'

'Not *all* her life,' Zeven added, 'not lately.'

'Don't you have enough on your hands with the two women you've got?'

'Never enough!' Zeven was curt and stepped away as Anselm became angry.

'If you've laid a hand on my dau—' Anselm took a swing at Zeven who clasped a hand around the man's forearm to stop the strike.

'If you harm my friends …' Zeven warned, raising both brows in challenge.

'Go and retrieve Taren before those bloody witches get hold of her!'

A burning, buzzing sensation swept over Zeven like a wave from behind, drowning out reality as he was ripped away from the conversation and catapulted through time and space to elsewhere.

A great rush of light swept over Taren and, much to her confusion, it filled her with warmth and joy. Was this part of the enchantment of the Phemoray?

Taren?

'Lucian?' Taren raised her head at the sound of his voice, to behold the most stunning natural formation she had ever seen.

It was a cathedral of trees, the trunks of which formed rows of pillars, their branches entwined to create arched windows and doorways in between. To her right, light was pouring through the structure, like a sunrise, but then the light source moved into Taren's line of sight. It had a human form at its core, but the surrounding glow was so bright that Taren couldn't see much more than a vague shadow.

Don't be afraid, he said, again in Lucian's voice.

'I'm not.' Taren suppressed an urge to laugh, as all the ill-will around her had been dispersed by a loving energy that felt very familiar. 'It is you, Lucian, isn't it?' She neared the being cautiously. Her eyes adjusted to the light and came to focus on, not Lucian, but someone who looked very much like him.

There is a part of me that was Lucian Gervaise, a long time ago, just as I will one day be a small part of the condensed memory of Azazèl-mindos-coomra-dorchi. But as I am now, I am known simply as Azazèl of the grigori.

Taren was mesmerised by his words, his beauty. 'The grigori?'

We are threshold dwellers ... between the cause of the spirit world and the effect in the physical world. Minor devas in the cosmic scheme.

Taren gasped as she realised what all this meant. 'I really made contact with Azazèl-mindos-coomra-dorchi?'

Azazèl nodded to confirm this. *Your planet is alive and well and existing in an entirely different universal scheme.*

He answered before she'd even formulated the question and Taren was again gasping for joy. 'Maladaan survived!'

Yes. He empathised with her relief for a moment.

'But it went through a black hole! Has it not been crushed into a singularity and damned for all eternity?' Taren asked.

Azazèl laughed. *A black hole in this universe forms a white hole in another, making it more of a cosmic gusher for matter. Your friend teleports himself and others from place to place, and every time he does so, every particle of his being reduces to its singular state to move and then reconstitute.*

'Which is pretty much how the inter-system gateways work,' Taren conceded.

It is the same with matter through a black hole, or, as with Maladaan, an inter-universal leak. So what we have in the Maladaan system is more of a wound than a hole.

'Do you mean to say the tear in space is mending?' Taren's mind boggled.

This unnatural phenomenon is more unstable and of an indefinite duration.

'How will we ever find Maladaan if the fabric of space repairs itself and closes over?'

There are problems with Maladaan remaining where it has relocated ... it shares the orbit of another planet that plays host to a human civilisation far more spiritually advanced than Maladaan's scientific populace will feel comfortable with.

'Can something be done?' Taren was concerned and feeling partly responsible. She wanted to be involved in the rescue, although she couldn't imagine what use she could be to beings like the grigori.

The beautiful being smiled at her fondly, as if knowing her mind and heart and where this conversation was going. *We cannot take action on a physical level, only you humans can do that. There is a role for you in the restoration of Maladaan, but first we must get you away from this hostile thought-form, which you are ill-prepared to deal with just yet.*

'Is it true that I am the daughter of this hate-filled queen and that my father is her worst enemy?'

You are indeed the first born of the royal line of the Phemoria, since the war between the sexes began, who was conceived in love.

The reply shocked Taren and, although she realised this being knew infinitely more than she did, she just had to query it. 'Are you sure? They claim to hate each other.'

Azazèl smiled that knowing smile again. *Soul-minds developing on your plane of demonstration are not always in touch with how they truly feel . . . their intellect, external agendas and pride get in the way and they will not admit how they feel, not even to themselves.*

Usually Zeven had to wilfully visualise something in order to utilise his PK ability, but he had no idea where he was going at present. He obviously hadn't orchestrated this journey, and that was a worry.

Before he had time to wonder what he was going to do to rectify the situation, reality came to a standstill and he was right in front of the slumbering form of Taren Lennox.

'Who are you?'

Zeven did an about-face to find a tall, veiled, regal-looking woman. 'Me? I'm no one.' He backed up toward Taren.

'No man has ever set foot in the Phemorian Royal Palace,' the woman said, her anger building.

'Is that where I am?' Zeven played cute and stupid. 'I must have taken a wrong turn somewhere.' He crouched down and took hold of Taren.

'Don't you touch her,' the woman warned him. 'It won't do any good to take her body. Her spirit is elsewhere.'

Don't listen to her, Zeven heard an internal voice advise, and was not given the option to query it before he was whipped off against his will to the next unknown destination.

When his world stood still, Zeven was in a dirt clearing in a dying forest. 'Stop doing that!' He drew a few deep breaths. 'Can we please just stop.' He suddenly felt the weight of Taren in his arms and dropped to his knees.

Taren was still sleeping like a baby, so Zeven raised his head to look around. He didn't consider himself particularly sensitive, but he felt that this place had the vibe of a bad nightmare. 'Where the fuck am I?'

You're always right where you need to be, said the voice inside his mind, as clearly as his own inner voice, but altogether more sure of itself.

'Am I possessed?' Zeven placed Toren aside and stood up. 'I'm certainly not pulling my own strings here, so what's the story?' he yelled, frustrated.

There was a crack of bark, as if every branch of every dying tree in the surrounding forest suddenly stretched. There was another such crack and another, as the dying forest re-formed into towering trees before his eyes. Horror and then wonder filled his eyes with tears as the trees moulded themselves into a cathedral-like structure, lush with vegetation and colossal in stature.

Zeven thought to wake Taren to witness the event and was shocked to find her missing.

Zeven!

He heard Taren call.

Where are you? He took a few steps in the direction of her voice and she appeared in a space between one of the tree-archways.

The question is more, where are you? She laughed, and it was good to see her conscious and carefree. *You're astral travelling!*

I am? He felt a pang of surprise and fear rush through him.

Who is your grigori friend? she asked, pointing behind Zeven.

My what? He turned to see a large celestial being trailing him and nearly had a fit! *I knew it! I was possessed*, Zeven accused the entity, who appeared remarkably like himself.

Well, of course you are possessed by your own soul-mind. The grigorian greeted Taren. *I am Sammael*, he said, bowing.

Another large grigori was trailing Taren. This being had Lucian's appearance. *Go now, quickly, away from this planet*, the glowing being advised Taren and she nodded to concur that she understood.

Are they aliens? Zeven was bemused and felt incredibly left out of the conversation.

Follow him ... Sammael pointed to Zeven, whereupon Taren moved towards him, a huge smile on her face as she reached out to touch him.

'Zeven ... wake up. Zeven!'

'What!' The pilot was startled back to consciousness but was pleasantly surprised to find Taren's smiling face awaiting him there also.

'How are you doing, champ?' She kissed his cheek, thankful she had awakened with her body and psyche reunited and in friendly company.

'What just happened?' Zeven sat up and was a little disappointed to note he was in the dead forest. 'You did see those glowing guys, right?'

Taren nodded with a grin. 'Yes, I most certainly did.'

'Well, who were they?'

'Spirits.' Taren's eyes glazed over as she replied and an expression of great affection lingered on her face. 'I believe they just saved me from doing something very stupid.'

A decaying branch dropped from a tree nearby and they leapt up, startled.

'We should go,' Taren suggested. Although it was broad daylight, she wasn't going to bank on the fact that the Phemoray could only frequent this place in the twilight hours.

'Yeah, well, I have a bit of a dilemma with where to take you.' Zeven briefed Taren on the situation and she was thrown into turmoil also.

'You've spoken with Anselm about me?' Taren struggled to remain calm and keep an open mind.

'You're all he talks about,' Zeven emphasised. 'He seemed genuinely desperate to speak with you ... but then I'm no great judge of character.'

'Sure you are,' Taren said, encouraging him to go easier on himself. 'And if you stay with me, what harm could it do to hear his side of the story.'

'It's a pretty strange love story Anselm has to tell,' Zeven warned.

'Have you met my mother?' Taren wasn't surprised in the least. 'Take me to him.'

Zeven took hold of her outstretched hands and then hesitated. 'Please don't do this on my say-so. I quite like the guy, but he could be a complete arsehole for all I know.'

'You commented before that he's like me,' she countered and Zeven had to laugh.

'Um, yeah.'

'Then I want to meet him,' Taren replied, and Zeven was then able to comply with her wish.

On arrival in the secure room, Taren and Zeven were confronted by Anselm and several of his armed operatives.

Zeven was immediately shot with a dart filled with sedative, and he dropped to the ground. 'I'm sorry, sweetheart,' Anselm said apologetically to Taren. 'Sorry again,' and raised his eyebrows in rueful sympathy. She felt a stinging sensation in the top of her arm and then numbness which spread rapidly throughout her body. She dropped like a stone beside Zeven. *I should have let him return us to AMIE*, she thought regretfully. Her eyes felt heavy and closed, but her hearing was the last sense to go.

'Get us off this damn planet,' ordered Anselm, as she was swept up by several men. 'Restrain her friend and bring him.'

'What about AMIE?' asked a subordinate.

'What about AMIE?' Anselm replied.

'Should we detonate the device on board?'

The query was almost enough to shock Taren from her sedation and she struggled to remain focused on the response.

'Once we are away ...'

Taren could not hold out any longer as her present was engulfed in a fitful blur.

PART 4

SERMETICA — DESERT PLANET

CHAPTER 23

PROVOCATION

Lucian felt he should have stayed in space — now Taren was missing again. What was worse, even with all the technology at his disposal, he was at a complete loss to do anything about it. If his brother and deceased wife — two mere mortals — managed to pull the wool over his eyes so completely, then what chance did he have against a planet of psychic man-haters and the combined secret service agencies of every other planet in the USS? Lucian hated that he had to leave Taren's rescue to Zeven, who may already have been tainted by secret service conditioning.

One thing was plainly obvious: Anselm didn't want Lucian in Taren's life any more than the Phemorians did, and Lucian resented these people's belief that he was a pushover and could be so easily disposed of and ignored.

The communicator on his hip sounded and broke into his mood as he gazed out the large porthole window in his office. 'Yes, Kalayna,' he responded, looking back at the planet they were fleeing.

'When I was flying us back,' she explained in a flurry, 'the handling of the craft felt imbalanced. It kept pulling off to one side. So I checked it out and,' she took a breath, 'there is an explosive device planted in one of the engines of the USS craft!'

'On my way!' Lucian raced up to the launch bay, his exasperation and anger mounting. When he arrived on the scene, Leal was already present.

'We can launch it on autopilot,' Leal advised and pulled Kalayna away from the entry hatch. 'I'll set it up, you ready the launch bay.'

Kalayna nodded, forcing a smile to acknowledge his bravery, and ran to the safety of the launch bay control room.

'Does it have a detonation timer?'

Leal shook his head. 'Only in the movies ... it's a remote detonator, which means it can go off —'

'— at any time.' Lucian understood well enough.

'So I'd appreciate it if you retreated to a safe distance, Captain. Actually ...' Leal had a brainwave. 'This might be the perfect opportunity to get those two dead Valoureans off our vessel.'

'Good call.' Lucian retraced his steps to quarantine, where the bodies were being stored, and Leal readied the vessel for launch.

Upon Khalid Mansur's return to his private quarters inside the Sermetican deep-space cruiser — his absence unnoticed by all on board — he moved to resume his post at the helm.

He'd been rather perturbed that the Phemorians had lost track of the crew who had been giving them so much trouble of late. However, thanks to his Phemorian lover's telepathic expertise, he now knew that Taren Lennox had fallen in with other psychically talented individuals. Their combined talents had enabled them to keep one step ahead of the game. *Not for much longer*. The viceroy grinned with satisfaction. He'd just been informed that Anselm was on his way back to the deep-space cruiser. Anselm had also had an explosive device planted on board the shuttle that had returned AMIE's captain to his institute in space.

The lengths that Anselm had gone to over the years to keep his bastard daughter hidden from her insane *femme fatale* royal lineage made her the most well-funded and resource-exhaustive operative that the secret services had ever had! Very few people knew about her connection to Anselm and nobody knew what she looked like, bar Anselm himself, just as nobody knew about Khalid's PK ability — that was their arrangement and it had been to both their benefit in the past. But Khalid Mansur had no intention of living in Anselm's shadow for the next fifty years.

There was an ancient prophecy that came into being around the time of the female uprising on Phemoria. The general belief was that it arose from a need to explain to children of that dire time why their families were being torn apart. The prophecy told of the ultimate being, the *Zagriata*, which in the old tongue of the Phemorians meant 'the restorer of love and balance', who would bring peace, not only to the desendants of the sexual revolution on Phemoria, but the entire universe. The prophecy was the secret hope of a divided people, that perhaps one day they, Sermetica and Phemoria, would repair the great divide caused by the horrid war. No one knew whether the prophecy was originally Phemorian or Sermetic, as both planets claimed ownership and that the ultimate being would be born of their people.

Khalid Mansur felt the prophecy was little more than a children's bedtime story that had been embellished with optimism over the years. If there was an ultimate being in this universe it was himself, as he had more power in his little finger than Taren Lennox would ever have. Still, the belief that Taren was the *Zagriata* had driven both Anselm and Qusay-Sabah Clarona to extreme lengths. Each of them wanted Taren allied to their people and planet. This made the little princess such a highly prized commodity that, if she was in his possession, he could hold two entire planets to ransom.

Khalid had been unable to will himself to the princess, because to do so he had to know what she looked like. And now he did — a vision his telepathic lover had been able to give him this day.

But first, get rid of the boyfriend and his psychic teamsters. The viceroy looked at his agent, who was still awaiting his response to the update.

'Detonate on my word.'

Anselm was furious when the communications officer on his vessel advised him that the viceroy was readying to detonate the bomb on AMIE — and attempts to communicate with the bridge on the deep spacer cruiser Khalid had been left in command of proved unsuccessful.

He's out of control. For the umpteenth time, Anselm cursed the day he'd taken Khalid into his confidence.

The politician arrived on the bridge of his vessel just in time to hear the cheer go up and see the dot that represented AMIE on their monitoring screen disappear.

'Clear the bridge,' Anselm ordered. The celebration dulled to confusion and the crew departed. Khalid stayed put — arms folded.

'I had no intention of detonating that device,' Anselm said once they were alone. 'I didn't want the Phemorians to know we were here!'

'It could have been an accident,' Khalid shrugged.

'I think you want to get rid of any evidence that might link you to the disappearance of Maladaan,' Anselm suggested, and Khalid broke into the crooked smile that always betrayed his guilt, something he never tried to hide from Anselm. They had so much dirt on each other neither dared blow the whistle on the other. 'Swithin Gervaise was answering to you and your operatives on Maladaan,' Anselm stated accusingly.

'That sample was an immeasurable energy source ... and it was contained in a canister that you can hold in your hand! Extraordinary! Our solar arrays on Sermetica are sustainable, but other planets need power and this appeared to be another resource which could be mined and sold off,' he explained rationally. 'I wasn't to know the whole damn planet was going to vanish when the substance touched down.'

Anselm was disbelieving. 'Why lead me to believe that AMIE's crew were to blame? If you'd told me the truth in the first place, we could have covered it up and all this could have been resolved on Frujia.'

'That is what I had *planned*,' Khalid lied, 'but I didn't realise these *scientists* were going to prove so elusive. If you ask me, they were a bunch of unregistered undesirables and I've just done the USS a big favour in blowing them up.'

Although Anselm knew of his Power, Khalid was still careful to never let down his guard; if he ever felt any sympathy for those with the Powers that he exposed, recruited or disposed of it never showed.

Needless to say, Anselm had not exposed *his* secret talent to his viceroy and went out of his way to ensure the PK adept would not discover Taren's identity.

'The mystery of what happened to AMIE will keep the Valoureans occupied whilst we get out of the Phemorian system ... you might remember, we have *no official* authorisation to be here.'

Anselm backed off from any further confrontation. They had breached USS law in order to execute this rescue; if word got out, it would not bode well for his political career.

'How fortunate that your vessel was so close to this system right when I needed access,' Anselm said thoughtfully.

'We both have secrets we want to keep hidden,' Khalid replied, 'and *that* is our insurance that they will stay hidden.'

Anselm had no reason to doubt his viceroy's allegiance. Khalid's auric body appeared to be free of any disease — cloudy patches being one of the first signs of a traitor. There was one very dark patch on his right hand — perhaps an embedded piece of shrapnel — but as this spot was not located over any of Khalid's light centres, Anselm felt it was of no great concern. The man was a cold, sometimes callous, ally, but he had always been reliable.

Lately, however, Khalid had been pushing the boundaries of his authority, and that made Anselm uncomfortable.

'If your mission is accomplished, I suggest you call the crew to their stations,' Khalid suggested. 'We should depart with all due haste before anyone confirms our presence. I shall take a more stealthy craft' — which meant he'd teleport himself — 'and meet you back on Sermetica.'

Anselm nodded, happy to have Khalid well away from the ship while he had his daughter and the pilot of AMIE on board. 'Keep me posted.'

'Naturally.'

As Khalid faded from sight, his vexing grin seemed to be the last part of him to vanish ... or perhaps it was just that it held Anselm's attention.

AMIE's loss was most distressing, as Anselm no longer had a safe haven for his daughter. He'd never slept better than during Taren's time on board the astro-marine institute when it was in some distant galaxy. With Maladaan gone, and now AMIE, his selection of hiding places was more limited. It was not going to be easy to break the news to her that yet another of her lovers had died because they became caught up in her destiny.

Taren didn't remember the sad deaths of the men she'd loved before Lucian. She'd been programmed to remember them all as bastards, so she would not have the stress of feeling responsible for their deaths. If she knew the truth, Anselm thought his daughter would probably never even attempt a relationship. He wanted her to know what it was to lead a happy, normal life; a desire that became increasingly hard to fulfil with every year that passed.

The explosion of the USS shuttle craft, only minutes after its launch from AMIE, set the entire ship shaking.

'That's it ... I've had enough!' Lucian decided as he dashed from the launch bay up to the bridge with Leal in hot pursuit.

'Shields. Shut everything down,' the captain instructed the co-pilot. 'We vanished off USS scopes once. We'll do it again.'

Leal was keen to do just that, although he had reservations. 'But how are we to escape the Phemorians if our systems are shut down?'

'One disaster at a time, please,' Lucian cautioned. 'With any luck some debris from the USS transporter will fall to the surface of Phemoria. When they discover the vessel is Sermetic, they'll have bigger fish to fry than us.'

The exterior shields blocked out the view, and then the interior of the ship dimmed as they reverted to minimal power.

'We could really use Zeven about now,' Leal commented.

'I fear the secret service is using him at present,' Lucian informed him sadly.

Leal suspected that with Taren and their pilot still missing, the captain was not going to be content to sit in the dark for very long. 'What do you plan to do?'

Lucian shrugged, his options limited. 'How long do you think it would take us to get back to Oceane?' he queried and Leal thought his captain was joking.

'A month using the inter-system gateways. Quite a few years otherwise. Why would you want to go back there?'

'Because I am sick of being a mortal among super-beings!' Lucian finally expressed his angst.

'You're not serious?' Leal wondered if the captain had taken leave of his senses. 'I would not wish this life on anyone —'

'I cannot hope to protect Taren as things stand,' Lucian said quite lucidly, 'for not only am I psychically ill-equipped, I am being discriminated against for that very reason. No one will tell me anything! I don't figure highly enough in the scheme of things to be kept in the loop as to what is happening in Taren's life ... but Zeven is informed! Why do you think that is?'

Leal could sympathise with Lucian's situation, but he had to point out the downside: 'Even if you were psychically gifted, it could be a passive type of Power that would not serve you as you hope ... then you're stuck with it as long as you live, with no respite.'

'I'd take that chance right now.' Lucian's communicator sounded and he responded to the call. It was Kassa.

'Have we lost power? What was that explosion?' the doctor queried, concerned for the patient she had in the medical quarters.

'Just a little evasive action, nothing to worry about,' came the captain's reply.

'So long as everyone is all right up there ...' Kassa tried to get him to be more specific.

'Yes, we're fine. Leal is fine,' Lucian said, guessing at her most pressing concern. *'How's Ringbalin doing?'*

'He's still out to it,' she replied, whereupon Ringbalin released a groan. 'I'll keep you posted.' She hung up and moved to Ringbalin's bedside, expecting he would be traumatised when he woke.

'No.' He tried to lift his hand. 'Don't go.'

'I'm right here. Ringbalin?' Kassa coaxed him from his slumber by gently stroking his face. As she made contact with his skin, she felt a rush of awe pass through her — if this was what Ringbalin was feeling, his consciousness was in a more beautiful place than she had expected.

His head wavered back and forth, as if trying to avoid consciousness, then his eyelids shot open. A few deep breaths later, the botanist laid eyes on Kassa and calmed.

'Ringbalin, welcome back,' she greeted him. 'How are you feeling?'

He dwelt on the question and his expression soured. 'Gutted,' he replied, suppressing his emotions. 'I killed those soldiers, didn't I?'

Kassa nodded. 'They would have killed you,' she said, trying to sanction what he'd done.

'And I'd be with Ayliscia.' He turned away as tears overwhelmed him.

Kassa only had to consider losing Leal to empathise with Ringbalin's pain. 'It was not your time, Balin.'

Ringbalin gasped and sat upright suddenly. 'That's what Armaros said.'

'Who is Armaros?' Kassa queried, having never heard the name before.

'Um,' he frowned, considering the question. 'You might say he's the sentinel of my higher consciousness.'

'*Ringbalin*,' Kassa gasped, intrigued. 'You've had contact with your higher self?'

'It seems so,' he replied, recalling the conversation he'd been having with three lofty beings just before he'd awoken. 'They were here, in the room, and probably still are.'

The comment gave Kassa a shiver in her bones; not a fearful sensation, but altogether delightful. 'Really? ...' She looked about, unable to psychically detect any presence, but she had never been a very talented medium.

'Apparently, the being we encountered on Oceane was an even higher manifestation of our combined higher selves,' Balin added.

Kassa's gaped in amazement. 'What are you saying?'

Balin was very calm, and stuck out his bottom lip as he considered how to explain. 'I'm saying that you channelled a causal being, Kassa ... not just a threshold dweller like Armaros, or a silent watcher who oversees him, but a fully fledged *deva* ... A universal architect,' he added for absolute clarity. 'That's clairvoyance.'

Kassa giggled, not sceptical but amazed. 'And your higher self told you this?'

He nodded. 'Some ... I just figured out the rest.' Balin hopped off the table and staggered on his weakened limbs.

'Where do you think you're going?' Kassa caught him, and guided him back to bed.

'I need to see the captain. Urgently.'

'Then let's bring the captain to you, shall we?'

Kalayna and Aurora arrived to check on Ringbalin just before the captain arrived.

'Oh, thank heavens he's awake.' Aurora breathed a sigh of relief and waved to the botanist from the open doorway that Kassa was blocking. 'Is he okay?'

'Now is not a good time,' Kassa explained as Lucian ducked under her arm and Leal followed.

'What's going on now?' Kalayna queried, sensing their haste to have a closed meeting.

'We'll let you know,' Kassa smiled sweetly as she closed the door.

Kalayna was annoyed at being left out, as was Rory.

'Why does everyone else get to be in there?' Rory pouted. 'Do you think they know something about Starman that they're not telling us? I hoped he'd be back by now.'

Kalayna suddenly burst into a grin.

'What?' Aurora called, as Kalayna hurried off towards her quarters.

'I still have my spy toys ...' She waved Aurora after her. 'I bet that the captain is still wearing the watch I bugged.'

'You bugged the captain?' she hissed, horrified, as she caught her girlfriend up.

'Part of the job,' Kalayna advised with a guilt-free shrug and Rory grinned.

'Cool.'

'I know you're thinking about going back to Oceane,' Ringbalin said to the captain and everyone's jaw dropped.

'Why?' Kassa asked, curious at this turn of events.

Lucian was so stunned that Ringbalin knew, he could not answer. Ringbalin decided to do the honours.

'Because our captain believes he can advance his psychic powers by breathing in the atmosphere on the planet, just as Starman did.'

Kassa was about to discourage any such thing, when Ringbalin intervened, eager to stay on topic.

'But, unfortunately, that's not going to work. I have it on good authority that this course of action will take far too long.'

Lucian was confused. 'To what authority do you refer?'

'Ringbalin claims to have had a conversation with his own higher self ... and yours,' Kassa explained, as simply as possible.

'And Zeven's, too,' Ringbalin added. 'They know about everything that has occurred —'

'Do they know where our planet has gone?' Lucian asked, sceptically.

'Yes, they do,' Balin replied matter-of-factly. 'And there may be a means to restore Maladaan to its place in our universe, but they need our help to do it.'

'We don't have the means to shift a planet through universes,' Lucian scoffed.

'But in the parallel universe where Maladaan now resides, there is the means,' Ringbalin said, and waved off that topic for now. 'The point is, if you do seriously want to enhance your psychic skill without traipsing across several star systems to do it, I believe I have a means to aid you.'

Lucian's scepticism fell away, although he couldn't imagine how Ringbalin would be able to help. 'The sample of air we took from Oceane was tiny, so —'

'But Taren brought a seedling of a tundrell from Oceane. I planned to develop it as a bonsai and it has been in quarantine in anticipation of that event ever since, as I have been a little preoccupied. The biophoton count of the tundrell hasn't altered one iota since the deva departed, so ... the atmosphere in its bio-containment area is basically what you'd find on —'

'Oceane!' the captain concluded, and kissed Ringbalin's forehead. 'You're a bloody genius.'

'Don't thank me, thank your sentient consciousness, Azazèl.'

'You can't be serious, Lucian,' Kassa interrupted, and swung him around to face her. 'A change like this could drive you, *of all people*, mad within hours ... we were very lucky Zeven didn't self-destruct.'

'If he can endure it, then so can I,' Lucian challenged.

'Yes, but ...' Kassa felt he was still not comprehending her concern. 'Your life will not be your own any more as you will no longer be isolated from the universal web.'

'She's absolutely right,' Leal confirmed, and Ringbalin nodded to concur.

'Once you are online, you will be invaded, bombarded, haunted or mysteriously compelled to do things by forces, spirits and people outside yourself.' She tried to force home the gravity of the consequences he was blindly taking on. 'Your personal agenda will come second to higher universal plans, for that is the price you pay for being connected.'

Lucian paused to consider her warning. 'And yet you are all content.'

'Because we have come to be at peace with our gift over many years,' Kassa explained, Leal and Balin again nodding in agreement. 'As you well know from my silence during the Amie affair, there are also burdens and secrets you must bear silently in order to protect yourself.'

'Not on my ship,' Lucian assured her and she smiled, thankful for his understanding.

'The secret services will not allow us liberty forever,' she was sorry to say.

'The secret services think we're dead.' Lucian brought her up to date on their situation.

Kassa looked at Leal who grinned. 'That's why we powered down.'

'I think I should take the advice of my higher self,' Lucian said, considering what Ringbalin had said.

'Oh, Azazèl didn't say you *should* do it,' Ringbalin pointed out. 'He just let us know there is a short cut should you be determined to follow through on your desire, as time is of the essence.' He noted the captain was looking a little discouraged. 'Azazèl also said that it would not be the first time that you had awakened your psychic potential.'

Lucian had no idea what Ringbalin was talking about now. 'But I have never —'

'Azazèl didn't refer to this life, nor even to this universe, I suspect,' Ringbalin clarified.

Lucian was rather overwhelmed, and sat down to gather his thoughts. 'Did *Azazèl* say anything else?'

'He said it is no accident that you feel compelled to risk your own well-being in order to protect Taren Lennox, because your souls are linked to the one destiny.' Ringbalin saw the captain's face soften as he seemed to find peace in those words.

'I feel sure that my destiny is not about fearing to discover my full potential as a human being. Do you?' Lucian posed to all those present.

'Well, no,' Kassa agreed. 'It's that you wish to accomplish this via an artificial acceleration process that troubles me.'

'If there is a price to pay down the road then so be it, if it means I can save the woman I love *now*.'

Kassa held both hands high in defeat. Lucian had never before referred to Taren as his love and it brought tears to her eyes; she was happy and sad for him at the same time. 'I cannot argue with that reasoning,' she murmured, her gaze drifting to Leal, who winked at her.

'I'd rather die for love, than live in fear and remorse,' Ringbalin assured Lucian.

With the approval of his crew, Lucian was feeling more resolute. 'I should do it now —'

'Please,' Kassa appealed, 'just sleep on this decision tonight. A few hours to think it over will not make much difference to any outcome.'

Lucian was reluctant to wait, although he knew it would be wise to take time to consider his move. 'I only have as long as it takes for us to reach Sermetica to figure out what my skill is and gain mastery over it.'

His three crewmates whistled in appreciation of the high level of difficulty in achieving mastery of a Power.

'That gives you about a month standard space-time,' Leal told Lucian, trying to sound hopeful. 'But I agree with Kassa. You should take a few hours to think this through.'

Lucian nodded. 'I will. Still, if Zeven managed to master his skills in weeks, how hard could it be?' he asked and his crewmates looked highly amused.

'Zeven has nowhere near mastered his talent,' Kassa corrected him, 'and in psychic circles ignorance will never amount to bliss.'

The first thing that struck Taren when she awoke was how high the ceiling was. The enormous suite in which she'd been deposited was elegant to the point of appearing presidential and, coincidentally, her eyes came to focus upon her alleged father. 'Anselm.'

'It pains me to hear you say my name like a stranger to be feared.' He remained where he sat, as Taren raised herself up to a seated position.

'Where is Zeven Gudrun?' Beyond having that question answered she was not interested in conversing with this man.

'He's safe —'

'Why should I believe you? I want to see him.'

'Sweetheart, please, will you just —'

'No, I will not just anything! And don't call me sweetheart!' Taren climbed off the huge bed to stand up for herself. 'I don't care if you are my father, you *drugged me* ... and one of my dearest friends! We were coming to see you of our own free will and then you turn it into a hostage situation! If you are not someone to be feared, then why would you do that? Or is this how one treats family members and their friends on Sermetica?'

Anselm was not riled and calmly responded. 'Zeven Gudrun is too powerful to let wander around unrestrained —'

'I am unrestrained,' she argued.

'You are not psychokinetic,' he replied.

Taren's eyes narrowed in challenge. 'You hope.'

'I know everything about you —' he said calmly, not fazed by her threat.

'I know you do,' Taren interjected. 'You are the keeper of my memories.'

'Gudrun told you,' he assumed.

'No,' Taren stated in all honesty, but made a mental note to question Zeven about whatever her father had revealed. 'But I could never be sure that the memory data you gave me had not been tampered with, so ...'

'There is a master memory file that cannot be tampered with,' Anselm stated, and Taren's mood lightened. 'Unfortunately, the file is to be found inside the MSS database on Maladaan.'

The wind escaped Taren's sails only for a second. 'Not to worry, I shall just have to retrieve it myself. Return me to AMIE with our pilot and —'

Anselm held up a hand to stop her there. 'There is a slight problem with that —'

Taren had realised she was in custody and not just visiting with dear old dad, but she thought she'd test her boundaries. 'Why should that be a problem?'

Anselm stood, but did not approach her. His face had a woeful expression and suddenly Taren didn't want to know.

'Oh, no.'

'AMIE has vanished,' he advised and the unexpected news paralysed Taren with shock. 'I cannot take you to a ship I cannot locate and which may no longer exist.'

Taren did not agree; she felt sure they had gone into hiding again. 'Zeven could find AMIE.'

'You're not listening to me,' Anselm said in frustration. 'Right before AMIE disappeared off our screens, reports from Phemoria told us that there was an explosion on board.'

The added shock of this announcement hit Taren like a brick wall. 'Lucian?' she wheezed, as her tears welled.

'The captain was on board at the time,' Anselm informed her. 'I'm so sorry.'

'You're sorry! You bastard,' she hissed, stepping away from him. 'All my dearest friends were on that vessel.'

'It was not my doing,' he pleaded, feigning total innocence. 'You have me to thank that you and Zeven Gudrun were not on board at the time.'

'I want to see him!' Taren yelled, getting hysterical this time. 'Until you bring Zeven to me, I will not hear anything you have to say.'

'Have it your way.' Anselm headed for the door, where he bade several agents to enter.

The men dragged Zeven's unconscious form into the room and deposited him on one of the lounges.

'As you can see, he's still unconscious,' Anselm commented as his men departed. 'But otherwise unharmed.'

Taren raced over to check on her friend, who seemed to be sleeping peacefully. Then she noted the electronic shackle that was attached to his right ankle: a psychic restraining device which all identified psychics were required to wear. The device scrambled a psychic's electromagnetic field and deadened their ability. 'What do you plan to do with us?'

Anselm was getting a little annoyed at being regarded as the enemy, and said, with some exasperation, 'If you would just hear what I have to say, you will discover that your fate is entirely yours to decide.'

Taren sniffed back her tears. 'Okay, then ...' She lifted Zeven's head, sat herself on the lounge and placed his head on her lap. '... talk.'

'Thank you,' Anselm said gratefully. He took a seat opposite Taren to say his piece.

'Mother does not send her regards,' Taren said dryly and Anselm gave a laugh.

'I'm not surprised. Her name means "cold in the morning" ... and that she was.'

Taren could see the muscles in his face tensing to suppress his disdain while he told of being seduced by the Phemorian queen who stole his DNA and conceived Taren without his consent.

'Why you?' Taren wondered, but suddenly realised the question might be insulting. 'I mean, you're very good-looking and powerful, but those qualities do not interest the Phemorians.'

Anselm smiled broadly. 'You're perceptive. You get that from me.'

'Answer the question.' Taren would not be swayed by flattery. 'Do you have the Powers?'

'You already know the answer to that question. If you would allow me to restore your memory now —'

'No ...' Taren flatly refused. 'What I would like to know is my MSS top-clearance code name.'

'Why?' Anselm was hesitant.

'Because I don't want you using it to control me, obviously.'

Anselm gave a half smile. 'It's baby-doll.'

'*What?*' Taren was almost insulted, but Anselm only shrugged.

'Well, you were only a baby when I had to invent it and I've not changed it since.'

Taren accepted his explanation. 'Who else knows this?'

'No one,' he assured her, and she was inclined to believe him.

'Keep talking.'

By the time Anselm had finished telling the tale of all he'd been through to protect her from the witches controlling her insane mother, Taren was feeling rather more agreeably disposed towards him. That he had been the unknown force behind getting her into the institute on Maladaan, and managing to have her assigned to AMIE, was also very much in his favour.

'It was your research that got you the assignment. I just helped get that research noticed by the right people,' Anselm concluded.

'And having put you through all that, you still love Qusay-Sabah Clarona,' Taren prompted and Anselm looked horrified.

'No, I do not love her!' he objected, puzzled by Taren's summation.

'But you did,' she challenged again.

'I never knew her long enough to fall in love with her,' he defended.

Taren shook her head, recalling the grigori assuring her that she had been conceived in love. *They will not admit how they feel, not even to themselves,* Azazèl said.

'What?' he queried. 'Why are you shaking your head? Do you know something I don't?'

'*Apparently*,' Taren said, as Zeven began to stir in her lap.

The first person Zeven saw was Anselm, whereupon the pilot sprang to his feet to get his bearings. 'Where am I?' He spotted Taren sitting on the lounge. 'Taren, you're here? I was looking for you ... I think?' He scratched his head and looked about. 'How did you find me? How did I get here?'

Taren hadn't been quite so disoriented when she'd awoken and she looked at her father with displeasure. 'You've edited his memory, haven't you?'

Anselm shrugged apologetically. 'I made him privy to information that I, *that we*, cannot afford to be leaked.'

'You edited my memory!' Zeven was furious. 'And what's this?' He pointed to the restraining device around his ankle.

'How about I leave you two to talk?' Anselm rose to take his leave.

'Thanks very much,' Taren said, annoyed, but she just couldn't bring herself to stay mad at Anselm. He was far too likeable and charismatic. It was better that the tragic news of AMIE was broken to Zeven by herself in any case.

Had Taren known that her father had been responsible for planting the explosive device on board AMIE, she undoubtedly would have felt differently. And as Zeven's memory had been tampered with, she would remain none the wiser, for now.

* * *

...rs alone in his room turning over the pros ...ychic acceleration, Lucian didn't want to ...nsequences any more! He'd done some ...he Powers and found there were twelve ...nct areas known: Clairvoyance/Clairaudience; Levitation; Shape-shifting/Physical Transformation; Mediumship/Channelling; Psychokinesis/Telekinesis; Prophecy/Precognition; Remote Viewing; Astral Projection; Telepathy; Transmutation; Teleportation; and the Healing Arts. There were thousands of talents that stemmed from combinations of these, some too horrifying to think about.

Lucian thought it was little wonder that regular folk feared those who had Powers and could only sleep soundly in the knowledge that they were all restrained. 'Pretty soon I will be one of those psychic lepers,' he considered, as he downed a shot of alcohol for courage.

He'd decided not to wait until morning; better to get this over and done with quietly, before the rest of the crew could talk him out of it.

He switched on the lights in the bio-containment lab and programmed the control console to admit him through each of the doors into the quarantine area.

As the final inner door opened and he passed into the tundrell's environment, Lucian breathed deeply of the sweetly warm humid air, and gasped mid-breath when he spotted Kalayna asleep on the floor.

He squatted beside her to see if he could wake her with a nudge. 'What *are* you doing here?'

'Mmmmmm ...' She stretched out and, laying eyes on Lucian, she smiled. 'Captain.'

'You should not be in here,' he said sternly.

'You should not be in here, either,' she whispered, grinning broadly. 'And yet, here we are.'

Lucian should have been furious, but he wasn't. He was transfixed by her youthful charm and tenacity. 'Why would you do this to yourself?'

'Because, like you, I am tired of falling victim to the will of others.' She sat up to look him in the eye. 'It's time I took my destiny into my own hands.'

Kalayna kissed Lucian and, although his mind knew he should be protesting, he felt so incredibly on fire ... he really wanted this girl.

'I'm online!' Kalayna gave a cheer between kisses. 'I've never felt this turned on before,' she confessed, amazed and delighted.

'Wait!' Lucian held her at bay in a moment of clarity, recalling Taren's misadventure with Zeven on Oceane. 'It's the air in here —'

'Yes,' Kalayna agreed, breathing in deeply before moving toward Lucian, who held her at arm's length.

'You don't find me attractive,' he said, trying to reason with her.

'Yes, I do!' she insisted. 'You have no idea!'

'But before this, you didn't,' Lucian challenged her.

'So! I was an idiot.' She shrugged off the oversight and backed the captain up against the wall and kissed him again. As tempting as it was to let her have her way, he caught her wayward hands and pushed her gently backward. 'I'm old enough to be your father and then some.'

At the mention of her father, Kalayna's sexual urges died. 'You really know how to kill the mood.'

'You need to leave this room,' Lucian said sincerely. 'And that's an order.'

'I'm done anyways, I reckon,' she smiled, as she'd been in here for a couple of hours at least.

'Would you tell me how you got past security to get in here in the first place?'

'I still have spy toys,' she grinned, 'and since Zeven broke my conditioning ...' The mention of his name made her feel horny all over again. '... I consciously remember how to use them.'

'I'll be confiscating those,' Lucian advised her sternly.

'Aye, aye, Captain.' As she backed up toward the inner exit door, it opened automatically. 'Good luck.'

'Go straight to Kassa,' he instructed.

'And then I'll send her here, shall I?' She wandered through the security door, which closed in her wake and, detecting no danger, the system allowed her to pass back into the observation room. She paused to look back at Lucian.

'There are not many men, or women, who have declined my favours, Captain,' she said with a tender smile of admiration and envy. 'You must love her very much.'

Lucian's eyes welled with tears just thinking about it, the tundrell's air spurring his senses and emotions into overdrive. 'Very, very much,' he agreed.

'Then we shall get her back.' Kalayna smiled and left.

Alone, Lucian's mind filled with memories of Taren, and as his lungs expanded to capacity to take in the supernatural air, tears of exhilaration and fear flooded his eyes. *Let's see them try and sever our connection now.*

CHAPTER 24

ANATHEMA

Qusay-Sabah Clarona was incensed about the security breaches around her daughter. She could barely contain her fury for long enough to address her viceroy as the woman entered the throne room.

'Who was he?' she demanded. 'How did he gain access to the Phemorian palace?'

'Zeven Gudrun, your majesty,' Jalila replied, bowing briefly to her queen. 'He is the pilot from the AMIE project, and nobody really —'

'The same pilot who escaped the collapsing Maladaan system,' the queen realised, her eyes narrowing in thought. 'You think that was just luck?'

'The two agents I sent after our treacherous spy, Dr Portus, have gone missing,' Jalila continued, ignoring the queen's question for the moment. 'But the remains of a small Sermetic shuttle have been raining down just south of the city this morning.'

'Anselm!' Now the queen had somewhere to channel her anger. 'How could such a craft be near our planet without a base ship?'

'It could not.' Jalila suppressed a grin. 'A Sermetic ship has obviously entered the Phemorian system without authorisation.'

'This must be reported to the United Star Systems,' the queen commanded.

'Already done, majesty,' Jalila said. 'All on board that vessel will be arrested as they pass through the inter-system gateway.'

'And if they go around it?' the queen quizzed. 'How shall we identify the offending ship then?'

'There is only one ship presently unaccounted for in the Sermetic armada, and I have the assurance of Khalid Mansur that everyone on board that vessel will be taken into custody as soon as it docks on Sermetica.'

The queen did not respond, a half smile gracing her lips. She mentioned nothing of what she suspected and the crown of Phemoria cast its psychic shield around her, so she was protected from Jalila's telepathic expertise.

'Splendid work, Jalila.'

'Thank you, majesty.' Jalila bowed deeply.

'Ready our fastest transport, please,' the queen requested. 'I shall leave for Sermetica as soon as possible.'

'Leave!' Jalila was caught completely off-guard. 'You wish to leave Phemoria, majesty?'

'That's right,' she confirmed, as if it were no big deal.

'Allow me to go on your behalf, majesty.'

'Not this time,' the queen said, feeling her viceroy's panic and resistance, but she did not let on that she sensed something was amiss. 'And what of the rest of the AMIE crew?' the queen asked, wanting to hear of Lucian Gervaise in particular.

'The AMIE vessel left dock late last night and, from all appearances, her crew left with her. Shortly after departure there was an explosion and AMIE disappeared from our screens.'

'And yet, all we have found is a Sermetic vessel,' the queen mused.

'My conclusion is that AMIE has formed an alliance with Sermetica.'

'I want that vessel found,' the queen commanded. 'That will be all.' She dismissed Jalila, who bowed and left to carry out the queen's orders.

The queen returned to her throne and shed her body to consult with the Phemoray.

The five veiled ones were awaiting the queen.

Qusay-Sabah Clarona bowed before her superiors. 'What do you think, great mothers? Is she treacherous?'

She is masked. She must carry a charm that blocks our sight, the women replied in unison. *An act that, in itself, reeks of treason.*

'Then my decision to retrieve my daughter myself is sound,' the queen concluded.

It is imperative that we get her back before she fully awakens to the extent of her Power, the Phemoray decreed. *Then there shall be no controlling her.*

'Does Anselm have the princess with him?'

Yes.

'And what of AMIE and her captain?' the queen queried.

Both survive.

'I shall find them and destroy them,' the queen assured, wanting that loose end tied up.

We advise against it. AMIE and her crew may still be of use to us.

The queen wasn't happy, but clearly they could be used as hostages to persuade her daughter to return to Phemoria. 'Your will be done.'

* * *

After a six-hour stint in the bio-containment lab, Lucian finally emerged. He would have described his state as completely euphoric had he not been dying to take a leak.

'I'm so mad at you,' Kassa said, checking his vital signs. 'And Kalayna, too ... you're both crazy!'

'I know,' Lucian mumbled, barely able to keep his eyes open.

'Off to bed with you then.' The doctor postponed her lecture for a time when he might have some chance of comprehending it. 'Ringbalin and I will give you a full checkup when you wake.'

Lucian didn't need to be told twice. He made straight for his quarters to relieve himself, and finally to rest. As he'd barely slept since they'd landed on Phemoria, sleep came easily for a change.

A little light-headed, Lucian stirred from his slumber. It took longer than usual for his eyes to focus, although he'd never had any problems with his sight, not even when he had a hangover. His stress subsided as the contours of his dimly lit room at last came into focus.

Against the wall, he saw his dead wife — her fatal wound still evident upon her neck — and panic crippled Lucian's being once again. 'Amie!' he gasped as he scampered backwards and out of bed.

You see me? she assumed, drawing nearer. *I was hoping one of the psychics on this ship would tap into their mediumship potential sooner rather than later.*

Amie's ghost had none of the vitality of his deceased wife's living presence; her skin tone and facial expression lacked colour and vibrancy, and her eyes were as dead as her corpse.

'Why are you here?' Lucian backed further away to keep a distance between them, horrified to see her again.

I never left! She sighed. *I cannot leave this project until I make recompense for what I did and that is near impossible in this condition. Although your girlfriend did prove of some use once hypnotised.*

'You've been here since you were murdered?' Lucian was feeling uncomfortable. Taren and he had enjoyed many intimate encounters in this room.

Amie nodded, forcing a smile. *Don't feel bad, I never deserved you anyway.*

'I don't feel bad, actually,' Lucian said, as he'd done nothing wrong. He realised this unique situation awarded him the chance to acquire information that only Amie could give him. 'Who were you working for? Swithin? Anselm?'

Amie shook her head on both counts. *Khalid Mansur.* Lucian was stunned. *He's been patiently waiting for the illegitimate daughter of Anselm and the Queen of Phemoria to be exposed. He always knew she existed, but Anselm kept her very well hidden. The Viceroy of Sermetica imagined that with her as a hostage he could conquer both planets without lifting a finger.*

Lucian's first reaction was horror, but then, Amie seemed to enjoy horrifying him. 'Taren is the daughter of the Queen of Phemoria?'

Looks that way.

The news was bewildering. 'That would mean that —'

— she is the Princess of Phemoria, Amie concluded for him.

Lucian had to sit down before he fell down — fighting off Taren's enemies to save her was one thing, but fighting royal parentage was something else again. 'That would change things. Why should I believe you?'

Have you not been listening? Amie stressed. *I'm stuck here until I fix this! Look at what that bastard Mansur decided should become of me.* She pointed to the gaping hole in her neck. *Do you think I wish him to live long and prosper?*

'Swithin said *he* ordered your death?' Lucian said, confused.

Ha! He wishes, I'm sure. She contained her amusement. *Only Khalid has the authority ... he found himself a new lover, I expect.*

'You were Khalid's lover?' Lucian gasped, and Amie shrugged and nodded.

Supposedly, she said, highlighting her betrayal. *I did love our life together, Lucian.*

'Married until your secret service lover recalls you from duty,' Lucian chided, unable to digest her reassurance. 'I don't remember that clause being in our wedding contract.'

It was a bad life choice, she conceded in retrospect. *What can I say?*

'What is so special about Khalid Mansur?' Lucian wondered.

Oh, he is special, Amie assured him, *just as you and most of the crew are special.*

'You mean to say he has psychic power?' Lucian was flabbergasted as Amie nodded. 'But he is the greatest prosecutor of psychics in the USS.'

Or so it would appear to the outside world, but, inside the secret service agencies, he recruits for his private army, Amie explained. *Did I not mention he has been looking for your girlfriend for quite some time?*

The door chimed and when Lucian looked in that

direction, curious as to whom his caller was, he saw straight through the wall to perceive his visitor. 'It's Kassa,' he said, startled by his own capability.

Don't tell her I'm here, Amie appealed. *She never did like me much.*

'Kassa!' Lucian called to her, glad to have the company of another living being.

'You're awake. Splendid,' Kassa noted with pleasure as she came through the door. Noting how far he was from the doorway, she was curious. 'How did you know it was me?'

'I saw you through the wall,' he replied, waving off further explanation. 'Amie is here. I can see her.'

Thanks, Lucian, Amie quipped, as Kassa looked around in surprise, her eyes narrowing with spite.

'You see her ghost?' Kassa clarified.

'I do,' Lucian confirmed and pointed to where Amie stood.

Kassa turned to stare in that direction, and although she saw nothing she did not hesitate to believe Lucian's claim. 'Do you have any idea how much trouble you've caused?'

'She does,' Lucian replied on her behalf, 'and it seems her soul is confined to this craft until she makes recompense.'

Kassa was mildly appeased by this. 'So there is a karmic order to the universe after all.'

'*Captain!*' Leal's voice sounded through Lucian's communicator, and Lucian answered the call.

'What's up?'

'*There's a very large Phemorian vessel headed our way. The Queen of Phemoria is on board and she is requesting we surrender our craft and allow her Valoureans to board.*'

'Shit!' Lucian wasn't in a position to resist.

He had no way of knowing whether Zeven had successfully rescued Taren from the Phemorians. Or whether the Phemorians had noted they were missing two Valoureans. If they were in deep space, far from a large light source, or in the night shadow of a planet, AMIE could hide from the approaching craft, and her surface would reflect only the blackness of the space surrounding. But this close to the twin system, the light reflected off AMIE's surface and she was exposed to naked sight.

'I guess we look at this as an opportunity to be updated,' Lucian advised Leal through the communicator.

'But they will execute Ringbalin if they discover he was responsible for killing their Valoureans,' Kassa said, worried.

Lucian held up a hand to calm Kassa while he finished talking to Leal. 'Advise the Phemorians that I agree to meet with the queen to negotiate terms for the surrender of my crew and vessel. Tell them I have some information that her majesty will find most interesting.'

'*Will do, Captain,*' Leal confirmed.

'But the Queen of Phemoria never meets with a man,' Kassa pointed out.

'Qusay-Sabah Clarona never leaves Phemoria either,' Lucian pointed out in return, as they awaited a response from Leal. 'This seems to be a day of firsts all round.'

'Speaking of firsts, how are you feeling?' Kassa queried at last.

'My sight is a bit strange,' Lucian complained, so Kassa pulled out her pocket torch to check his eyes. 'It's a bit blurry, then it comes sharply into focus —'

'That will be the balancing act going on between

your two physical eyes and your third-eye vision,' Kassa theorised. 'Like a camera lens adjusting to objects in the foreground and background, your sight is now adjusting to see objects in the physical realm as well as objects in the etheric world.'

That explanation seemed fair enough to Lucian. 'How is Kalayna faring?'

'She's fine ...' Kassa hesitantly began, 'although she had quite a crush on you when she came to see me last night.'

I thought you were in love with the princess? Amie chimed in.

'It was just something in the air,' Lucian said defensively. 'I'm sure she's all better now. What I'm more interested to know is if the air had any effect on her psychic skills.'

'She hasn't come back to me with anything, but I believe Aurora is fairly cross with Kalayna so she might be a little preoccupied!'

'*Captain,*' Leal's voice interrupted. '*Her majesty wishes to see our botanist as well.*'

'They suspect,' Kassa concluded, worried for their crewmate.

'I'll go.' Ringbalin made his presence known, having heard the latest news as he arrived at the door. 'I heard the Phemorians have found us and I want to surrender myself to them.'

'No, Balin,' Kassa appealed. 'Your intentions are honourable, but the Phemorians will not judge you fairly.'

'I judged those Valoureans rather harshly, so possibly it would be fair,' Balin said somewhat sharply.

Only Lucian perceived Ringbalin's dead lover as she followed him into the room, half her head missing from her death wound. Kassa noticed the captain wince in surprise and suspected that Ringbalin had a ghost of his own in tow.

'It doesn't matter what spin you put on it,' Ringbalin stated. 'I killed those women.'

'Confirm that request, Leal.' Lucian forced out the words, having no time to debate the issue. 'I will fly us across to the Phemorian craft.'

'*Confirmed, captain,*' Leal replied slowly, sounding none too happy about it.

'Thank you, captain,' Ringbalin said. 'I am grateful for your understanding.'

Don't wish yourself dead to come after me, Ayliscia's ghost cried out to Balin.

'My understanding is that you might have a death wish due to your recent loss,' Lucian told Ringbalin on Ayliscia's behalf and Ringbalin was taken aback by the captain's insight.

Ayliscia's ghost looked at Lucian, amazed and excited. *You see me, Captain Gervaise?*

Lucian served Ayliscia with a slight nod as Ringbalin responded. 'I do not plan to do anything heroic or stupid, if that is your concern.'

'No, my concern is losing you,' the captain replied. 'AMIE would not be here without you. We need you alive and in Module C if the project is to continue.'

'I'll be sure and look you up when I get out of prison,' Ringbalin replied, ignoring the captain's warm sentiments.

'You're not going to prison,' Lucian said emphatically. 'Not if I can help it.'

'I murdered two people!' Ringbalin snapped.

'In self-defence,' Kassa argued.

'No!' he roared. 'I meant it ... I wanted it ...' Ringbalin began shaking violently as tears overwhelmed him. 'They didn't stand a chance.' He collapsed to his knees, clawing at his chest. 'I just want to rip my heart out.'

Ringbalin keeled forward, weeping, and Kassa dropped to her knees beside him, reaching out her hand. Ringbalin immediately warned her to stop right there. 'To touch me is to expose yourself to my pain and I would not wish that on my worst enemy.'

It was my fault that he was driven to kill. He is the gentlest of souls, captain. Don't let my people take him. Ayliscia looked on, helpless to prevent his pain. *You might be able to make a trade for his life,* said the tall mutilated spirit as she approached Lucian, *with this information ... the queen's viceroy, Jalila Lamas, is Khalid Mansur's lover.*

Lucian's jaw dropped at the implications, but it was his dead wife who protested.

I knew there was someone! Amie was infuriated to learn who she'd been tossed aside for. *I suppose they plan to rule the universe together ... Phemoria and Sermetica anyway.*

Ayliscia chose to ignore Amie. *You must warn the queen.*

When Lucian had entered bio-containment to spend time with the tundrell from Oceane, he'd been expecting enlightenment, but not quite this much at once. 'Perhaps I should go alone?'

'Yes,' Kassa said, relieved.

'No,' Ringbalin interrupted, pulling himself together. 'I must go. My higher self advised me to follow my conscience. Yes, thinking about Ayliscia makes me want to die so I can be with her, but I will not do anything to bring death upon myself, I swear it.'

'Balin, you don't have to die to be with Ayliscia...' The captain ventured to expose his new talent for the sake of easing his comrade's pain. 'She is standing right beside you.'

'What?' Balin was wonderstruck and looked at the captain, puzzled and intrigued.

As the captain nodded to confirm the truth of his words, his eyes drifted to one side of Balin to indicate where Ayliscia was and Ringbalin calmed himself. 'She has given me some information that we might use to aid your cause with the Phemorians.'

'Really?' Ringbalin wiped the tears from his face, not wanting his dead lover to see him so distressed. 'She can hear me?'

'Oh, yes,' Lucian assured him and Kassa quietly withdrew some distance to give Balin a little privacy.

Tell him I shall love him always and will stay with him until he finds love again, Ayliscia requested of the captain.

Lucian, although he felt a little awkward playing the messenger, passed on her message as requested.

'Then we shall be together forever,' Ringbalin vowed, 'for I shall never love another as I love you.' He bowed his head as tears threatened to overwhelm him once more.

Ayliscia shook her head to disagree and leaned close to kiss her lover's head. As soon as she appeared to make contact with him, Balin drew a deep breath of surprise.

'It's true,' he said, and looked at the captain in amazement. 'She is here, I can sense her!' Ringbalin laughed with happiness through his tears.

'I wouldn't lie to you about something like that,' Lucian assured him.

'I didn't think you would, captain, but —' Ringbalin gasped as he realised the answer to the question he was about to ask. 'You've been in bio-containment with my tundrell.'

Lucian nodded.

Ringbalin forced a smile and thought how brave Lucian was, to expose himself to social ostracism for the sake of love.

'So, as Ayliscia cannot bear to see you fall into the hands of the Valoureans,' Lucian posed, trying for a humorous tone to dispel the awkward mood, 'let us go see if the Phemorians will strike a deal.'

Ringbalin gave a determined nod and Ayliscia smiled, satisfied that they had turned her lover's death wish around.

As the captain and Ringbalin exited their shuttle on the Phemorian vessel, the men were immediately taken into custody by Valoureans.

'How dare you request an audience with her majesty?' a tall luscious blonde, who appeared as deadly as she was beautiful, hissed at Lucian.

'Then with whom am I to negotiate?' he asked politely.

'We ask the questions,' she barked, motioning for her soldiers to take hold of the men.

'I'll come freely,' Ringbalin said, knowing it was not safe to touch him. 'You shouldn't —'

'We also give the orders, short guy,' the blonde shouted and two Valoureans took hold of him, one on either side.

Lucian heard the soldiers who were dragging Ringbalin along start to sniffle and he couldn't help but smile.

The blonde in charge got fed up and turned about to find both her warriors weeping. 'What are you two whimpering about?'

'I don't know,' explained the warrior to Ringbalin's left. 'All of a sudden, I feel so incredibly sad, and sorry for him.' She looked at her prisoner.

'Uh-huh,' confirmed the soldier to Ringbalin's right.

'I'll do it,' and the blonde took hold of Ringbalin, who could only sigh, knowing a warning would be a waste of breath.

Before they'd made it to wherever they were going all six guards with them were in tears.

'We don't have to take him to the captain,' the blonde in charge suggested. 'We could hide him somewhere.'

'Yes,' they all agreed.

'No!' Ringbalin suggested. 'My captain needs to see the queen.'

'Impossible,' they all said.

'Then, please, take us to your captain,' Lucian requested. The warriors looked to Ringbalin, not prepared to act until he gave the nod.

'Please, ladies,' Ringbalin begged them. 'Our business is most pressing.'

Reluctantly, the Valoureans complied, wiping tears from their faces as they led them away.

'Do you think you can pacify their captain so easily?' Lucian asked in an aside to Balin.

Ringbalin shrugged. 'Probably, but that would rather defeat the purpose of me confessing my crime, don't you think?'

In the large ornate council chamber there was only one throne-like chair, which was presently unoccupied. The captain of the Valoureans stood before the throne, hands on hips, her face hidden behind her war mask, which depicted the face of an angry woman. Under normal circumstances the mask would have had Lucian's full attention, but above the head of the masked woman was a ball of seething red energy within which Lucian could see tortured women screaming. It was extremely disturbing to watch and totally distracting.

The two men were forced to kneel before the captain of the ship.

'By request of the Queen of Phemoria, the honourable Qusay-Sabah Clarona, you must surrender your craft and return with us to Phemoria, Captain Gervaise.'

'This sounds like an arrest,' Lucian noted. 'On what charges are we being held?'

'Your crew are wanted for questioning in regard to the disappearance of two Valoureans —'

'Who shot down my project's marine biologist, Dr Portus, in cold blood ... those Valoureans?' Lucian said angrily, turning the charge around and their host appeared surprised by the news.

'Agent Portus is dead?'

'Shot in the back by her own people,' Ringbalin said, emotion filling his voice. 'Why? She loved her people, her queen —'

'She loved you, did she not?' the captain of the guard asked, cutting him short.

'Not nearly as much as I loved her,' he replied, allowing his tears to flow freely down his cheeks.

The guards who had touched Ringbalin were sympathetic to his cause and sighed, still caught up in his pain.

Lucian became dizzy, and was forced to close his eyes as he felt a huge wave of energy hit him. Before his equilibrium had even returned, he felt the illumination of something very powerful indeed. He opened his eyes to perceive three beings of light enter the room, passing straight through the wall to do so.

Looks like we are just in time, said one of the lofty beings whose form rather reminded Lucian of Zeven. The being looked at the female guards all pining after Ringbalin. *Still breaking hearts I see, Armaros.*

Lucian was doubly shocked to note that the spirit so addressed, Armaros, was very like Ringbalin.

Well, for this incarnation it was infectious, Armaros replied with good humour.

Let's focus on getting her majesty severed from the influence of that cursed thought-form, shall we. The third being turned his attention to the masked warrior and the seething mass above her head became agitated.

In the third being, Lucian saw himself, and recollected Ringbalin's assertion about the sentient spirits he spoke with during his emotional blackout.

The crown is the amulet that binds her to the entity. Any idea how we might get her to remove it, Lucian's twin being posed to the others.

I think I can come up with something. Armaros approached Ringbalin. *I could do a walk-in.*

Lucian's sentinel shook his head. *Only as a last resort. We are not supposed to directly interfere.*

Alarm bells were going off in Lucian's head. If these beings spoke the truth, then this was not the captain of the Phemorian guard they were addressing, but the Queen of Phemoria herself. Lucian couldn't see the crown on her head to which the beings referred, concealed as it was by the mask.

'You killed to avenge your lover,' their masked hostess accused Ringbalin as she neared him.

'No,' he told her honestly. 'It is not my nature to destroy, not for any reason.'

'You are male,' she retorted, 'and therefore a born killer and a liar.'

'I cannot lie,' Ringbalin humbly replied in his defence, not wanting to contradict the warrioress directly. 'It is a physical impossibility for me to lie to anyone who is touching me, for my feelings have resonance.' He motioned to the guards who had brought him into the room, who all had tears in their eyes.

All three beings of light appeared to be inspired by Ringbalin's manner of responding. *This could be promising,* Armoros said, delighted with his charge. *Yes, be honest,* he encouraged.

'Then you could still be lying, for I am not touching you,' the masked woman pointed out.

'Nor do you want to whilst questioning me about the death of Ayliscia Portus,' Ringbalin advised, 'as the pain I felt from that loss was enough to kill two Valoureans.'

'So you admit it,' the woman said, her contempt evident, while the seething mass above her churned in agitation.

'I admit that seeing her head shot off before my eyes incensed me,' he said, his tears welling anew. 'Can you understand the pain of realising that the most precious thing in your life, someone you cared for more than yourself, someone you'd nurtured and loved beyond life, has been taken from you in a heartbeat in the cruellest way imaginable?'

Lucian held his breath as the woman in the mask stared down upon Ringbalin's tear-stained face. The mass above her head became alarmed and began hissing at her, displeased.

He lies, the evil thought-form insisted. *You know better than to trust a man.*

The masked warrioress crouched before the botanist and held out her hand. 'Convince me.'

No! screeched the thought-form in panic.

'Majesty!' Several guards made a move to prevent their queen making physical contact, but Qusay-Sabah Clarona held up a hand to prevent their advance. Her cover now blown, she removed her mask.

'Your majesty,' Ringbalin bowed, having never met royalty before. 'I had no idea ...'

'Give me your hand,' she ordered.

'Let me, majesty,' the blonde guard volunteered. 'If his emotions have already slain two Valoureans then —'

The queen gestured for silence. 'Shall you be the man who finally slays the Queen of Phemoria?' she asked Ringbalin, her hand still upturned and awaiting his contact.

'Not I, majesty.'

As Ringbalin placed his hand upon the queen's, the seething entity above her began howling in pain. Lucian found the noise harrowing to the core.

After only a moment, the queen was forced to close her eyes as Ringbalin's feelings bombarded her. She choked in an attempt to prevent her tears welling, but she could not stop the rising flood of emotion.

I know you see me.

Lucian was distracted from the churning red force exploding with grief above the heart-warming scene to find his spirit self staring him in the face.

Remove the crown from the queen's head, if you wish to save the woman you love.

Lucian was flabbergasted by the request. The guards would kill him without question for such a stunt.

As long as she wears the curse of her foremothers she will be blinded to the truth and will do you no favours.

Did this mean that she would favour his cause if he assaulted her? Lucian wondered.

There is no point having psychic power if you do not use it! His spirit self became impatient. *You've been dying to burst out of your comfort zone for months, and now is the time ... take control, captain!*

Lucian was the closest person to the queen; he could accomplish the mission given him. He looked at the angry thought-form whose restless ghosts had stilled and were staring at him awaiting his move. Was the mass aware of the spirit beings instructing him, or was it detecting his intention to dethrone it?

In that moment Lucian heard his own heart beating and his world seemed to slip into slow motion.

Almost as soon as his first muscle tensed for movement, the tortured females within the apparition hissed at him in protest and he could not ignore them. He perceived their presence with his psychic senses which he could not turn off at will, having not yet mastered that art. Lucian now grabbed hold of the crown and it felt as if a thousand burning needles stuck into his hand to prevent him keeping hold. He clutched tighter as his hand went numb with the pain and managed to cast the offending item across the room before gripping his burning hand.

As soon as the crown was removed from the queen's head she burst into tears.

Lucian prepared to be seized by the Valoureans he felt closing in from behind. Taking a quick look around, he noticed the spirit beings had conveniently vanished.

'Leave them!' the queen commanded. 'Leave us.' She struggled to regain her composure as her guards left the room. Her eyes turned to Ringbalin, whose hand she still held in her own. 'I do understand how you feel,' she said, her emotions beginning to overwhelm her once more. 'I had forgotten I had ever been hurt, or that I ever felt anything at all.'

Her eyes turned to Lucian, who bowed his head, ready to be reprimanded.

'What compelled you to remove my crown?' the queen asked directly and Lucian was unsure how to respond.

Tell her the truth. He heard the voice of his spirit self inside his mind and drew a deep breath to follow the advice.

'I am a medium, majesty.' Lucian felt a little uncomfortable, not used to describing himself in this way. 'A spirit advised me that the crown was impeding your majesty's will.'

'It has been anathema to me,' she advised. 'You are a medium, you say?' She rose to her feet to challenge this. 'Taren Lennox informed me that you had no Powers.'

Lucian explained to the queen the side effect of Oceane's atmosphere, and of the plant they had which was still generating the virgin atmosphere in a bio-containment lab on board AMIE.

'You became a leper to your kind for the sake of a woman?' The queen could hardly believe a male in his right mind would do such a thing. The move was social suicide outside of Phemoria.

'I believe Taren is in grave danger,' he confessed.

The queen observed Lucian, her stern expression melting away. 'It seems I have several reasons to thank you.' She looked at the crown on the floor with apprehension and relief. 'I have been unable to remove that crown since the day the Phemoray placed it on my head. Ironic that a man should remove it when I have been discouraged from meeting with any male. Fifty years I have had those demons in my head directing my thoughts, my decisions —' She gulped in a deep breath then gave a great sigh of relief. 'All the hatred, pain and torment,' she paused to search her being, 'has gone!' But then the queen began to think back over her reign: the lies she'd told, the deceptions she'd woven, and then moaned in alarm. 'Anselm saved our daughter from that sad fate. Oh, dear mother,' she cried, grasping her chest as her heart pained her, 'I nearly sacrificed our daughter to the Phemoray's will, too.'

'So it is true,' Lucian said sadly. 'Taren is Princess of Phemoria.'

'Yes,' the queen conceded, 'but, fortunately, that fact is not well known.'

'It is more widely known than you think,' Lucian told her. 'Where is Taren now?'

'Your pilot came for her,' she explained. 'The Phemoray seem to think that Anselm has her. I know he will not harm her, as he's spent his entire life protecting her from me,' she confessed with great regret.

'Do you know if Khalid Mansur is with them?' Lucian asked, and the queen's eyes sparked with anger.

'From all reports, he is on Sermetica,' she said warily, 'but with that dark cloud you never can tell.'

'The ghost of a lover he betrayed told me that Khalid Mansur has psychic power,' Lucian conveyed, 'and is building an army of psychics. He hopes to control Taren and use her as a means of blackmailing

Anselm and your majesty into stepping down from your positions.'

The queen did not find it hard to believe the man's ambitions.

'Agent Portus also claimed that he is the lover of your viceroy, Jalila Lamus.' Lucian was not a revengeful kind of man, but he truly enjoyed ratting on the viceroy.

'I knew she was treacherous!' The queen quietly seethed for a moment and then smiled, as for the first time in her reign she felt in control of her own mind. She was now one step ahead of the game and she was astounded that she had two men to thank for that.

For days, Taren and Zeven had been confined to quarters together. She had told him of AMIE's disappearance and he was as eager as she to get in a space vehicle and go look for them.

'If I could just get this damn thing off my ankle, I wouldn't need to steal a spacecraft,' he complained for the umpteenth time. 'I miss my girls.' Sadness replaced frustration and he went quiet again.

'*Why* can't I use this precognition of mine at will?' Taren complained. She felt completely useless, but knew she needed to lift their spirits ... they could not create anything positive from the defeated state they were wallowing in. 'You know, I think I once achieved a tiny feat of PK.' She left her place by the large window and came to sit beside Zeven on the lounge.

'Really?' he replied, mildly interested.

'Yep, I'm pretty sure I made the clock on my bedside jump. A little bit,' she emphasised.

Zeven gave a slight smile.

'It was magnetised ... which would have increased the difficulty factor.'

It suddenly dawned on Zeven why Taren was telling him this. '*You* can snap this thing off my ankle?'

Taren held up both hands in defence. 'I didn't say that ... but I can try.'

And try Taren did, over and over, with no success.

'Well,' she concluded, 'that was good for a bit of a laugh.' Not that Taren had done much laughing. Zeven was fairly amused, however.

'I thought you were going to burst a vein with concentration, for a minute there,' he chuckled, and Taren hit him.

'Be constructive, can't you?' she appealed. The Queen of Phemoria had told her that she was destined to be a great psychic, so why could Zeven do this better than she could?

'Okay, let's start with the obvious. Are you imagining the device dropping off my ankle?'

'I taught you the importance of visualisation,' Taren reminded him, 'so, *yes*, I am.'

Zeven sat up to take another look at the device. Observing a band of light that indicated the restraint was operating, he asked, 'Maybe it only opens once it's switched off. Have you envisaged —'

'Brilliant,' Taren awarded, looking at the restraining band. The second she imagined how the device would look when defunct, it switched off and clicked open.

'All right!' Zeven could hardly believe it, but was startled when the door unexpectedly opened. He quickly dropped his leg to the ground and kicked the device under the lounge.

It was Anselm who entered and he appeared bemused. 'Something odd has happened.'

'What is it?' Taren rose to meet him to draw attention away from Zeven.

'Your mother has contacted me via my private channel to inform me that she knows we're in the Phemorian system and that I have you on board.'

'Has she threatened to attack?' Taren asked.

'Quite the contrary,' he frowned. This was the confusing part. 'She has withdrawn an order to detain this craft at the inter-system gateway and has requested a meeting before we touch down in Heavensgate.'

Sermetica's capital, Heavensgate, was so named because it was quite literally a city in the clouds. The surface of Sermetica was too hot for a comfortable lifestyle, so most Sermetic cities were built on giant platforms that hovered in the troposphere where the conditions were cooler.

Each city in Heavensgate was actually a huge craft, powered on solar energy that was collected through the specially designed windows of every high-rise building and intricately domed complex that comprised the platform cities. Such cities were originally designed as moveable mining rigs, but, following the revolution on Phemoria, the same basic design had been used on a larger scale to create the floating cities of Sermetica. These floating cities could move to different destinations upon the planet, but were too huge and open to move through space.

Taren had only ever seen pictures of Sermetica and was excited at the prospect of seeing the giant floating cities first-hand. 'Did you agree?'

Anselm felt the answer was obvious. 'Better that than cause an interplanetary incident that rehashes the ancient war.'

'I thought Qusay-Sabah Clarona never met with men?' Taren realised how puzzling the queen's behaviour was!

'Not since the last time she saw me, so I'm told,' Anselm confirmed.

'So when is this auspicious event to take place?' Taren asked, playing up the drama, clearly more excited about the prospect of her parents meeting than Anselm was.

'This afternoon, on the other side of the inter-system gateway.'

Taren noticed Anselm seemed nervous, when he was usually so calm and collected. 'Do you think the Phemoray will accompany her?'

'Always,' he said spitefully. 'That is the curse of being a Phemorian queen.'

'Did you know her before she was associated with them?' Taren asked, curious as to the queen's prior character.

'Briefly,' he replied, his voice lacking the usual resentment. 'She was very much like you are now ... smart, ambitious, beautiful, charming —'

'I want to be there,' Taren decided, 'at the meeting.'

'No,' Anselm insisted. 'I have no defence against the Phemoray. No one has —'

'I do,' Taren argued and Anselm gave her a startled and questioning stare. 'I have a benevolent spirit watching over me —'

Her father scoffed. 'Personal guardians are a fiction of children's bedtime stories.'

'Actually, they are our spiritually evolved selves,' she stated. 'Mine has saved me from the Phemoray once already. Zeven arrived after my astral form had been moved to safety.'

Anselm looked at Zeven, who stared blankly back at him and shrugged. 'Give me my memory back and I'll be happy to tell you what I knew,' he said.

'Trust me,' Taren implored Anselm, 'there are higher forces at work here.'

Anselm took a deep breath, disposed to believe her. 'We'll be passing through the gateway very soon. I'll return to fetch you to the meeting before the queen comes aboard.'

'I'd greatly appreciate that,' Taren replied. She was done with allowing others to decide her destiny.

As soon as Anselm had departed, Zeven ducked under the lounge to retrieve and pocket the restraining device and then got to his feet. 'Let's go.'

'Go where?' Taren wondered.

He gawked at her. 'To find AMIE. Remember that?'

Taren looked to the door through which Anselm had just exited. 'I really do want to be at that meeting.'

'Why? Please don't tell me you care about that snake or your insane mother!' Zeven was still annoyed about his missing memories.

Taren looked at the pilot, imploring him to understand. 'In fact, I do trust Anselm. There's something deep within me that knows him. As for my mother ... my higher self told me that my parents had loved each other. Perhaps if they meet again, after all this time, they'll be reminded.'

'But they've both done things —'

'We've all done things,' Taren rebuked him. 'Hell, we made a whole planet disappear!'

'That wasn't our fault —'

'*Yes, it was*. If we had never taken that sample, none of this could, or would, have happened. *Our* fault!'

Taren said firmly, pointing emphatically to Zeven and herself. 'And it's up to us to put it right.'

'Are you mad?' Zeven posed in all seriousness. 'I mean, I've heard some visions of grandeur in my time but that one beats all.'

'When I was a mere mortal I expected to move mountains,' Taren enlightened him, 'but now I am a super-being I expect to move planets, cross galaxies, shift universes! We have to think outside the box. You cannot measure what we are capable of by what has been achieved by others before us. There have been none like us before, and if there were, they never united.'

'Yeah, they did, and drove the entire male population of Phemoria off the planet!' Zeven reminded her. 'That's why the rest of the civilised galaxy fears psychics.'

'That rift can be mended, I know it,' Taren said. 'I know the source of the disease now ... although I'm not quite sure how to heal it. Getting Anselm and Qusay-Sabah Clarona on speaking terms would be a good start, don't you think?'

Zeven stood back a moment, for it had really only just hit him. 'You're actually starting to sound like a princess. In a good way,' he added, so she would not mistake his meaning. 'All the issues you're passionate about are fricking huge undertakings ... ultimately, all I'm worried about is whether I have a job to go back to and if I'll get laid tonight.'

Taren frowned and smiled. She knew he was deeper than he cared to admit. 'Well, I'm worried about those issues, too.' She considered how much time she had to spare ... 'I guess we could go check on AMIE and be back before the meeting starts.'

'Good call.' Zeven approached and took hold of her hands. 'You ready?'

Taren nodded, and Zeven closed his eyes to focus.

As it seemed to be taking a while, Taren became concerned. 'Are you okay?'

'Damn it!' Zeven let her hands go. 'It's not working.'

'Maybe your field has yet to stabilise,' Taren suggested.

'What if they did something to me and it's gone?' Zeven stressed.

'But I thought you wanted it gone?' Taren queried, not understanding his distress.

'I know I did,' Zeven whined.

'Be careful what you wish for,' Taren reminded him again.

'But I dig it now,' he appealed, as if Taren had some say in the outcome. 'My whole life I've loved to move with speed and for a while I didn't need a vehicle to do it!'

Taren was pleased that he'd finally embraced change. 'I'm sure you just need to allow your electromagnetic field to come back into balance. Why would they have bothered restraining you at all?'

'You're right.' Zeven stopped panicking and sat down to begin trying to move things with his mind.

CHAPTER 25

TRYST

When her communicator sounded, Jalila knew who the caller was. The timing was not convenient, as she was currently with a number of Valoureans in the royal vault of the queen's craft, where they had been asked to place the crown of Phemoria.

'Leave me,' the viceroy demanded, ushering the guards out so she could answer the call, but one of the Valoureans remained obstinate. 'Her majesty specified that no one was to be left alone —'

'She did not mean me, you idiot. Now go, before I tell the queen that you have a crush on one of her new prisoners,' Jalila threatened, and as the viceroy could have her discharged in a heartbeat, the Valourean turned and followed the others.

Jalila answered the call. 'I'm alone,' she advised, and hung up, swinging the vault door closed.

Khalid was with her in an instant. 'Why has the queen withdrawn the arrest order? How am I going to disgrace Anselm without a charge against him?'

'I don't know what changed her mind. She's been very secretive and is acting out of character.'

'Does she suspect something?' he quizzed. 'We really don't need her to wake from her self-absorbed coma right now.'

'If she did suspect, I would have been arrested by now,' Jalila reasoned, 'and she certainly would not have given me the job of escorting her crown to the vault.'

Khalid looked around, only just noting where they were situated. 'The crown of Phemoria is *here*.' Khalid smiled with delight, as Jalila directed him to a large silver-white metal case, tightly locked, with an electronic touch pad.

'The case is made of osmium and the lock is DNA-activated,' Jalila explained.

'How nice,' he said, wriggling his fingers with anticipation.

'You're not going to open it!' Jalila was mortified at the thought. 'It is said to be cursed to all bar the true Queen of Phemoria.'

'And one day soon, my lovely, that will be you,' he stated and Jalila smiled in anticipation.

'We'll just keep it in safe keeping until then, shall we?' He placed a hand upon the case containing the royal treasure.

'You cannot take it,' Jalila objected. 'I am alone in here. If they discover it missing, I'll be the prime suspect!'

Khalid held up a hand and manifested a case that looked identical to the one he was intent on stealing. He swapped them over immediately. 'That ought to confuse them for a bit. I intend to uphold the arrest order,' he told her. Jalila went to object, but Khalid placed a finger to her lips to stop her speaking. 'Hopefully, the little princess will get lost in the confusion.'

'Ah,' Jalila said, enlightened.

'Just make sure they arrive at Heavensgate and I shall take care of the rest.'

'But ...' Jalila began to query how he expected her to ensure such a thing, but he vanished, along with the case containing the crown of Phemoria.

Several hours passed before Zeven finally got a glass to fall over and smash in response to his will. 'All right!' he cheered as it shattered all over the marble floor.

'*Starman,*' Taren complained. 'I'm barefoot?'

'Uh ... oh, sorry.' He looked back at the scene of his offence; the shattered pieces of glass gathered together and appeared to jump onto the table. 'I guess we're good to go.' He rose and reached for her, but Taren backed up.

It had been quite some time since they had passed through the inter-system gateway and she figured her parents' meeting must be imminent. 'I can't go. Nobody gets to choose their family and the universe knows no one in their right mind would pick my parents, but I've spent too long wishing I had family to walk away now that I've found mine.'

Zeven had to respect her reasoning, but he knew he had to go. 'I'll be back,' he assured Taren, having decided it would be okay to part from her. There wasn't a place in the known universe she could go that he could not find her with a thought. 'If I find myself adrift in space, I'll be back even sooner.'

'They're alive,' Taren said, confident in her heart that it was true. 'But be careful anyway.'

'You be careful,' Zeven said. 'You have a lot more to contend with than I do!'

Taren nodded to convince him she'd be fine. Zeven closed his eyes and thought of Aurora.

Touchdown found Zeven in the corridor where the bio-containment labs were located, between the launch bay and AMIE's bridge, and he breathed a great sigh of relief to be in familiar surroundings.

A woman sobbing drew his attention to Aurora on the floor beside him, curled up in a ball, crying her eyes out. 'Why are you crying?' he asked, squatting down in front of her and gently gripping her shoulders.

'Because I am not brave enough to do what Kalayna did,' she wept, completely oblivious to who it was she was talking to as she wouldn't look up.

'What did Kalayna do?' he asked, crouching lower. He finally gained her attention, whereupon she ceased crying and burst into a huge smile. 'Starman!' She launched herself into his embrace and kissed him repeatedly. 'I was so worried,' she said, hugging him in between her kisses. 'I've missed you so much.' She kissed him again and began ripping the clothes from his body.

Zeven couldn't have been happier, but having his wits a little more about him he decided the corridor was really not the place. He swung open the door of the bio-containment lab observation room and they stumbled inside, panting and shedding layers as they went.

'Unbelievable,' Kalayna uttered, looking over the proof in her hand, yet she still couldn't accept what she'd done. 'This is a miracle.'

She'd built a prototype weapon from the bits and pieces of spy equipment she still had, plus the spare parts she'd found in the hangar storeroom. 'This has to be my Power,' Kalayna reasoned. She'd always had a good grasp of engineering and perhaps, given a few years to draw blueprints and fiddle with construction, she might have been able to create the same device that she'd just thrown together ... overnight! It was a handheld weapon that sent out pulses from the rounded nose, pulses which scrambled a psychic's electromagnetic field for a short period. At least, that's what Kalayna expected the device to do, but of course she needed to test it.

As she left the launch bay, Kalayna headed towards the bridge in hopes of finding Leal there. She was polishing up the silvery outer casing of her new toy when, out of the corner of her eye, she noted shadowy movement through the window of one of the darkened bio-containment labs and she moved to take a closer look.

Starman was ravishing Aurora on the floor of the lab and Kalayna's heart sank. Her first reaction was to feel hurt and left out, and she briefly entertained the thought of testing her new weapon on Starman, but she had learned that blind rage was not the way to handle heartbreak.

The sheer bliss she saw on their faces filled her heart with joy. She really did care for them both very deeply and she knew they cared about her. She could walk right in there and join them and neither would have objected, but Kalayna would feel like she was intruding … and that's what she'd been doing all along, she suddenly realised.

Since meeting Aurora, Kalayna felt she'd really discovered herself; she had her own fascinating life to lead and was no longer controlled by anyone else. She had to admit that a good part of her attraction to Aurora was the AMIE project, and Aurora had been more distant since discovering that Kalayna was a sleeper agent for the secret service. Kalayna may have had no conscious knowledge of being a spy, but Aurora now felt that Kalayna had only targeted and seduced her for secret service purposes. The fact that Kalayna had dared to enter the bio-containment area without permission had infuriated Aurora all over again. The relationship with Aurora was definitely over this time, and Kalayna didn't blame her for a second. Aurora had been pining for Zeven the entire time he'd been missing and obviously Starman had been pining for Rory too.

It had been a lovely tryst, but now that Kalayna knew the truth about herself, it was clear to her she had no claim on either Aurora or Starman.

They got each other. I got a Power and a really cool job . . . pretty sweet deal.

She reined in her emotions, backed away quietly and continued along her own desired course of action. She still needed to test her prototype.

When Anselm arrived to collect Taren for the meeting, he was naturally curious about where Zeven Gudrun had gone and how he'd escaped.

Taren just smiled broadly. 'Just goes to show, you don't know everything about me.'

'He didn't attempt to find AMIE, surely,' Anselm asked, distressed, as he'd had plans for the pilot. 'Not without a spacesuit? I told you there was an explosion —'

'You worry too much. Starman is fine.' Taren waved off his concerns.

'Starman?' Anselm was set at ease by her certainty. 'Is that what you call him?'

Taren nodded. 'And he sure does live up to the name. Shall we go?'

As Anselm led her to the conference chamber, Taren noted how handsome and how fit her father was for a man of his years. 'I hear you are very popular with the ladies, Father.'

Anselm suppressed a smile. 'I hear you're having an affair with Captain Gervaise.'

'Mother doesn't approve,' Taren grinned, and then frowned. 'Do you think she ordered the attack on AMIE that caused the explosion?'

Anselm went to answer, but they'd reached the conference room and his guard pressed the switch that opened the doors for them. The politician waited until they were inside and the doors had been closed before he replied. 'The truth is ... I was the one who had the explosives planted.'

'What!' Taren backed up.

'I needed to ensure Gudrun's cooperation in your rescue, but I never intended for the device to be detonated. I did not give that command.'

'Then who did?' Taren challenged, just as the doors opened and a guard entered to announce the queen's arrival.

'Khalid Mansur,' he uttered in an aside, then stood up straight to prepare for the arrival of the queen.

In the light of this new information, Taren feared that Lucian might actually be dead along with all of AMIE's crew ... and she had her parents to thank for it. She raised her woeful face to tell the pair of them exactly what she thought of them, and was shocked to the core to see Lucian and Ringbalin escort the veiled Qusay-Sabah Clarona into the room.

'Lucian!' Taren flew to embrace him and he caught her up and swung her around. As the lovers kissed, everyone else in the room was notably uncomfortable.

'Leave us,' the queen commanded her Valoureans.

'Wait outside,' Anselm directed his men.

'Jabez,' the queen said, informally greeting him as she had not done since she'd taken up her office. 'I appreciate you seeing us so discreetly.'

'By "us" do you mean you and your witches?' Anselm asked warily, although her demeanour was not as cold and unemotional as he remembered.

'These men released me from the curse that bound me to the will of the Phemoray. Now I am my own ruler,' she told him.

Anselm looked at the tiny blond man standing beside the queen, rather than to the captain who was still preoccupied kissing his daughter. 'Then we are greatly indebted to you ... I think?' He looked back to the queen whose nature was now something of an unknown. Would she be back to the wonderful, idealistic woman he'd once known and been fascinated with, or would she be someone entirely different again?

'Could we speak alone?' the queen asked, obviously uncomfortable having to make the request.

'More alone than this?' Anselm was intrigued.

'We can leave.' Taren had heard, and considering this meeting was proceeding somewhat faster and better than she'd expected, she took hold of Lucian's hand and led him to the door. Ringbalin bowed out also.

Once the door had closed, Anselm motioned about them with his palms upturned. 'We are alone, majesty,' he smiled, curious. He also wondered if he should have brought a weapon to the meeting.

Qusay-Sabah Clarona raised a hand to touch his cheek. 'I have missed that smile,' she confessed, to his great surprise, but he determined not to be seduced by her again.

'Really?' He backed up a few paces. 'I have not given you a second thought.'

'Of course. I was so completely forgettable,' she said in a sarcastic tone.

'There was nothing to remember,' he retorted. 'You drugged me and stole my DNA.'

'I drugged you?' the queen recoiled, offended. 'You got yourself drunk and completely forgot the most wonderful night of my life!' The pent-up emotions of fifty years came flooding forth in a burst of tears, although she realised she really couldn't recall him being drunk that long-ago evening.

Anselm was bemused, as she seemed so passionate about what she was saying. 'You told me you stole my DNA and that we were never lovers.'

'I lied!' she confessed. 'When you woke with no memory of that *spectacular* night, I was so angry I didn't want you to know you'd had me at all. Soon after that I was crowned Queen of Phemoria and the Phemoray took control of my affairs ... until today.' Qusay-Sabah Clarona pulled the veil from her head so that he might see in her face that she meant what she said.

Anselm was overwhelmed to see how beautiful she was ... to his eyes she had barely aged a day. Her lips were still the most rosy and luscious he'd ever seen. Her long, dark hair was pulled back into an ornate arrangement at the crown of her head and shimmered in the light as it cascaded over one shoulder and fell to her waist. Her large pale violet eyes were awash with tears and yet she appeared serene and dignified.

'I truly loved you, Jabez, and I am sorry for all the pain my curse has caused you and our daughter.' She fell to her knees before him and Anselm's reserve melted away. 'Please, forgive me.'

'We have both been deceived, I fear.' Anselm knelt also — if she was so upset about his forgetting their night of passion then she had not arranged for his memory loss, and something, or someone, else was responsible. The secret services had the capability, even back then, so perhaps one of his own people had erased the memory.

'Khalid Mansur ...' The queen startled Anselm with the name, as Khalid was Anselm's first suspect as the saboteur. '... wishes to kidnap our daughter and use her to blackmail us.'

Anselm didn't doubt this was the truth. Actually it was making more sense than just about anything had in fifty years. 'Forewarned is forearmed,' he said, taking her hand to aid her to rise.

'Nothing is more important to me than Taren's safety,' the queen assured him. 'Words cannot express my gratitude to you for saving her from my sad fate.' She bowed her head, indicating the heaviness of the burden she carried. 'Now I have to devise a way to save the rest of my people.'

'I will help you,' Anselm said, and with a fingertip under her chin, he raised her face to look into her eyes. 'You're not alone any more.'

With his words, the queen's tears began flowing anew.

'I sincerely apologise for forgetting the conception of our daughter, but I can assure you there is no one more sorry for that memory loss than I.'

His apology made her smile. It was an eon since she'd been charmed by anyone. 'I still remember every little detail,' she said softly. 'If you'd care to remember ...' she added in a seductive manner, and held her right palm up, her fingers splayed wide apart.

Anselm was curiously aroused by the offer. 'You can convey your memory to me?'

She nodded, delighted that he seemed disposed to accept her proposition. 'If you wish it.'

'I can't think of a better way to spend an afternoon.' He led her to a lounge where they could be more comfortable.

Out in the corridor, Taren advised Ringbalin that she needed to speak with Lucian alone.

'I understand that you do.' He suppressed a smile.

'Will you be okay?' Taren didn't like leaving the pacifist alone among a throng of Valoureans.

'We'll see no harm comes to him,' a tall blonde Valourean was quick to say, and her company all agreed with great enthusiasm.

'Very good,' Taren replied. She looked at Ringbalin, knowing that he must have touched them with his gentle, compassionate love for all things, just as he had obviously touched her mother. 'Will you please let me know the minute they are out of conference?'

Balin was a little unsettled by the request. 'As I have been given a royal pardon, I really do need to be getting back to Module C as soon as possible,' he said to Lucian.

'Noted,' Lucian confirmed. 'I'll see what I can arrange once the conference is over.'

'In that case ... I'll let you know as soon as it is.' Ringbalin frowned, resigned to waiting. He'd expected to find Zeven on board the Sermetic craft and so get spirited back to AMIE. 'Where has Starman got to?'

'On board AMIE, I expect,' Taren explained as she backed away to lead Lucian to the quarters she'd been occupying. 'One guess as to what he's doing right now.'

Ringbalin was amused. 'I won't expect him any time soon then.' He looked back to the females around him.

'Tell us about Module C,' the Valourean in charge suggested, and she could not have picked a better topic to keep Balin's mind occupied.

'How did you do it?' Taren was bursting with anticipation to know how Lucian and Balin had freed her mother, but the captain was distracted by a couple of Sermetic agents walking by and came to a standstill. 'What is it?'

'All these guards have throngs of ghosts following them about.' His eyes were glued to the apparitions that Taren couldn't see.

'Lucian ...' Taren took hold of his face and directed his attention back to her. 'Are you seeing ghosts?' Inside, her heart welled with excitement and warmth to the point of overflowing.

He gazed down at her and nodded. 'I breathed the air of Oceane —'

Taren was overwhelmed with emotions. 'For me?' Her eyes filled with tears for she knew how reserved he was about all things supernatural.

'I love you, Taren whatever-your-second-name-really-is,' he replied, a little teary-eyed himself. 'I don't suppose they'll let me marry you now that you are royalty and a prominent politicians daughter —'

'*They* don't get any say in it ...' Taren wanted to annihilate that obstacle just in case he ever really did get it into his mind to propose. '... because I am not giving myself to any man but you.'

She kissed him with such enthusiasm that Lucian had to hold her back to make a suggestion. 'Ah ... you have a room, I believe.'

Taren realised they were attracting an audience in the corridor. 'Let's go.' She grabbed hold of his hand

and led the way to the whistles and encouragement of the onlookers.

'I suspect Khalid Mansur wishes to kidnap you,' Lucian informed Taren once they were alone.

'Well, why not?' Taren said frivolously. She wasn't worried, as she had no idea who he was beyond being her father's viceroy. 'Everybody else has had a crack at it.' She stripped the shirt from Lucian's body and kissed his bare chest.

'He has Powers,' Lucian warned, although he couldn't help smiling as clearly nothing mattered to Taren beyond their union this very second.

'So do we.' Taren envisaged the clothes vanishing from her body onto the floor, whereupon she felt her person lightened of the load of fabric.

Lucian was delighted and sincerely impressed. 'Will you marry me?'

Taren knew he wasn't being serious, but moved in closer to engage her desires. 'In this universe and the next,' she affirmed with a kiss.

Khalid had not hidden the cursed crown in Heavensgate. He had a secret place where he stashed his riches.

In a deep crevice in a wide, remote canyon on the surface of Sermetica, there was a place known as Dead Man Downs. There was an abyss of embittered thought-forms to be found there, remnants of a human holocaust.

After Phemoria's revolution, several shiploads of men had been launched to Sermetica. There had been no one qualified to operate the craft, no supplies, little oxygen and water, but plenty of fuel to make it to their destination with no known survivors.

Dead Man Downs was where those craft crash-landed.

Inside the least damaged of the shipwrecks, there were quite a few skeletal remains, but that didn't bother Khalid. He felt the bones added to the dark ambience. Since the craft had plunged to the bottom of the canyon, it was forever in shade, and inside the wreck, some of the rooms, especially the executive lounge, were still usable, even comfortable. However, Khalid did not come here for the décor; he came for the *atmosphere*, which was electric with fear, anger, pain, suffering and other negative emotions that filled him up and made him brave enough to be more ruthless and cunning than the next man.

Khalid willed the lights and air-conditioning on, although none of the ships systems actually worked any more and had long ago run out of power. He placed the case containing the crown of Phemoria on the coffee table, to observe it while he mixed a drink. 'This should be interesting,' he muttered to himself. He took a seat on a lounge and rested his crossed feet beside the metal case on the table. 'Disengage lock and open lid.' He sipped at his drink, pleased that this spectacular theft had been so easy.

The sound of angry females emanated from the case as it opened and a huge seething ball of red energy burst forth from the crown and simmered furiously near the ceiling of the luxurious lounge.

Khalid Mansur, it hissed, as five veiled women appeared nearby.

'Ladies, how nice of you to come.' Khalid held up his glass in mock salute. 'I don't know if you are aware of this, but your planet is up for a bit of a change in management.'

How have you stolen the crown of Phemoria?

'Does it matter?' he asked cheerfully. 'What does matter is that you have something I need ... Phemoria. And I have something you need ... a ruler for your planet and the crown by which we shall control that ruler.'

A man will never control Phemoria!

'Really? Then I'll bury this crown in a desert and the Phemoray will become nothing more than a brooding pile of ill-will in the wilderness ... much like the wretched souls you condemned to this sweltering abyss. Better still, I could bury your crown here and you would spend an eternity at the mercy of the men who owe their damnation to you,' he threatened. The women took his threat seriously and humbled themselves.

No, we beseech you.

'I appreciate that it would not work in our favour if I were to be known as the ruler of Phemoria. It is the world's resources and political backing that I desire. So, fear not, I will not rule directly ... I will impregnate your princess and deliver her and the crown to you, to control until my daughter comes of age to rule.'

The Phemoray were not in a good position to argue. *But you are her uncle.*

'Who better than a Prince of Phemoria to father your next queen?' he spat out, and the female apparitions bowed their heads. They had no choice while the crown was in his possession.

We accept your terms.

'Thought you might,' Khalid grinned, and ordered the lid on the royal case to close. The Phemoray and their angry mass of female thought-forms vanished. 'This take over just keeps getting sweeter all the time.'

* * *

'So how did you do it?' Taren finally asked, having expended all her accumulated sexual yearning for the present.

'Three spirit beings talked me into snatching the queen's crown from her head.' Lucian looked down at Taren, who had her head resting upon his bare chest.

'You saw Azazèl?' Taren asked in astonishment.

'I don't know. The only name I caught was Armaros,' Lucian replied, to Taren's confusion. 'Have you seen these beings?'

'Light-filled spirits, one of whom, Azazèl, appears very much like you? Yes, I've seen them. They saved me from the Phemoray,' she told him, delighted and amazed. 'But I was astral travelling at the time ... you saw them whilst still in your physical form, which means you're a *medium*.' She was so very elated for him.

'I see through walls, too,' he added, revelling in her excitement.

'X-ray clairvoyance!'

'So my higher self saved you from the Phemoray, even when I could not,' Lucian said, finding the idea very reassuring.

'Azazèl is not just *your* spirit self, but *our* spirit self,' she enlightened, and Lucian was pleased and discomforted at the same time. 'Overwhelming, isn't it? He told me we were ... the male and female sides of himself.'

'No wonder I was so attracted to you when we first met.' Lucian's mind boggled. 'What were the chances of us ever finding each other?'

'Very good apparently,' Taren said with a grin. She went on to explain what little Azazèl had revealed to her. 'We, and others of our soul-group, are constantly drawn together to accomplish what none of us could accomplish alone.'

Lucian smiled, liking the sound of it. 'That rather removes the loneliness out of life.'

Taren agreed and calmed down enough to remember the point of this conversation. 'So Azazèl advised you to remove my mother's crown. Why?'

'It said the crown was cursed and while she wore it she would be of no assistance to me,' he explained.

'You trusted a spirit?' Taren was flabbergasted.

Lucian shrugged off her disbelief; he knew he'd been a total sceptic. 'He was yelling and threatening me with failure if I did not comply,' he joked about his blind faith, but Taren was incredibly proud of him.

The door chime sounded, and Taren and Lucian both scrambled around quickly, finding clothes and trying to put them on. 'Wait a second.' Taren thought them both dressed and then moved to unlock the door.

'That's sure going to come in handy,' Lucian said, as his panic subsided at finding himself fully dressed once again.

Ringbalin was startled when the door was answered so quickly. 'Your parents are asking to see you.'

'Are they still being civil to each other?' Taren winced, not fancying her chances, but hopeful nonetheless.

'From all appearances they are in fine spirits,' he told her happily.

Taren looked to Lucian as he joined her by the door; he was as amazed as she. 'Could the ancient feud actually be coming to an end?'

'Let's go find out.' Lucian took hold of her hand and they followed Ringbalin's lead to the council chamber.

CHAPTER 26

SNATCH

Taren was stunned to find her mother unveiled and smiling, and her father beaming with delight.

'You will be happy to know that a new relationship of cooperation has been formed between Sermetica and Phemoria today,' Anselm informed Taren, unable to keep his eyes off Qusay-Sabah Clarona.

'I can see that,' Taren replied. 'So does this mean no more having my memory erased, no more hide-and-seek —'

'Not exactly, no,' Anselm was sorry to say. 'You will be under guard until I can find Khalid Mansur and address certain claims that have been made against him.'

'What?' Taren had other plans. 'No way, I —'

'I'm only talking about a few days,' Anselm beseeched her.

'Look, I'm really pleased that you two have worked out your differences, but how about we consider what I want for a change?' Taren posed and her parents felt they owed it to her to hear her out.

'All right,' Anselm conceded. 'What is it you want?'

'I —' Taren was interrupted when a guard entered with Kalayna in tow.

'Sorry, Mr President, but she insisted.' The guard kept one hand on Kalayna's shoulder, just in case her intrusion was not welcome.

'No, it's fine,' Anselm said. He knew her and knew she was embroiled in all this too.

'Thank you.' Kalayna watched the guard leave and then turned to them. 'I would not have come if my news wasn't urgent,' she began and thought about where best to start. 'Since my agent programming was broken, I've been remembering some things from my past. The most repugnant of which was my recruitment into the SS by Khalid Mansur. Right before he wiped my memory, he confessed to being responsible for me losing my job. He killed my father to get to me —' She began shaking as tears of fury flooded her eyes.

Ringbalin moved in to place a hand around Kalayna's shoulder and his calming energy gave her the strength to continue.

'But I also recall him doing something that I did not see again until I met Zeven Gudrun. He didn't know I saw him and knew I wouldn't remember in any case.' A smile threatened to form on her lips. 'The man has PK,' she advised. Some in the room knew this already, but most did not.

'That changes things,' Taren said, concerned that a man who wished to kidnap her could find her with a thought at any time.

'Hence the twenty-four-hour guard,' her father concluded.

'Is Mansur after Dr Lennox?' Kalayna guessed.

'So it is rumoured,' said the queen.

'Never fear.' Kalayna felt very proud to be able to provide reassurance, showing them her handheld silver device. It was shaped like a very large, slightly squashed cigar. 'This is what I call a psychic neutraliser. It performs the same function as the restraining bands, but from a distance of up to thirty metres.'

All present were completely astounded, and Ringbalin backed away to give her the floor to demonstrate.

'I can see why Khalid went to such great lengths to recruit you,' Taren commented, feeling safer already.

'I have a gift,' she grinned, excited. 'I am a thaumaturge.'

No one was any the wiser, bar the queen. 'That is an ancient art. I've never come across anyone in modern times who claims to have such a gift.'

'Kassa said that thaumaturgy was known as the "art mathematical", the ability to construct complex mechanical devices that are ahead of their time, which is how the inter-system gateways were constructed, or so it is theorised. It's like I can pull blueprints out of the future with my mind, and within existing machinery I can see the components that will fulfil the brief, then the engineer in me constructs the device and ... ta-da!'

'Have you tested it?' Anselm wondered.

'I have,' Kalayna said. 'A shot from this weapon will incapacitate psychic ability for a little under two hours.'

'About the same time it takes for a field to re-stabilise after wearing a restraining band,' Anselm noted. 'How does it work?'

As her tutorial drew to a close, Kalayna was suddenly fearful and she felt an ominous presence near her.

Khalid materialised behind Kalayna and, with a knife to her throat, he removed the psychic neutraliser from her hand. 'You're all supposed to be dead,' he snarled, firing the new pulse weapon at Anselm, the Queen of Phemoria and Taren — all those known to him to have psychic talent. They staggered and gripped hold of each other as the force of the pulse bullet knocked them backwards. 'I don't appreciate having my secrets betrayed,' he told Kalayna as he sliced his blade across her throat. Blood streamed from her wound as Kalayna dropped to the floor and Khalid faded to invisible once more.

Ringbalin rushed over to help Kalayna, but the cut was too deep ... she was already dead. 'No, no, no!' He could not believe he was bearing witness to another tragic and brutal slaying inside a week and he collapsed into tears.

Lucian grabbed hold of Taren's hand, whilst straining to try and spot their foe. *If I'm a medium, why can't I see him?*

Taren was suddenly yanked from Lucian's grasp and Khalid reappeared as he dragged her further away — his knife at her throat. Lucian, Anselm and the queen all took a step towards them in protest.

'Khalid, don't do this,' Qusay-Sabah Clarona appealed to him. 'She is your niece —'

This news shocked everyone in the room, including Anselm. 'Khalid is your brother?'

'My half-brother,' she admitted.

'On any other planet I would be ruler and you, dear sister, would be nothing but marriage fodder for political gain. But, *no*, I had to be born a bloody Prince of Phemoria, to be completely disinherited from birth. Well, I intend to change all that,' he advised them. 'Speaking of which, the little princess and I really do have to go, as we have a wedding to arrange.'

Lucian launched himself towards Khalid, who vanished with Taren, and the captain fell to the floor empty-handed. 'Sonofabitch,' he yelled, finding his feet to express his frustration. 'What will it take to keep this woman in my life?'

The queen and Anselm could only sympathise with his feelings. This unexpected turn of events had them all baffled and distraught.

'We'll find them,' Anselm assured Lucian.

'I have agents who can —' the queen began to say, but Lucian, who was still sore at these two, for a great many things, snapped.

'*Stop* helping us!'

'I didn't detonate that bomb on your craft, captain,' Anselm said, to set the record straight, 'that was Mansur's order —'

'I don't care any more.' He looked at his dead technician, of whom he'd grown very fond in the time he'd known her. 'Your kind of assistance gets people killed! My project had a full complement of crew and between the two of you I have lost all bar five! I'll find Zeven Gudrun, and we'll handle this.'

'And just how do you propose to aid Taren?' Anselm was dubious as to the captain's capacity to be of help.

Without disclosing too much, Lucian replied, 'Do you believe in guardian spirits?'

Anselm would have completely disregarded the implication had his daughter not told him just recently that she had one.

'I do,' replied the queen, with a nod to grant him permission to act on her behalf.

Anselm sighed, persuaded to have a little faith. 'What do you need us to do?'

* * *

Zeven and Aurora lay naked on the observation room floor, amid a pile of their discarded clothes. In the wake of their passionate outpouring, which had lasted several hours, on and off, their muscles had begun to fail them and so they had paused to catch their breath.

'I just can't go on ...' Aurora gasped for breath. '... although I still want to.' She found enough energy to roll over and kiss Zeven before collapsing once again.

'I think we've pretty well exhausted every possible sexual aspect of this lab anyway,' he laughed, only now feeling a twinge of guilt for stealing this brief interlude amid the chaos AMIE was embroiled in at present. 'I suppose I should let someone know where I am.'

Aurora was reluctant to let him go again. 'No,' she protested as she rolled over to prevent his escape. 'Stay with me forever.'

'I intend to,' he assured her with a kiss as he slid out from beneath her.

'And Kalayna, too?' Aurora sounded disheartened. She was thinking he would like Kalayna so much better now that she had a Power like he did.

'Hey,' Zeven was alarmed to see her tears returning. 'I care about Kalayna but if I had to choose between you, I'd choose you.'

'You do have to choose.' Aurora's emotional state deteriorated before his eyes as she explained how they had spied on the captain, and how Kalayna had used the information they gleaned to acquire herself a Power. 'The only reason she picked me up in that bar in the first place was because she'd been programmed to.' She collapsed into Zeven's arms and wept.

'Just you and me from now on then,' he whispered, and his sincere resolve had a calming effect on Aurora. 'And that's the way it should have been all along.'

Aurora raised her teary sights, astonished to hear him say so.

'I should have asked you out that night and I'm really sorry I didn't.'

She smiled broadly. 'Apology accepted,' and she kissed him again.

Quite often, Aurora's kiss would induce a kind of euphoria in Zeven, but what he felt right now was not like that. At the same time it was all too familiar.

You've been summoned, announced an overconfident voice inside his mind, one that had possessed him before against his will.

Sammael, don't you dare ... Zeven protested and before he could grab one stitch of clothing, he was being hurtled through space to an unknown destination.

Lucian, although he was not a spiritually savvy person, had had the foresight to realise that if the spirit he'd encountered was, in fact, his higher self, then as a medium he could call on this spirit for counsel and aid, which he did.

Azazèl and his comrades had responded to the call at once and charged Sammael with rousing Zeven Gudrun.

Zeven materialised before the President of Sermetica, the Queen of Phemoria and his captain in the council chambers ... nude.

As the pilot materialised, Lucian noted the spirit step out of him and leave the poor fellow wavering in his stance.

Sammael. Azazèl was annoyed at his comrade. *We are not supposed to directly intervene. We are supposed to inspire and guide —*

He's lying naked with a beautiful woman, he is not listening to any guidance I might have in regard to leaving, Sammael responded, defending his action to Azazèl and Armaros, and neither being could argue his logic.

When Zeven realised where he was and who was present, he immediately covered his private parts and imagined himself clothed. The weight of the fabric manifesting on his form was a great relief.

'Your ... um, highnesses ...' He nodded to the last two people he would have expected to see in the same room as his captain. His eyes drifted to a bloodied stain on the carpet and his concern trebled. 'Where is Taren?'

'That's exactly what I need your help to find out,' Lucian advised solemnly.

'You don't know?' Now Zeven really felt guilty. He should have got back to her sooner.

'She's been kidnapped by Khalid Mansur —' Lucian began.

'Say no more,' Zeven said and closed his eyes to focus.

'No, wait ...' Lucian grabbed hold of Zeven's arm to warn him about the new weapon in Khalid's possession, whereupon the captain was whisked away to the surface of Sermetica with Zeven.

CHAPTER 27

GHOST SHIP

In the midst of her daughter's peril and with naught to do but await an outcome, Qusay-Sabah Clarona felt it was time she had a little heart-to-heart with her viceroy. The queen retreated to a small antechamber off the main council room to speak with Jalila alone.

Not long ago she would have handled her viceroy's treachery differently, but at that time her instincts and thoughts were being controlled by the Phemoray. Today, her reasoning mind and judgment were her own.

'My queen,' Jalila said in greeting and bowed to hide her apprehension at being summoned into such an intimate situation with her royal highness.

'Come in, Jalila. Sit down.' The queen motioned for the other woman to take a seat on the lounge beside her, which she had never, in her fifty-year reign, invited her viceroy to do.

Jalila warily complied with the request and attempted to read her queen's thoughts — usually this was impossible, as the crown of Phemoria cast a psychic shield around whoever wore it, but the queen was not wearing the crown today. Jalila honed in on the queen's inner dialogue to hear ...

What is it that you fear I know?

Jalila suppressed an urge to gasp as she sat beside her monarch. 'Is something the matter, majesty?'

The queen forced a smile to inform her. 'I have found love ...'

This was the last thing Jalila had expected to be discussing. 'That is well, majesty.'

'... with a man,' the queen added. 'I believe you too have a male lover,' the queen advised and watched the colour drain from her viceroy's face. 'I don't know what Khalid promised you, but he has kidnapped my daughter, and plans, I assume, to produce a daughter with her through whom he can finally control Phemoria.'

Jalila was horrified and infuriated and immediately stood up, unsure how to react. 'Shall I summon the Valoureans?' She decided to keep her poker face.

'He told you that you would rule, didn't he?' the queen surmised, and didn't await an answer. 'The truth is, he hates women and is protected by a like-minded masculine thought-form ... just as the Phemoray granted me additional power and protection because of our mutual hatred for men.'

'And now that you love a man?' Jalila posed.

'Has my power gone?' The queen guessed at her interest. 'You love a man, yet your power is unaffected,' she bluffed, challenging Jalila, for the queen was still psychically bereft from being hit by Kalayna's psychic neutraliser.

'*Love* is a very strong word. I would have said *use*. Make no mistake, majesty, I love Phemoria and any alliances I have formed have been for the benefit of our people.'

'Khalid does not care about our people,' the queen stated, quashing her viceroy's belief, 'and although I thought I was acting in their best interests during my reign, I see now that I was certainly not. How many happy families have been destroyed due to our absurd laws!' Thinking about the loss of her own family for fifty years brought tears to the woman's eyes. 'I won't be ruled by the forces of hate any longer, I can assure you. If I could have taken that crown from my head, I would have handed it to you long ago, happily. The Phemoray are a curse and I will be overjoyed to be rid of them.'

Jalila was stunned and wasn't entirely sure how to respond. 'I agree,' she stated uncertainly. 'That is why I sought Khalid, to help rid the planet of your royal line and the witches you answer to.'

The queen smiled, appreciating her viceroy's honesty. 'I can well understand why you did what you did,' the queen said. 'I would have done the same thing in your place … but I gather Khalid did not mention he is my half-brother, and part of that royal line you seek to expunge.'

The news winded Jalila. Hardly able to breathe, her fury at being lied to began to surface nevertheless.

The queen had recently come to wonder if Jalila had an amulet to protect her from psychic scrutiny. It was only after witnessing how easily Khalid had kidnapped her daughter from under the noses of so many psychics that the queen now suspected that Jalila had acquired her protection from her association with Khalid. 'All Khalid really wants is to claim the inheritance he believes is rightfully his. I now suspect that Khalid has an amulet that prevents him from being discovered psychically and you are the only one who might know what that amulet is … I believe you carry such an item also.'

'Why should I help you?' Jalila folded her arms defiantly and allowed her true colours to show. 'So that Phemoria can remain a sovereign-ruled nation, at the mercy of one power-hungry insane family? No, I don't think so.'

'If you help me ...' The queen stood to look into her viceroy's eyes so that she might know she spoke honestly. '... the royal line of Phemoria will end with me and I will hand over to someone our citizens choose to elect.'

Jalila's arms dropped to her side once more, as she was pleased with this arrangement. 'No offence, but can I have that in writing.'

'You shall have it,' the queen stated, and held her hand palm out towards her viceroy as a peace offering. Jalila placed her palm against the queen's to seal their deal.

Jalila then reached inside her vest to expose a metal amulet she wore. 'This was a gift to me from Khalid. It was made from the melted-down ignition keys of the ships of Dead Man Downs and it has shielded me from the psychic sight of the Phemoray. Khalid claims to have one just like it, but I have never seen it on his person. If he is separated from the amulet, he will be open to psychic attack and able to be found with a thought just like any other soul in existence.'

The queen was very grateful to Jalila for disclosing this information, and was about to state as much, when Jalila added: 'You should also know that he has stolen the crown of Phemoria.' The fact that Khalid had taken it and left her to explain the disappearance made her seethe even more now. If she'd only known the truth about him, she would have slit his throat long ago.

The queen shuddered. Why had Khalid stolen the crown? 'It is well known that the crown will kill a man —'

'Khalid is well aware of the legend,' Jalila confirmed.

'Please, no,' the queen whispered as her panic trebled. 'He can't mean to put it on Taren's head?' The thought of her daughter suffering as she had suffered was intolerable. 'The Phemoray would never align themselves with a man.'

Jalila wasn't so sure. 'Not even if he's giving them what they want?'

Before Taren had even manifested in the next location, she could feel the cold dread of the place they were approaching.

Much like the Abyss of the Obstinate on Phemoria, the ruined spaceship in which she found herself was oppressive in the extreme. Even with her psychic powers defunct, she could sense this place had seen great human suffering — a pile of skeletons in the corner seemed to confirm her instinct.

'Welcome to Dead Man Downs,' Khalid advised, dumping her on a lounge and moving to the bar. He placed his new weapon upon it and fixed a drink.

Taren had read the dark and sordid legend of Dead Man Downs and never in a million years thought it would in any way relate back to her.

'Being a scientist you are aware of cosmic order, and this place is the polar opposite for that witch pit on Phemoria. Every soul here is a male who hates the women of Phemoria to the core, just like I do.'

Taren really didn't like where this conversation was headed. 'What do you want?'

'I want you to give me a daughter,' he advised, raising an empty glass to her. 'Drink?'

Taren's heart started beating rapidly; she was appalled by the suggestion. 'But you're my uncle.'

'Half-uncle, really.' He tossed the empty glass aside, not bothering with her drink. 'Hold her down, boys,' he instructed his ghosts as he gulped down a shot.

'What the ...' Taren yelped as she felt a great force bear down on her, pinning her back against the lounge. She struggled, but it just became stronger. 'What happened to the wedding?' Taren panicked, overwhelmed by her predicament.

'I've never really been one for formalities, so I thought we'd just skip to the consummation part,' he quipped, stripping off his jacket.

Taren felt ill. 'Azazèl!' she cried out as Khalid undid his belt. *Think girl, think.* There had to be a way to turn this situation around. *The banishing stone.* She still carried it on her person, just as Dr Portus had advised her to do. It was in her pocket, which fortunately was located right next to where her hand was pinned down the side of her body. She scrunched the fabric up with her fingers to draw the pocket over her hand and searched frantically for the stone.

'We're all alone, sweetheart,' Khalid said triumphantly as he came towards Taren. 'There's just you, me and the ghosts of a thousand vengeful men.'

She felt the stone at her fingertips. Grasping it in her hand, Taren held it tight and closed her eyes in an attempt to block out the nightmare.

The pressure immediately lifted and her world slowed to a dreamlike state. She remembered her previous experience beneath the spell of the banishing stone as a veil rose between herself and her physical reality.

Beyond the misty veil, Taren witnessed her present reality unfolding ever so slowly. When Khalid moved towards her, Taren rolled off the lounge to avoid being trapped beneath him and noted that she seemed to be shedding a lot of light in the darkness of this place.

She is of the line of those Phemorian whores who launched us to our death! Taren heard a man say, but it was not Khalid.

Within the misty veil of the banishing stone's spell, she saw the ghosts of dead men venturing out of the shadows and into the light she was exuding — so many gaunt, harrowed faces.

A bit of light ain't going to stop us from tearing you apart! said another.

Where ... the ... fuck ... did ... she ... go? Khalid demanded slowly, infuriated out of his mind.

Taren wasn't sure who was more ominous: Khalid or his ghostly crew.

The ghostly hordes gave a war cry and rushed towards her, but an atmospheric disturbance in both the inner and outer world, sent the spectres into retreat as a wave of force radiated out from around Taren.

Before she could wonder how she would defend herself without her Powers, Starman and Lucian manifested with their backs to her.

'*Where ... is ... she?*' Starman droned as he looked around in slow motion, as did Lucian.

'*How ... the ... fuck ... did ... you ... get ... here?*' Khalid spotted them and did up his trousers.

Taren came up behind Lucian to make him aware of where she was, when she noted Khalid extend his hand towards the bar. Taren dropped her stone back into her pocket to ensure Zeven heard her warning. 'Starman, the weapon on the bar!'

Zeven was startled to see Taren appear and by the time he'd comprehended her warning, the weapon was already airborne and heading for Khalid. 'Mine!' Starman exerted his will, and the weapon changed course to land in his possession. 'This is a weapon?' He boggled at the design of it.

'So you're the one.' Khalid sized up his competition with disdain.

'I guess so,' Zeven said, flattered that his reputation preceded him.

'One of my abandoned bastards, no doubt,' Khalid taunted and Zeven was totally pissed off at this claim.

'Just because we have the same ability doesn't mean —'

'PK only runs in the royal line of Phemoria, so either you're one of mine or you're an abandoned son of Qusay-Sabah Clarona,' Khalid advised him with a grin. Zeven was rather taken aback by the news, so Taren was not about to mention that the queen had denied having any sons.

'Enough,' Lucian growled. He grabbed the weapon from Zeven's hand and fired at Khalid, who vanished before the pulse hit him.

Khalid's laughter echoed through the abandoned chamber. 'You can't defeat me here, this is my domain.' The lights and air-conditioning cut out. 'Get 'em, boys!'

Even in the darkness Lucian could see the ghosts as they sprang from the walls all around them, and the first to shoot past Starman served him a hard punch to the jaw sending him reeling.

'Bugger this!' Starman found his sensibilities quickly and willed the lights and air back on — he was stunned to find the room empty of any but his colleagues. Zeven received another punch to the jaw, much to his invisible adversary's amusement.

A few of the phantoms took a dive at Lucian and Taren, but the captain saw them coming and dropped to the floor with Taren.

'How do we combat a foe we can't see?' Starman yelled, frustrated in his attempt to get close enough to his comrades to get them out of there.

'Duck!' Lucian warned, as the pilot was about to be hit again and Zeven was quick enough to dodge the strike.

'You can see these guys?' The captain only smiled, and as the walls had ears and eyes at present, Zeven decided now was not the time to catch up on the personal gossip.

'What we need is a diversion,' Lucian commented. He spotted a case on the table, recognising it as the container for the crown of Phemoria, having seen the crown put to rest in it. He grabbed the case down from the table, and noting the lock he turned to Zeven. 'Starman ...' The lock cracked open. 'Many thanks.'

'No!' Khalid was heard to protest, but Lucian opened the lid of the case, releasing a seething mass of violent female energy onto the battlefield. Lucian fired Kalayna's weapon in the direction Khalid's voice had come from and Khalid was rendered visible.

'There you are,' said Zeven ominously. In the room, small whirlwinds were building created by the massing of angry spirits.

You dare threaten us! The seething mass of feminine

energy turned its attention to Khalid. *Reap the wrath of the Phemoray*.

Khalid backed up and bolted through a door and Zeven attempted to go after him.

Protect the master! The ghosts of Dead Man Downs flew to engage the Phemoray in battle.

'Starman,' Lucian called over all the atmospheric disturbance going on in the room. Objects were now flying everywhere! 'He'll know these ruins and he has phantoms supporting him here.'

'I know what he looks like now. I can find him with a thought! I need to get him while he's incapacitated.' Starman jumped over a chair that had come flying at his legs.

'We need to return Taren, this weapon and the crown of Phemoria into safe hands,' Lucian yelled as the stormy disturbance grew more violent.

Zeven suppressed his urge for instant revenge and headed back to Lucian and Taren. When he reached them, Lucian closed the lid of the case.

The angry female thought-forms vanished and the atmosphere instantly stilled.

'Why not leave the Phemoray to fight out their fate?' Zeven wondered.

'Not our decision to make,' Lucian said, 'and certainly not Khalid's. These souls are tortured enough. There must be a better way to end their suffering.'

Taren and Zeven nodded to accept his reasoning, and then looked at each other to ask: 'Are you all right?'

Taren smiled and gave a nod. She considered the idea that they might be related in some way. 'Thanks for coming back to check on me.'

'I was compelled,' Zeven grinned, still embarrassed that he'd presented himself butt naked before two of the most powerful people in the USS.

The air in the room began to stir once again and Lucian beheld the ghosts of Dead Man Downs massing above, making ready to descend upon them and retrieve the crown case. 'Time to leave ... now!'

'Back to the queen then?' Starman assumed as he gripped hold of the captain and Taren.

'With the greatest haste,' Lucian stressed as the mass of angry entities let loose a war cry and hurtled towards them.

Swithin was beyond fed up with being imprisoned. He'd been jailed without charge by everyone at one time or another: the MSS, the USS, the triple-S, the Phemorians, and even his own project! Since his brother had handed him over to the Phemorians, he'd lost count of the interrogation rooms and cells he'd seen the inside of.

This current holding cell was the pits, and he hadn't seen or heard from anyone in what seemed like an eternity! He would almost prefer being beaten shitless by Valoureans to this state of affairs. At least they were something good to look at while you were dying.

'What the fuck have I got to do to get a feed around here?' he yelled for the umpteenth time from his reclining position on the bunk, wondering if they'd docked somewhere and he'd been left behind to rot. 'At least this cell has a crapper,' he consoled himself and closed his eyes to listen to his stomach rumble some more.

'Not like you to settle for so little.'

Swithin was startled to standing by Khalid's voice, and was even more startled to see him inside his locked cell. 'How did you get in here?'

'You might be more excited to learn how I am going to get you out,' Khalid proffered.

'Why would you want to do that?' Swithin knew Khalid would never act out of the kindness of his heart.

'How well do you know AMIE's systems?' the viceroy asked.

Swithin had a chuckle. 'Still trying to dispose of any evidence linking you to Maladaan's disappearance, huh?'

Khalid smiled. He had a plan. 'I know that Gudrun was the hot shot who snatched Aurora DeCadie from our custody and if he came for her once he'll come for her again.'

'I'd say you're right about that,' Swithin concurred, understanding the bait but not the trap.

'But in order to maintain the element of surprise I need to act swiftly,' Khalid said, pushing for Swithin to commit.

'Well, seeing as you are the only damn bastard who has spared me a thought lately, I believe I have to accept your proposal,' Swithin decided and was rather alarmed when Khalid took hold of his arm.

'Splendid,' Khalid commented. 'And try not to throw up.'

'What?' Swithin froze, petrified by the force of every molecule in his body being swept away elsewhere.

When Swithin became aware of being whole and stationary once more, he began trembling violently and staggered away from Khalid. 'You're one of them,' he croaked, nearly choking on the fear and trepidation that rushed through him.

'You're a genius,' commented Khalid. 'Which way to the bridge?'

'But I've seen you torture your own kind,' Swithin said, still reeling from his rude awakening, 'you sick fuck.'

'There is no *my* kind. I'm an *original* ... or at least I was before this lot arrived back in civilisation. So, start cooperating, or I'll implode all your vital organs. Did I mention I'm in a bit of a hurry?'

CHAPTER 28

HEAVENSGATE

Just prior to Taren being reunited with her parents, they had given the order for their vessels and AMIE to proceed full speed towards Heavensgate. Jalila had disclosed Khalid's plan to arrest Anselm, but now that Qusay-Sabah Clarona was his ally, Anselm was eager to return to his capital and ensure that any confusion or threat of rebellion was sorted out quietly and quickly.

When Lucian and Zeven came back with Taren to report that Khalid was incapacitated in the wilderness for a few hours, the president felt he had an even better chance of avoiding an embarrassing incident.

Qusay-Sabah Clarona was relieved to have the cursed crown of her realm returned to her in its case. 'This is the second time I find myself greatly indebted to you, captain.'

'Not half as indebted as I am to you for your daughter,' he replied graciously and the queen was touched by his sentiment.

Anselm chose to overlook Taren's lack of memory of him and hugged her tight. 'Praise the ancient powers,' he said and kissed her forehead.

For the first time, Taren felt in her heart that Anselm was truly her father and she embraced him back. 'I'm good, truly,' she told him as she freed herself and looked at the queen, who was obviously restraining her need to hold her daughter.

'It was the stone you sent me that turned the situation in my favour and bought me some time.' Taren smiled warmly at her mother, as she pulled the stone from her pocket, using her sleeve as a glove to prevent it making contact with her skin.

The queen's emotions overcame her, and tossing formality and fear aside she rushed to embrace her child. 'Thank the universe I did something right.'

'Oh, I don't know ... I think you've done a whole lot right just recently.' Taren was overwhelmed to be finally holding her mother. 'Welcome home to yourself,' she whispered, reducing both of them to tears.

'That's a handy little gadget,' Zeven commented to the captain, interested in looking over the weapon they had retrieved from Khalid. 'Is it something new the USS came up with?'

'No,' the captain said sadly, and handed it to Zeven. 'Kalayna designed it.' Lucian nearly choked on his words and Zeven was confused by the captain's lack of enthusiasm.

'Kalayna designed *this* ... whoa! That's awesome! Isn't it?' The sorrowful look on Lucian's face made Zeven's heart sink. His eyes turned once again to the bloodstain on the carpet, and instinctively Zeven knew the blood belonged to Kalayna. 'What happened?'

Lucian held up both hands in the hope of calming Zeven before he lost his temper. 'If I tell you what happened, you will wish to seek revenge, and we need you right now.'

Zeven's jaw clenched as this confirmed that Kalayna had been killed. 'What happened?' Zeven repeated, backing up as objects in the room began to quiver.

'I need you to focus on the problems at hand,' Lucian repeated more firmly.

'Zeven, please!' Taren appealed, whereby the objects threatening to take flight stilled.

'I'll find out on my own,' he stated and he turned his will toward locating Kalayna.

Zeven landed in Kassa's medical quarters and stared at a body bag. Outside in the waiting room, he could hear Aurora weeping as she conferred with the doctor.

It was difficult to accept that Kalayna was in that bag. He'd brought her back from the brink of death once and had hoped he could do it again.

'I've tried.' Ringbalin's comment startled Zeven to about-face, where he found the botanist sitting quietly in a corner. 'But healing only works on living things. Once the spirit has taken flight the game is up.'

Zeven clenched both fists and his entire body in an attempt to restrain his grief. 'Who did this?'

Ringbalin was surprised by the question. 'Did the captain not tell you?'

Zeven's eyes narrowed as his patience was coming to an end. 'Who?' His constrained, hushed tone demanded an answer and Ringbalin sensed he'd best not deny the pilot satisfaction.

'Khalid Mansur.'

Zeven focused his will on Khalid target, trembling with the conviction that was pulsing through his veins; he'd never wanted to hurt someone so badly in all his born days.

'I had rather expected you to pop straight off and seek revenge,' Ringbalin commented when, minutes later, Zeven was still standing before him.

'So did I,' Zeven grumbled, confused.

'Perhaps Khalid has a psychic shield protecting him from being sought by psychic means,' Balin offered up a possible explanation.

'What the heck,' Zeven objected. 'Nobody ever mentioned there was such a thing.'

'It usually takes the form of an amulet, or in the case of the Phemorian queen, it took the form of a crown.'

'An amulet,' Zeven queried. 'Like a medallion?' He didn't recall spotting any such item around Khalid's neck.

'Could be,' Balin agreed. The pilot threw his hands up in frustration.

'Do you think such an item would shield him from the effect of the psychic neutraliser as well?' and with the thought that Khalid might have been faking his disability, Zeven realised leaving Taren had been a mistake. He would have sped straight to her, but Aurora opened the door and saw him.

The girl flung herself into his arms, elated to see him alive and devastated by Kalayna's death. 'Please don't vanish again —'

'I have to go,' he was sorry to say as he peeled Aurora off himself. 'Taren is in danger.'

Kassa, who looked on from the doorway, gave a heavy, sympathetic sigh. She could feel how torn Zeven was, along with Aurora's fear of losing the man she'd loved for so long and finally won. They both grieved the loss of their intimate friend. And losing two crew members in tragic circumstances was a giant reality check for them all in regard to their own mortality.

'You're in danger,' Aurora appealed, her tears causing her make-up to run black lines down her face. 'If you must go, take me with you. I hate waiting to see if you'll come back in one piece next time.'

'Don't I always come back in one piece?' Zeven said in his own defence. Aurora hated that reassuring smile of his, as she had no resistance to it. She allowed him to kiss her, let her hands go and vanish.

'I thought he'd never leave.' Khalid's voice made all present jump.

'Damn it!' Lucian grumbled at Zeven's departure, and then calmed when he realised that, through his spirit contacts, he could probably get the pilot's arse dragged back to him when required.

'I could try going after him,' Taren proffered, although she was still not very confident with her PK abilities. And that was only if she had fully regained her Powers.

'Let him go. Azazèl will know where to find him.' Lucian took hold of her shoulders to prevent her disappearing again. 'Right now, we have about two hours to figure out how we are going to hide you from Khalid.'

'The triple-S have psychic containment quarters beneath their offices in Heavensgate,' Anselm offered, moving over to them. 'These rooms prevent psychics escaping or entering unauthorised —'

'You're not going to lock me in some containment area!' Taren objected.

'It's the only place we can possibly hide you from Mansur,' Anselm insisted.

'No, it isn't,' Taren argued. 'You never did hear me out about what I want —'

A chime from the door exasperated Taren, and Anselm's guards entered to let him know that the ship had been given authorisation to dock at Heavensgate.

Anselm thanked and dismissed his men ahead of turning back to Taren. 'Please can we do this my way, and once you're safe, I promise I will help you do whatever you want.'

Taren smiled, and looked at her mother who nodded to show that Anselm spoke for her too. 'I will hold you both to that promise and Lucian is my witness.'

The captain nodded, none the wiser to what she had in mind.

'Very good.' Anselm was now eager to get them to their destination. He rounded everyone up and began moving them towards the door. 'I look forward to hearing what we've agreed to, once I have Khalid restrained.'

'I'll have my Valoureans go ahead of us,' the queen suggested.

'My agents are all psychically gifted and trained,' Anselm told her proudly.

'But they are all wearing restraining devices. It will take hours to stabilise their magnetic fields,' Qusay-Sabah Clarona argued.

'Fake,' Anselm smiled sweetly.

'Why am I not surprised?' The queen grinned at his cheek, in retrospect. 'Fortunate that we are on the same side now.'

'Very fortunate,' Anselm replied, pausing to admire her, which delayed the departure of the entire party.

Whilst the queen had been meeting with her viceroy, Anselm had been doing some investigative work in the secret service database that stored erased memory. He had been stunned to find that he — 'Jabez Anselm' — had a file. The memory file was over fifty years old and pertained to a six-hour period, the same period during which he had lost his heart to Qusay-Sabah Clarona. It had come as no surprise to him to discover that the memory extraction order had been authorised by Khalid Mansur.

'It is my great regret that I was not there to save you from the Phemoray, Clarona.' Anselm now knew that he had called her this as it was the part of her name he liked the most ... it meant 'morning'.

Taren's heart fluttered to see her parents so smitten with each other, and she felt sure they would have kissed had it not been for present company.

'I shall never have the wool pulled over my eyes like that again,' Anselm vowed to his long-lost love.

His words stirred a desire within Taren to ensure her parents' future happiness and the happiness of all involved in this twisted web of deceit, lies and ancient prejudice. A light-headedness caused Taren's vision to blur and she staggered.

'Taren? What is it?' Lucian grabbed hold to steady her, but she became a dead weight in his arms. 'She's going into a trance ... *she's going to change the future ...*'

Lucian's voice did not fade as Taren continued to perceive her present situation from above her inactive form.

'We'll have to carry her,' Anselm suggested.

'No, we shouldn't move her, or make a move ourselves,' Lucian laid Taren down on a lounge. 'I've learned that if Taren goes into trance, something dire is about to happen. Best wait and heed her advice.'

'And what if she takes hours to awaken?' Anselm posed. 'We need to get her to a safe area now.'

'And miss an opportunity to heed her warning?' Lucian pushed his view, not prepared to risk it.

At this point, reality split in two: one stream where they waited for Taren to wake; the other where they did not. Taren's consciousness pursued the time stream of the latter scenario ...

When their party disembarked from their craft, they were met by a large contingent of agents and officials from the USS, who were all surprised to see their president disembark from the vessel with the Queen of Phemoria, who had issued the arrest warrant for everyone on board. The queen explained that there had been a huge misunderstanding as Sermetica and Phemoria had been engaged in sensitive political talks on board the vessel and its presence in the Phemoria system had, therefore, not been officially announced. The USS officials present could only be delighted to see the Queen of Phemoria on speaking terms with the President of Sermetica. Obviously, this held the promise of a better relationship between Phemoria and all the other planets of the USS.

'Along with my viceroy, Jalila Lamis, the Chairman of the USS and I have been discussing a new democratic future for Phemoria,' the queen announced. This news was an enormous shock to everyone, but, equally, everyone buzzed with delight.

'But what of the Phemoray?' asked a senior official, who'd been dealing with their unusual and threatening demands for decades.

'The reign of the Phemoray has come to end on Phemoria. They will never return to power for as long as feminine rights are upheld on our planet and throughout the United Star Systems,' she declared to the USS press, who were there expecting an arrest, not a major political coup. The announcement caused a further frenzy of excitement and amid the turmoil no one heard the sniper's bullets until the Queen of Phemoria was hit, and seconds later the President of Sermetica dropped dead alongside her.

The gathering at the space dock erupted into pandemonium, while Taren's consciousness took flight from Heavensgate and sped towards AMIE ... no one had noticed it was now headed back towards the inter-system gateway.

On the observation lounge at the rear of the bridge of AMIE, Leal, Kassa, Ringbalin and Aurora were sitting bound and gagged. It was Swithin Gervaise who sat behind the controls and alongside him stood Khalid Mansur.

'So, only you and I know the code to override the systems now?' Khalid queried Swithin, who grinned.

'Correct.'

'Excellent.' With a thought, Khalid sent Swithin's heart into cardiac arrest, and the rest of the crew looked on horrified as Khalid approached to address Aurora. 'You had better hope your boyfriend notices this ship's change of course before you pass back through the inter-system gateway. Our sub-station is having a little meltdown today. It seems the exit passage has mysteriously jammed on the Maladaan system.'

Aurora's eyes parted wide in fear, as did the eyes of her friends and colleagues alongside.

Taren's perception floated up and away from the space institute and she sped forward into the inter-system gateway that AMIE approached. Upon entering, she was swept up in the vacuum of the ancient quantum tunnels and spat out in the remnants of the Maladaan system; she was immediately swept backward by a wave of energy. After a while, she was sucked forward into the expansive darkness where her home planet had once been located. The passage through this darkness was fleeting, as up ahead there was a quasar-like pulsing of colourful light at the centre of a gap in the darkness that had the appearance of a great glowing eye. The tide carried her through the eye where she was shot out into the universe parallel. The ebb of space nearly drew her back through the eye, but she fought free of the rip and continued along with the flow of invisible matter toward the nearest star system.

There, Taren spied her missing home planet, minus its many satellites, but from all appearances it was otherwise perfect. But on the far side of the sun, directly opposing Maladaan, there was another planet in the same orbit. This was a breathtaking aquamarine-green globe of immense natural beauty. There was but one city on the entire globe and it was grand in the sense she had of magnificent cities only known in her universe through ancient myth and archaeological ruins.

Taren's consciousness honed in on one building, one room, one individual in particular. He was youthful, dark-haired, dark-eyed and handsome, and he smiled broadly at her and said: *'Welcome back to Kila . . . Goddess knows, I really need you.'*

Taren did not recognise this man and yet she felt as if she had known him forever and was compelled to help him. As she felt her consciousness threatening to shift once again, her heart began beating rapidly in protest — she didn't want to leave this place, this mysterious person with whom she felt such an affinity.

She was hurled backwards along the time stream, kicking and screaming, through the universal crossing, the remnants of the Maladaan system, the shattered entry of the inter-system gateway, and back to Sermetica.

'I am her father! I've been dealing with Taren's psychic episodes far longer than you,' Anselm was saying to try and get his way. 'And I say we move now.'

Taren's consciousness landed with a huge body slam and she awoke in a panic. 'Thank heavens,' she gasped as she took in her surroundings. 'You're still here.' Taren turned to her parents. 'There are snipers waiting for you to disembark.'

'What?' Anselm had expected to be confronted by an embarrassing incident, not an assassin!

'Check that Swithin Gervaise is still in custody,' Taren suggested.

'What? Why?' Anselm was perplexed. 'Is he the sniper?'

'No!' Taren groaned, as she needed to be more succinct about what she said. 'Khalid is about to conscript him to his cause,' Taren said quickly, stressed at being questioned. She had too much to address at once, and more to remember. 'Swithin knows AMIE's systems,' she explained, as her eyes turned to Lucian. 'AMIE's changed course. She's heading for the inter-system gateway.'

A chime from the door announced a visitor, and an agent entered to inform everyone that the inter-system gateway had had a malfunction and was closed until further notice.

'What kind of malfunction?' Lucian was alarmed.

'I don't know, they didn't say,' the agent shrugged.

'Check on Swithin Gervaise for me,' Anselm requested as the guard departed, 'and abort the docking in Heavensgate. We're to remain where we are until further notice.'

'Yes, sir,' the agent confirmed and as soon as the doors closed Taren spoke up.

'Khalid has locked the exit passage of the gateway to the Maladaan system.'

'But there is no exit passage in the Maladaan system!' Lucian stressed. 'Where is Leal?'

'I saw him bound and gagged along with the rest of the crew,' Taren said, holding back tears, until she saw their saving grace materialise before her. 'Zeven!'

'I thought you'd be seeking revenge on Khalid.' Lucian was greatly relieved to see him.

'I would be, if I could find the sonofa—' When Zeven spotted the Queen of Phemoria, he refrained from finishing the sentence.

'Khalid has an amulet protecting him, but not even his lover has seen it on his person,' the queen said. 'It's possible he might have had it implanted in his body.'

'It's in his right hand,' Anselm said, finally realising that the evil charm would explain the dark blockage he had perceived in that area of Khalid's light-body. The charm would have hindered Anselm's psychic sight and shielded Khalid's full aura, but because the amulet was a physical object, Anselm had detected it.

Anselm's agent returned to let them know that Swithin Gervaise had indeed escaped.

'Then Khalid is already on board AMIE,' Taren concluded regretfully. 'He'll kill Swithin as soon as he has finished reprogramming AMIE's systems to respond only to a private password.'

Swithin was not presently Lucian's favourite person, but he did not wish him dead.

'But I just left AMIE and everyone was *fine*,' Zeven complained, becoming agitated when he realised he might be in the wrong place at the wrong time yet again! 'You've taken another little trip into the future, haven't you?' he demanded, confronting Taren. 'What about Aurora?'

'Khalid knows you'll only go after live bait,' Taren replied.

'So it's a trap, is it?' Zeven was livid, but with a deep breath, he managed to keep his emotions under control and think rationally. 'This amulet of his is made from metal?' he asked the queen, who nodded. Zeven looked thoughtfully at a sculpture sitting on a table that featured several metallic balls. He held out his hand towards the piece and issued the intention of *magnetism*. The balls tore away from the sculpture to land in his hand, and he grinned at Lucian. 'I think I have an idea how we can take Mansur out, but ... it's risky.'

Lucian, who'd been with Zeven at Dead Man Downs, was having the same idea. 'What other option do we have?'

'Well, do share with the other children,' Anselm requested, eager to bring this situation under his control. 'I know we've given you grief in the past, captain, but if you allow us to assist you in this, you won't regret it. I have a few old scores to settle with Khalid myself.'

Lucian nodded in agreement. 'Actually, your cooperation, and the queen's, will be essential.'

Qusay-Sabah Clarona stepped forward, honoured to be included. 'Whatever you need, captain, just ask.'

CHAPTER 29

CROSS

'You had better hope your boyfriend notices this ship's change of course before you pass back through the inter-system gateway. Our sub-station is having a little meltdown today. It seems the exit passage has mysteriously jammed on the Maladaan system.'

Aurora's eyes parted wide in fear, as did the eyes of her friends and colleagues alongside.

Khalid laughed at their distress as he vanished into thin air.

Leal and Kassa backed up to each other in an attempt to loosen the other's bonds. It was agony for the doctor to sit by and watch whilst a human being was dying in front of her. *Swithin won't last much longer.*

Leal wasn't getting anywhere with their restraints and it frustrated him. *Neither will we if don't get off this vessel.*

Do you think that lunatic is still here?

I can't sense him, Leal bethought her, *but then I didn't sense him the first time he snuck up on me.*

He must have a shield, Kassa concluded. Then her eyes caught sight of the captain, Taren and Zeven as they crept into the bridge from the direction of the holding bay. Taren was holding her FFRD and observing the readout. She nodded to Lucian and handed the device to him.

'*Arman!*' Aurora tried to call to Zeven through her gag.

He snuck over and hugged her briefly before he began to untie her bonds.

'Don't go anywhere,' Aurora said, and Zeven gripped her hand tight.

'I'm not going anywhere without you,' he swore and she immediately calmed.

Lucian headed straight to Swithin who'd collapsed onto the floor. 'Quick, release Kassa and Ringbalin,' he directed Taren.

'You really do have a fucking death wish ...' Swithin forced out the words, amused and touched that his brother still cared enough to want to save his life. 'Forget me ...'

'Don't talk,' Lucian urged him, surprised by how much he did not want to lose his only sibling.

Swithin grinned, bound to have the last say in the matter. 'The ... system ... password ...' Swithin choked up completely and fell limp as Kassa was freed from her restraints.

'Swithin!' she called ahead of reaching him and checking his vital signs. 'He's still alive, thank heavens. He's the only one who knows the password to AMIE's systems,' she explained. 'I'll need equipment to keep him alive though.'

'I'll get a trolley and your bag.' Leal raced from the flight deck.

Both Kassa and Lucian were breathing a sigh of relief when Taren gasped and vanished from their midst.

'He's got her.' Lucian paused and pulled Kalayna's psychic neutraliser from his equipment belt as well as Taren's handheld FFRD.

'You knew he was still here,' Kassa could tell by his tone and the fact incensed her.

'He may be able to escape the psychic sensors of human beings, but you cannot hide a negative charge, such as Khalid carries, from the quantum world.' The captain thought this would explain their reasoning, but it was not nearly enough detail to pacify the doctor.

Now that Kassa's suspicion — that the FFRD had let him know Khalid was still here — was confirmed, she was even more aggravated. 'Why expose Taren to such danger?' she demanded of Lucian.

'They'll be back,' Lucian said. Or so he was hoping with all the willpower he could muster.

'Why would Khalid come back?' Kassa wanted to know. 'He has what he came for.'

'Khalid doesn't know that Taren has PK,' Lucian whispered into her ear. Kassa grinned and then gasped as she noticed the needle begin to move to the negative on the FFRD.

'Here they come,' Lucian warned Starman, who nodded to confirm he was ready.

When Taren reappeared she was alone, yet she appeared to be tightly gripping something. 'Stage left.' Taren motioned to that side with her eyes, and Lucian fired his weapon. Although Khalid was not rendered visible, Taren lost her grip on him as he was sent reeling backwards from the strike.

Zeven stood to make his move and, focusing on the amulet in Khalid's hand, he attracted it into his possession.

The weapon in Lucian's hand suddenly shot off in the direction of Khalid.

Khalid fired upon Taren, who was knocked down by the pulse. A pain in the palm of his right hand drew Khalid's attention, and he watched with horror as the amulet tore through his skin and sped into Zeven's outstretched hand. Khalid materialised and was furious at the loss of his psychic shield, but he still had his PK ability and a weapon, which he fired at Zeven.

Zeven pushed Aurora aside as he was knocked down by the force of the blast. He gripped the amulet tight, even when it began to burrow through the skin of his hand as Khalid willed his amulet back to himself.

Leal came screaming towards the flight deck with his trolley and medical supplies, but upon seeing the chaos before him he drew to a halt.

'Now,' Lucian advised into his communicator.

'You!' Khalid pointed to the captain. 'Time to die!' He desired for Lucian to join Swithin and was baffled when the man only smiled and motioned to the viceroy's lower leg.

Whilst Khalid had been distracted with Zeven, Taren had clamped a standard secret service restraining band around their foe's ankle and scurried back towards Lucian, beyond Khalid's reach.

Zeven held high the small metal amulet with his bloodied hand, pleased that Taren had restrained Khalid before he'd lost any fingers. 'I order the phantoms of this amulet back to their source.'

A disturbance whipped through the bridge, streamed into the amulet Zeven was holding up and was gone.

'Deserters!' Khalid cried in the wake of being abandoned, an ordinary mortal once more.

'It seems you are now as vulnerable as the rest of us,' Lucian concluded.

'Ha!' Khalid was clearly shaken in the wake of his unexpected defeat. 'None of you have the stomach for killing.'

'No,' Lucian replied, agreeing that this was quite true, 'not us.'

Upon the captain's cue, Qusay-Sabah Clarona moved to confront her past with Anselm at her side.

'Even if they kill us, we'll be together,' Jabez assured her with a squeeze of her hand.

The queen was gladdened by his sentiment, but summoned all her strength and determination — she would ensure it did not come to that. 'They have no power beyond that which we give them.' Clarona opened the crown's containment case and the seething red mass rose up above her. 'Ladies of the Phemoray,' she acknowledged.

'You lost the crown of Phemoria,' the thought-form hissed. *'You are no longer our queen.'*

'That is correct, I am no longer your queen, nor shall I ever be again. Your rule of Phemoria is at an end. You have no power over me, nor will you cast your spell and influence over any of my descendants.'

The mass of feminine energy seethed away quietly. For thousands of years their crown had been passed on without question, their ultimate authority assured. The crown had never been removed from the head of the ruling monarch, not since the first queen had willingly placed the crown upon her head, where it resided until the day she died. The crown was then immediately placed upon the head of the next Queen of Phemoria, so no monarch could ever warn the next ruler of the crown's dark enchantment. The Phemoray had had the power to prevent their patron taking the crown off, but they did not have, nor had ever needed, the power to make her put it on. *'We serve Phemoria!'* The thought-form cast an appeal for its continued existence.

'*No*, Phemoria has served *you* and your agenda, which should have been ancient history long ago.' The queen dictated the terms of their future service. 'But I shall award you an opportunity to truly serve Phemoria and exact your revenge upon he who held you to ransom at Dead Man Downs ... but harm another living soul in the process and it will be the last thing you ever do.' The queen still held the lid of the crown case in her hand and threatened to close it.

Your majesty is most gracious. Thy will be done. The angry thought-form split into many and all soared quickly through the roof of their transport.

AMIE's infrastructure shook and the power flickered on and off, causing all in the bridge to hold their breath in expectation of what was coming.

'What is that?' Aurora scurried over to Starman's side.

'The sound of retribution,' Lucian forewarned Khalid, who was unaccustomed to feeling vulnerable.

'No!' He guessed at what was coming, but could scarcely believe it to be his fate. 'You justice types believe in a fair trial and so forth ... you wouldn't condemn an untried man.'

The seething red spectres quietly seeped through the ceiling behind their target.

'You slit Kalayna's throat before our eyes.' Taren's patience had come to an end. 'You ordered the death of Amie Gervaise, tried to rape me, dethrone my mother, disgrace my father, murder my closest friends *and* you were largely responsible for the displacement of my home planet! I cannot imagine how justice will ever be done. I've not got the stomach for torture, nor the time and energy to waste on extracting revenge ... but my foremothers do.'

Bury us at Dead Man Downs, would you?

At the sound of the harsh voices of the Phemoray, Khalid was startled to about-face, and upon sighting the angry spirits he attempted to flee. The thought-form gave hot pursuit and to the screamed protests of their target, they swooped Khalid Mansur up and vanished with him.

An immense wave of relief swept over the crew of AMIE, but there was no time for celebration. Leal rushed to Kassa with the equipment she needed to try to save and revive Swithin. Zeven rushed to the helm, hoping, against all odds, to crack the system code and save their vessel. Warning lights were flashing on the communications console.

'That will be the gate-station telling us to abort our course,' Leal commented as he left Kassa and joined Zeven, who was feeling aggravated with himself.

'Why did I have to get hit?' He knew his PK was going to be useless for hours. 'I could have pulled us back from this.'

'Time to abandon ship, lads,' Lucian advised. 'We'll use the recon transport to get everyone out.'

But nobody wanted to abandon AMIE.

'My greenhouse,' Ringbalin pined.

'Our home,' Kassa added.

'Your dream,' Taren put in, sorry that all Lucian's hard work had come to this.

'*Your lives*,' the captain said emphatically, 'are far more important. Let's get Swithin on this trolley, then everyone to the loading bay ... that's an order.'

Leal healped Lucian load his brother's stretcher on board their recon vessel, next to the enclosed stretcher that carried the body of Kalayna, and another containing the body of Dr Portus. As Kassa climbed in alongside, Lucian put his hand on her arm. 'Will he live?'

'If he does, it will be of precious little good to anyone,' Kassa said, feeling bitter and wondering why Lucian still gave a damn.

'Promise you'll do your best,' Lucian begged her.

'That's my job, captain,' she replied to reassure him.

Zeven fired up the recon vessel as Leal strapped into the co-pilot's seat — there was plenty of room in the rear cabin for the rest of the crew. Ringbalin and Aurora joined Kassa aboard, but when it came time for Lucian and Taren to embark they looked at each other to say, 'I'm staying ... what? No!'

'This is exactly what I've wanted,' Taren said, breaking their stalemate. 'I've glimpsed what lies beyond this gateway and it's not a black hole. It's a tear, and it's closing! I know in my soul that Maladaan is still alive and well in that universe, parallel to ours, but if I wait and argue this out with my parents I fear the tear will mend before I get clearance to go ... I don't have time for a committee. I won't ask anyone to trust my vision —'

'The captain goes with the ship. I've worked my whole life to experience something like this and even if I don't live to tell of it, I'll have accomplished a little of what I set out to do,' Lucian retorted.

Taren realised he was telling her she didn't have a say in him staying behind or going, and clearly he was not trying to talk her out of it either.

'No wonder I adore you.' Taren had never thought she'd meet anyone as bent on exploration and discovery as she was, and they kissed to seal their deal.

'Go, Starman.' Lucian stepped away from the smaller transport with Taren under his arm.

'No way.' Zeven was out of the recon vessel and on the launch pad. 'I'm staying with you. Leal can fly the others out.'

'Starman, you promised!' Aurora appealed from her seat in the back of the recon vessel. 'I'm not ready to cross into another universe! I just want a safe, sane existence where I don't have to fear for our lives every couple of hours.'

'We don't have time for this,' Leal interrupted, eager to lock and leave.

Zeven was torn between Aurora, and Taren and Lucian.

'You can find us with a thought, remember.' Taren encouraged him to go with his lover.

'Even in the next universe?' Zeven doubted that.

Taren shrugged. 'Let's experiment, shall we?'

Zeven gave a reluctant nod and then hugged Taren tight. 'See you in the next one then.' He squeezed out the words with difficulty — Zeven had never felt this strongly about a woman he hadn't slept with. 'I really loved the way it was. I'm going to miss it *a lot*.' As he couldn't prevent a tear from escaping, Taren brushed it quickly away.

'Take care,' she said and kissed him. She urged him back towards the transport, but Zeven couldn't leave without shaking Lucian's hand.

'It's been an honour and an education,' he told the captain, but it was only now, as they said goodbye, that they both realised how much they'd come to rely on one another.

'You exceeded my expectations ...' Lucian embraced the young pilot, and Zeven returned the sentiment. '... and never faltered in your loyalty.' Lucian held him at arm's length. 'I'm greatly indebted.'

'Starman!' Leal called urgently as the inter-system gateway was drawing closer and Zeven hauled arse to strap himself back into the pilot's seat.

'I always said you two were the perfect couple,' Kassa called. 'Take care of each other!'

'And come back!' Aurora made a desperate appeal for the impossible.

'What can I say?' Ringbalin raced to the closing door to add his piece. 'You're beautiful people ... love your work!' The door slammed closed, so Ringbalin waved through the window.

Taren was choked with emotion as the doors of the craft locked and she waved frantically to her departing space family.

Lucian was having trouble containing his emotions himself, but he squeezed Taren and urged her to accompany him back to the bridge.

'Alone at last.' Lucian observed the expansive surface of the inter-system gateway which was only minutes away from making contact with their craft.

That was one consolation and Taren found a smile to bestow on her lover.

Not quite all alone.

The sound of his deceased wife's voice rather rained on Lucian's parade. He looked about and saw her standing by the console, where last he'd seen her alive.

'Amie,' he announced for Taren's benefit and Taren's delight turned to shock.

'Your dead wife?' Taren queried, discomforted. 'You've been talking to your dead wife?'

'She's just leaving, I suspect.' Lucian looked back at her sternly.

I'm going, Amie informed. *I just wanted to say thank you . . . you did good.*

'I didn't do it for you —' Lucian pointed out.

I know, she was a little sad to admit. *But thanks anyway.* She blew him a kiss and vanished.

Lucian forced a smile as she departed. 'She's gone now.' He expressed both great relief and great pain in the statement.

'But I'm still here.' Taren embraced him tightly, so grateful for everything. 'What say we blow off this universe and see what the next one has to offer?' She swallowed her fear of actually going where only her consciousness had ventured before.

'Sounds good.' Lucian played along, as petrified as she was. 'Ship, set a course for the universe parallel. *Hey*, look at that,' he said, faking amazement as he motioned to the systems monitor, 'it's already been done for us.'

Taren turned the captain to face her. 'I guess there's nothing left to do but enjoy the ride.' Taren moved in for a kiss, but, in the event they got carried away, she thought to add, 'But should something go horribly wrong —'

'It won't.' Lucian was the voice of reassurance for a change, as he had noted three larger-than-life spirits out of the corner of his eye. 'We have guardian spirits watching out for us.'

Taren had forgotten about the grigori, even though they had been the ones who had inspired her to take this risk. With the reminder, all her fears departed and she placed her trust in the higher power she hoped to one day understand. In the man before her she saw her beautiful guardian, and if she was to meet her end this day, it would be in the divine bliss of his love.

I think they can probably take it from here, Azazèl commented, to distract his comrades' attention away from the intimate moment, but he felt proud of a job well done.

Aye, Sammael agreed, *you never did have any problem in that department.*

Well then, Armaros rose into the air to leave, feeling they were now intruding. *Let us see this ship safely to its next destination.*

As Azazèl fondly observed his split-soul manifestations in the throes of passion, he suggested, *Take the scenic route.*

That's a given, Armaros jibed as he led his fellow threshold dwellers upwards.

The triad soared beyond AMIE as she penetrated the entry barrier of the inter-system gateway and swept along the quantum tunnel ahead of their charge, towards the crossing that would grant entry to the universe parallel.

BIBLIOGRAPHY

Bletzer, June G, PhD: *The Donning International Encyclopedic Psychic Dictionary*. The Donning Company Publishers, Virginia, USA. 1986.

McTaggart, Lynne: *The Field: the Quest for the Secret Force of the Universe*. HarperCollins Publishers, London. 2001.

McTaggart, Lynne: *The Intention Experiment*. HarperElement Publishers, London. 2007.

PLANETS OF THE UNITED STAR SYSTEMS

Maladaan
Capital City: Esponisa
Ruler: President Woodford Tallak
Climate: Polluted
Landscape: Overdeveloped
Highrise-modern cityscapes
Known as the technology capital of the USS

Frujia
Capital City: Kotan Bathaar
Ruler: Chief Matan-tu-hoo
Climate: Hot, tropical
Landscape: Scattered island archipelagos
Small tourist colonies
Known as the pleasure capital of the USS

Sermetica
Capital City: Heavensgate
Ruler: President Jabez Anselm
Climate: Controlled
Landscape: Desert-mineral rich
Mobile-airborne cities in the clouds
Known as the mining capital of the USS
a.k.a. the Planet of Men

Phemoria
Capital City: Tonissia
Ruler: Queen Qusay-Sabah Clarona
Climate: Moderate
Landscape: Forest and ocean rich
Beautiful ancient cities, unspoilt by time
Known as the cultural capital of the USS
a.k.a. the Planet of Women

Oceane
Capital City: none
Ruler: Azazèl-mindos-coomra-dorchi
Climate: Wet and steamy
Landscape: Largely ocean and small rocky land masses
Unknown to the USS

THE POWERS

1. **Clairvoyance** (clear vision) — to see into the ethereal dimension without using physical eyes, to reach into another vibrational frequency and visually perceive 'within the head' or 'in outer space' something significant to this incarnation, eyes opened or closed. To see psychically a full blown picture, part of a person or scene, an object, lights, words, colours, auras, geometrical figures, thought forms, deceased friends, living friends, etheric world intelligences. Visions are shown regarding past, present or future. **Clairaudience** (clear audio) — to perceive sounds or words when no person is present. Sounds are inaudible to the normal hearing, can appear to come from 'within the head' or 'out in the atmosphere'.
2. **Shape-shifting/Physical Transformation** — to physically transform oneself into another human being, animal, bird, fish or object for a temporary period and to be able to perform the task of that animal or object and use the mind, memory and senses of the adopted form as if it were one's own.
3. **Levitation** — to elevate oneself or an object in the air. The object or the self is kept suspended for a length of time without the use of physical means. Performed by a psychic in a semi-trance or full-trance state of consciousness. Levitation is always

willed and desire controlled. This is accomplished by the undivided concentration of the subconscious mind or the guides. The psychic's subconscious reverses the attraction of gravity in the subject or object.

4. **Mediumship** (mediator; go-between) — one who serves as an instrument through which the personality of an intelligence in the etheric world can help earthlings. The intelligence enters the medium's body to speak. **Channel** — bringing psychic information or healing energy to others. Comes through in physical and mental psychic skills while the person is in a deep or semi-trance state. The intelligence advises the psychic and the channel passes on the information in their own voice.

5. **Psychokinesis** (PK) — to deliberately change the position, form or elements of objects of a specific energy field with disciplined concentration of the conscious or subconscious minds. To physically and intentionally direct one's will to act on elementary atoms of the third dimension in a definite manner.

6. **Precognition** (speaking before) — a word meaning psychic message from the future. All psychic information pertaining to future events that comes spontaneously or willed.

7. **Remote Viewing** — to perceive clairvoyantly something that is happening at the present moment that is out of range of the physical eyes. This sometimes involves astral projection.

8. **Astral Projection** — to will one's soul-mind to leave the physical body en-clothed in an astral body and travel to distant localities.

9. **Telekinesis** (TK, tele 'over a distance'; kinesis 'movement') — a psychic production of movement or motion over distance. To act psychically on third-dimensional matter and change its position, form or elements. Phenomena is always pre-planned, willed and desired by the medium.
10. **Telepathy** (tele 'distance'; pathos 'sensing', 'to feel afar') — the touch of consciousness of one person upon another person with the ability to discern what that person is thinking and feeling at the present moment: thoughts, visions, hypnotic energy, body movements, subconscious data, feelings, illness, emotional states, psychic messages or the train of inner dialogue. Both individuals can be alive or one deceased. Can be voluntary or involuntary, selective and deliberate, or spontaneous and undesired.
11. **Transmutation Teleportation** — to transfer one's body, another's body, or an object through ethereal space from one physical locality to another, via the use of the will. To dematerialise one's own body by rearranging the atomic structure until it is ethereal in nature and attuned to a higher vibrational frequency, and to re-materialise one's body into the mundane.
12. **The Healing Touch** (Remote; Holistic; Spiritual; Sympathetic; Psychic; Magnetic; Mental) — all holistic healing requires that the practitioner takes into consideration every aspect of the patient's lifestyle and emotional attitudes to find the cause of an ailment. To use etheric world energy to cure a patient, or etheric world information to diagnose an ailment.

ACKNOWLEDGEMENTS

I'd like to thank David, Sarah, John, Mum, Dad, Gillybean, Kyle and Joey, Steven and Lorraine, Mo and Ken, Shane, Wendy Connie and Oliver, Geoff and Terry, Michael, Sue M, Chez, John-Mark, Harold, Lisa, Claire-Bear, Karen, Sally, Sue W and Kath — for keeping me sane, making me laugh, supporting me, and reminding me what life is all about.

Loads of thanks also to everyone on the Traci Harding Community Message Board (the THC) and Trazling — especially, Chez, Willow, Temmies, EJ, Whirls, Fi, ED, Thirsty and all my moderators and helpers.

A special thank you to Sue M, Chez and Whirls — my pre-readers.

A very big kiss and hug to my agent, Selwa.

And a huge chug on the shoulder to everyone at HarperCollins Publishers — especially, Linda, Stephanie, Annabel and Jordan — thanks for thirteen wonderful years!

I would also like to acknowledge the fantastic work of Lynne McTaggart, who inspired this book and the entire trilogy. You'll find the details of her books in the Bibliography. I have not read anything so mind-expanding in ten years.

HARPER Voyager Online

MAKE VOYAGER ONLINE YOUR NEXT DESTINATION

VOYAGER ONLINE has the latest science fiction and fantasy releases, book extracts, author interviews, downloadable wallpapers and monthly competitions. It also features exclusive contributions from some of the world's top science fiction and fantasy authors.

DROP BY the message board where you can discuss books, authors, conventions and more with other fans.

DISCUSS SF/F in depth: take part in the Voyager Book Club which runs every two months, or look up some of the available reading guides to your favourite books.

KEEP IN TOUCH with authors via the Voyager blog, which is updated every week with guest posts from authors and all the latest news and events on sf/f in Australia and around the world.

FOLLOW US on Twitter and Facebook.

ENJOY the journey and feel at home with friends at www.voyageronline.com.au

HARPER
Voyager

www.voyageronline.com.au